Sibling Revelry

TERRY SYKES-BRADSHAW

Published by

**Braughler
Books**

Printed in the United States of America

To my almost twin sister, Kathy … who celebrated with me through the good, cried through the bad and helped me survive the seriously ugly. And always knew the difference. Thank you a million times. This one is for you. *Te quiero mucho.*

ACKNOWLEDGMENTS

First I must confess that any resemblance in *Sibling Revelry* to real people is purely intentional. I'm grateful to my family for allowing me (not that I actually asked them) to take liberties with their identities. They really can't complain because at least I gave them good hair and really cute clothes.

Since writers can be notoriously insecure I appreciate all the support and encouragement I've gotten along the way. Many thanks go to . . .

. . . my friends, Edie and Grace, who plied me with gallons of coffee as well as other more potent beverages and listened to me whine during the long process of completing this book.

. . . Agnes for cheering me up and cheering me on. You all (Keena, Sue, Sandy and Veronica) have been awesome. I never would have made it without you.

. . . Second Tuesday Writers who listened and offered their constructive critiques. And to my Book Club who read the first draft and made suggestions that helped the final outcome to be so much better.

. . . my wonderful family --- Kathy, Chris, Helen and Alyssa --- who were always there to provide inspiration, love and comic relief. I love you all.

. . . my sales department, my mother, Elinor, and my sister, Kathy, who believed in the possibilities even when I didn't. I love you both to the moon.

Special thanks and a round of applause go to my favorite cover photographer — Kathy Bradshaw. You do fantastic work, little acorn, and always make me look good. *Je t'aime.*

Finally, last and definitely not least, I owe a huge thank you and a large apple pie to my husband Bill who gave me hugs and kicks in the pants in equal amounts no matter how cranky I got. I love you first, last and always.

It took ages but here we go again. I hope you enjoy reading *Sibling Revelry*.

SIBLING REVELRY
BY TERRY SYKES-BRADSHAW

"*Mom? Mommy? Oh, God where are you? We're okay. Don't worry. He hasn't hurt us, but he says….*" Casey's voice on the answering machine quavered. Wasn't she shopping with Tessa? What was going on?

A male voice cut her off. Cold, flat and unemotional. "*I have taken your daughters. They are alive…for the moment. If you do exactly as I say, they will not be harmed. If not…*"

The frightening voice went on, but all I could hear was my heart pounding in my ears. My lungs collapsed. I couldn't breathe. No air in the room, in the country of Spain, in the entire universe.

A hand tugged at the receiver I had clenched in my freezing fingers. "Kate? Who is it? You look like death?"

Chrissie, my twin sister. I stared at her. I didn't want her to hear the sinister voice, but she had to. I jabbed at the telephone buttons. My fingers were shaking so badly that I missed the first time. I finally managed to get the message to play again. This time on the speaker.

As the terrifying voice filled the hotel room, Chrissie's eyes, glazed with horror, locked on mine.

"*I have taken your daughters. They are alive, for the moment. If you do exactly as I say, they will not be harmed. If not … I will kill them both.*

"*I have left instructions for you at the front desk. Do not call the police. You will not see your daughters alive again if you do. I am getting impatient. Do as I say. Do not try to fool me.*"

We stood paralyzed for a few seconds. Casey and Tessa were in danger. We had to do something.

"It's him," Chrissie breathed. "Isn't it?"

My mouth was glued shut. I could only manage a nod.

"I'll go to the front desk," Chrissie said and, shoeless, flew out the door.

I paced the room unable to sit still, nauseated with fear. Cold rivulets of sweat dripped down my sides. By the time Chrissie burst back into the room, waving a sheet of paper, I was hyperventilating.

"What does it say?"

"*Come to the bullring. Alone. Do not call the police. Your daughters are waiting for you.*"

I tossed Chrissie's sneakers to her. "Put them on. There's no time to waste."

She stuffed her feet into her shoes and we exploded out the door and clattered down the steps. We raced through the cobble-stoned streets dodging cars and pedestrians. Casey's face floated before my eyes. I imagined his hand holding a gun to her head as she begged for mercy.

"Hurry," I gasped.

"I am." Chrissie huffed out her words. "Will…we…make it?"

"We have to."

I shoved my hair out of my eyes. My vision was blurred with sweat. We finally reached the building and hurried inside. The huge wooden door leading to the bullring was secured with a heavy iron latch. I struggled with it and then popped the release and slammed the door open with my palm using strength I didn't know I possessed.

Chrissie saw the girls first. Her scream echoed off the high ceiling. I peered ahead of me, my heart racing.

A large dirt floor. Empty bleachers circling it. In the very center, two tiny forms twisted toward us.

Our daughters. Casey and Tessa. Bound and gagged. Their eyes wide above the gags.

And just behind them a mammoth black bull pawed the ground and snorted as he tossed his head from side to side. Would he attack them with his giant horns? Or were they in more danger from the man dressed all in black who had a large gun pointed directly at their heads?

This could *not* be happening.

PART ONE
PRE-FLIGHT

It all began with a margarita.

Toss in equal parts sun and sand and a pinch of dread about our next big birthday and you have the recipe for trouble. Of course, we didn't realize it at the time. For the first time in the three days we'd been in Florida, my twin sister, Chrissie, and I had grabbed some alone time at the beach. Most of our immediate family had gathered at Captiva for a surprise birthday celebration of our mother's 75th birthday. We were occupying several adjacent condos and personal space was at a premium. Finally when family togetherness turned into claustrophobia, Chrissie and I snuck away. We bought margaritas at the condo's convenient Tiki Bar and settled ourselves for a long afternoon at the beach.

I was mindlessly contemplating the waves or perhaps it was my wrinkly "elephant" knees when I was struck by a horrible thought. If you ask her, Chrissie will tell you that I screeched. She tends to exaggerate. I didn't screech. I don't screech. Ever. I can be a bit excitable at times, so perhaps I was impassioned. Yes, that's it. Impassioned. Anyway, I'm telling the story and she isn't.

So, I looked up from my examination of my knees and said to her, quite calmly, "I just realized that we have only three months until our birthday." Okay, I'll admit my voice sounded a bit shrill even to my own ears.

Chrissie leaned back in her beach chair and took a long sip of her drink. Eyes closed she drawled, "Seriously? You're just realizing that? It's the same day every single year."

I sighed. "I know, I know. I think I was in denial. But now it's staring us in the face."

"You're really bugged by this one, aren't you?"

I licked salt from the rim of my glass and looked at ... was that an age spot on my hand? "Any time we have a birthday ending in zero, I feel the sands of time drifting through our hourglass."

"I don't know about your hourglass," Chrissie said, "but mine is just fine. Thank you very much."

"I'm not going to debate it with you. I'm just saying we need to celebrate with something special."

"Can't we just ignore it and hope it will go away?"

"Maybe we could, but they…" I gestured at two slim figures loping down the beach away from us. "… aren't going to let us off that easy. Anything they come up with will be over the top."

"Like an intimate gathering in Michigan's football stadium for 111,000 of our nearest and dearest friends and relatives," Chrissie said.

I nodded. "With Michigan's marching band playing the birthday song."

We watched the waves roll in for a few moments. Finally, Chrissie said, "We could go to that twin festival thing again. We haven't done it in a while and I don't mind coming to Ohio."

"Let me think about it. Okay. No. The last time you made us wear matching outfits."

"Hel-*lo*. Twinsburg? Twin Festival? The operative word is twins. We're supposed to look like twins. They give prizes and stuff."

"Yeah, well, I looked like the plus size model of you."

"You did not, but come up with something else then."

"I'm not *totally* opposed to piercing another body part or getting another tattoo."

"Ow!" Chrissie grimaced. "I don't care if that tattoo guy is offering a buy one, get one free deal. That stuff is for the young and foolish."

"And now we are aged and wise beyond our many, many years," I said. "I guess it would be inappropriate to run off with a gigolo … although it's tempting at times. But we could have liposuction or a face lift."

Chrissie thought it over it for a nanosecond. Then she shook her head.

5

"Don't be ridiculous. I don't consider surgery an ideal way to spend our birthday."

She picked up my book, the new Evanovich mystery, from where I'd dropped it in the sand and handed it to me. "I suppose you want to bring out your inner Stephanie again," she said.

I shuddered. "No way. I'm thinking of something way more calm and age appropriate."

"That just sounds boring," she said.

"We'll come up with something," I said and picked up my book. "All I know is that it needs to be the two of us. I'm leaving crime solving to the experts."

I had no more than immersed myself in the adventures of Stephanie Plum when one of the two joggers we had seen earlier, my daughter Casey, trotted up. She collapsed on the beach towel next to me and nearly upended my margarita. I snatched it, slopping icy liquid on my hand and said, more sharply than I intended, "Watch it, Casey!"

Casey flipped her sunglasses up and gave me a long assessing stare. Then she laughed. "Someone's cranky."

"She seems to have issues with our upcoming birthday," my sister said.

"Ah," Casey said. "That explains it."

"Explains what?" Tessa, Chrissie's daughter, appeared and flopped on the sand. "What are you guys talking about?"

"The twins are discussing their birthday," Casey told her. "You know the big …"

I clapped a hand over Casey's mouth before she could say *that* number out loud. "We are not discussing it with you! Your aunt and I will figure out a suitable celebration without help from either of you, thank you very much."

"Grumpy isn't she?" Casey said.

"Speaking of birthdays," Tessa added, "where is the birthday girl? I thought

Nonny was coming to the beach with the two of you."

"Your fathers got home from the golf course and Nonny stayed at the condo to fix them something to eat," Chrissie said.

"That sounds like her," Tessa said.

"And it sounds like your father and your Uncle Scott," Chrissie continued. "They turn helpless whenever Nonny's around."

"Not that she minds waiting on them," I said. "She never let Dad spread his own peanut butter, let alone make an actual meal."

"Speak of the devil," Tessa said and pointed up the beach. "Here comes the birthday girl now."

We followed Tessa's gaze and saw our petite, white-haired mother struggling across the sand toward us carrying a cooler and a picnic basket. As she trudged in our direction she stopped every few yards to put down the heavy cooler and chat with other sunbathers. Casey and Tessa bounced to their feet and jogged down the beach to meet her and help her carry her picnic things.

"She never met a party she didn't want to be in charge of," I said to Chrissie, "including her own."

It was clear that Mom was resisting the girls' help and when they reached us she was still arguing with them. "I can manage," she said. "I'm not some helpless little old lady who can't drag her own cooler."

"Obviously," Chrissie said.

I jumped out of my chair so that she could sit in it and had to argue with her about that too. "Some people are too independent for their own good," I told her. She ignored me and opened the cooler and picnic basket to reveal the contents. Cold drinks and snacks that she distributed cheerfully.

"What a lovely day," Mom chirped. "Do you all have on sunblock?"

"Mother," I protested, "we aren't children."

Then I felt guilty about being testy. "But thank you for asking."

Chrissie added, "And thanks for the picnic."

"My pleasure," Mom said. "So, what did I miss?"

"Well," Tessa said, "The twins are trying to figure out what do for their next birth…" Chrissie shot her a warning look, but it was too late.

"A party?" Mom sat up abruptly, her cracker poised midway to her mouth. "This family party for me has been so much fun. We could do it again for you two. Remember your birthday picnics?"

Chrissie and I groaned. "How could we forget?" I said. "Those picnics are family legends, but I think we've outgrown that."

Chrissie just nodded.

Mom slumped in her chair. "Oh, I thought you two loved your picnics."

"We did when we were kids." I made a face. "But that was a *long* time ago."

"And we plan to celebrate this one by ourselves," Chrissie said. "Kate's in mourning for our lost youth."

Mom wrinkled her nose in distaste and pointed her finger at the tiny rose tattoo on Chrissie's shoulder. "I should hope you've also outgrown those youthful tattoos."

Chrissie jerked her T-shirt on and covered her tattoo as she looked helplessly at me over Mom's head. Clearly our birthday plans were now going to be open to group debate. I tugged my own shirt more securely around my shoulder where a twin to Chrissie's rose flourished. I moaned inwardly.

Everyone seemed to have an idea of what we should do for our birthday. The three of them debated our choices and ignored us as we sipped our drinks and nibbled on crackers and *brie*. Casey and Tessa kept exchanging odd looks and finally I said, "What's going on, you two? Have you already planned some major carnival?"

"Us?" Casey said with exaggerated innocence.

"Don't be silly," Tessa added. "It isn't always about you two, you know. We have our own lives to lead."

Casey patted Tessa's hand but Tessa yanked it away and bent forward to scrutinize a piece of sand clinging to her tennis shoe, her blonde hair falling over her face. Neither of them said a word for a few minutes as they sat shoulder to shoulder in the sand. Then Casey punched her cousin lightly on her tanned shoulder. "We really should help the aging twins plan their celebration, don't you think?" she said.

Tessa bit her lip and then said, "What about Tahiti?"

"No? What about Bali?"

"Where is Bali anyway?"

"Indonesia."

"Seriously? Still a no?"

"A cruise around the world?"

"On a ship?"

"Duh. What did you think in a rowboat?"

"A safari in deepest, darkest Africa?"

"No, I've got it. A trip down the Nile with a side trip to the Pyramids?"

As we finished our second margaritas and the late afternoon chill set in, we got sillier and sillier. As amazing as the suggested itineraries sounded, nothing really "spoke" to us. It was like turning the pages of a coffee table book to admire the glossy, beautiful photos of places you dream of visiting. Enticing yes, but with no emotional attachment.

At last Casey sat up and wrapped her arms around her knees. She turned to me with a grin and said, "I've got it. Why don't you and Aunt Chrissie go to one of those elder hostel places? I'm sure you'd fit right in."

"Elder? I'll show you elder." I lunged at Casey, but she squirmed out of reach, laughing.

"Elder hostels," Chrissie added, "are for *old* people."

"Now, Mom," Tessa said, "we didn't say you and Aunt Kate are old. You're vintage!"

"Classic," Casey said.

"It sounds like fun," Mom said. "You know that your Aunt June has done the elder hostel things several times."

"Aunt June?" I fumed. "Aunt June is your age."

"And what do you mean by that?" Mom fluffed her white curls and glared at me. "Are you trying to tell me I'm old?"

I had struck a nerve. Time to quit. I began to gather up the picnic remains and stuff them into the basket. "I'm cold," I announced. "Time to go back to the condo and get showered before dinner."

Chrissie mock shivered. "Definitely."

Swiftly we collected our things and started up the beach toward the condo. Mom and the girls dashed ahead of us, racing for the first shower. Chrissie and I trailed behind, walking at the edge of the water. The incoming waves washed over our toes and our feet made a slapping sound in the wet sand. Still seething over the elder hostel crack, I stomped along. I'm not … splash … old … slosh … enough for … splat … an elder hostel. The cold sand splattered on my bare legs. My margarita glass is way more than half full, I thought crossly. Plenty of salt left on my rim. I've still got lots of time… And I stopped so suddenly that an octogenarian clad in a revealing bikini nearly rear-ended me. I had it. The perfect celebration. "I'm so sorry." I said to the *past* vintage woman as I yanked Chrissie away from the ocean and into the sand. I blurted out my idea.

"Backpacking," she exclaimed. "Are you kidding me?"

"No. Think about it. I've always wanted to do it. It would be exciting and romantic. And…"

"Insane? Why didn't you do it when we were young?"

"Because Scott and I got married and I didn't think backpacking across Europe with two babies in tow would be all that romantic. But now? You and I could do it."

"No way. You go backpacking. I'll find something grown-up to do. Like Club Med."

"Talk about boring. You know you want to."

"I do not. And, if you really think about it, neither do you. You can't go out for the day without taking more supplies than your average backpack holds. What about your infamous shoe collection?"

"Okay. I hear you." I drew designs in the wet sand with my index finger. X's and O's. "So, what if…"

"What if instead of backpacking we took cars and trains?" I squiggled my bare toes in the sand. "And stay in hotels?" I twisted my wedding ring around on my finger thinking furiously. "Paris. Rome. Madrid. Think about it, Chrissie. Just the two of us. No husbands. No kids. Wine, culture, shopping."

I held my breath.

Chrissie vaulted to her feet, brushed the sand off her butt and looped an arm around my neck. "Ooh, baby," she said. "You had me at shopping."

"Welcome to the *Bubble Room*. My name is Keith and I'll be your Bubble Scout for your dining experience this evening." The gangly kid wearing what appeared to be a khaki Boy Scout uniform greeted us at the door of the quirky Captiva Island restaurant. He ducked his head as he ushered us through the doorway nearly dislodging the giant set of Mickey ears perched on his mop of red curls.

"Oops," he said. "Watch your step." As he guided our family past the seven-foot statue of Mickey guarding the entrance and into the restaurant, he looked over his shoulder. "We're passing through the Santa's workshop that was originally located at Macy's in New York City. Please watch out for the elves." He chuckled.

Indeed, we were surrounded by thousands of twinkling colored lights and Christmas decorations. Mechanical elves wielded hammers while Santa nodded his head and boomed, "Ho ho ho."

"Ooh, this is so cute," Tessa cooed, craning her neck to take it all in.

"Look, Tess," Casey said, "it's a poster of Betty Boop. And, over there." She waved her hand. "Isn't that old jukebox cool?"

Since there were 14 family members in our party, we had been able to reserve a large table in a separate room. A toy train chugged around a ledge just below the ceiling and Hollywood pin-ups were featured on the walls. Bubble lights cast colored shadows on the table as we arranged ourselves around it. Mom took the place of honor at the head of the table.

"I love this place," she said. "Isn't that Myrna Loy over there on the wall? And there's Clark Gable."

Keith took our drink order and scurried off to the kitchen leaving us to gaze around in amazement. My husband, Scott, and Chrissie's husband, Max, and our brothers, Bill and Bryan, and Bill's two teen-aged sons sat together at one end of the table arguing over which team would win the next NFL playoff game. The girls were grouped at the other end chattering about places to shop and what we might order for dinner.

Mom seemed enchanted by our selection of the *Bubble Room* as the venue for her big birthday dinner. "Good choice," I whispered to Chrissie. "We did well."

She nodded and sipped her glass of wine. She quickly glanced up and down the table before she whispered back, "But I'm looking forward to ours."

We grinned at each other. "I know," I said. "I'm thinking Chateaubriand on the *Champs Élysées.*"

Casey, sitting on my right, had appeared to be absorbed in conversation with her 12-year old cousin, Olivia, Bryan's daughter. But she jerked her head in my direction and raised her eyebrows. "What about the *Champs Élysées*? Are you thinking of going to Paris?"

Suddenly all conversation at the table died and our entire family focused its attention on Chrissie and me. Mom put her elbows on the table and propped her chin on her hands as she leaned toward us. "Do you girls have something to tell us?"

"Today didn't seem like the time to announce it," I said. "It's your day not ours."

"But yes, we did kind of decide on our birthday destination," Chrissie added.

Mom fluffed her hair and beamed at us. "I think that sounds delightful. You two will have a wonderful time in Paris."

"I'm insanely jealous," Casey said. "Paris is my absolute favorite city in the entire world."

"We'll bring back souvenirs," Chrissie said.

Tessa poked her arm. "Nice, Mom. Generous of you."

The guys weren't that interested and went back to their heated football discussion, but the girls gossiped about our tentative itinerary.

"I'd go with you," said Casey, "but I'll be in LA with Lester by your birthday."

"Really?" Tessa asked. "I didn't think you were moving so soon."

"We've given up our apartment and all we have to do is load up the moving trucks."

"Awesome," Tessa said.

"Yeah. Awesome," I echoed with a decided lack of enthusiasm.

Casey frowned at me. "Don't be sarcastic, Mom. I know you and Dad don't like Lester."

I couldn't really argue. We never had much liked Lester, her boyfriend and roommate. He's one of those weak-chinned guys who makes me feel vaguely slimy when I'm around him. Scott refers to him as "ferret face" which is letting him off easy if you ask me.

But I love Casey so I keep trying to find the good in the boy. Hard work, but she's my daughter.

"It's not that we don't like Lester, sweetie," I said to her. "We want you to be happy."

"The implication being that Lester won't make me happy?" Casey took a huge gulp of wine and turned her back on me.

Oops.

Tessa tossed her head, her blonde bob swinging. "I can go with you."

Chrissie carefully set her glass down on the table and looked Tessa in the eye. "I don't remember inviting you, but no, you can't. You'll be involved in that internship Dad set up for you," she said. "Have you forgotten that?"

"No, of course not," Tessa said. She slumped in her chair. "How on earth could I forget something as fascinating as an internship in a law office? Silly me."

Chrissie scrutinized her face and then shrugged. "Yeah, silly you."

In a stroke of good timing Keith materialized with our dinners and in the ensuing commotion, our upcoming birthday trip was momentarily forgotten. Not before, though, my mother caught my eye and said, "More murder and mayhem, sweetheart. I know you love a good adventure."

"Not this time, Mom," I said. "We're going to have a cultured and civilized trip to celebrate our advanced years."

Mom rolled her eyes and attacked her sirloin. How annoying. I get involved in one teensy murder investigation and she acts like I'm a magnet for trouble. Honestly.

Mom tossed her purse on the floor and collapsed on the couch still clutching her box of dinner leftovers. She groaned dramatically and said, "I'm stuffed. That was absolutely delicious. *The Bubble Room* is … hmm." She trailed off with a sigh.

Chrissie and I plopped down on either side of her and the three of us sprawled comfortably, our heads against the back of the couch, our feet propped on the coffee table. No one spoke for several minutes, each of us absorbed in her own thoughts.

Finally, Mom heaved a great, satisfied sigh and struggled to a sitting position. She plunked her box on the coffee table and said, "I should put this in the fridge."

"No. I'll do it," I said.

"Let me," Chrissie said.

But no one moved as much as a toe. The only sound in the room was the monotonous ticking of the battery powered flamingo wall clock and distant laughter from outside. Several more minutes passed before Mom sighed again. "Dinner was wonderful. I loved it. But this is even better. Peace and quiet and my two girls all to myself."

"Um-m-m." I kicked off one flip flop and let it fall on the floor. "The silence won't last forever. They'll all descend on us soon."

Chrissie sank into the corner of the couch and put her feet in Mom's lap.

A few more beats of silence and then Mom, her eyes still closed, asked, "You really did make a decision about your birthday?"

"It was Kate's idea," Chrissie said, "but I think it's perfect."

"Paris sounds so lovely. Particularly in May. Your dad and I had such wonderful trips there. I always thought we'd go again."

Uh oh. My eyes popped open and I looked over Mom's head at Chrissie.

Before I could open my mouth, Mom continued, "This will be so special for the two of you. I'm excited for you."

Chrissie raised an eyebrow at me and I shrugged. Before I could formulate a response, though, Casey and Tessa burst into the room followed by a giggling Olivia clutching a dripping chocolate cone and a huge conch shell. "You'll never guess what happened at the ice cream place, Nonny," Olivia said, licking her cone and holding the shell out to her grandmother.

Saved by the ice cream cone! I patted the couch and held out my arms to Olivia. "Olivia, sweetie, come sit over here and tell Aunt Chrissie and Nonny and me all about it."

15

Hours later I was curled up in bed next to Scott dreaming that I was sprinting down an airport concourse naked except for my flip flops. The plane would leave without me if I didn't get there in time, but I moved as if I was slogging through tapioca. I can't run in these things, I huffed, and kicked my flip flops aside. When I reached the gate I realized that I had no idea what the destination of my flight was. Suddenly I heard a band strike up a chorus of "New York, New York", and I frantically tugged on the arm of a fellow passenger. "What's happening?" And Scott yanked his arm out of my grip and, mumbling incoherently, turned over dragging the blankets with him.

I rolled over onto my back, my heart still pounding as the strains of "New York, New York" pierced my sleep fogged brain and I realized that it was Casey's cellphone chiming in the distance. Lester's ringtone. Good, I thought, as I drifted back to sleep. Casey had been leaving messages and texts for him all day. She'd be happy to hear from him. I fell into a deep and, this time, dreamless sleep lulled by the soft murmur of my daughter's voice in the adjoining room.

I had no idea of how much time had passed when I was awakened by a soft tapping on the bedroom door. I poked Scott. "Scott, did you hear anything?" He gave a soft snort in response.

A few seconds ticked away and simultaneously I heard sniffling and Casey whispering, "Mom? Mommy?"

Oh, my God, the small voice. I winced as I rubbed my eyes and tried to focus. This couldn't be good.

"Casey? Honey? What's up, babes?"

More sniffling from the doorway.

"Casey?" I threw back the covers and patted the bed. "Come here and tell me what's going on."

Casey tiptoed across the shadowy room. Wearing a skintight "I Love New York" tank top and boxers with her eggplant hair standing up in gelled peaks, she looked like a baby bird. My baby bird. She sank onto the bed and a single tear slid down her cheek.

"Okay. Tell me what's wrong."

She drew a wobbly breath. "We had a fight."

I hugged her and pulled her close. She didn't resist as more tears streaked down her face.

"We'll wake up Dad," she said.

"The Michigan marching band couldn't wake Dad, but let's go out into the other room if you'll be more comfortable."

I led her into the living room, switched on a lamp, shoved her gently onto the couch and handed her a tissue. She blew her nose noisily and crumpled the tissue in her hand.

"Now, tell me what you and Lester fought about," I said as I sat beside her and wrapped us both in an afghan.

"Nothing. Everything. It's all my fault."

"Case ... you and Lester have had fights before. You'll make up in the morning."

Casey scrubbed at her eyes with the damp tissue. "Not this time. It's o-o-ver." She gulped. "It's all my fault."

"Casey. Stop. I can't help if you don't tell me what happened."

"Well-l-l." She swallowed as if the words were painful. "Yesterday was his last day of work. Big party for him last night."

I nodded.

"I texted him all day and left messages on his cell and at home and at work. I just wanted to talk. Was that wrong of me?"

"Of course not."

"Well, apparently it was. He said. He told me. I mean. He didn't...he doesn't...we aren't..."

She shredded the tissue and then said in a rush, "Going to LA together. He wants his space. Space!" She laughed a bit hysterically. "Oh, I can go. Just not with him. He said I'm too demanding."

"Oh, sweetie," I said. "He's a snake." More harsh words occurred to me but I bit them back at the same time I slapped down a brief mental, "Yay."

"I'm a bad person. I talked and talked, but he won't budge. I'm a nag. If I hadn't texted and…"

"Casey, listen to me," I said. "You are not a bad person. Lester's a jerk. You're better off without him."

"But what am I going to do-o-o-o-o?" she wailed. "I quit my job. The apartment is rented. My furniture is in storage. And Lester doesn't wa-ant me. I'll be homeless. I'll have to live in a cardboard box on the street."

"Don't be such a drama queen," I said. "You don't have to live in a box. You can live with Dad and me. We'd love to have you."

"Oh, right," she said. "You and Dad don't want a 23 year-old reject loser living with you. Besides my room is Dad's den now."

"We'll figure something out. I promise."

"But, Mom, I really wanted to go to LA."

"I know, I know, but you can let me take care of you for a little while. Home cooking and TLC."

I thought she was about to agree when a stricken look crossed her face. "Your birthday! You and Aunt Chris are supposed to go to Paris."

Call me crazy, but I had no choice. I sent a silent plea to Chrissie for understanding and said, "Well, maybe you can't explore LA with Lester, but you can explore Europe with your wonderful mother and aunt. We'd love to have you along as our official photographer."

She considered my offer for a second. "Europe? I've always wanted to go back to Paris . . . but . . . I ca-an't. I'd ruin it for you."

"Don't be ridiculous, babycakes. I won't take no for an answer."

In my mind the matter was settled. I hoped that Chrissie would be onboard too.

Not nearly enough hours later I woke with a jolt, a nervous knot in the pit of my stomach. Casey and I had talked and cried until exhaustion drove us into unconsciousness. Now I dragged myself out of bed and stumbled toward the kitchen driven by an urgent need for coffee…strong and a lot of it.

In the kitchen I was surprised to find my sister perched on a barstool staring into space, a mug of coffee cooling in front of her. She looked up as I staggered into the room, her long face a warning of something distressing to come.

"What're you doing here?" I asked her. "How did you get in?"

"Waiting for you. Tessa let me in." Tessa was sharing a room with Casey in our condo while Mom was bunking in the extra room in Chrissie and Max's place.

She hopped off the barstool, poured me a mug of coffee and said, "Drink. You're gonna need it."

I took a sip and then another trying to lift the fog from my brain. Chrissie watched, one foot tapping rapidly against the rung of the stool.

"Okay, shoot," I said when I felt ready to deal with whatever was coming. "What has you up and out at this…" I glanced at the clock. Seven o'clock? "…ungodly hour?"

Chrissie blew out a breath. "Tessa and I went for a walk on the beach."

"And?"

"And she told me that she's dropping out of school."

"She is? I thought she loved school." Tessa is a first year law student at the University of Michigan, always a high achiever with top grades and a multitude of extracurriculars. Every parent's dream child.

Chrissie poured some milk into her coffee and took her time stirring it. "There's more," she said.

"Now you're just freaking me out. She's not. She couldn't be. Pregnant?"

"No-o-o. Maybe worse. She's dropping out of law school." I heard an

19

implied drum roll in my sister's voice. "To become an exotic dancer." Her voice rose to a wail.

I gave a snort of laughter and then covered my mouth to stifle it.

Chrissie glared at me. "It's not funny."

"It kind of is."

"I'm so glad you are finding humor in this," Chrissie said.

"Oh, lighten up. I'm sure that a kid as dedicated as Tessa will be a huge success in her chosen career."

"Ha ha. I knew something like this was bound to happen."

"You did? Why?"

"You know that Tessa never really wanted to go to law school. Her father sort of pushed her into it."

"Max did? I always assumed since she was a champion debater in high school that she'd be a fantastic lawyer."

"She would. But she'd rather be an exotic dancer. Go figure."

"That's a big leap. Get it? Leap? A dancer leaps!"

"Yeah. Hilarious," Chrissie said dryly. "But I think that's the point. To take as big a leap away from Max and his goals for her as possible. He's not going to be thrilled when he finds out."

Max is a bit of a stuffed shirt in a sweet kind of way and I could easily imagine his reaction to the news.

"I'm sure Tessa has perfectly good reasons for her decision. Do you want me to talk to her?" Chrissie knew that Tessa and I have always enjoyed a special relationship, born of a shared desire to take the path less traveled. I, of all people, might understand her. She'd always worked hard . . . maybe too hard . . . to live up to her parents' expectations and I had wondered for years if she would ever break free and assert her independence. Now, it appeared, she had.

"Please talk to her, Katie. I need your input on this one."

"The little birdie is flying away from the nest," I said.

20

"The little birdie is taking a jet plane out of the nest," Chrissie corrected me. "And naked at that."

I had to laugh at the woebegone expression on Chrissie's face.

"I'll try."

I found Tessa in the girls' room packing for the return trip to Ann Arbor. She had nothing on but her bra and panties and the music blaring from her iPod speakers. I stood in the doorway for a few moments watching as Tessa undulated and shimmied to the music. I had to admit she had a gorgeous figure and all the moves to make her an outstanding dancer. Exotic or otherwise.

I knocked on the door and Tessa grinned as she noticed me. "Hey, Aunt Kate."

She motioned me in and turned down the volume on her iPod, but her hips wiggled as she stuffed a tiny tank top into her bag. I shoved aside a stack of thong panties, perched on the edge of the chair and waited.

She picked up another top and air-folded it before she stopped shaking her cute little booty and winked. "I'll bet my mom sent you to talk me out of, and I quote, 'this craziness' of mine."

"Busted," I said.

"Tough assignment. I've made my decision and I'm sticking to it. I'm finished with law school."

"I hear you about law school. I think it would be excruciatingly dull, but is exotic dancing really the way you want to go? I mean, when you're my age will you still want to be . . . um . . . stripping for a living?"

Tessa's eyes went wide. "Stripping? Is that what she thinks? Honestly, Aunt Kate, I'm not stripping. I'm not that bold. Trust me. I'll be covered at all times. At least the important parts. Tell Mom that, will you? I don't think she was paying attention."

"Well, if it's not stripping what kind of dancing will you be doing?"

"Pole dancing."

"Seriously? How did you find that particular career?"

"I took a class in pole dancing at the rec center. I needed a break from my mind-numbing law courses and I've always loved to dance."

"Uh huh." I pictured Tessa at two wearing a pink tutu, her blond ringlets topped by a pink ribbon, dancing at her first ballet recital. I smiled.

"It's the newest thing in exercise and it's really fun. Candi, the instructor, and I got to talking one day after class and she mentioned a place that needed dancers and I decided to try out. And I got the job."

"Uh huh." I pictured Tessa at 21 wearing nothing, her blonde bob topped by a pink feather, gyrating around a pole. I cringed.

"Why don't you stay in school and become a lawyer? Make your parents happy. Become a Jazzercise instructor on the side."

Tessa laughed. "You and your Jazzercise. Do you know what Jazzercise instructors make these days?"

"Not a lot," I said. "Mostly they do it because they love it."

"Excuse me but," Tessa said, "barely enough to cover their asses, er, assets. I could potentially make six figures dancing with tips and salary."

I whistled. "You have a point, darlin'."

Tessa was hellbent on dancing and, hey, she'd probably be a crowd pleaser. It was the particular crowd that concerned me. I knew that I was going to have to pull out the big guns. Bribery was not off the table.

"Would you be open to a counter proposal?"

Tessa quirked an eyebrow at me in a gesture that reminded me of her mother. "Show me what you've got!"

"I'll give you quitting law school. Your mom and dad won't be happy about it, but they'll come around. I'll get them to see your side of it. But they won't budge on the stripping, I mean, pole dancing."

"I was planning on dancing this summer to make enough so I can rent an apartment in New York City for a few months."

"Well, I can't promise you New York, but I can offer you an all-expense paid trip to Paris and other exotic spots with your mom and me."

So, shoot me, I hoped that having Tessa along would cheer Casey up. If not, what's another happy celebrant? I gazed out the window at the palm fronds swaying in the breeze while I waited for Tessa to make up her mind.

Finally Tessa dropped onto the bed opposite my chair and looked me in the eye, her blue eyes twinkling. "You don't have to work so hard, Aunt Kate. You had me at Paris."

Chrissie wasn't hanging out in my condo's kitchen or in her place next door so I pulled on my swimsuit, grabbed my beach bag and headed for the pool. It was still early and the pool area was deserted except for one swimmer about my mother's age who was swimming slow laps, her flowered cap bobbing with each deliberate stroke. No Chrissie. As I rounded the corner and passed the Tiki bar, though, I spotted her stretched out on a deck chair underneath a red and white striped umbrella in an isolated corner of the enclosure. She was wearing a bright red swimsuit and a broad-brimmed straw hat and her book lay open on her stomach. She appeared to be asleep. My flip flops slapped the cement surface as I made my way to her secluded corner, but Chrissie didn't budge.

I tweaked her toe. "Hey," I said.

"Hey," she said and didn't move.

I plopped myself down onto the other chair nestled under the umbrella, picked up her bottle of sunblock and started slathering it on my arms and shoulders. When I finished I draped my towel over the chair and sprawled comfortably. I had expected her to be curious about what I'd found out from Tessa but obviously she wasn't going to ask. "You can thank me anytime," I said at last.

"Thank you," Chrissie said automatically. The lone swimmer splashed to the edge of the pool and I concentrated on her progress. Finally, Chrissie said, "What am I thanking you for exactly?"

"I talked to Tessa."

That got her attention. Chrissie sat up and shoved her sunglasses up on her head. She gaped at me. "Don't keep me in suspense here, Kate, what did she say?"

"Do you want the good news or the bad news first?"

"Just tell me."

"Okay, I'm sorry. Tessa was adamant about law school. She hates it and isn't going back after this semester."

"Go on."

I poked her arm. "However, your sister possesses miraculous powers of persuasion and Tessa has agreed not to accept the dance position."

When Chrissie didn't respond, I said, "Hey. I'd appreciate a round of applause. Maybe even a standing 'O' here."

"Oh, I'm sorry, Katie. That's great. Max won't be thrilled about law school, but at least I don't have to break it to him that his only daughter is a stripper."

"You weren't listening, Chris. It wasn't stripping. It was pole dancing."

"Oh, that's so much better. So how did you accomplish this miracle?"

"Well-l-l," I said. "I had to resort to bribery. I invited Tessa to join us on our birthday trip to Europe. All expenses paid."

"You're paying for Tessa?"

"Nope. You are." I took a long sip from the sweaty glass next to her. "And it's a small price to pay to get her to keep her clothes on."

Chrissie hopped up and hugged me. "The three of us will have fun. I know Tessa's just a kid, but…"

"Wait, Chris," I interrupted her. "There's one other tiny confession I have to make. It won't be three of us. It's more like four. I invited Casey."

"I thought she was moving to LA with Lester. She's not? You can explain

24

that later, but, well, there's something I should tell you too in the interests of full disclosure. I was going to wait, but …"

"Shoot."

"Have you talked to Mom today?"

"Not today. Why?"

"We had coffee and she was going on and on about how wonderful our trip was going to be."

"Uh oh."

"And," Chrissie said, "she told me how special it is to go on a trip with someone you love."

"Uh oh."

"She said it was so exciting being in Paris in the spring and she had all these memories of Dad and their trip."

"Uh oh."

"Quit saying that," Chrissie said.

"You asked her to join us, didn't you?"

"Like I had a choice. Could you have just flown off and left her here? Especially now that the girls are coming too. It would ruin the trip to think of her alone and pining away."

"Mom's never alone. And she doesn't pine. But I see your point."

"She tried to say no and I had to argue with her about it before she gave in."

"Uh huh," I said. "How long did it take you to convince her? A minute?"

"Longer than that. She doesn't want to be a burden."

The last time that Mom was a burden was, well, never. My dad died four years ago but Mom is self-sufficient and certainly appears to be enjoying her life. It would be fun to have her along, I guessed.

"So, it's a party of five," Chrissie said. "This sure isn't the vacation we planned, is it?"

"Planning is for sissies," I said with uncharacteristic optimism. "The five of us will have a blast."

"Uh huh," she said.

Chrissie hugged me goodbye at the airport the next day as the family prepared to return to our homes. Scott and I were heading back to Ohio and Casey was going to New York to collect her possessions before moving in with us. Tessa planned to take her finals and then go to Florida and stay with Chrissie and Max until our birthday trip. And our brothers and their families were driving home to Michigan.

"I'll call you," I said to Chrissie, "after I talk to Mary Linda."

My Jazzer-friend, Mary Linda St. Clair, owns *You're Out of Order*, a small business dedicated to creating order out of chaos. We decided to use her services to plan our trip.

"Keep in mind," Chrissie said, "I want to do Spain too. Not just France."

"Got it," I said. "Equal parts Spain and France. I was thinking of Paris and Nice."

"And Barcelona and Madrid," Chrissie added.

Suddenly I had a brilliant idea. "We could stay in one of those paradors in Spain that my friends keep recommending."

"Paradors?"

"Inns owned by the government that are converted from deserted castles, monasteries or palaces. Things like that."

"Oh, wow. Cool."

"Mary Linda told me that the Parador in Ronda is amazing."

"Ronda?" Chrissie blanched. "The village famous for the bullring?" She shook her head. "No way. You know how I hate bulls."

"First," I said in my patient big sister voice, "I don't know why you're so afraid of them. It's not as if you've ever come out on the wrong end of a bullfight or something. And second, we're not bunking at the bullring or running with the bulls. I promise you won't have to see a single scary bull if you don't want to."

"Sarcasm isn't necessary," Chrissie replied. "But you win. I'll go to Ronda if you think we shouldn't miss it."

"Oh, Kate," she said as she hugged me one last time, "I think I'm glad that Mom and the girls are coming along."

"Me, too," I said. Maybe.

"Remember our motto," Chrissie added. "She who buys the most cute outfits wins."

PART TWO
IN FLIGHT

"Ah, Business." Chrissie purred with the same blissful satisfaction she might have used to describe a triple chocolate fudge brownie.

I stepped into the aisle of the Paris-bound Delta 767 to allow her to squeeze past me to her window seat and then slid into the seat next to her. I kicked off my shoes and stretched my legs out. "I can barely touch the seat in front of me," I said.

A trim flight attendant stopped beside us and held out the tray she was carrying. "Would you like champagne or a mimosa while we get settled?"

"Definitely," I said. "Thank you." I plucked a glass from the tray, handed it to Chrissie and took a second for myself.

"Business Class is so worth bankrupting our frequent flyer mileage accounts," Chrissie said.

"You mean Max's and Scott's accounts, but we've earned it. Long life, very long life, should be rewarded." I hoisted my glass and touched hers. "To an amazing trip!"

Chrissie looked up from the menu she was reading. "To glazed salmon with quinoa and arugula," she said.

I squirmed in my seat, checking out the other passengers and the cabin and turned back to my sister. "I can't believe we're finally here."

"I feel kind of bad about our birthday groupies relegated to the cheap seats," Chrissie said.

Mom and Casey and Tessa were traveling in the crowded, less comfortable and far cheaper coach section of the plane.

"I tried to convince Mom to take my Business seat," I said, "but she wouldn't budge."

Chrissie snorted. "I've seen political announcements with more sincerity than your attempt to convince her."

"Ha ha," I said. "I tried. And I only feel a tiny bit guilty. If I know Mom she'll have the entire coach section singing Kumbaya together before we land."

Chrissie snickered. "You're so bad."

Shortly after takeoff, we accepted a pre-dinner glass of wine and a ceramic cup of warmed nuts from one of the accommodating flight attendants. I balanced my glass on my knee while I rummaged in my carry-on bag for my iPod and my book. "Rats," I said straightening up with an iPod in my hand.

"Problem?" Chrissie asked.

"Sort of," I said. "This is Casey's iPod. We must've gotten them mixed up on the plane from Ohio."

"Are you sure it's not yours?"

"The playlists on this one include 'Sad Songs' and 'Our Songs'. Definitely not mine."

"No show tunes?"

"Not unless the show is *Les Miserables*. Casey's been in a black mood since she's been home. It's been like living with a pod person."

"The trip will snap her out of it," Chrissie said. "Give her something to focus on instead of Ferret Face, I mean, Lester."

"I hope so. In the meantime, I'm going to go get my iPod."

I slid out of my seat and started toward the back of the plane, dodging the drink cart and other passengers. When I reached the last row of Business Class, opposite the galley, my path was completely blocked by several flight attendants engrossed in a heated discussion with a seated couple. I couldn't understand what was being said since most of what I could hear was in French. The man, slight and balding with a bad comb over and a nervous twitch contorting his eyebrows, gestured wildly. His female companion, perhaps trying to be invisible, slouched in her seat, a magazine shielding her face. I caught only a glimpse of fuzzy, blondish curls.

Nosy as always, I pretended to be absorbed in reading the inflight magazine while I lurked in the aisle and eavesdropped brazenly. Finally one of the attendants noticed me and gave me an apologetic shrug. "*Pardon, madame. Un moment.* We need to take care of a situation."

"*Pas de problem,*" I said. I congratulated myself on my French.

The little drama concluded as I watched the flight attendants officiously escort the couple from the Business seats. I shook my head and did a mental shrug, but I was in a rush to get my iPod and return to my seat before my meal was served. I tossed my magazine toward the seat the French couple had vacated and a glimmer of something shiny caught my eye. I looked down and saw a gold hoop earring lying there. I scooped it up and hurried after the couple as they unceremoniously exited the rarified air of the Business Class and vanished into coach. "Wait," I called.

I reached them as they were settling into seats a few rows into coach. The man was in the window seat still gesticulating and ranting in rapid French. The woman had her back to me, struggling to stuff her oversized bag into the overhead bin. I tapped her on the shoulder and she stiffened and then spun around to face me. Her eyes were blazing and she looked ready to pounce. I flinched and stumbled backward. But when she saw me holding the earring out to her, her ferocious expression sagged into one of confusion. Our gazes locked for a few seconds and an inexplicable flash of recognition passed between us.

I couldn't explain the odd feeling of familiarity. Of course, I knew I had never met the moderately attractive, blonde. But I froze in place for a few seconds as I checked her out. Wearing black leggings and a nondescript black tunic sweater, she was definitely not fashion forward. Her hair was a mass of unruly curls and lacked any sense of style. In fact, she could have benefited from the use of a comb. Incongruously, though, her shoes were bright red peep-toed stilettos. Possibly Louboutin or Jimmy Choo. Certainly designer. Believe me, I

30

know my shoes. When she observed me ogling them with what I am sure was a covetous stare, her lips curved into a small half smile directed at a fellow Sister in the Fellowship of Shoe Lovers.

I pressed the earring into her hand and she murmured an embarrassed, "*Merci,*" before she slouched into her seat and I hurried off in search of my family.

Hmm, I thought, now that was odd, and promptly pushed the strange encounter to the back of my mind. I'll think about it later, I told myself.

I headed toward the back of the plane where I knew Mom and the girls were sitting. I was so focused on getting there that I nearly shrieked in surprise as I hurried past the exit row and a hand snaked out from the aisle seat and grabbed me. Willing my racing heart to slow down, I looked down and saw Tessa grinning up at me. "Hey, Aunt Kate," she said, "where're you going in such a hurry?"

"Tessa," I said, "what are you…" I looked past her. "…and Casey doing in exit row seats? I'm positive that you were a lot further back."

And then, when I realized that Mom wasn't with them, I said, "And where's Nonny?"

Tessa giggled and gestured. "Back there."

Sure enough, there she was a few rows back seated next to a distinguished white-haired gentleman and so engrossed that I doubt she would have noticed me if I sat on her lap. Leave it to Mom to turn a plane trip into a blind date.

"How did this come about?" I asked.

"Oh, Nonny has her ways," Tessa said. "She was so cute wheeling, dealing and flirting."

I had to smile. Indeed, she did have her ways.

I handed Casey's iPod to her and she quickly passed mine to me. Just then Mom tore her attention away from her handsome seatmate and saw me lurking in the aisle. She waved gaily and motioned to me to join them.

"Hi Kate," Mom said when I reached her seat.

I leaned down to give her a quick peck on her cheek and managed to give her companion a quick once over. I estimated that he was about Mom's age and well-dressed in pressed jeans and cashmere sweater.

"Kate," Mom said, "this is my new friend, Bobby MacTavish." She smiled up at him. Coyly, I might add.

"Bobby," she added, "this is Kate, one of my twin daughters."

As Bobby attempted to stand up I realized that he was too tall to accomplish this in the cramped coach seats. Hunched over, he extended his hand. "Aye, I'm delighted to meet you."

His heavy Scottish accent took me by surprise. Then he grinned at me and I could see why Mom was attracted to him. That accent and that smile! Sexy and charming. Perfect for a plane date that would end upon landing.

When I returned to my seat I found Chrissie enjoying another pre-dinner glass of wine. "Whoa," I said. "You're getting ahead of me."

"Well, the flight attendant offered me more wine and I decided it would be rude to refuse." Chrissie beamed at me. "Did you see the girls and Mom? Is everything okay with them?"

"Let me get me a glass of that and I'll tell you everything." I signaled the nearest flight attendant. "You will not believe it."

By the time we were sipping after dinner liqueurs, we had not only devoured every crumb of our delicious Business class dinner but had also chewed over and dissected every delicious morsel related to our mother's love life or potential love life.

Chrissie leaned her head against the headrest and contemplated her glass as she swirled the chocolate liqueur in it. "So," she said, "you really think Mom is hooking up with some low life Scot?"

I ran my tongue around the rim of my glass. "In the first place, Chris, Mom is not hooking up. And in the second place, this Bobby didn't seem like a low life to me."

"What then?"

"I told you he's good looking in a mature gentleman kind of way. Kind of Sean Connery with white hair. And he was nice. Well-mannered and…"

"And what else?"

"You want me to say it? Okay. Bobby is hot. And Mom seemed captivated."

Chrissie sipped her drink, leaned toward me and whispered, "It's not that I don't want Mom to have fun. I mean, Dad died four years ago and she must get lonely. But a pick up on a plane? Not so much."

"Relax, Chris," I said, "she'll never see him after we land in Paris. Even if she did, is that such a terrible thing? She and Dad got married when she was a teenager, so I'm sure she never sowed so much as a single wild oat. It's past time."

She gulped her drink and gave me a rueful smile. "Yeah, yeah, yeah. I'd go back to check him out, but I'm way too comfy right here."

"Oh?" I said. "Is that what they're calling it now? Comfy? In my day, we called it 'tipsy.'"

"Don't be ridic-u-lous." Chrissie enunciated deliberately. "I am not tipsy. In fact…" She signaled an accommodating flight attendant. "…I think I'll have a teensy weensy bit more Baileys."

I studied her face for a moment and then shrugged. "Better make it two. I don't want you to get comfy alone."

PART THREE
C'EST LA VIE
Chapter 1

Shortly after we landed at Paris' Charles DeGaulle Airport, Chrissie and I were fidgeting at the end of the jetway while we waited for Mom and the girls to appear. Chrissie had decided not to run the gauntlet of food carts and groggy passengers clogging the aisles before landing, so she hadn't met Bobby MacTavish yet and was impatient to do so. She peered expectantly at the mob of deplaning passengers, standing on tiptoe to get a better view.

"What's taking them so long?" she fumed. "The plane must be empty by now."

I rummaged in my bag for my passport and baggage claim ticket only partially aware of the crowd oozing past us. I was so absorbed in the contents of my purse that I almost missed seeing the French couple who had been evicted from Business Class early in the flight. The man, looking grumpy and irritated, was speeding along with his frowzy companion tottering on her stilettos in his wake. She caught my eye as I looked up, gave me a tiny smile and raised one finger in a salute. I nodded and nudged Chrissie. "That's the couple I told you about, Chris." I pointed. "You remember?"

"Those shoes are to die for," Chris said. Obviously she retained only the most important details of my story. "Could be Prada."

Before the shoe debate could go further, I spotted Mom and Bobby. She was still chatting and forced to do a little jog to keep up with Bobby's long-legged stride. Occasionally he would pause and lean down, perhaps to better hear her. Mom was so absorbed that she nearly walked right by us.

I stepped in front of her and she jumped.

"Hey, Mom," I said. "Here we are."

"Oh, dear," she said and laughed. "I didn't see you."

34

"Where are Casey and Tessa?" I asked.

"Right behind us. Oh, there they are."

We all turned toward the plane. Casey appeared first, deep in conversation with a tall young man who tossed a shock of thick, shiny hair out of his eyes as he bent to speak to her. I stared.

"Um," I said. "Do I know the boy with Casey? He looks familiar."

Tessa came into view next, clinging to the arm of a cheerful looking young man who bore a strong resemblance to Casey's escort. They made a striking couple, both blonde, blue-eyed and athletic.

Chrissie grabbed Tessa's arm. "Hey, Tessa."

"Oh, hey, Mom, I didn't see you." Tessa said with a chuckle, still distracted by her good-looking companion.

"Oh, my," I said as it registered. "Those two look just like…."

"Bobby," Mom finished. "They should. They're his grandsons, Robert and Mac."

Mom and the girls hastily introduced the MacTavish men as we moved toward the endless line snaking through customs and immigration. As Casey, Tessa and Mom said their good-byes to their plane dates and we prepared to go our separate ways, Chrissie whispered to me. "I see what you mean. Bobby is cute and Mom does seem to be attracted to him."

"I know," I whispered back, "but she'll never see him again. I guess a little flirtation among senior citizens helped pass the time on the flight."

"Maybe," Chris said with a nod toward the girls, "but what about them?"

Tessa and Casey and the two MacTavish grandsons stood to one side and peals of merriment drifted our way. Tessa threw back her head and howled at something Mac said, while Casey leaned against Robert as she tugged her shoe on. The look she gave him was way too seductive to make me think this was just a casual flirtation.

"Let's not worry about it," I said. "Our adventure is about to begin and no

Scottish interlopers are invited. No matter how sexy and charming."

"Ooh, la la," Chris said.

I admit that I was relieved when we disentangled ourselves from the MacTavish men. Their uninterrupted charm had become a tad cloying and I was anxious to get on with our adventure. It was our birthday, after all, and I wasn't about to let some love fest take over. Enough is enough, I huffed silently.

Chrissie who knows me better than anyone said, "Don't be grumpy. It's just us now."

By the time we reached the baggage area, most of the other passengers had claimed their luggage and departed, but I thought I caught a glimpse of red stilettos disappearing down the passageway. The baggage area was nearly deserted and our bags were among the lonely few left riding in infinite circles on the carousel. We snatched them, hurried outside and looked around. It was a chilly grey morning, the sun still not up. Taxis and buses littered the drive and pedestrians dragging roller bags wove their way around them. I took a deep breath.

"I swear I can smell croissants," I said.

"All I can smell is exhaust fumes," Casey said. But her grumpy tone contrasted with her sparkling eyes and chipper smile. The pod person had gone into hibernation and I hoped would never return.

Mom started dragging her bag down the sidewalk. "Come on, everyone. The train is down this way."

"Uh uh," I said. "We're taking a cab into Paris. I'm not up for a train ride."

"But, dear," Mom explained, "cabs are much more expensive than the train. We need to be frugal."

"We absolutely do not," Chrissie said. "Casey, flag down that cab and tell him where we're going."

"You rock," Casey said and hailed the nearest cab.

We piled into a cab with a *Taxi Parisien* sign on top and Casey gave the driver our destination in fluid French. The fact that we were squashed into a tiny vehicle didn't dampen our enthusiasm as we gazed in awe at the French countryside as we sped past. Tessa, giddy with lack of sleep and excitement at being in Paris, pressed her nose against the cab's window. "Look out there everyone," she said as she pointed at a field empty except for a few stolid farm animals.

"Tessa," Casey said with exaggerated patience. "Those are cows."

"Yes," Tessa said, "but they're *French* cows." She paused for a beat. "And do you know what French cows say?"

Not waiting for an answer, Tessa crowed, "Moo la la." She giggled hysterically at her own joke. "Get it? Moo la la?"

Chrissie and I moaned. "Someone," Chrissie said, "needs a nap."

"Do not," Tessa said. "I'm connecting with my inner mademoiselle. Je parlee Fran-say. *Oui*?"

Our driver put a hand over his mouth in an attempt to cover a smile and Casey leaned over the seat and said something to him in rapid French. The two of them laughed.

"Hey." Tessa said. "Do not talk about me in French."

"Okay," Casey said, "I'll talk about you in English." She patted Tessa's cheek. "You, *ma petite*, are an idiot."

"Girls, give it a rest will you?" I said. "Enjoy the view."

Finally we arrived in Paris itself and had our first much-anticipated glimpse of the city. It was the morning rush hour and taxis, buses, trucks and miniature cars whizzed in every direction. The chaos extended to the sidewalks where we could see Parisians toting paper-wrapped baguettes and cups of coffee.

"Can you believe it? We're finally here," Chrissie said.

"Casey, ask the driver to give us a mini-tour before he takes us to the hotel,"

I said.

"Mom, do you have any idea how much that could cost?"

"I don't care. We need to absorb the flavor of Paris."

And Casey spoke quietly to the driver who simply shrugged and maneuvered his vehicle smoothly through the traffic. I caught a glimpse of the Eiffel Tower in the distance and shivered with excitement. "There it is," I said and waggled my hand to point it out.

"Awesome," Tessa said.

"Totally," Casey echoed.

Our brief tour ended as the driver turned onto the *Rue Mouffetard*, the charming 5th *Arrondissement* street on which our hotel, *Le Hotel Mignon*, was located. As we tumbled out of the taxi, I noticed the local market jammed with booths a short distance away. The narrow street was clogged with shoppers picking up produce and baked goods.

As the driver piled our luggage onto the sidewalk, Chrissie examined the hotel façade with a worried look on her face. "I thought we opted for cute and quaint here in Paris. This just looks rundown and claustrophobic."

"Not to worry," I said. "I trust Mary Linda not to lead us astray. Let's check it out."

The hotel lobby was not much larger than my walk-in closet, but clean and cozy with wood paneled walls and a tile floor spread with thick throw rugs. The large, buxom woman behind the reception desk greeted us warmly and introduced herself as Madame Reno. It took only a few minutes to get checked in and take the ancient elevator to our fourth floor rooms.

I struggled for a moment with the heavy key and old-fashioned lock and then shoved the door open to reveal perhaps the smallest hotel room I had ever seen. I heard hoots of laughter from the adjoining room as the girls and Mom discovered the same thing.

"Unbelievable," I said.

Chrissie shoved me aside and gasped. "Where are we going to put our stuff?"

"Good question." I looked dubiously at our two roller bags, large carry-ons and purses.

Our room was furnished with twin beds occupying the entire space between the windows and the wall opposite. An armoire sat at the end of the beds and allowed only two feet of walking space. It was cheery, though, with bright orange duvets and sunlight streaming through the windows.

"I didn't plan on being quite this intimate with you," Chrissie said.

"Let's see the other room," I said.

Next door we discovered their room was not much different from ours except that a full-sized bed and a single bed were crammed into the limited space. Tessa and Casey sprawled on the larger bed giggling while Mom efficiently stowed her clothes in the armoire.

Mom sighed. "I knew we wouldn't have much room but …" Her voice trailed off as she eyed the pile of luggage.

"Stop worrying, Nonny," Casey said. "We won't spend much time in the room anyway and it's charming. I love it."

"You would," Tessa said.

"I didn't know …" I began and Tessa interrupted me.

"Aunt Kate, I'm not complaining. Really. *Mouffetard* is perfect. I can't wait to explore the market."

"Chill, Mom," Casey said. She threw back the curtains and gestured. "That's Paris. We don't care that our rooms are kind of compact. I think we should get our act together and get out there."

"I second that," Tessa said. "Let's go before jet lag hits."

"I could use *café au lait* and *un croissant*," Chrissie added. "Give me five minutes."

A few seconds later Chrissie stood, hands on hips, surveying our room. She grinned at me. "This must be like it was when we shared the womb."

"Yeah, your stuff spread all over and no room for me."

"And that's why you muscled your way out ahead of me."

"I thought I was first because you were primping. Wanted to impress the doctor. Middle child syndrome."

Chrissie chuckled and spun around to face me. "Oh, Katie, this is awesome. Can you believe it? We're in Paris." She hugged me and twirled me around, almost colliding with the door.

"You unpack," I said. "I'll use the bathroom and then we can switch places. It's the only way we'll get anything done." I pushed her toward her suitcase.

I had no more than unzipped my jeans and lowered myself onto *la toilette* than Chrissie wailed, "Oh, no. Oh, no. Oh, no, no, no!"

I tried to leap to my feet, but with my jeans around my knees, I tripped and crashed into the counter sending the bottles I had just arranged clattering into the ceramic sink. I smacked my elbow against the wall and banged my hip on the doorframe as I lurched back into the bedroom. "What?"

Chrissie stared with horror into her suitcase lying open on the bed. "Spiders?" I asked, thinking of one thing that terrifies my sister. "Is there a black widow or a tarantula in your bag?"

Goggle-eyed, Chrissie pointed. "Look."

Jeans still unzipped, I reeled across the small space and peered over her shoulder. At first I couldn't imagine what had her so upset, but then I got it. The bag was full of men's clothing! Fashionable, perhaps. Maybe even expensive… was that a black silk shirt? But definitely not Chrissie's style.

"Those aren't my clothes," she said. "This isn't my bag."

I rubbed my sore hip and pondered. "You should've taken my advice and gotten another color bag." I waggled my fingers toward my cherry red bag. "Black bags are hard to identify."

"I'd agree with you except for one tiny thing," she said as she tugged on the designer baggage tag bejeweled with a sequined letter 'C' that was affixed securely to the handle. "This is my tag. It's just not my bag that it's on."

"Mom? What's going on?"

"Aunt Chrissie!"

"Kate, open the door this instant."

I unlocked the door and Casey, Tessa and Mom fell across the threshold. I pointed at the open suitcase. "Christine has a bit of a problem."

While Tessa and Mom scrutinized the dark clothing in the bag, Casey hovered just inside the room with her back pressed against the door, her arms crossed over her chest. She fidgeted with her bracelets and shifted her weight from one foot to the other.

Finally Tessa looked up and grinned. "Geez, Mom, I know this is a huge birthday, but I didn't think you would sink into mourning."

"Funny," Chrissie said. "Make jokes if you want, but I want to know where my bag is."

I scratched my head as I tried to come up with an answer. "Well, maybe your baggage tag fell off and…"

"At that exact moment another tag fell off another bag," Chrissie interrupted, "and the handler switched them?"

"Could have happened that way," I said.

"Oh, sure it could, Kate," Chrissie said. "And there's a pot of gold at the end of the rainbow. You live in fantasy land if you believe what you're saying."

"So, Miss Smarty Pants, what do you think happened?"

"That's a very good question," Chrissie said. "Maybe I should call the airline and see if someone else has reported a missing bag."

"Casey can do it," I offered. "She speaks French."

Casey abandoned her post at the door and grabbed the receiver of our room phone and put it to her ear. "No dial tone. I'll go down to the front desk and let Madame Reno help."

"I'm coming with you," Tessa said. Clutching Chrissie's boarding pass and claim check, the two of them sprinted out the door --- women on a mission.

Mom was unusually quiet as she poked tentatively at the clothing in the suitcase.

"Mom, don't touch that," I said.

"Do you think I'll get cooties?"

"I guess not, but …"

Mom continued her cautious examination of the contents. "Good quality," she muttered. "Hmm, nice brand." Suddenly she froze, her hand poised in midair. "What the dickens…"

I followed her gaze to the corner of the suitcase. The grey lining was pulled back revealing a layer of green paper beneath. The layer of green paper was stacked tightly into a brick. With the words "one hundred dollars" clearly visible across the bottom.

"Oh, my God," I said. "H-how much is in there?"

"I'm gonna count it," Chrissie said and reached for the stack of bills.

Mom slapped her hand away. "No, you are not. We need to contact the authorities. The gendarmes. The police."

"Hang on," Chrissie said. I recognized the stubborn look on her face. "Not quite yet."

"What do you want to do?" I asked.

"Let's just see if someone has turned my bag in. Then we can decide what comes next."

We were still gaping at the contents of the switched bag when Casey and Tessa barged into the room sending the door slamming against the wall. Startled, we all jumped.

42

"Relax, Mom. Geez. Don't have a heart attack," Casey said. "Sorry, Aunt Chrissie. No luck. I talked to a very nice clerk at Delta Baggage Claim, but she said there hadn't been any bags turned in. She suggested that we take this bag to the Delta office on the *Champs Élysées* and file a missing bag claim. I'm really sure your bag will be turn up."

Chrissie shook her head. "If I give this one up, I've got nothing. I think I'll keep it until mine shows up. Besides I don't feel like dragging this one all over Paris so that some drug dealers aren't inconvenienced."

"Mom, don't be a drama queen …" Tessa began, but stopped when Chrissie stepped aside to reveal the stack of money nestled in the bag.

"How much?"

"We don't know."

Casey peered over Tessa's shoulder. "Is that *money*?" she said her voice rising several octaves. "I thought …." She broke off.

Something wasn't right. Casey was pale and her lower lip quivered as she stared into the bag. But I didn't have time to figure her out at the moment.

"You thought?" I said.

Casey refused to meet my eyes. "I don't know. Never mind. It's not important." She turned away from the bag. "I'm really sorry about your bag, Aunt Chrissie."

Chrissie patted her cheek. "I know you are, Case. But you didn't have anything to do with it."

"Well, that's not…" Tessa began and broke off when Casey shot her a poisonous look.

"Just don't touch anything," Tessa said. "You'll mess up any fingerprints."

"You watch too much CSI," I said.

"You're a fine one to talk," Chrissie said. "Remember your cruise…"

We debated for a few minutes until Chrissie said, "That's enough discussion. It's my bag that's missing and I say we go to the Delta office and file a claim.

43

Then we can decide what to do next."

"I still say we have to call the police," Mom said. "That's a lot of money and it's probably stolen."

"I know," Chrissie said, "but let's see what happens at Delta. If my bag is there, we can let them deal with the police."

I hopped off the bed. "Okay, then let's head out. Bags to find. Crimes to solve."

Tessa and Casey hesitated for only a few seconds before they mocked me with matching eye-rolls. "You'd think she does this all the time," Casey said to Tessa. "One tiny crime and she's an expert."

Tessa chuckled. "I say we should follow our resident detective. We'll grab our things and be back in a flash." She turned to her grandmother. "Coming, Nonny?"

Mom was perched on the edge of the second bed pleating and un-pleating and then smoothing the edge of the bedspread. "Um," she said hesitantly. "Um, I guess not."

"Oh," I said, "you've got your stuff already. Then we're set."

Finally Mom made eye contact. "No. I mean I'm not going with you."

"You're not?" Chrissie said.

"Oh, come on, Nonny," Tessa begged. "I know you must be exhausted but we won't be out that long."

"It's not that, Tessa," Mom said. "I'm not exhausted at all. It's just that…"

"It's just that what?" I asked. "Is there something else you want to do? Go to the Louvre?"

She regarded us solemnly. "I … um … I have a date."

Chrissie and I whirled around and confronted our petite, white-haired mother, for heaven's sake. "You have a what?"

"A … um …date."

"With whom? Who on earth could you have a date with in Paris, for crying out loud?"

"With Bobby," she replied. "Bobby MacTavish."

With Bobby? Of course. Obviously we hadn't seen the last of him after all.

"You can't just date some guy you met on a plane," Chrissie said. "You don't know anything about him."

"Yes, I do. He's from Troon, Scotland, and he's a baron. He's royalty. He plays golf."

"Oh, sure," Chrissie said. "How do you know he wasn't just telling you tall tales?"

"Yeah," I said, "do you have any proof that what he says is true?"

"Like what?" Mom said a bit huffily. "An ID card saying, 'I am a legitimate Baron'. Give me a little credit, the two of you. I didn't just fall off the turnip truck. I know a real gentleman when I meet one, thank you very much."

I sat down next to her on the edge of the bed and put my arm around her shoulder and gave her a squeeze. "Don't be upset. We're just worried about you."

"Well, don't be. I can take care of myself. You have better things to do than worry about me. Like find Chrissie's bag."

She had a point there. Two, actually. I knew she could take care of herself, but I didn't have to like it.

"Bobby is going to meet me in the lobby in …" She checked her watch. "… ten minutes. We're going to do some sightseeing. He's going to show me his Paris." Her cheeks were flushed and her eyes bright.

I raised my eyebrows. "Well, then," I said, "we're going down with you to check out his story for ourselves."

"That will *not* be necessary."

"Oh, yes, it will," Chrissie insisted. "Either that or we all go with you on your … um … date."

Mom sighed but gave in. "Okay, you win. Let's all go meet the Baron."

"Nonny's got a gigolo," Casey murmured to Tessa.

Mom stopped. "I heard that," she said. "And I could do worse."

Laughing, we trooped down to the lobby to meet Mom's date.

When the elevator door opened a moment later the five of us were struck dumb at the sight of tall, dignified, white-haired Bobby MacTavish waiting for us wearing full Scottish regalia. He had abandoned his sweater and jeans in favor of — maybe he was a Baron after all — kilts. A few seconds ticked by and Casey recovered her power of speech first.

"Och, lassie," she whispered in a terrible Scots accent, "Nonny has found herself a hot gigolo."

"A hot, Scottish Baron gigolo." Tessa giggled.

"With cute legs," added Casey.

"Girls," Mom said as stepped off the elevator, "be nice."

But Casey was right. Baron Bobby did have nice legs. Sheathed in navy blue knee socks they were straight and strong and…oh, God, was I actually ogling the legs, albeit sexy ones, of some geriatric Scottish hottie? I tore my eyes away from the aforementioned legs in time to see Bobby take Mom's hand and bestow a kiss upon it. Good Lord, my mother was giggling like a schoolgirl with a crush. I wasn't sure I could take much more.

Bobby's eyes twinkled as he explained his unique attire. ""I wouldn't usually show up on a first date with a wee American wearing kilts. Today, though, I dressed to impress some potential financial backers." He shrugged, a kind of helpless, go figure, lift of the shoulders. "I hope I didn't — as ye Americans say — freak ye out."

"Not at all," Mom said. "We were just caught off guard."

Casey whispered to Tessa, "Are you wondering what he has on under those kilts?"

Tessa punched Casey's arm. "You're so bad. And, of course, I am."

Mom and Bobby were absorbed in flirting (My mother flirting! That freaks me out!), but Chrissie and I overheard the exchange between the girls and shushed them. "Don't be rude," Chrissie said. Then she snickered. "We'll discuss it later."

"Bobby," Mom continued as if she hadn't heard the snickers, "you've met my daughters, Kate and Christine. And my granddaughters, Casey and Tessa."

Bobby nodded and as he turned toward us I automatically stuck my hand behind my back and noticed that Chrissie had done the same. Neither of us intended to have some kilt-wearing stranger put his lips on our hands — no matter what our mother thought of him. Bobby grinned as if he could read our minds and bowed deeply. "I am delighted to be in the company of such lovely women," he said. The accent that I had found so charming on the plane now sounded false and grating to my skeptical ears.

To his credit, though, Bobby sensed our reluctance to send Mom off with a stranger and suggested that we go to a small café nearby to get acquainted. We accepted gratefully and soon the six of us were settled with large cups of coffee and a basket of pastries at an outdoor table at *Le Bonne Crumbe*, the *patisserie* across the cobblestone street from our hotel.

By the time we finished our second cups of *café au lait* and devoured our fill of *croissants* and *pan au chocolat*, my reservations about Baron Bobby were somewhat assuaged. I found myself liking the guy in spite of myself. He was an interested and interesting conversationalist, asking intelligent questions and actually listening to the answers, his piercing blue eyes fixed on whomever was speaking. He spun fascinating tales (possibly true) about his life and family with a self-deprecating sense of humor I found appealing.

Bobby, or Robert MacTavish of Troon, Baron of Troon, his official title, disclosed that he was kind of a lower echelon member of the Scottish royalty. "Barons aren't that big a deal," he told us. "It's a title that has been passed down since about the 15th century, I believe. It doesn't net me much but a seat in

Parliament and an old family barony in Troon."

"Cool," Casey said. "What's a barony?"

"Oh, the family farm, more or less," Bobby answered. "In our case there isn't much left of the old barony. My ancestors sold off bits and pieces until all that remains is a rundown heap of stone." He chuckled. "Even so we like to refer to it as the castle."

"Awesome," Tessa said. "I'd love to see it. Does Mac live there?"

Well, at least her motives were crystal clear.

"Guests are always welcome," Bobby said. "Especially beautiful lassies like yourselves." He smiled but it didn't quite reach his eyes.

I felt a faint stirring of apprehension, but pushed it aside when Mom, suddenly businesslike, sat up and brushed off her jacket. "Now, then, children," she said, "it's time for Bobby and me to get on our way. The day will be over before we know it and my jet lag will kick in even sooner."

When Bobby went inside to pay the bill, Mom turned to Chrissie and me. "So, do I have your blessing?"

"Well-l-l," I said. "If you're sure you …"

"…want to go and sow some wild oats," Chrissie added.

"Then have fun and don't stay out too late. We have an early day tomorrow," I said.

"We do?" Chrissie asked. "I didn't think…"

I kicked her ankle under the table. "We do."

Mom shoved back her chair and stood up. "Wild oats?" She bent to give each of us a quick kiss and laughed. "Listen to you. Please don't worry about me."

Bobby reappeared, his white hair gleaming in the sun. "Miss Laura, your chariot awaits."

"Let's go then," Mom said.

Tessa pulled urgently at Mom's arm. "Nonny, remember what we talked about."

Mom patted her own white curls and grinned. "I'll be fine, Tessa."

Tessa gave her a thumbs up and Mom sauntered away, her hand on Bobby's arm.

"What was that all about?" I asked Tessa.

"No biggie," she replied. "I'll tell you aboot it later."

As Bobby and Mom disappeared around the corner, Casey commented, "Aren't they a bonnie couple?"

"Enough with the accent," I said. "Are ye lassies ready to explore Paris?"

"Not quite," Chrissie said. "I have to run back to the room for a second."

"I'll come with you, Mom," Tessa said.

Casey watched them cross the street and disappear into the hotel. Then she put her open guidebook down on the table and turned to face me. "Um, Mom, I need to tell you something. And don't freak out until I'm finished. Okay?"

My mom-radar was suddenly on high alert. "Go ahead. I'm listening."

Casey fidgeted with a creased corner of the guidebook's cover and squirmed in her chair before she sucked in a huge breath and said, "The thing is, I might have had something to do with Aunt Chrissie's bag going missing."

For just a moment I thought she was kidding, but she wasn't smiling and her jaw was clenched. What on earth had she done?

"How exactly?" I said with a calm I wasn't feeling at all.

Her gaze fixed on a spot somewhere over my left ear, she said, "I ran into an old acquaintance on the plane. From that photo shoot I did for my grad school project."

"The one where you took pictures of people on the street and in Central Park?"

She nodded. "Do you remember Fifi? She was the one I shot on a park bench watching a street performer in the park."

And just like that all the pieces fell into place. Of course, I remembered that shot. It had always been my favorite in the show. A lone woman on a park bench with a sad and faraway look on her face while all around her others passed by. A poignant shot. And now I knew why I felt I knew the French woman in the red stilettos on the plane. She was Fifi. The park bench woman.

"I know the one," I said. "She was on the plane wasn't she?"

Casey bit her lip. "I ran into her by the restrooms and naturally we started talking. I got the feeling that she was upset about something."

"I saw her and her companion being thrown out of Business Class right before I got my iPod from you. That would have been what was bothering her, I'd guess."

"I'm sure that was part of it," Casey said, "but she told me she was terrified of going through customs in Paris. She said she and her boyfriend were bringing back some things they got in New York that were sort of illegal to bring into France."

My stomach lurched. Drugs? "Did she say what?" I asked.

Casey looked at me with the wide-eyed "oops got me" look I recognized from her childhood. She shook her head. "She didn't say exactly, but I got the impression it was booze or some kind of electronic thing."

"Go on," I said.

"Not much to say. I offered to trade her suitcase for mine so she could get her stuff with no problem."

"You did *what*?"

Casey's hand trembled as she raked her fingers through her hair. "I know. You don't have to tell me how stupid I was. But, Mo-om…you would not have believed how upset she was."

I put my hands on either side of her face and turned her head so she had to look at me. "Casey. Sweetie. That's *illegal*. You could go to jail."

Casey feigned a huge fascination with the street traffic. Finally, I couldn't stand it. "How on earth did you pull off a switch like that anyway?"

Casey grinned. "That's the cool part."

"The *cool* part? That's what all the inmates in Cellblock C say."

"You don't have to be sarcastic."

"Under the circumstances sarcasm is a far better response than my other choice --- screaming hysterically."

Casey's brown eyes filled with tears, one drop glistening on her eyelashes. She was so pathetic I couldn't be mad at her. "Okay. I'll save the hysterical screaming for another time. Tell me the *cool* part."

She regarded me seriously for a few seconds, perhaps waiting to see if I'd start screaming after all. Then she said, "Turns out that Fifi and I have the same kind of black bag. So it would be pretty easy to make a switch with no one being any the wiser."

"There might be a little issue of baggage tags to deal with," I said.

"Here's the cool thing. It seems that her boyfriend is a bit of a magician. Fifi assured me that he could switch tags with no problem."

"Casey," I said, "that makes no sense. Your bag, and Fifi's too I assume, looks identical to about a million others. How were they going to find it on the carousel?"

"I have that really awesome tag with the letter 'C' in rhinestones. Easy to spot."

"The one you got from your Aunt Chrissie," I said.

She nodded. "Exactly. The one she gave me that is identical to hers."

"Ohh," I said.

"Uh huh. I forgot about that when I told Fifi how to identify my bag. So, obviously, they saw a bag with the 'C' tag on it and assumed it was mine."

"Only," I added, "it was Chrissie's not yours."

Casey toyed with a few leftover crumbs on the table. "I feel awful, Mom."

"You should," I said. "How did you and Fifi plan to exchange bags after you got through customs?" I paused. "*If* you got through customs without being arrested, that is."

Casey waggled her fingers in the air as if flicking away bothersome bugs. "Oh, well. We figured we'd meet up on the sidewalk afterwards, but if that didn't happen I told her the name of our hotel. She and her boyfriend would bring my bag there."

"Brilliant," I murmured. "And now we have a bag full of money that you smuggled into France. You are at the very least an accessory to a crime, if not the actual perpetrator. God, Casey, this is really serious."

Tears spilled down her cheeks and she blew her nose into a napkin. "I'm sorry." She blubbered. "What should we do?"

At that moment we saw Tessa bounce out of the hotel and cross the street heading toward us. "Did you tell Tessa?" I asked.

Casey nodded mutely.

"What did she say?"

"Not much. Tessa has her own issues."

Before she could explain that cryptic statement, Chrissie appeared. Both she and Tessa seemed subdued and preoccupied as they joined us.

"Is everything okay? You seem a bit down," I asked.

"Me? Down? I have no idea what you're talking about. So where is the nearest Metro stop anyway?"

I made a possibly ill-advised decision to keep Chrissie in the dark for the time being. Maybe, I hoped, her bag will have been turned in at the Delta office and we can exchange them with no problem. Head in sand has always been a great position for me. So burdened with self-doubt, I followed as Casey led the way to find the Delta office.

Chapter 2

As we emerged from the Metro, the Paris version of the subway, onto the *Champs Élysées*, we were awestruck. Elegant shops nestled next to sidewalk cafes patronized by well-dressed Parisians and under-dressed tourists. Cinemas and office buildings as well as a myriad of tiny shopping malls dotted the sidewalk crowded with pedestrians. Miniature cars and bigger trucks scooted along with little regard for speed limits or the population.

Wide-eyed, Tessa twirled in a circle to take it all in. "The *Champs Élysées*! I can't believe I'm actually here. Oh, everyone, look at the shops."

"Business first, Tessa," Chrissie said. "And then shopping. Lead me to my suitcase."

Casey checked the address she had scrawled and a few doors up the street we found the Delta office nestled behind a row of sidewalk trees in huge pots. A pleasant looking woman of about thirty greeted us. "*Bonjour.* How may I help you?"

"I ended up with the wrong suitcase," Chrissie said. "And I hoped that mine might have been turned in here."

The Delta clerk accepted Chrissie's claim check and punched things into her computer. Then shaking her head at what she saw, she picked up the phone and spoke to someone else.

Casey listened to the conversation. "It doesn't look good, Aunt Chris. I think she's not having any luck locating your bag."

Sure enough, the clerk turned back to Chrissie and said apologetically, "There is no record of either your bag being turned in or of another one reported missing. I am so sorry. If you'll give me a way to reach you, I'll keep checking and let you know if I find it."

"But my clothes …"

The clerk rummaged in a desk drawer and then handed Chrissie some slips of paper. "If you will fill out the paperwork, Madame, I will do a search. And please buy whatever you might need and then bring the receipts to Delta. We will be happy to take care of the bills."

As we regrouped on the street outside the office, Chrissie was more resigned than angry, probably worn down by jet lag and stress. "I don't suppose they'd consider designer clothing a necessity," she said.

"Who cares?" Tessa said. "We have to shop on the *Champs Élysées*. I'm not shedding any tears for my poor, poor, mommy."

Casey's eyes glimmered. "Let the shopping begin."

"Oh." I pointed. "Look, a lingerie store."

"Let's go," Chrissie said. "I absolutely have to have underwear, don't I?"

"Just don't embarrass me by acting like tourists," Casey said and led the way down the crowded street.

In a remarkably short time we had all succumbed to the lure of the lingerie and parted with a hefty number of Euros. We fled the elegant lingerie shop burdened with silken bags. Chrissie gazed at her bags with an astonished look. "Oh, God. We shouldn't have done that."

"Perhaps," Tessa suggested with a grin, "a 50 Euro bra was a bit over the top. That's like $75, isn't it?"

Chrissie frowned. "I think perhaps I got carried away. But, have you ever seen a more gorgeous piece of lingerie?"

"It might actually give you cleavage," I said. "Well worth the 50 Euros."

"It's a French bra." Casey started to giggle. "And you know what it would say?"

"What *would* it say?" Tessa asked, happy to play straight man.

"*Boo-o-b* la la," Casey said and doubled over with laughter.

And we all were laughing as we meandered down the *Champs Élysées* clutching our boob-tie.

We peered in windows of elegant shops, dodged pedestrians on the wide tree-lined sidewalk and gawked like the tourists we were. Even Casey was happy, undeterred by our blatant rubbernecking. Suddenly, Tessa grabbed Casey's arm and pulled her to a stop in front of one of the numerous sidewalk cafes. "Oh, my God, Casey. Is this the *Fouquet's*?"

"It says so, doesn't it?"

"It's really famous and stuff. Celebrities drink and eat here. I mean like Jackie O."

"Yeah, and it's *tres* expensive and *tres* touristy," Casey objected.

"Can we please, please, please get a drink here?" Tessa begged. "I'll pay. I will."

Overcome by Tessa and fatigue we agreed to have a drink, just one drink, at the renowned *Fouquet's*, and wilted into four chairs surrounding a round table. A flower box full of bright red and yellow flowers separated us from the sidewalk and the hordes of tourists. One look at the menu, though, had us rethinking our choice. "Ten Euros for a glass of wine?" Chrissie said. "No way, José. Or make that, no way, Jean Pierre."

"Oh, come on, Mom," Tessa pleaded. "We're already here. Just one teensy glass won't break the bank. And I said I'd pay."

Chrissie puffed out a breath. "Okay. You win. But just one glass. And you will sip that. No gulping. Maximize the experience."

"*Quatre verres de vin blanc*," Casey said to the waiter and he sauntered off to put in the order.

"What's next? After the wine, I mean. Maybe we should go back to the hotel and see if Chrissie's bag has shown up there," I said.

Casey gave me a sideways glance out of the corner of her eye. "Good idea, Mom. I'll bet it's there."

Chrissie took a tiny sip of her wine. "If it is, we'll find out soon enough. And if it's not..." She shrugged. "... we can decide what to do then."

"I agree," Tessa said. "Why interrupt a perfect day of drinking wine and shopping with a tiny thing like Mom's missing bag?"

"I'll bet you'd be singing a different song if it was your bag, Tessa," Chrissie said.

Tessa started to protest but Casey interrupted her. "And the *Arc de Triomphe* is really close. We need to go there too."

So, thoughts of the bag shoved aside for the moment, we sipped our wine and lounged on the *Champs Élysées* soaking up sun and atmosphere --- a woman and her dog wearing matching pink faux fur jackets; the striking blonde wearing leather, head to toe, with jewels the size of footballs in her ears and on her fingers. An elderly woman pushing her equally elderly husband in a ribbon be-decked wheelchair -- a large black cat wearing a bejeweled collar trotting beside them. The smell of garlic mingling with exhaust fumes and the perfumed scent of flowers in the box. Magic. We lingered as long as we could but eventually it was time to move along.

"The waiter keeps giving us the evil eye," Tessa said.

"Probably because we're taking a table that customers with a bigger budget might want," Casey said with a wink. "Typical French waiter."

We paid the bill and were gathering our purses, cameras and shopping bags when we heard a roar on the busy avenue. I looked up and caught a glimpse of the rear of a large motorcycle as it careened past weaving in and out of traffic. A sidecar was attached to the motorcycle and I could just see the head of the passenger peeking out and --- I froze. No way, I thought. Not a chance in the world. I whirled around and found my three companions staring at the speeding motorcycle in disbelief.

"Was that ..." I began.

"Couldn't have been," Chrissie said.

"It was," Tessa said. "It was ..."

"Nonny!" Casey finished with more glee that I thought necessary.

After all, if we had seen what we thought we had, my conservative ---

Republican, for crying out loud --- mother was hot-rodding around Paris in the sidecar of a motorcycle piloted by a sexy, possibly psychotic, certainly daring, senior citizen Scotsman.

Casey and Tessa capered on the sidewalk waving and shouting. They exchanged high fives and collapsed into their chairs, laughing like a pair of hyenas. I eyed them as realization dawned.

"You two know something," I said.

"Us? Not us. We know nothing."

Chrissie was gaping at the street with a dazed look on her face and suddenly she clutched my arm. "They're coming back."

Indeed, the motorcycle had circled the *Arc De Triomphe* and was roaring back down the *Champs Élysées* toward *Fouquet's*. As it drew abreast of us, I focused my attention on the passenger in the sidecar. Red helmet. White hair curling out beneath it. And then the red-helmeted passenger waggled the fingers of one hand furiously. I thought I would keel over. Mom! I'd recognize those curls anywhere.

"All right, you two." I glared at my daughter and my niece. "I want answers. Now."

"Tessa…" Chrissie took a single menacing step toward her daughter. "We mean it."

"Okay. Geez, Mom. Aunt Kate. Chill. It's not a big deal."

"Your grandmother is speeding all over Paris in a motorcycle driven by some maniac Scotsman and it's no big deal?" Chrissie's voice rose.

"Don't burst a blood vessel, Christine," I said. "Let's hear what they have to say. Sit."

Chrissie dropped into her chair and fixed her gaze on Tessa, waiting.

"Okay," I said, "this had better be good."

Tessa and Casey exchanged looks and then Tessa shrugged. "Yeah, we knew about it. Robert and Mac told us that their 'Grampa Rabbie' keeps motorcycles in Paris and London and Glascow for when he's in those cities on business."

"Traffic is crazy and parking is insanely difficult," Casey continued, "so it makes sense."

"Besides," Tessa added, "we talked to Nonny about it last night on the plane. We made her promise to wear a helmet."

"Well, then that makes it okay," I said. I dragged a hand through my hair. "Couldn't you have at least clued us in?"

"Why?" Casey asked in the same tone used in reasoning with a small child. "She wasn't worried."

"Yeah," Tessa said, "Nonny is cool. For a grandma."

"If her own driving doesn't scare her, I don't see why a motorcycle would," Casey put in.

Casey had a point. Mom's nickname was "Hot Rod Nonny" and she'd more than earned it. Her need for speed was legendary among her grandchildren.

I drew a deep calming breath. "I suppose we're making a big deal out of nothing."

Chrissie nodded. "I think I may have overreacted."

"Ya think?" Tessa laughed. "Mom that was major overreacting."

Chrissie's lips curved into a tiny smile. "Well, that was one hell of a wild oat if you ask me."

"Totally," I agreed. "I didn't think she was ready for a walker, but a motorcycle? I wasn't prepared for that one."

"Come on, you two," Casey said. "There's nothing you can do about it and the *Arc de Triomphe* awaits."

Not much later, I was standing on the sidewalk facing the *Arc de Triomphe* mesmerized by the cars racing in a circle around it. I must have been more mesmerized than I thought because I realized with a jolt that Casey was speaking to me.

"What do you think?" she asked me. "Mom? Mom! You didn't hear a word I said."

"Of course, I did." But I didn't have a clue. "What was that again?"

"I said," she repeated with exaggerated patience, "that you and Aunt Chrissie look like you're asleep on your feet. We need to get some dinner and then tuck the two of you into bed."

My eyes were gritty with lack of sleep and I fought to keep them open. I had been literally asleep on my feet. One look at my twin's drooping eyelids and vague expression told me that she wasn't faring any better.

"It's been at least twenty-four hours since I woke up in my own bed in Ohio," I said. "I guess I am about to crash. Dinner sounds wonderful. How about *Pizza Pino*? I know there's one around here."

"Moth-ER!" Casey was scandalized. "That would be like eating at *Pizza Hut*. We can do better."

"Your father and I happen to love *Pizza Pino*."

Casey shook her head in mock despair. "You would. I have a better idea. Why don't we go back to *Rue Mouffetard* and find a cute local place. Then you'll be only a few seconds from your room."

"Lead me to it."

Chapter 3

Casey selected a restaurant around the corner from our hotel called "*Le Bouffe Tard*" as much for the name as for the ambiance. The place was quaint and the menu looked appetizing but Chrissie and I most appreciated being off our feet. Food was just a bonus. We had just finished our *omelettes* and *pommes frites* and a *pichet* of *vin blanc* and were getting a second wind when Casey's cell phone began to play some random rock tune. Casey fished in her bag, pulled out her phone and slapped it to her ear. "*Bonjour*," she trilled. "Uh huh. Of course, I remember you." She mouthed the name "Robert" and Tessa sat up straighter as she listened to Casey's end of the conversation.

When Casey disconnected, Tessa demanded, "That was Robert? MacTavish? What did he want?"

"He invited me and you to go clubbing with him and Mac. I said we'd love to go and they're picking us up around eight-thirty." She checked her watch. "That gives us time to catch a nap and change our clothes."

"I don't think …" Chrissie began and Tessa held up her hand.

"Don't go there, Mom," she said. "Casey and I are adults and we can go out with a couple of nice guys if we want."

"Nonny did," Casey said.

Good point. So we paid the bill and headed back to the hotel. Sleep sounded very appealing.

For most of the day I had done a good job of burying any unpleasant thoughts about Chrissie's missing bag and Casey's involvement in the disappearance. Paris is an excellent distraction, it turns out. But as we approached the *Le Hotel Mignon* the knot in my stomach grew to massive proportions. Would we find drug dealers camped in our room? Or even worse, would the police be waiting in the lobby to arrest Casey and haul her off? By the time we entered the lobby,

I had worked myself into a full-blown anxiety attack … palms sweaty, heart hammering.

To my huge relief, though, the lobby was deserted except for the desk clerk. Which left our room as a potential hiding spot and I wasn't anxious to discover what might await us there. But obviously Chrissie wasn't sharing my reluctance. She elbowed me aside and snatched our room key from the desk clerk as if it was the last Coach purse on the clearance rack. She barely acknowledged his greeting and whirled toward the elevator where she stood punching at the up button.

Tessa put a hand on Chrissie's shoulder. "Whoa, Mom. Don't break a nail."

Chrissie shrugged off Tessa's hand and pushed her way into the elevator before the door was completely open. The three of us squeezed in behind her and had to hurry to avoid being squashed as Chrissie stabbed at the button and the heavy ornate door began to close.

When we reached our floor Chrissie burst out of the elevator and was halfway down the hall before we caught up with her. She paused outside the door to the girls' room, gave Tessa a quick peck on the cheek and started toward our room without a backward glance.

I grabbed her sleeve. "Wait, Chris. Hang on. What's the rush? We should check on Mom before we go to our room. See how her day went." I wanted to delay as long as possible the fate awaiting us in our room.

"Oh, okay," Chrissie said, "but make it snappy."

Irritated at Chrissie's attitude, I flicked a glance at her as Casey unlocked the door and flung it open with such force that it crashed against the wall. "Shh," I said. "Don't wake Nonny."

"Uh, uh," Casey said. "Nonny's not here."

"Of course she is. Look in the bathroom."

Casey unlatched the bathroom door and peeked inside. "Nope. No Nonny."

Chrissie lifted the edge of the bedspread and peered underneath the bed.

"What is she thinking?" she said. "She should be in bed by now."

Tessa laughed. "In it, Mom, not under it. Besides it's only 6:30."

Chrissie gave a tiny shrug. "Okay, fine."

And then, Mom apparently forgotten, she tugged at my arm and started dragging me toward our room. "Come on, Kate. Let's go."

I could almost feel the nervous energy crackling off her. I pulled my arm away from Chrissie's grasp and hugged Casey. "It appears that I'm going to my room now. Have fun tonight. Don't get into more trouble."

"Mo-om," Casey protested.

That stopped Chrissie for a moment. "More trouble?"

But without waiting for an explanation she hurried toward our room, key in hand. She struggled with the stubborn lock, muttering under her breath until it released and she shoved the door open and marched inside. She stood hands on hips, surveying the tiny space. She flicked on the light. "I knew it."

"Knew what?"

"The suitcase is gone."

"Gone? Which suitcase? Are you sure?"

"The suitcase. And, of course, I'm sure. Where would it hide in this tiny space?"

My red suitcase was still standing alone in the corner where I left it. "Your real suitcase must be here. It has to be. "

Chrissie snorted. "Obviously not. Why would you think it would be?"

"Well, I had a feeling it would be." I had thought Fifi and her boyfriend were supposed to return Chrissie's bag. Then another explanation occurred to me. "We've been robbed." I rushed to the armoire and started pawing through clothes until I unearthed my tiny jewelry bag. I breathed a sigh of relief as a quick inventory told me everything was still there.

Chrissie shook her head. "I think this is all about the mystery bag. I feel like I'm someone's target."

"Don't be ridiculous," I said. "And even if you are right…and I'm not saying you are… what do you think we're involved in?"

"Beats me," Chrissie said, "but let's ask them when they return."

"What makes you think whoever 'they' are will come back?"

"Because," she said with her head stuck in the armoire. "I think they might want this." She stepped aside to reveal the small safe tucked inside. Its door was open --- a pile of neatly stacked bills in clear view.

Horrified, I stared at my sister. "Are you stark staring mad?"

"Why would you say that?" she asked with infuriating calm.

"Because that money doesn't belong to us. Someone is going to want it back." I picked up the phone receiver. "Maybe I should call the police."

"Oh, no you shouldn't." Chrissie flew across the room, snatched the phone from my hand and slammed it back into the cradle.

Dumbfounded, I stood with my mouth open. What was wrong with her anyway? She was all over the place. Behavior totally unlike my usually unflappable --- middle child --- twin. I was trying to figure out her problem when she turned her back and dropped onto the bed. She refused to make eye contact with me and picked at the duvet as if she was mining it for gold dust. Finally, when it seemed the silence had stretched out for an eternity, she said, "I mean, you don't even know how to use a French phone do you?"

"It's a phone, Chrissie," I said, "not a nuclear weapon. I think I can handle it." I paused. "Besides I wasn't going to call the police. I have to tell you something first."

She shook her head. "I have something to tell you too."

I sank down next to her on the bed and put my arm around her shoulders. "What's going on?"

She continued to shake her head while her fingers busily mutilated the duvet. "Would you believe me if I said that I want to find out who took my things…my new hot pink suede jacket and the cutest pair of jeans you ever saw and…." She looked me in the eye. "I want my stuff back?"

Her words had a ring of truth to them, but I knew it was more than that. "Christine Marie Stevens Montgomery, I didn't know insanity ran in the family."

"I prefer to think of it as tenacity," she said.

"Chrissie, come on. I know you. This vacation is supposed to be about shopping and sitting in cafés drinking coffee and wine. Not an exercise in crime solving. Tell me."

And just like that she gave in. She flopped backwards on the bed with her arm over her eyes. "We can't call the police, Katie, because if we do they will arrest Tessa and ship her off to prison and I won't see her again until we are very old ladies."

"What?" I shot to my feet. "Tessa? But she's not the one … It's Casey who would go to prison. What on earth are you talking about?"

Chrissie narrowed her eyes. "What are you talking about?"

Suddenly my throat was parched. I uncapped a bottle of water and poured two glasses. I handed one to Chrissie and took a swig from the other. Then I collapsed on my bed, plumped up the pillows behind my back and took another gulp of water. Chrissie watched in silence as I fidgeted.

Finally, she said, "Are you quite comfy now?"

"Yeah, I am. I'll go first." I didn't dare look at her as I rapidly, and with as little fanfare as possible, related Casey's story about her bag swapping adventures. When I finished, I waited apprehensively for Chrissie's reaction. She had every reason to be furious with Casey. I certainly was. When she didn't say anything, I snuck a peek at her. She looked calm enough until her lips twitched. She put her face in her hands and I saw her shoulders shaking. Was she crying? I knew it had been a stressful day and this was undoubtedly the last straw.

"I'm sorry, Chris. Casey is too. She feels awful…." I broke off when Chrissie looked up at me and burst into giggles.

"Oh, God," Chrissie said. "That is so Casey. It's Beauregard the dog all over again!"

I started to laugh. "That flea bitten mutt that she rescued from the chopping block was the reason I had to have the entire house fumigated."

"But she couldn't," Chrissie said, "let him be put to sleep…even if he was 150 in dog years and the ugliest mutt in the world."

"That's my girl," I said. "Always rescuing someone or bringing home a stray. Heart of gold, brain of oatmeal."

"I suppose that if we look at the up-side of this situation," Chrissie said, "at least we don't have fleas."

"Are you sure about that?" I said and stuck my head under the sheet. "Is that a flea I see? I think it is."

When we finally sobered up, I wiped my eyes on the edge of the sheet and said, "Now it's your turn. Why is Tessa going to be hauled off to prison to occupy the cell next to Casey's?"

"It's not funny. But here goes…" she began and then stopped. "Wait a second."

She bounced off the bed and with her back to me, rummaged in the armoire. When she turned around she was brandishing a bottle of white wine and a corkscrew. "I was going to save this for later," she said, "but I think we need it now."

"Where did you get that?" I asked. "Oh, never mind. It's a brilliant idea."

Chrissie deftly opened the bottle and poured two glasses of wine with a flourish. A cloud passed over my twin's face and she took a gulp of wine before she said, "You will not believe this, but apparently Tessa is wanted by the French police!"

"Tessa? No way. That isn't possible." I scratched my nose. "Is it?"

"It is. Do you remember last spring when Tessa spent a month in Paris with a group of students from Michigan on a work/study internship?"

I nodded. "And?"

"It seems that some of her group got involved in a demonstration for women's rights outside the *Palais du Justice*. Tessa hadn't planned to join them. She claims she intended to do some shopping instead. At the last minute, she says, she changed her mind."

Chrissie wrinkled her nose and took another sip of wine. "It seems that a guy was involved. He was *really* cute and she'd been hoping he'd notice her the entire time they were here. So when he asked to join the demonstration, she said she couldn't refuse."

I snorted. "Of course, she couldn't. Leave it to Tessa to turn a demonstration into a date."

"It was supposed to be a peaceful demonstration --- a gathering of college students to protest some French legislation discriminating against women. But Tessa says shortly after they arrived, it turned ugly. The police tried to disperse the students and the students resisted."

She sighed. "According to Tessa, she accidentally got arrested."

My eyebrows shot up. "Accidentally got arrested? Sounds like our Tessa."

Chrissie blew a lock of hair out of her eyes. "Yep. One of the policemen grabbed Tessa's friend by the arm and twisted it really hard. So hard that Tessa thought he would break the boy's arm. So, again according to Tessa, she 'very politely' mentioned to the policeman that he was hurting the boy. And that the boy had done nothing to deserve it."

"Oh, boy."

"Oh, boy, is right. You can imagine that the policeman wasn't thrilled with Tessa's interference and the next thing she knew, both she and the boy were put into the police wagon and taken into custody. They were fingerprinted and had a mug shot taken." Chrissie paused and smiled a wry smile. "Tessa said it was an awful picture. Her hair was a mess and she was all sweaty. I think that bothered her more than the fact that she was being arrested for disturbing the peace."

"Sounds like Tessa."

"Anyway, they were allowed a phone call and the group chaperone came down to the police station and got the charges dropped. Or dismissed. But not before the arresting officer told Tessa and the cute boy that they would be treated much more severely if they ever got into trouble in France again."

"And that's why," I said, "you don't want to call the police."

Chrissie drained her glass and poured herself a refill. "I know it's pretty remote, but I figured that if I called the police and they found out Tessa was involved…even if it wasn't her suitcase and she had nothing to do with the money…they would throw the book at her. I couldn't take the chance."

"What a mess," I said.

I wandered over to the window, pulled the curtain back and stared out at the pedestrians hurrying along the sidewalk. Sounds of laughter floated up to me. I leaned my forehead against the cool glass as I tried to process all this. When I turned back around Chrissie hadn't moved.

"Casey really screwed up this time," I said. "We obviously can't call the police or she'll be implicated for sure."

"I'm not upset," Chrissie said. "She wanted to help a friend."

"Whether it was against the law or not? If only she'd thought first maybe we wouldn't be in this mess. And you'd have your suede jacket."

"I'm kind of sad about that," Chrissie said, "but you know what Mom always says? You can't see behind you because those eyes in the back of your head are always covered with your hair."

I started to laugh and then it struck me. "Mom. We have to tell Mom."

"Are you sure? I hate to ruin her trip worrying about the girls. Couldn't we wait until we're on the flight home?"

"Oh, sure. She would never forgive us. And, besides, she could be in danger. We all could."

Chrissie stared vacantly into space for a moment and then polished off her wine and stood up. "So, Katie, what do we do?"

I thought about it for a second and said, "I think we have to find Fifi and her boyfriend and demand that they return your bag the way they were supposed to. And we'll give them the money and that will be that."

"Brilliant, Kate. Let's just do that. How exactly?"

"I'm working on it. Casey must know Fifi's last name and maybe she even has an address or phone number. We can find out in the morning."

Chrissie locked the money in the safe and stuffed it back into the armoire. She threw some underwear over it, dusted off her hands, snatched her make-up bag and marched into the bathroom. She looked over her shoulder at me and said, "I can't think about this anymore. I'm getting ready for bed. I hope I'm not murdered during the night."

She slammed the bathroom door. Suddenly I was too exhausted to do any more than crawl fully dressed under the covers and pull them up to my chin. I was asleep before I could summon one more coherent, or even incoherent, thought.

Chapter 4

Hours later I woke from my coma-like slumber disoriented and groggy. It took me a few moments to clear the fog from my brain and figure out where I was. I rolled over to check the time on my travel alarm and realized that the numbers were crystal clear. Oops. I hadn't taken my contacts out before I crashed into oblivion. And I had to pee. So I swung my legs over the edge of the bed, jerked myself to my feet and, grabbing my nightshirt on the way, tottered toward the bathroom. Chrissie was sound asleep in the adjoining bed wearing, I noticed, my favorite pair of pajamas. Oh, well. Share and share alike.

I had almost finished in the bathroom and was brushing my teeth when I heard through the paper-thin wall a thudding noise as if someone had dropped something.

"Oops," I heard someone murmur, followed by the sounds of shuffling feet and jingling keys.

Casey and Tessa! They must just be getting home from their dates. I yanked my nightshirt over my head and heaved open the door to the hallway and discovered, not Casey and Tessa, but my mom weaving — yes, definitely weaving — toward her room. She didn't notice me as I watched her stab the key in the general direction of the lock. Failing to insert it the first time, she poked at it ineffectually once again.

"Mom," I called softly as I tiptoed in her direction. "Psst, Mom."

She looked up and her face lit up with delight. "Katie. Thith lock ith broken."

I took the key from her and fit it easily into the lock. "Here let me help you."

Mom beamed at me. "Thankth, Katie. I 'preciate your help."

"Um, Mom, are you just getting home from your date with Bobby?"

"Yessss. Jush gettin' home." Her words were slightly slurred.

I fixed a suspicious gaze on my cute, little mom. "Are you drunk?"

"Course not." She giggled. My mother never giggles. "Well, maybe jush a little."

Appalled, I pushed her gently into the room. "Less not wake the girlsh." She giggled again.

I squinted. Even without my contacts, I could see that the beds were empty. "Casey and Tessa had dates with Bobby's grandsons. I guess they aren't back yet. And Chrissie is zonked out in our room."

"Oh, goodie," Mom said. "Then come in and I'll tell you all 'bout my day. We can have a schleep...I mean...sleep over."

I steered her to her bed and she sank onto it with a sigh of relief as she kicked off her shoes and tossed her purse aside. With her white curls awry and her clothes the slightest bit disheveled, she resembled a mischievous elf. I shook my head in disbelief.

"So, what did you and Bobby do today?"

Mom inspected a spot somewhere over my left shoulder and then whooped happily, "Chrissie...we thought you were thleeping."

I turned to see my twin standing in the doorway rubbing her eyes and peering at us sleepily. "Am I missing the party?"

"I think we both missed the party," I said. "But apparently Mom didn't." I made a face at Chrissie trying to telegraph my thoughts. "Mom was about to tell me about her evening."

Chrissie caught on immediately and winked. "Don't let me interrupt. Go ahead, Mom."

"Hmm," Mom murmured. "Oh, yes. It was so romantic. Bobby took me to the Eiffel Tower for dinner."

"Wow," we said together.

"That's not only romantic, but expensive," I added.

Dreamily Mom gazed at us. And then she lurched awkwardly to her feet. "Gotta go," she said and took an unsteady step toward the bathroom. She stumbled and caught herself. "Oopsie daisy. Guess I shouldn't have had that second bottle of wine."

Shocked, I said, "Second bottle of wine?"

Chrissie added, "You had two bottles of wine?"

"Course not, Christine. Bobby and I shared them. I probably had about one."

A frightening thought occurred to me. "And then he drove you home on that motorcycle?" My voice rose in terror at what could have happened.

"Course not," Mom said. "He brought me home in a taxi. No one should drive a motorcycle when he's been drinking. Do you think I'm an idiot?"

We bit back any smart responses we might have been considering since Mom was beginning to look pretty droopy. We waited until she used the bathroom and then eased her into her bed and turned out the lights. "You can tell us all about it in the morning," I said as we tiptoed toward the door.

As we stepped into the hall, Mom called after us. "It really was wonderful, girls. Bobby knows how to treat a girl."

Yeah, I'll bet he does, I thought churlishly. That geriatric Lothario.

"Tessa and Casey are planning to sleep in tomorrow. Don't get up 'til you're good and ready," Chrissie said.

"Mmm hmm," Mom mumbled as she drifted off to the land of dreams.

"Probably gonna dream about a kilt-clad knight in shining motorcycle gear whisking her away," Chrissie said.

"It boggles the mind," I answered.

Her back to me, Chrissie relocked and bolted the door to our room and then turned to face me. She struggled to keep a straight face and then burst out laughing.

"I do not believe it. Mom was sloshed, blotto, three sheets to the wind."

She sank to the floor with her back against the door and buried her face on her knees, her shoulders shaking.

"She was not drunk," I said. "She was tipsy. Shouldn't have had that second bottle of wine."

"Crocked, hammered, soused." Chrissie wiped her eyes. "Smashed, blitzed, buzzed."

"She is so grounded," I said. "Totally unacceptable behavior."

"Do you think Baron Bobby came on to her?"

"Or did she lead him on?"

Gasping for air, Chrissie said, "Well, you know those wrinkled knees must have been real tempting."

I snickered. "And you know what happens when you touch a man's knee."

"He goes crazy. Can't control himself. Lust on the loose."

"Never, ever, ever touch a man's knee," she scolded me, mimicking Mom's voice.

And we lost it.

When we finally managed to regain our composure, we agreed that we weren't capable of further discussion. Giddy with fatigue, we tumbled into bed and I let sleep crash over me like an ocean wave.

I resurfaced hours later clinging to the vestige of a dream in which I was piloting a boat in a roiling sea while bad guys chased me on water skis. Relieved to find myself safely on dry land, I yawned, stretched and rolled over to peer with half-closed eyes at my travel alarm. Only seven in the morning. But strangely I was wide awake and raring to go.

Chrissie was propped up in bed fully dressed and scribbling in a notebook balanced on her knees.

"Hey," I greeted her. "Aren't you the early bird?"

"Time and shopping wait for no woman. Particularly when that woman has nothing to wear." Chrissie, wearing the same outfit she'd traveled in, was definitely rumpled.

"You could always borrow something of mine, you know," I said.

"I'll stick with my jeans for now. Your things probably won't fit me anyway."

I sat up in bed and glared at her. "Are you trying to tell me I'm fat?"

"No," she said, "I'm trying to tell you that you are four inches taller than I am. Don't be so sensitive."

"I'm not. I just hate that you are always 'the cute twin.'"

"Uh huh. And you're 'the clever twin'. Imagine how stupid that makes me feel."

"I didn't call you stupid."

"You don't have to. Everyone thinks I'm cute but dumb."

"Yeah, yeah, yeah," I said. "We've had this same conversation a million times before. Get over it."

Chrissie grinned. "No, you get over it."

"Well, you can at least borrow a sweater or something if you want," I said. Pretty generous.

"Nah, I'm good for now. I'm wearing my new sexy undies and I'm feeling great."

"Okay, it's your call. I'll shower and get dressed and we can let the shopping begin." I paused halfway to the bathroom. "I thought we were going to try to find Fifi and her boyfriend and track down your bag."

Chrissie looked up from her scribbling. "We are. But the girls are sleeping and I obviously need something to wear until we find my stuff. Don't I?"

She held up a shred of notebook paper. "This was stuck under the door. From the girls. Says they got in 'really late' and will meet us around one. That leaves plenty of time to shop for new clothes."

"Although," she added, and shook her head in mock despair, "I'm really gonna miss my cute stuff. That suede jacket was gorgeous. I got such a deal on it at Nordstrom because it was missing a button. I replaced the buttons with these awesome gold coin ones I found at '*Renew You*'. You would have been so jealous."

"I'm sure," I said. "But we'll find something to replace it. Remember our motto ... 'it's all about us.'"

Once again shopping in Paris provided the perfect diversion. Whoever coined the term 'retail therapy' certainly knew what she was talking about. We let worrying about missing bags and our daughters' escapades take a back seat to wandering in and out of boutiques and the enticing department stores. And, after several hours, Chrissie and I were sprawled at *Le Bonne Crumbe*, surrounded by packages and shopping bags. We were sipping *café au lait* and nibbling on croissants as we took inventory of our purchases.

Chrissie groaned. "My feet are killing me but it's worth every blister to have my new Paris wardrobe." She fingered a glossy bag.

"I agree," I said, peeking in one of the bags. "I'm kind of glad your suitcase went AWOL or I wouldn't have found this..." I held up a leather jacket. "Or this..." A cherry red cashmere hoodie. "*J'aime Paris*."

"I'm ready to go upstairs and change my clothes," Chrissie said. "I feel like a new woman. To borrow one of your Jazzercise terms, I'm pleasantly fatigued but ready to go."

"It looks like someone else is ready for action." I pointed at Tessa who bounded out the hotel door and toward the café.

When she spotted us, a huge smile split her face and she hurried over to our table. "*Bonjour Maman. Tante* Kate. Isn't it a *tres* lovely day?"

"You're certainly in good spirits," Chrissie said. "Have a good time last night, did you?"

"*Oui*." Tessa bubbled. "We totally did." She bought herself a *café* and a *pan au chocolat* and planted herself at the table clearly willing to spend hours -- if that's what it took -- filling us in on every detail.

"Ach, lassie," I interrupted her finally, "where is the other lassie and your grandmother?"

"Hmm," she mumbled, her mouth full of pastry, "they're getting it together."

"Let's go up to our room and drop off the packages. We can see how they're doing."

Laden with shopping bags and purses, we struggled across the street toward the hotel entrance. As Chrissie reached for the brass door handle, a skinny Frenchman with a bad comb-over bolted out the door. His elbow connected with Chrissie's shoulder and her bags went flying as she staggered to regain her balance. "*Pardon*," he muttered as he fled down the street. "*Desole.*"

"Well, that was rude," Chrissie said as she retrieved her scattered bags.

I stared after him as he disappeared around the corner. He looked sort of familiar. Where had I seen him before? Oh well. I promptly forgot about him as we hurried inside.

We found Casey and Mom putting the finishing touches on their make-up. Neither seemed any the worse for the late hours and amount of alcohol they had consumed. Mom was far perkier than either Chrissie or I had anticipated. "Girls," she greeted us. "How was your morning? Did you buy some clothes, dear?"

Why is it that no matter how old you get, you are always girls to your mother?

"You certainly look cheerful," I said to her. Her eyes were bright and her white curls were perfectly arranged. She had either forgotten or was choosing to ignore the fact that when we last saw her she was giggling and burbling on about the wonders of Bobby.

I perched on the corner of her bed watching her fasten the clasp on her bracelet. "So, Mom, are you seeing Baron Bobby Hot Legs today?"

She clipped on her gold hoop earrings and leaned closer to the mirror to apply lipstick and then pirouetted to face me. "Bobby has business meetings today, but we'll probably --- how do I say this? -- hook up tomorrow."

"Mo—ther," I protested. "Do you even know what that means?"

Mom winked, picked up her purse and then patted me on the head. "I'm ready when you all are."

Chrissie had ducked into their bathroom with her shopping bags and now she emerged decked out in some of her new Paris finery. Her dark-washed jeans fit like a pair of jeans are supposed to fit and displayed her figure to perfection. Topped by her new midnight blue cropped leather jacket and red silk t-shirt she looked like a million bucks. Or Euros, if you prefer.

Tessa gave her mother a once over and then a thumbs up. "Wow, Mom. You look fierce."

Casey chimed in. "Shut up. Aunt Chrissie, you're hot."

I felt the tiniest twinge from the green-eyed monster, but I slapped it in the head and beamed at her. "I almost wish…" I cut my eyes to Casey. "…it was my suitcase that got swiped. That outfit is smokin'."

Chrissie struck a pose and then burst out laughing. "Having to shop in Paris wasn't drudgery, I'll admit. Hey Kate, let's drop the rest of our stuff in our room and hit the road. I can't wait for Paris to see the new Christine Montgomery."

The second we stepped into our room Chrissie stopped dead in her tracks. A moment before she had been laughing, but now her face was a thundercloud. My stomach did a flip flop. "What?" I asked.

"They've been here again," she said. "They came back."

I didn't have to ask who she was talking about. Fifi and her boyfriend or maybe the drug dealers/money launderers/murderers. "What makes you think they've been here?"

Casey, Tessa and Mom crowded into the room behind us and it was claustrophobic and clammy. Chrissie stepped over the shopping bags strewn at her feet and squeezed between the beds. She pointed. "There," she said. And wedged between the window sill and her bed was a suitcase.

"I told my Mom that she'd bring it back," Casey said.

"Who would bring it back?" Mom asked.

"Oh," Casey said, "it's a long story."

Casey reached around her aunt and pulled the bag out of the corner and tossed it on the bed. "Safe and sound."

Chrissie unzipped the bag and stepped back so that the rest of us could see the contents. Underwear, neatly folded, and a pair of pajamas. Chrissie glowered at Casey. "Hardly safe and sound. It's my bag all right, but they took my nice things and left only my ratty PJs."

Casey turned pale. "Oh, Aunt Chris, I'm so sorry."

"Honestly, Casey," Mom said. "What do you have to be sorry about? Someone please tell me what's going on."

No one said anything for a couple of heartbeats while we absorbed this new development. I had a terrifying thought and I scooched between them to reach the armoire. "Chrissie," I said, "do you suppose they found what they were really looking for?"

"Oh, my God. I hadn't thought of that. Yet."

Chrissie stuck her head in the armoire and punched in the combination on the safe. In her anxiety she hit a wrong number and had to begin again. No one spoke as she jabbed at the keypad. Finally, we exhaled as the lock clicked and the door cracked open. Chrissie peered inside. "Nope. It's still here."

"What is still here?" Casey and Tessa asked in unison.

Chrissie stepped aside so that the stack of bills was in view. "The money."

Casey's mouth dropped open. "Aunt Chrissie, you got your bag back and they were supposed to get the money. Now they're going to come after us."

Chrissie turned her back and carefully relocked the safe. "How was I supposed to know that they were coming to return my bag and ask politely for the drug money? What about that, Casey? Or didn't you consider the danger in this whole plan?"

Casey hung her head and fidgeted with her bracelet. "I'm sorry."

"Kathleen. Christine. I want to know what on earth is going on," Mom said. "The four of you are acting like guilty children."

"It's a long story, Mom," Chrissie said.

"Why don't we get out of here and find someplace to get a bite to eat and we'll have a family meeting," I said.

"You're not going to believe it," Chrissie concluded.

"God," Casey said to Tessa under her breath, "They're doing the twin talk again."

"Tell me about it," Tessa said.

Chapter 5

I popped the last bite of crepe into my mouth, wiped my fingers on a napkin and leaned back in my chair. I chewed slowly watching the others and then swallowed. "So," I said, "Does anyone have anything to add?"

The five of us huddled around a table outside a crepe place a block from our hotel. As we scarfed down crepes we took turns divulging what we knew about the mystery of the missing bag. As Mom listened to each revelation the look on her face changed from concerned to shocked to horrified.

"So," I repeated. "No one has anything else to say?"

Chrissie and the girls shook their heads silently. I watched Mom and waited for her response. She was gathering her thoughts, I was sure, for her cross-examination. Finally, when the silence became nearly unbearable, she took one last sip of coffee and plonked the cup on the table. She fixed each of us in turn with a laser gaze and then said with a studied calm, "And why, might I ask, have none of you told me any of this before now? I do not need protecting, you know." Mom gave a quick shake of her head. "What do we do now? Since calling the police is obviously out of the question."

Chrissie toyed with two paper straw coverings --- folding them accordion style and then unfolding them. "We-l-l," she said, "Kate and I agreed that first we ought to try to find Fifi and her boyfriend and get some answers from them. Casey might be able to give us some leads as to their whereabouts."

"Listen to you, Mom," Tessa said. "You sound like a two-bit-private eye. Whereabouts? Honestly, are you two nuts? You can't just go around tracking down crooks. Not if you want to live!"

"No shit, Sherlock," Casey said, and then glanced quickly at her grandmother who didn't seem shocked by Casey's language. No. She was too focused on how stupid her two daughters were.

"Let me understand," Casey continued. "The two of you hid the money in the safe so when someone came to return Aunt Chris' bag and get the loot, they ended up with nada. If you'd just left it in the suitcase, we'd be off the hook. So, presumably, they still want their money and will do whatever it takes to get it."

Mom turned green. "Murder us in our sleep, no doubt. Maybe we should call the cops, after all, and take our chances."

"Right," I said. "Take our chances and see whether one, or both, of your granddaughters is hauled off to a French prison to share a cell with a homicidal felon named Giselle."

Casey put her head in her hands. "Oh, God. I really screwed up, didn't I?"

Tessa patted her on the head. "You did, but I have to admit, it's sort of nice having you be the screw-up. Usually that's my role."

Chrissie snapped at Tessa. "You aren't blameless in this either, young lady. You could have told me about your brush with the law long ago."

Mom's face registered indecision and fear while the four of us eyed her. Finally, she said, "We don't have a choice. If they'd gotten their money back, it would be different. But, unfortunately, we have to find them before they harm us."

Speechless, we stared at her for a moment. And then we all started talking at once.

"What?"

"But how do you…?"

"Are you kidding me?"

"You are seriously out of your mind."

Finally, Mom rapped her fork on her coffee cup and barked, "Quiet everyone. Let me explain."

When she had our attention, she continued. "I wasn't married to a newspaperman for all those years without learning something about the criminal mind. Your dad always said in order to score the best story or, in this case, trap the crooks, all you need is a little information, a bit of intelligence, and a lot of patience. Basically, we let them chase us until we catch them."

Casey shook her head. "That might work on television, but not in real life."

"Unless you have a better plan, Casey," Mom said, "you'd better pay attention to mine. They want the money. We have the money. We wait until they make their move and then we foil their plan."

"Uh, huh," Tessa said. "And how do we do that?"

Mom frowned. "Quite obviously these are not the most intelligent criminals. Casey can identify them."

"Which is why we are in danger, Mom," Chrissie said with exaggerated patience. "We don't know where they are but they know where we are. And we don't know if Fifi and her boyfriend are in it alone or working with someone else."

"Besides," I put in, "it isn't a requirement that a criminal have an advanced degree in quantum physics. Lack of intelligence doesn't make them less dangerous. In fact, it might make them *more* dangerous."

Stubbornly, Mom said, "Which is why we bring in our secret weapon."

"Secret weapon?" I said.

"What secret weapon?" Chrissie asked.

Mom's face lit up with self-satisfaction. "Bobby," she said. "Bobby is my secret weapon."

"Bobby?" I said. "How is some geriatric Scottish baron going to be any help to us here in Paris?"

"I'm not exactly sure," Mom said, "but he knows people in politics and business. I'm betting he'll be able to help us out of this predicament without having to resort to calling in the authorities."

I thought about it. Mom made sense. "Bobby just *might* be our baron in shining kilts," I said.

I looked over my shoulder to see the pedestrians on the street. Nothing. But I could almost feel eyes watching us. I sighed. "I guess we can try it this way. Casey, you have Robert's cell number, don't you?"

She nodded.

"Call him," I said, "and see if he knows how to reach Bobby."

"I got us into this and I'll help get us out," Casey said as she pulled her cell phone out of her bag.

A few minutes later Casey dropped her phone back into her bag. "No luck. But I'm sure that either Robert or Bobby will call when they get my message."

"So," I said. "I guess we wait."

"It could be a long wait," Casey said. "There's no reason to just sit here."

Tessa broke in. "No way. We're in Paris. It's a beautiful day. We can't waste it hanging out here. We haven't even gone to Notre Dame yet."

"It's too dangerous," I said.

"We could be shot or kidnapped or drugged," Chrissie said.

"Don't be silly," Casey said. "Bobby will call and we can tell him what's going on. Meanwhile, we can do Paris."

And with the resilience, or perhaps naiveté, of youth, she and Tessa scooped up their bags and stood up, prepared to let the sightseeing begin.

I caught Chrissie's eye and arched an eyebrow at her. Unblinking, she stared back.

"Okay," I said to Casey finally, "your aunt and I agree that we can do a bit of sightseeing while we wait for Bobby to call."

"But," Chrissie added, "on one condition. That as soon as he does call, we will stop what we are doing and meet with him."

"But we have to be very careful. Let's not do anything stupid," Mom said.

"Too late for that, I'm afraid," I said.

"Amen," Chrissie said.

82

Chapter 6

The area surrounding Notre Dame was crawling with people that afternoon. Tourists snapped photos and clustered around tour guides gesturing at the magnificent cathedral. Vendors hawked everything from T-shirts to flowers to snow cones. I got chills imagining evildoers stalking us.

As we wandered along the Seine and strolled past the artists set up beside the church, I kept glancing over my shoulder --- feeling like we were slow moving targets. Mom and the girls appeared happily oblivious, but Chrissie had a white-knuckled grip on her purse strap and her eyes darted from side to side as we edged our way past the line of easels. I accidentally brushed her arm and she stiffened and whirled around.

"Whoa," I said and gave her a consoling pat. "Take it easy."

She bit her lip and smiled sheepishly as she met my eye. "I'll try."

We paused on the plaza in front of Notre Dame as Casey rapidly shot a series of photos. When she finished we slipped through the ornately carved door and entered the giant cathedral. It was hushed and peaceful after the commotion on the busy plaza and I sank onto a pew bench gratefully. I gazed at the brightly colored stained glass windows surrounding me. All that grandeur was soothing. Surely nothing bad could happen here. After all God was on duty. Wasn't he? Chrissie slid in beside me and we contemplated the windows in silence. But as I was beginning to relax I felt someone staring at us. And it wasn't God either. I whipped around and caught the startled eye of a middle-aged woman seated in the pew behind me. I stared at her until she leapt up and scooted out of the pew, giving me one last frantic look as she disappeared up the aisle.

"Kate. Hey, Kate." Chrissie clutched my arm. "What's the matter with you? You scared that woman shitless."

"Oh my God," I said. "I did, didn't I? I think I'm losing my mind. I see bad guys lurking everywhere."

"Me, too," Chrissie said. "What are we going to do?"

"Hope that Bobby calls soon?"

"Oddly enough, I would feel better if he did," Chrissie said.

But as the afternoon dragged on without a call from Bobby, we toured Paris with one eye on the sights and the other eye focused on the crowd of potential murderers. We wandered along the cobblestone walkways from *Notre Dame* to *Sainte-Chapelle*, a 13th century Gothic Chapel nestled next to *La Palais du Justice*.

"It really is awesome," Casey said. "Right, Mom?"

I merely nodded and nudged them toward the staircase winding its way to the upper chapel and the magnificent display of thousands of Bible figures formed by tiny panes of deep red and blue stained glass. As we began our ascent I squinted into the shimmering sunlight coming from the skylight. Wait. Was that…? Yes, it was. A red stiletto, presumably attached to a feminine leg, could be seen on a step several feet above my head. Could it be Fifi? I grabbed Chrissie's shoulder and pointed. Her eyes widened and she bolted up the steps with me on her heels. Before we could catch up, the red stiletto vanished taking its owner with it.

Chrissie and I burst from the staircase into the upper chapel and scanned the space. With my hands on my thighs I bent over and tried to catch my breath. "Where did she go?" I huffed.

Chrissie ran a hand through her hair and turned in a circle. "Beats me. I thought we'd caught her."

I felt a movement behind me and turned to see Mom and the girls and said in a hushed voice, "Fifi. We thought we saw her on the stairs, but…" I gestured at the chapel space. "… I don't see her now."

Mom rapidly lost interest in the pursuit of Fifi and gazed around at the stained glass windows. "This is stunning," she breathed.

The sun shining through the stained glass soaring far above our heads cast red and blue shadows on us. It *was* gorgeous, but I was too distracted by our alleged Fifi sighting to really appreciate it. Instead of focusing on the windows I scrutinized feet, hoping to spot the errant red stiletto once again.

"We are pretty pathetic, aren't we?" Chrissie whispered. "Chasing a red stiletto shoe?"

"It probably wasn't Fifi," I whispered back, "but even if it was, what were we going to do? Rip off her stiletto and use it to beat her into returning your bag?"

"I've heard worse suggestions," Chrissie said, "but I think we're losing our minds. We need serious help." She paused. "And I need my bag."

"We're right next door to the *Prefecture de Police*," I said. "Maybe we should go there and tell the police our story. They could help us."

"Or," Chrissie said. "They could arrest Tessa or Casey. Do we dare take that chance?"

I looked over my shoulder at Casey and Tessa --- Casey, snapping photos from every conceivable angle and Tessa with her head angled back so she could see the cathedral ceiling, her lips parted and her eyes bright. Casey took her camera away from her eye and caught me staring. She grinned and did a little jog step.

"No," I said to my twin, "We can't risk it."

Casey wandered over, her camera slung over her shoulder. "You two sure look gloomy," she said.

I fixed her with the "mom look". "I wonder why."

Casey wrapped one arm around my shoulder and the other around her aunt's. "I, dear twins, have the solution."

"Do tell."

"Yep. Ice cream."

"Ice cream?"

"Not just ice cream. 'Oh my God I've died and gone to dessert heaven' ice cream."

"*Berthillon*," I said. "The best ice cream in Paris."

"Not just Paris," Casey corrected me. "In the world. And we are mere steps from such decadent goodness."

Chrissie scowled at us. "What are you two talking about? We have some serious issues here. We don't have time for ice cream."

"I know," I said, "but every problem goes better with ice cream. You can never go wrong with *chocolat*. Particularly from *Berthillon*."

Chrissie tapped a fingernail against her front teeth. "Okay. Lead me to it."

Decision made in favor of ice cream, Casey skipped across the floor to round up Tessa and Mom and drag them away from their stained-glass gazing.

We ambled along the cobblestone street past the shops and hotels lining *Rue Saint Louis en l'Ile*, pausing to peer at clothes and pottery and artwork and jewelry displayed in the shop windows until we reached *Berthillon*. We joined a long line of hungry tourists and Casey translated the list of flavors for us as we inched toward the counter.

"*Pistache, praline aux pignons, vanille, chocolat au nougat, fraise, framboise*," Casey said. "Oh, here it is. I'm having the *peche*."

"I'll take *Noix de Coco*," I said.

Casey laughed. "It's all about the coconut with you, isn't it, Mom?"

"*Oui*," I said. "But, of course."

While we waited our turn to order Mom struck up a conversation with two women in front of us.

"This is Jane and Diana," Mom introduced us after she chatted for a few minutes. "They're retired school teachers from Michigan. I'll bet we know some of the same people."

She turned her back and returned to an animated conversation with the teachers. By the time they reached the counter, Mom had undoubtedly pried some of the most intimate details of their lives out of them.

"Oh, dear," the older of the two said as the young French woman handed her a large cone, "this isn't what I thought it would be."

"Well, Jane, what did you expect?" her companion asked.

"I didn't know that *praline aux pignons* had nuts! I'm allergic to nuts."

The woman pivoted and held out her cone to Mom. "Here you take it. I heard you say that you were going to order *praline aux pignons*. I'll order plain chocolate."

"Oh, I couldn't," Mom said. "Let me pay you for it."

The woman pressed the cone into Mom's hand and spoke to the young clerk. Holding the now dripping cone Mom dug around in her purse one-handed looking for money. By the time she found it, the two women had walked away eating their cones without a single backward glance.

"Wait," Mom called after them. "Let me give you some money."

But the praline woman gave an airy wave of her hand and disappeared around the corner, leaving Mom holding the cone.

"Now that was odd." Mom licked the cone. "Mmm. Good."

Our own cones in hand, the rest of us joined Mom on a nearby bench. I tasted my coconut and then sat up with a jerk.

"Do you really think you ought to eat that, Mom?"

Mom's eyes were closed. She sighed. "This is delicious. Of course, I should eat it."

I frowned. "Didn't your mother ever tell you to never accept ice cream from a stranger?"

"I believe that would be candy. And those two women weren't strangers. They were from Michigan." Mom continued to swirl her tongue through the ice cream.

"Oh, sure," I said. "And there are no criminals in the entire state. Haven't you heard of Detroit?"

"Don't be snarky, dear," Mom said and smiled.

"Good one, Nonny," Tessa said. "Don't be snarky, Aunt Kate. Those two women looked perfectly harmless."

"They were wearing tennis shoes," Casey added.

"Oh, silly me," I said. "I should have known that anyone wearing tennis shoes is perfectly harmless."

"Only someone wearing red Jimmy Choo five-inch stilettos should be feared," Chrissie added.

"Fear the red stiletto." Casey laughed.

For a few minutes we licked our cones in silence enjoying the ice cream and the *Ille Saint Louis* ambiance --- cobblestones and quaint whitewashed architecture. I leaned back against the bench and allowed myself to relax --- just a little.

Mom nibbled her nearly finished cone and then suddenly stiffened. She ran her tongue along the wafered edge. "There's something in my ice cream."

"Must be a nut," I said. "Jane didn't want the nuts."

"No. Not a nut. It's something else."

Mom fished with one finger in the melted puddle at the bottom of her cone and pulled out an object and held it up. "It's a hunk of metal."

Casey offered her napkin to Mom who dropped the metallic object into it.

"I could have broken a tooth," Mom said. "Or choked. They shouldn't serve ice cream with pieces of metal in it. I'm going to take it back. Give it to me, Casey."

Casey unwrapped the offending object from the napkin and started to hand it to her grandmother. Her eyes widened and her mouth dropped open.

"Oh my God," Casey said. "Look at this. It's not just some random hunk of metal."

Mom stared at her. "What is it then?"

Casey dangled it from her fingertips. "It's a skull and crossbones."

A silver skull and crossbones charm? In Mom's ice cream? We all gawked at it speechless. Finally Tessa recovered her voice.

"How did it get there? And why?"

"Beats me," Mom said, "but it wasn't meant for me. It was meant for Jane."

"And where exactly is Jane?" I asked. "Gone. Disappeared. Nowhere to be found."

"What are you trying to say, dear?" Mom asked.

"I think that Jane put that charm in your ice cream," I said.

"But why would she do that? She's a retired schoolteacher from Michigan. Not some super spy."

"And you know this exactly how?"

Doubt washed over Mom's face. "I guess because she told me so. But why?"

"And how?" Chrissie said.

"I'm going to go talk to the clerk," Casey said and held out her hand for the charm.

"I'm coming too," Mom said.

Chrissie, Tessa and I stood up.

"You aren't leaving us behind," I said.

Casey elbowed her way through the line of tourists at *Berthillon* apologizing in both French and English until she reached the counter. The clerk was not the same one who had waited on us, but Casey displayed the skull and crossbones charm and explained the situation in fluent French. The young woman behind the counter held up her hand in protest and shook her head.

"*Non,*" she said. "*Non.*"

She backpedaled as far as she could in the confined space retreating from Casey and the skull. The clerk spoke in rapid French to the other employees who were scooping ice cream. Then she spoke again to Casey with much head-shaking and hand wringing. Finally, Casey shrugged and stepped away from the counter. We followed her to a quiet spot a few steps away and gathered around her.

"The girl said that she didn't know a thing about the charm, but she offered us a refund. She also said that she had just come on duty and that the other girl --- the one who waited on us and on Jane and her friend --- was temporary help. This girl said she had never met her or even seen her before today. She was extremely sorry and also seemed a bit freaked out by the charm," Casey said.

"This is all very weird," Tessa said. "Do you think that someone actually wanted one of us to get that charm? And not Jane?"

"My guess is yes," I said.

"But how would anyone know that we would be at *Berthillon* at that exact time?" Chrissie said.

"We weren't exactly quiet at *Sainte Chapelle* when Casey suggested we go for ice cream," I pointed out. "And it was crowded. Anyone could have overheard her."

"And followed us," Casey added.

"But why?" Mom said. "What could anyone gain by planting a skull and cross bones in my *praline aux pignons*?"

"I'd say it was to frighten us," Chrissie said. She took the little charm out of Casey's hand and examined it. "Give us our money or you'll turn up like this."

"I agree," I said. "And it's working. I'm definitely frightened."

Mom gently removed the charm from Chrissie's fingers and tucked into a pocket of her purse. "I'm keeping this to show Bobby."

"If we ever see him or hear from him again," Chrissie said. She shoved her sunglasses up on her head and scrutinized the pedestrians hurrying up the street.

"Maybe," I said, "he's in on this. It sure seems convenient that he met Mom on the plane."

Mom glared at me. "Bobby is not in on this. Whatever this is. I am a better judge of character than that."

We scowled at each other until Casey said, "This isn't helping. Let's get out of here and go somewhere else."

"Leaving the scene of the crime," Tessa said with a grimace.

No one seemed to be paying any attention to us, but I felt those eyes again. "Good idea, Casey. Let's go."

Nobody uttered a single word of protest as Casey marched down the street away from *Berthillon*.

Chapter 7

An hour later as late afternoon turned to dusk and then dusk to twilight, we watched in awe from the top viewing level of the Eiffel Tower as the lights of Paris flickered on like fireflies in the backyard on a hot summer night. Casey leaned against the railing and flung her arms out wide. "Now, *this* is what *I'm* talking about," she exclaimed. "It's like winning the sightseeing lottery. Takes your mind off anything else."

We gazed in awe until Tessa broke the spell. "I agree, but I'm cold. And hungry. Have we seen enough?"

"Spoilsport," Casey said, but she shivered and didn't object as we tore ourselves away from the view and headed for the elevator and then the street.

"Let's try that cute bistro," Tessa said as we picked our way through the crowd of pedestrians clogging the sidewalk. She led the way to an outdoor table nestled next to a space heater and we plopped down with sighs of relief.

"This is awesome," Casey said. "The Eiffel Tower looks like a fourth of July sparkler with all those lights."

"Nice of them to turn it on for us," Tessa said.

Mom turned to look over her shoulder at the Eiffel Tower and heaved a sigh. "It was a wonderful afternoon. It would have been perfect, if only…"

"I know," I said. "If only we hadn't spent the entire afternoon feeling like we were being followed, it would have been exactly what I dreamed about before we left home."

Mom pulled the silver skull and crossbones charm out of her bag and held it up to examine it. Its eyes glowed eerily in the candlelight.

"Creepy," Tessa said.

"This is a situation which calls for wine." I signaled to a waiter. "Some things call for chocolate, but wine is definitely in order here."

Somehow in spite of the day's events, we did succeed in enjoying a long and lazy supper. After we finished our food and sipped after dinner liqueurs and coffee, Chrissie jumped to her feet and dusted off her jeans. "I'm going to use *la toilette* before we leave."

"I'll go with you," I said. "We'll be the first shift."

I pushed back my chair and trailed Chrissie into the interior of the restaurant.

It was dark and crowded. Smoke wafted heavily in the air and my eyes watered. Chrissie led the way toward the stairway in the back leading to the *toilettes* in the basement. I lagged behind grimly rubbing my eyes when suddenly she stopped and ducked her head. Abruptly she melted into the darkness at the edge of the well lit bar area.

"Don't look now," she said.

But it was too late. I was already checking out the crowd. The bar was jammed. Every seat was taken and people stood around holding drinks and talking loudly. I singled out a tall, skinny guy in a suit and tie gesturing excitedly. His back was toward me but when he turned I realized with a shock that I'd seen him before. Bad Comb-over Guy. The same one who had nearly knocked Chrissie down leaving *Le Hotel Mignon* earlier. And then it hit me. Not only had I seen Bad Comb-over Guy at our hotel, I had also seen him on the plane. With Fifi.

"Good Lord," I said to Chrissie. "Look who's at the bar. It's…"

"Shh," she said. She grabbed my arm and skulked away with her back to the bar and her head bent, pulling me toward the stairway.

She trotted down the steps without looking back and I clattered after her. She spotted the *toilette*, yanked open the door and pulled me inside. It was tiny. A minute commode sat in the corner next to a washbasin the size of a shot glass. I doubted that I could sit on the commode without banging my knees on the opposite wall. But size was not an issue for Chrissie. She had other concerns.

"In the bar," she said. "Did you see?"

"Yeah, Bad Comb-over Guy."

"What? No. My jacket. A woman was wearing my new hot pink suede jacket that was in my bag! The one that's missing!"

"Seriously? A woman has on a jacket that looks like yours?"

"It *is* mine," she insisted. "I'm positive. But I can prove it if we get closer. I told you about the buttons."

"Describe the woman wearing your jacket."

"Blonde frizzy hair. One of those '80's fluff chick styles. About my size. And wearing *my* jacket."

Her tightly pressed lips and set jaw told me that Chrissie wouldn't budge on this. The only course of action, apparently, was to go back to the bar to verify her jacket sighting. It was hot and claustrophobic in the cramped bathroom and we were starting to perspire.

"Let's go," Chrissie said and shoved open the door. We tripped over each other in our haste to escape and barged into two haughty waiters taking a cigarette break in the narrow hallway. The two exchanged knowing looks as we emerged sweaty and somewhat disheveled. One murmured something in French to the other and they both laughed snidely and made rude gestures.

We brushed by the pair and Chrissie looked back over her shoulder. I wouldn't have been surprised if they had been incinerated on the spot, the look she gave them was so blistering. Seething she clomped up the stairs. I hurried after her --- my heels reverberating on the tile.

"Dirty minded waiters," she fumed. "I have half a mind to go back and tell them in no uncertain terms that we are sisters — not lovers."

Then, waiters forgotten, she headed back to the bar. Chrissie surveyed the area and, concluding that no one was paying any particular attention to us, edged closer. Hovering in the shadows Chrissie pointed. "There. Do you see her? I swear it's my jacket."

It didn't take an ace detective to pick out the fluff chick in the jacket with her back to me. "Whoa," I said.

"So you see it too?"

"Yes," I breathed, "it's incredible. I've never seen suede quite that color. Where did you…"

"Kate. Focus," Chrissie hissed.

"I am," I hissed back. "Are you positive she isn't wearing a jacket that looks like yours?"

"Wait 'til she turns around and check out the buttons."

I was still unconvinced. How likely was it that a woman who might have been involved in the theft of Chrissie's suitcase would show up in the same bar as we were and wearing the evidence? How stupid would she have to be? I was conducting a debate with my inner skeptic when Pink Jacket spun around to speak to someone. I caught my breath. This could not be possible.

"Do you see the buttons?" Chrissie whispered.

"Forget the buttons," I whispered back. "That's not some random fluff chick. That's Fifi."

"Fifi? Casey's Fifi? Red stiletto Fifi?"

"The very same. I spoke to her on the plane. It's Fifi." I let my gaze travel down to her feet. "And look, Chris, she's wearing the red Jimmy Choo's."

Chrissie stiffened. "Who wears red stilettos with a hot pink jacket? I thought Paris was the fashion capital."

I clapped a hand over her mouth. "Shush. Now who needs to focus?"

Then I gasped. Fifi clutched the shirt sleeve of Bad Comb-Over Guy and tugged until he bent his head. Then she said something in his ear. Obviously they were together. Just as they had been on the plane.

"Chrissie," I hissed. "She's with Bad Comb-Over Guy. And she was with him on the plane too."

"So? Do I know him?"

"You haven't been formally introduced, but he nearly knocked you over leaving the hotel this afternoon."

"And?"

"And that was just before we discovered your suitcase had been returned."

"Oh, my God. This is too big a coincidence to ignore."

I was set to storm the bar and confront them — demand an explanation --- when a saner head, my twin's, prevailed. "I have a plan," she said under her breath. "Let's get out of here and I'll explain."

Chrissie grabbed a couple of menus from a side table and we used them to cover our faces as we skirted the bar area and scurried outside to our table. Casey had her cell phone plastered to her ear and held up a finger as we approached.

"Okay, I'll tell them," she said as she closed the phone and dropped it into her purse. "That was Robert and he said...."

"Not now, Casey," I said. "We're leaving."

Chrissie threw a wad of Euros on the table. She scooped up her camera and guidebooks and stuffed them into her tote bag. "Now."

"But Mom," Tessa protested. "I'm not finished with my coffee."

"No time for that, Tessa. We're leaving now. Before they spot us."

"Before who spots us?" Mom asked.

"We'll explain when we get out of here," I said. "Hurry."

I picked up Casey's camera and thrust it at her. "Don't dilly dally."

She wedged it into her camera bag and slung the strap over her shoulder. "Okay, okay. Chill. We're coming."

The three of them grabbed the rest of their stuff and hurried after Chrissie and me onto the sidewalk. Chrissie scanned the area and then herded us several yards down the block to reconnoiter behind one of those large green kiosks that are everywhere in Paris. From this vantage point we could see the restaurant, but were hidden from view.

"Here's the deal," Chrissie said. Taking turns we quickly explained about Bad Comb-Over Guy and Fifi. "And," Chrissie concluded, "We're going to follow them when they come out."

"Are you two insane?" Tessa said. "What do you plan to do if you catch them?"

"Yeah," Casey added. "Why didn't you just talk to them in the bar?"

Chrissie rolled her eyes. "And do what? Ask them to please come back to the hotel so we can return the money to them?"

"And say, oh, by the way, please return Chrissie's new and very trendy wardrobe to her?" I added.

"This way," Chrissie said her eyes trained on the entrance to the restaurant, "we can find out where they live and then have something to tell Bobby --- if he ever calls."

Casey smacked her forehead with her hand. "Oh, yeah. We raced out so fast I didn't get to tell you. Robert called."

"And?"

"He said Bobby had been in some high profile meetings all day and didn't have his phone. But that he --- Robert --- would make sure he got the message that we need to talk to him."

"More waiting for Bobby?" I stepped back as two pedestrians ambled past.

"No," Casey continued. "Robert said to call when we got back to the hotel and he and Mac and Bobby would come by. Tess and I are going clubbing with the guys, but Bobby can hear our whole story before we go. Okay?"

"Maybe we should just go back to the hotel now and skip prowling the streets of Paris in pursuit of some thieves." Mom shivered. "It's cold."

To prove her point a chill wind swept around the corner. It was cold and dark and the idea was undoubtedly crazy. Still we pulled up our collars and huddled behind the kiosk to wait for Fifi and Bad Comb-Over Guy.

Fifteen minutes went by and it seemed like an eternity as the temperature dropped and the wind whistled around the edge of the kiosk. Tessa looked up at the sky and a large drop of rain splattered on her nose. "Oh, geez, you guys," she whined. "Now it's raining. This is so stupid."

Chrissie looked at me. I nodded back. "We, Aunt Kate and I, are going to follow them. The rest of you wimps can go back to the hotel if you aren't up for the challenge."

"My feet hurt," Casey moaned. "Let's just quit." She kicked off her shoes and stood barefoot.

"You're being a brat. Put your shoes back on," I said. "We might have to leave in a hurry. We aren't waiting for you."

"Not asking you to," Casey grumbled, but she put her shoes on.

Fortunately, at that moment Fifi and Bad Comb-Over Guy appeared. The pair stopped just under the awning and surveyed the street. The rain had turned from drizzle to downpour and Fifi made impatient gestures at Bad Comb-Over Guy. She doesn't like this weather any better than we do, I thought. Finally, she tossed her head, yanked an umbrella out of her bag, put it up, and strode off down the street. As she passed us I heard her muttering in French. Bad Comb-Over Guy lifted his shoulders in a Gallic shrug, put up his own umbrella and shuffled after her. I pressed back against the kiosk and held my breath but neither of them gave us a glance.

"Looks like they're having a fight," Casey said.

"My jacket," Chrissie said, "is going to be ruined. You can't wear suede in the rain. Everyone knows that."

"Then why did you bring it?" I asked. "Everyone knows Paris can be very rainy in the spring."

Chrissie gave me a withering stare and followed the pair as they walked away. We tailed them through the wet streets trying to stay out of sight. Occasionally they would stop and face each other gesturing wildly. Definitely not happy.

Each time they stopped we melted into a shop doorway and pretended to window shop.

"This is so stupid," Tessa groused.

"A wild goose chase," Casey agreed.

Chrissie turned on them as we limped through the rain. "Stop whining. We could be sipping cognac in a bar if it wasn't for the two of you. We could just call the cops and see what happens if you like. Besides, I told you to go back to the hotel if you wanted."

"No, no," Casey said as she splashed through a puddle. "Whither though goest."

Fifi and Bad Comb-Over Guy skirted the Eiffel Tower and hurried through the *Parc du Champs de Mar*. We emerged from the park onto the *Rue Saint Dominque*. After the darkness of *the Parc du Champs de Mar*, it was a relief to find it much brighter here with restaurants and streetlights scattered along the sidewalk. The street, though, was almost deserted on this rainy night so we kept a distance between us and our prey. If one of them had looked back, we would have been spotted easily. But they didn't. They just scurried along.

Suddenly they halted in front of a large wooden doorway nestled between a liquor store and a supermarket. Bad Comb-Over Guy pulled a key from his pocket and unlocked the door. Fifi shoved him out of her way and stormed into the building. They both slipped inside and the heavy door thudded shut behind them, leaving the five of us watching from the street.

We waited a moment with rain pelting our heads and then Tessa grumbled, "Now what? I'm not going to stand out here in the rain all night and wait for them to come out."

Chrissie dug around in her bag and pulled out a notepad and a pen. She peered at the brass numbers affixed to the door, jotted them down and tucked the notebook safely away. "We don't have my stuff, but now we have an address to give to Bobby. That's more than we had before."

Casey grinned. "Aunt Agatha Chrissie. We're hot on the trail of your missing wardrobe."

Drops of rain dripped down Mom's glasses. She pulled them off and wiped them on the sleeve of her sodden sweater. "We've had enough detective work for the night. I'll spring for a cab."

"Really?" I said. "You will? Like for the entire ride home?"

"You rock, Nonny." Casey clapped her hands as a cab appeared and, soggy and grumpy, we piled into it for the trip back to the hotel.

Chapter 8

As soon as we reached our room Chrissie and I stripped off our waterlogged clothes, hung them over the shower bar and bundled up in the thick terry-cloth robes provided by the hotel. We wrapped our icy fingers around steaming mugs of herbal tea generously provided by Madame Reno, the front desk clerk.

Chrissie rummaged in her carry-on bag and pulled out a small bottle of whisky. She twisted off the cap and poured a liberal amount into her mug. Then she offered me the bottle.

"Booty from Business Class," she said.

"Well, aren't you the little walking liquor store." I held out my mug. "Count me in."

Chrissie blew on her tea before taking a cautious sip. "Hmm." She took another larger sip. "I wonder how long it will be before Bobby and the grandsons appear on our doorstep."

"We'll ask Mom when she comes over from her room. I presume that Bobby is through with his business by now." I glanced at my watch. "It's late. Past midnight."

"Too late for the girls to go clubbing," Chrissie said, "but when did they ever listen to their mothers?"

"We wouldn't be in this mess if they had," I told her.

We were interrupted by a tap on the door and Mom's voice, "Hel-lo. Girls? Are you decent? Bobby and the boys are here. Can we come in?"

I hopped off the bed and belted my robe more securely before I unbolted the lock and opened the door. There was a small crowd in the hallway --- Mom and the girls and Bobby and his grandsons, Robert and Mac. The MacTavish men were dressed in jeans and sweaters --- all tall and ridiculously good-looking. I stepped aside to let them in. Our room seemed too tiny to accommodate all those long legs and broad shoulders and testosterone.

"I know we agreed to consult Bobby," Chrissie said, "but I don't know about them." She angled her head in the direction of the grandsons.

"We trust them," Tessa said.

"And we told them most of the problem last night," Casey added.

I opened my mouth to object and then closed it. What difference did it really make?

After a few minutes of fumbling, everyone found a place to sit --- Chrissie, Tessa, Casey and I curled up on one bed. Mom and Bobby perched on the other and the grandsons sprawled on the floor.

"So," Bobby said. "What is this situation which your mother says is troubling you?" The expression on his face was more curious than concerned. He quirked a white eyebrow in our direction.

"Well," I began, "it started with a chance encounter on the plane...."

We all took turns and with a lot of interrupting and correcting each other, we managed to explain the problem.

"We don't want to call the police," I said in conclusion. "And we don't know what to do."

"Is there anything you can do to help us, Bobby?" Mom asked. She squeezed his bicep and I tried not to notice.

Bobby sat on the edge of the bed, elbows on knees, chin propped on his hands. He was very quiet. So quiet that it was unnerving. What was he thinking? Did we want to know? Had we made a huge mistake in divulging our secrets?

Finally when I thought we might expire from the suspense he looked up and did that eyebrow quirk thing in Casey's direction. "Well, lassie, you have certainly stirred up a fine kettle of haggis."

Casey hung her head and played with her bracelet. "I know. I'm really sorry. I was so stupid. Am I going to be arrested?"

Bobby's lips twitched briefly --- it appeared he was biting back a smile. "Ah, lassie, I doubt that it will go that far. One of my mates from school is on the

Paris police force. I think it best if I speak to him --- off the record, as you Yanks say. Maybe I can find out how they will handle it and what he can do to help you all. If you'd like me to do so, of course."

"Oh, Bobby, that would be wonderful," Mom cooed.

He smiled at her. "Of course, I can't promise anything, but I would be delighted to try."

Eventually we left it at that. Bobby would get in touch with his "mate" and then he'd fill us in. We agreed to meet the next evening at *Bouffe Tard* to find out what he learned. Casey and Tessa left with Robert and Mac to go clubbing, leaving the four of us to figure out details.

"So, tomorrow night. Say nine-ish. At *Bouffe Tard*?" I said.

"I think that will be agreeable," Bobby said. "But I'd prefer that you ladies didn't expose yourselves to any danger. I suggest that you stay in the hotel tomorrow. No sense risking injury."

Chrissie and I glanced around the claustrophobic hotel room and exchanged "that's not going to happen" looks.

Mom aimed a reassuring smile at Bobby. "Don't worry, Bobby, we won't be in any danger. I promise."

Her hand on his back she guided him out of our room. At the door she looked back over her shoulder at us and winked.

Chapter 9

In spite of Bobby's instructions, Chrissie, Mom and I decided to spend the day absorbing the special ambiance of Paris. It was too tempting to miss. Hoping to check out as many sites as possible, we got an early start. The morning flew by. After a quick stop at the *Louvre*, we lingered a bit with the Impressionists at the *Musee d'Orsay* and then strolled through the *Tuilleries Gardens*. A posse of little boys wearing school uniforms kicked a soccer ball in our direction. When it rolled into our path, I gamely kicked it back.

Mom clapped as if I had scored the winning goal at the Olympics. "I hope the girls are having as much fun as we are," she said. "I can't believe I'm in Paris in the *Tuilleries* with my girls! Playing soccer. "

"And so far," Chrissie said, "no one has shot at us."

"Dumb luck?" I suggested.

By early afternoon we had roamed as far as *Le Marais*, the old Jewish section of Paris, and poked into quirky shops along the way. In *Place des Vosges*, a bit of green park surrounded by arcades filled with shops and cafes, Mom randomly selected a café for lunch. It was a bustling, sunny place with a counter across the back of the building for take-out and a few tables covered with red and white checked tablecloths scattered in the front room. We sat down at the only empty table --- Mom and I facing the courtyard and Chrissie facing the rear of the restaurant. Shrugging off our jackets, we perused the menus our cheerful hostess provided.

"This is nice," I said as I surveyed the place. "Good choice, Mom."

"*Merci*," she said. "Hmm. What do I think I'd like?"

"Maybe the quiche," I said.

"Or the *croque monsieur*," Mom added. "What do you think, Christine?"

Chrissie divided her attention between the menu and the activity at the back of the café. "I think I'll have the omelet…" she began and then stopped. Her eyes went wide. "I do not believe it. It's them. Again."

"Them?" I said.

"Them. Fifi and Bad Comb-Over Guy. At the counter back there." She flicked her head toward the rear.

Both Mom and I turned to look.

"No," Chrissie said. "Don't look now." She hid her face behind her menu and peeked around it to observe the pair. "They aren't going to get away this time. I'm going to talk to them."

She shoved her chair back and stood up.

"Not without me, you're not," I said and pushed my chair back. "Stay here, Mom, and guard our purses."

We marched toward the counter where customers were standing three deep waiting to be served. We hesitated a moment and then Chrissie edged her way through the throng and snuck up behind Bad Comb-Over Guy. She reached out and tapped him on the shoulder. "*Pardon, Monsieur.*"

Bad Comb-Over Guy glanced over his shoulder and went rigid as the blood drained from the top of his oddly coiffed head to his neck. He turned as white as the powdered sugar on his almond croissant as if he had just taken a sucker punch to the stomach. He gaped at us and opened his mouth as if to speak. And then closed it.

"Surprise," Chrissie whispered.

At that moment Fifi completed her transaction with the cashier and, holding a white bakery bag, whirled around and spotted the three of us in a frozen tableau. Before either Chrissie or I could react, she grabbed Bad C's shoulder and gave him a shove.

"*Allez,*" she said and raced from the café with him on her heels.

"Oh, no." Chrissie made a grab for his sleeve but missed. Her elbow connected with the arm of a heavyset woman, knocking her purse out of her hand. The woman immediately began screeching. Other customers turned to see what was happening. In the ensuing commotion Chrissie and I managed to slip away.

"We can't let them get away again," I cried as we hurried to our table to retrieve Mom, our purses and our shopping bags.

The three of us burst out the door and onto the arcade walkway. It was empty. But wait…I spotted Fifi and Bad Comb-Over scrambling into a taxi at the corner. Before we could reach it, the taxi sped away into the traffic.

Chrissie stepped off the curb and frantically waved her arm at a passing taxi. A moment later the taxi screeched to a halt beside us and Chrissie yanked open the door, pushed Mom in ahead of her and clambered in. Heart pounding I piled in after her.

When the driver looked at her questioningly, Chrissie said the words she had probably dreamed of saying her entire life. "Follow that taxi!"

The driver gave her an uncomprehending look. "*Je ne parles pas anglais bien.*"

Frustrated, Chrissie tried again. "*Allez, Monsieur.* Fast fast." She gestured excitedly at the other taxi stalled at a red light a half block away.

Suddenly, inspiration struck. "Le Amazing Race. *Comprende?*" she said.

"Wait, just a second," I said, "we're not…"

Chrissie's elbow in my ribs nearly knocked me out of the cab and back onto the curb. "Work with me," she snapped. And to the driver she said again, "Amazing Race. Follow that taxi."

His face lit up as it dawned on him what Chrissie was saying. "Ah, *oui, Madame.* Zee race. No problem." And he shifted into gear and pulled away from the curb with the tires squealing in protest.

I closed my eyes and clung to the leather strap on the door of the taxi. My nails bit into my palms and I fumbled with the seatbelt taking three tries to latch it. I was thrown against the door as we careened around corners at high speed. I snuck a peek and realized we had run a red light --- narrowly missing a huge street washer. Our taxi scraped by a parked mini car --- mere inches separating us.

"Please God," I breathed. "Let us live."

"We're going to die," Mom whispered.

Chrissie leaned forward, resting her arm on the back of the driver's seat so she could encourage him. Not that he seemed to need any encouragement. When I dared look, I saw him gripping the steering wheel his face screwed up in concentration. He was certainly taking this chase thing seriously.

"*Allez*," Chrissie cried. "They're getting away."

When it seemed that the wild ride would never end I felt the cab slowing. I forced myself to look out the window as we sped across a bridge and rounded a corner. I caught a glimpse of the Eiffel Tower and then we jolted to a stop.

Half a block away I saw Fifi and Bad Comb-Over Guy emerge from their taxi and sprint toward a small ticket booth. Chrissie tossed a handful of bills at the driver, shoved us out of the taxi, and raced after the pair. "*Merci*," she called over her shoulder to the driver.

Unfortunately for the success of the Great Chase, at that moment a tour bus parked at the curb unloaded its trench-coat-clad passengers. They swarmed the area in front of the ticket booth while their guide arranged their entrance into the attraction.

"Where are we?" Mom asked as she tried to wiggle through the crowd.

I looked around and recognized exactly where we had landed. "The Sewer," I said. "This is the Paris Sewer Museum."

"Eew," Mom said.

Chrissie was undeterred. "Come on. We're losing them."

By the time the tour guide finished his business and we purchased our entrance tickets, there was no sign of our prey. "Damn," Chrissie fumed. "Just our luck."

Mom hesitated at the top of the steps just inside the door. "Are you sure about this?"

Chrissie started down the steps leading into the sewers under the street. "We aren't letting them get away again."

The tourists from the tour bus blocked our path and we had to muscle our way around them. "Maude," one camera toting senior citizen said to her friend, "take my picture." She backed into Mom, nearly sending her sprawling.

"Oh, dear," Camera Woman said. "I'm so sorry." She brushed at Mom's jacket as she clutched Mom's shoulder.

Chrissie stepped between them and tugged on Mom's arm. "Come on, Mother, we don't have time for idle chit chat."

Mom nodded an apology for her daughter's rudeness and clomped down the steps after Chrissie. At the bottom of the steps we stopped to survey the area. No Fifi. No Bad Comb-Over Guy. All we saw were damp cement tunnels leading into darkness. Chrissie limped toward the tunnel and stopped to kick off her shoes. "Ouch. Blisters," she said. And clutching her shoes in one hand, continued into the shadows.

It became more murky and eerie the farther we went. The only sounds were running water and the distant murmur of conversation. We felt very alone. I peered anxiously into the darkness and wondered if it was possible to become hopelessly and forever lost. The dampness was creeping into my bones. I shivered.

We came to a cement gutter with water trickling down it. I shuddered to think where the water had come from. There was a scrabbling, scratching sound and I was horrified to see a large rat scurrying into the tunnel opposite us. I let out a tiny surprised shriek.

"What?" Chrissie said. I pointed and she clung to my hand with icy fingers. "Ick. Is that what I think it is?"

"You dirty rat," I called to it. The rat ignored me.

We raced through the maze of tunnels following the arrows until we reached a better-lit room filled with exhibits. The history of the Paris sewer system was presented in a series of plagues and displays. Mom halted in front of a plaque. "Girls," she said. "This is really fascinating. Did you know that these sewers date from the 11th Century?"

"That's great, Mom," Chrissie said, "but we don't have time to read all of this now. We have to find Fifi and her boyfriend."

"Chrissie, this is crazy, don't you think?" I said. "How on earth can we find them in here?"

"I'm hoping that the only way out is past us."

She led us through a maze of exhibits toward a gift shop on the far wall. I could see a large --- what I sincerely hoped was --- fake rat hanging above the gift shop sign. I shuddered again. There were more tunnels leading away from the lighted area and Chrissie steered us in that direction. As she turned to head back into the darkness, I noticed the restroom door open. And out stepped Fifi followed by Bad Comb-Over Guy. They conferred briefly at the gift shop entrance. I squeezed Chrissie's arm and pointed. She gave me a thumbs up and smiled. Stocking footed, she limped toward the pair, sidled up noiselessly behind them and calmly tapped Bad Comb-Over Guy on the shoulder. As he whirled to face her she said, "The jig is up, Monsieur."

Chapter 10

Fifi spun around slowly and met my eye over the top of Chrissie's head. Her body was tightly coiled as if she might sprint away into the nearest tunnel. We stared at each other unmoving. A single curled lock fell over her right eye but she never broke eye contact.

"*Bonjour,* Fifi," I said softly.

"Ah." Her body sagged. "From the plane." One hand went to her gold hoop earring. "Madame returned my earring."

"*Oui,*" I said. "I did. But I believe you know my daughter, Casey Kelly, as well."

"Casey? You are the *maman* of Casey?" Fifi's face lit up.

I exhaled. I hadn't realized I had been holding my breath. "*Oui.*"

Bad Comb-Over Guy took Fifi by the elbow and started to urge her away. Fifi shook off his hand. "*Non, mon amor.* It is time. We must explain all to Madame and her friends."

Fifi's boyfriend tugged on her arm. "Come, Fifi. They will call the *gendarmes.* We will go to jail."

Fifi shook her head and refused to move. "*Non.* Casey helped us. Now we must talk to them." She took his face between her hands. "*S'il tus plait, mon amor.*"

Finally, he gave in. "*The Café Tour Eiffel* is near. It will be quiet now."

A short time later we were gathered around a table at a brasserie just across the Seine from the Sewer Museum. We ordered drinks and waited in awkward silence for the waiter to serve them. Bad Comb-Over Guy toyed with his glass of absinthe, turning it one way and another so that light reflected green and shadowy on the white tablecloth. He studied us from under his brows and then sprawled back in his chair. He took a long sip of absinthe and finally spoke. "It was just a job. Nothing to do with you at all."

"Nothing? You used my daughter to get a ton of cash into the country. Illegally. How does that have nothing to do with us?" I glared at him, irritated at his placid demeanor. Really? He got Casey into a lot of trouble and he's acting like it's no big deal?

"And." Chrissie protested. "You took my suitcase." She scowled at Fifi. "She stole my clothes."

Fifi blushed but her lips were pressed tightly together and her eyes flashed. She said nothing.

The silence descended again. We nursed our Diet Cokes while Fifi and Bad Comb-Over sipped the thick green absinthe. His eyes darted about as if he expected gun-toting compatriots to burst in at any moment. I squirmed and nervously inspected the room.

He took another sip of his drink, banged his glass down and spread both hands flat on the table. "I can explain. First, let me introduce myself. I am *Le Grande Laurent*." He drew himself up and puffed out his chest. "Perhaps you have heard of me. I have just returned from a tour in *Les États Unis*."

We shook our heads and Laurent sank lower in his chair looking deflated. "Oh. Is not so *importante. Je suis une illusionniste*."

"An *illusionniste*?" I said. "A magician? Like David Copperfield?"

"*Oui*." He beamed. "Monsieur Copperfield is my *idole*. And Fifi …" He gestured at her. " … is my assistant."

She tipped her head.

"So, Monsieur Laurent," I said. "What made you decide to bring a suitcase of money into France and then switch it with my sister's bag?"

"I will tell you the entire story. Then you will perhaps understand." He straightened his tie and took another sip of absinthe.

"First of all, I should tell you that Laurent is my stage name. *Si'l vous plait* to call me Georges."

"Okay, Georges then." Chrissie leaned forward in anticipation. "We're waiting."

"Our manager, Luc, he arrange for a tour of the States. He told me we would make *beaucoup* Euros. Huge opportunity."

"Well," Georges continued, "Luc, he is either *tres* stupide or he is crook. We tour in not so much big city in the States but in little town. We do not make *beaucoup* Euros. I am spending the money on the hotel and the travel and not getting rich. *Non.* I am going broke. Our last ... is it gig?" He looked at us questioningly. And we nodded. "Is in New York City. Very big. Fifi and Georges are *tres* excited. Finally we are playing the big city. But club is small."

He shook his head sadly. "Not much audience for us. So after last show Luc comes backstage and tell us that two gentlemen want to meet us and buy us drink."

"We think we have fans," Fifi interrupted. "But no. Is business. We meet them and they buy us drinks and offer us a job."

Georges frowned and his expression turned dark. "They say all we have to do is take suitcase back to Paris for them. No question. They will give us 20,000 Euros."

He turned both hands palms up. "What can I do? I need Euros to pay bills." He jerked his head at Fifi. "Fifi requires much of clothes and restaurants and things."

Fifi opened her mouth. Then snapped it shut. She sipped her absinthe in silence, but the temperature around the table dipped several degrees.

"Who were these men?" Chrissie asked. "Where did they get the money they wanted you to smuggle into France?"

"Of course they would not tell us that." Fifi's expression implied that only an idiot would ask that question.

"Did you happen to get their names?" I asked.

Georges rearranged his comb-over. "*Non.* Not exactly. They call each other

Mister Smith and Mister Jones."

"But," Fifi put in, "I hear one call the other by the name Guillermo. And they both looked Spanish. Dark. *Mysterieux*."

"Villains," Georges said. "But I tell them we will take the suitcase. They give us 5000 Euros and promise the rest when we give them the suitcase in Paris."

"I get it so far," I told him, "but why didn't you just bring in the bag yourself? Why did you need Casey?"

Georges fidgeted with his glass --- rolling it between his palms. "Small problem."

"*Grande problem*," Fifi said.

"Fifi! Shh! *Oui. Grande problem*. I was pickpocket as a boy and I have the record with the police. When I pass into our country I must always be looked at with …" He held his hands far apart. "*Grande attention*. They look into my bags and check me out with great detail." He puffed out a breath. "I cannot possibly enter France with a bag full of money."

"Then why did you say you would do it?" Chrissie asked. "If you knew you would get caught?"

Fifi put her elbows on the table and leaned close to Georges. "I'd like to hear the answer to that question myself." Her English was nearly unaccented.

Georges narrowed his eyes. "Tush. Fifi. Let us not have that fight again." He appealed to us. "She think I make huge mistake."

Fifi glared back. "What I think doesn't matter. Obviously."

As I stared at them, I had a flashback to the plane. "So, that's what you were arguing about on the plane? The suitcase?"

A wary look crossed Fifi's face. "That was part of it."

Georges gave his head a quick shake. "Luc, our manager, he tell me we have seats in the Business Class. When we get tickets. *Non*. We are not. But I tell Fifi that mistake is made and Luc wouldn't trick us. So we take seats in front of plane."

113

"And got thrown out," I said. "I saw the discussion with the flight attendants."

Fifi rolled her eyes. "I told him but he wouldn't listen. I was very angry with him. First the suitcase and now this." She raised her shoulders in supplication. "You see?"

And we did. For a brief moment a look of complete understanding passed between us four women. Men!

"So," Fifi continued, "I was so upset and I ran into Mademoiselle Casey. I recognized her from New York and we start talking."

"And that's when you asked her to switch bags with you and Georges?" I asked.

"*Non,*" Fifi said, "I did not ask. Mademoiselle offered to help."

I peered at her, trying to gage her honesty. I tossed my crumpled napkin on the table and sat up straight. "Fifi. Seriously. Casey is just a kid. You had to know that she could get in a lot of trouble."

Fifi dropped her eyes. "*Oui.* I know. But I am desperate. I wanted to say no, but I couldn't."

I turned to Chrissie and Mom. "It seems that Casey and Fifi arranged to switch bags and that Fifi and Georges would recognize Casey's bag by the red rhinestone 'C' on her luggage tag."

Georges cleared his throat. "So we get off plane in Paris and see bag with 'C'. I grab it quickly and then I have much luck. My bag appear. I grab it *aussi.* I change tags very fast." He waved his hands in a flourish. "*Voila.* Job is done. I put my bag back on carousel."

Chrissie's eyebrows shot up. "So they took my bag by mistake. They got mine not Casey's. I gave her the tag that is identical to mine."

"So then what?" I asked. "You have Chrissie's bag and she has yours holding all that money."

Georges shrugged. No big deal. "The customs agent stop me as I know he will. He search your bag, Madame, and ask me many question. But Fifi say it is her clothes and they let us go. Fifi and Mademoiselle agreed to switch the bags back at your hotel. We see you get in taxi and follow you in other taxi to *Le Hotel Mignon*."

We all bent toward him. We were getting to the good part.

"I think I will make switch when you all go out. *Pas de problem*. I don't expect next development." Georges frowned at Fifi. "Fifi she fall in love with the clothes. She tell me I must let her keep all of it. Payment for all she suffered from me."

Fifi and Chrissie exchanged a long look. "*Tres belles*," Fifi said. "*Je l'aime*."

Chrissie grinned. "Awesome jacket, eh, Fifi?"

Georges tapped the table with his glass. "So when I finally do get chance to make exchange, it all go wrong." He paused and glowered at us. "I do not get money. Where is money?"

The smile slid off Chrissie's face. "And why should we tell you that? What's in it for us? She..." She scowled at Fifi. "...has my wardrobe."

Georges wiggled in his chair. "Because they will kill me if I don't give them the bag and the money." He held out his hands beseechingly. "*S'il vous plait, Madame*."

"*Non*," Fifi interrupted. "It is time to call the *gendarmes*. *Je suis finis*. I am finished with this charade."

"No," the three of chorused.

"You can't do that," I objected. "They will arrest Casey." I caught Fifi's eye. "Do you want that?"

Fifi dropped her eyes. "But what do we do?"

Mom had remained silent through all of the discussion. Now, though, she coughed to get our attention and said, "We need to find out who these men are and what they are up to."

"They want their money." Georges broke in.

"Don't you want to find out more about them? I'd feel much better if they were arrested and put into jail. I think that's the only way that you and Fifi will be safe." She looked at Chrissie and me. "And the only way that we can be sure that the police will be easier on Casey."

Fifi and Georges stared into each other's eyes for a long time. Finally, Fifi sighed. "*Oui.* No police."

Mom smiled approvingly. "Good. So we do have one clue. The apartment where you stayed last night. Do you own it?"

Fifi's face lit up. "*Non.* The men gave us the key to the place. It must belong to them."

"Or," I suggested, "to someone who can lead us to them."

"Us?" Chrissie smacked her forehead with her hand.

Mom fluffed out her white curls and winked. "No. Bobby will find them."

"I hope so," I said. "Did you tell the men we still had the cash?"

Georges wiggled in his seat, uncomfortable under my unwavering gaze. He refused to meet my eye. Finally, he mumbled in a barely audible voice, "The two came to us the day the plane arrived and want the bag. I explain to them my minor difficulty and I would have it the next day. They were not pleased but they tell me I have one day only."

"But why tell them we had it?"

"They were not nice. They threaten to harm Fifi if I do not tell."

Chrissie pinched her nose between her fingers. "So. Let me sum this up. These thugs want their money and know we have it."

Georges nodded.

"Wonderful."

Mom chewed her lower lip as we watched Georges wrest open the heavy leaded glass door to the café and usher Fifi out onto the sidewalk. She sucked in a deep breath and then beckoned our waiter over. "Monsieur, we'd like *trois* —"She held up three fingers. "*omelettes au fromage.* And *un—*"She held up a single finger. "*pichet de vin rouge*." As he disappeared to put in the order, Mom commented, "I'm starving. This private eye stuff sure makes a girl hungry."

"I totally agree," I said.

"Do you think we'll ever see Fifi or Georges again?" Chrissie asked.

"Don't know," I said. "I'm not sure they will think it's much of an advantage to keep in touch."

"After all we've meant to each other too." Chrissie said.

"We promised not to call the police which pretty much keeps them in the clear," I said and grimaced. "It's only the bad guys they have to fear. And we aren't much help there."

We polished off our omelets and lingered over the last of the wine. Mom swirled the wine left in her glass and sagged against the back of her chair. "This has been an exhausting day. Crime solving is hard work. I can't wait to get back to the hotel and kick off my shoes. Take a nap."

"It will be kind of interesting to get Bobby's take on all of this," Chrissie said. "And that nap sounds like an excellent idea."

Terry Sykes-Bradshaw

Chapter 11

Madame Reno was at the desk when we breezed into the lobby of the hotel. She glanced up, smiled broadly and crooked her finger beckoning us. "*Madames. Bon Seure.*"

As we approached she held up one hand and ducked under the desk muttering under her breath. When she popped back up she was waving a white business-sized envelope. "A man leave this for you, Madame."

We exchanged quizzical looks as I took the envelope from Madame Reno's hand. "*Merci*, Madame Reno."

I examined it. An ordinary white business envelope. Our room number printed on it in masculine handwriting. "It must be from Bobby changing the time or place of our meeting tonight." I handed the envelope to Mom. "You should read it."

She slid a fingernail under the flap and started to open it but the elevator arrived at that moment. She clutched it in her hand as we rode upstairs to our room. We dumped our things on the beds with a sigh of relief.

"What does Bobby say? Read us the note." Chrissie kicked off her shoes and slumped onto the edge of her bed.

Mom slipped the note out of the envelope and started to read. The blood drained from her face. She didn't move a muscle. Her fingers crumpled the page as she stared at it.

"Mom?" I said. "Does Bobby have bad news?"

"It … it … it's not … f-f-from, B-b-obby," she stammered.

I guided her to the edge of my bed and pushed her gently onto it as I took the wrinkled page from her. Then froze as I read it. I looked up at Chrissie.

"What?" she said. "You two are scaring me."

I took a deep breath. "It's from them." I smoothed the crumpled page. "Listen! '*Madames. We want our money. We are serious. Be very sure of that. Do* *not try to trick us. Bring the money to the steps of Sacre Coeur tomorrow morning at 10 o'clock. Wait there for further instructions. The money must be in two **J' aime Paris** tote bags. Do not call the police. No harm will come to you or your daughters if you do as we say."'*

I sank onto the bed and put my head in my hands. "Oh, Casey," I cried. "What have you done?"

The color was back in Mom's face and she was recovered enough to shift into protective Nonny mode. "Don't blame Casey. She was only being the Casey we know and love."

"I know," I said. "She wanted to rescue Fifi and Georges. Now who is going to rescue her?"

Mom stood up and smoothed her slacks. "Bobby. When we meet with him, he'll find a way out of this. I know he will."

Bouffe Tard was rocking when we got there — jammed with patrons playing some sort of trivia game where each question appeared on a large television screen. Most of the tables were filled with noisy drinkers shouting answers -- and insults, according to Casey --- to each other over the loud music. It was a chaotic but the hostess led us to a table on the fringe of the action. I had a perfect view of the front door so I could see who was coming or going. But we had to raise our voices to be heard as we replayed the events of the day for Casey and Tessa. That made me nervous that we might be overheard by the wrong people. I looked around but no one appeared interested in us or our conversation.

Still, we were relieved when Bobby appeared at the door of the bistro. He surveyed the crowded bar and when he spotted us threaded his way through the throng to reach our table --- his grandsons trailing behind. The three men oozed class, nobility, and a heavy dose of sexuality. They created a minor stir among the other customers — particularly the women.

When Bobby reached our table he bent down and cupped Mom's face in his hands and planted a kiss on her lips. Mom blushed to the roots of her white curls and shoved him away. "Bobby, I don't think…"

"Of course, my dear. I apologize to you and the lassies."

I was so caught up in Bobby's entrance and the flames sparking between him and Mom that I failed at first to notice the fourth man in the entourage. I stared at him. In trench coat, fedora and sporting a David Niven mustache, he was a dead ringer for Inspector Clouseau, the bumbling detective of Pink Panther fame. I am pretty sure that my mouth dropped open in amazement. I know that Chrissie's did. Bobby winked at us.

"Lassies," he said. "Let me introduce my old and dear friend, Inspector Claude Bouchard of the *Prefecture of Police*. I believe he might be able to help with your dilemma."

The inspector bowed to each of us, took our hands and kissed them. "*Enchante, Madame. Enchante, Mademoiselle.*" When he reached Mom he held her hand just a second longer, admiring the large family diamond on her finger. "Your ring is exquisite."

Embarrassed, Mom rapidly buried her hand in her pocket. "*Merci,* Inspector."

"My son is a jeweler. I am fond of beautiful gems," Inspector Bouchard explained.

The men dragged chairs over from an adjoining table and ordered drinks from the waitress who was eyeing Robert and Mac as if they were dessert. When she disappeared in the direction of the bar, Bobby nodded at the Inspector. Any resemblance to the inept Clousseau was dispelled when Bouchard began to speak. He was, in fact, the anti-Clousseau, suave and debonair and immediately in charge.

"*Madames et Mademoiselles,*" he said, "I understand that you have gotten yourselves into a bit of difficulty. Let me make sure I have all the facts." He fumbled in the pocket of his trench coat and pulled out a tattered notepad and flipped through several pages. He looked from Casey to Tessa and said, "Which one of you is Casey Kelly?"

Casey slunk lower in her chair, lifted one hand in a tiny wave and mumbled in a barely audible voice, "I am."

Inspector Bouchard regarded her solemnly. "Perhaps you can tell me exactly what happened."

"I … um … I," Casey began and then she stopped, pulled herself together and sat up straight. She met the inspector's eye and started speaking in rapid French.

If the inspector was surprised to discover that Casey was fluent in his language, he didn't show it. He listened attentively and scribbled in his notebook. He asked an occasional question, but was otherwise silent. When Casey finished he tugged one ear thoughtfully and contemplated the ceiling. Finally he said, "Does anyone have anything to add before I tell you how I think we should proceed?"

We all looked questioningly at Casey. "I told him everything I could remember about meeting Fifi first in New York and then again on the airplane and how I agreed to bring in her bag. And I told him about following them to that apartment last night. I think I covered it."

"Not quite," I said. "There are a few other things he should know."

And Chrissie, Mom and I took turns recounting our adventures that day. Bobby and the grandsons listened to the tale with increasing dismay while Inspector Bouchard jotted notes in his pad. When we stopped for breath, Bobby broke in. "I thought I told you to stay close to the hotel, Laura," he said in a tone that suggested he should be obeyed.

"I know that, Bobby," Mom said. "But I do as I please. When I please."

Bobby appeared shocked — as if, I guessed, very few dared to defy him. Or maybe he just didn't dream that Mom was such a little rebel.

He heaved a giant sigh and steepled his fingers on the table in front of him. "Oh, right. Is that all?"

"Not quite." Mom fished in her bag and pulled out the note Madame Reno gave us and handed it to the inspector.

"Hmm," he said and handed the crumpled page to Bobby.

Bobby read the note rapidly and handed it back to the inspector. An odd look passed between the two of them. What were they thinking?

"So?" I said.

Inspector Bouchard smoothed the page. "I think that's exactly what you should do."

Tessa had been listening quietly, but now she exploded — blue eyes sparking dangerously. "What? That's craziness. My mother and my aunt and my grandmother are not going to consort with criminals. No way."

Chrissie patted her cheek. "Shh. Tessa. It's okay. I'm pretty sure the inspector won't let anything happen to us." She faced him. "Right?"

"*Non*," Inspector Bouchard said. "If I am correct these are the same men we have been after for quite some time. We would be very grateful for the help in catching them." He cut his eyes to Casey. "So grateful that I am positive we can manage to drop any charges which might be registered against Mademoiselle Casey."

"That's blackmail, Claude," Bobby protested.

The inspector cast an inscrutable look at Bobby and didn't say a word.

I pictured Casey wearing an orange jump suit, her eggplant hair hanging in greasy strands across her woebegone face. A tear came to my eye. "We'll do it," I said.

Chapter 12

I hardly slept that night. It was past midnight when Inspector Bouchard and Bobby came to our room carrying *J'aime Paris* tote bags filled with marked bills. When the inspector counted the bills in the safe, we were astonished to discover that we had been hiding over $750,000. As I watched him count out an equal number of marked bills and stuff them in the bags, I had an awful thought. "The crooks know that we have the money. They must be watching us. They'll know that the inspector was here."

Inspector Bouchard tugged at his earlobe. "*Non.* Do not worry. I am a master of disguise. No one would recognize me."

"Somehow," I said, "I don't feel all that reassured."

Mom wrung her hands. "This is too dangerous. Call the CIA. Call the FBI."

Bobby draped an arm around her shoulder and gave it a squeeze. "Don't worry, Laura. Claude is very good at what he does. He won't let anything happen to any of you."

I don't think anyone was convinced, but we couldn't risk Casey's freedom. Or Tessa's. So we agreed to meet at the steps leading up to *Montmarte* and *Sacre Coeur* at 9:30 the next morning. Chrissie and I would haul the tote bags and the others would provide moral support. As Bobby escorted Mom back to her room, she waved feebly. I wondered vaguely about their relationship, but gave it up as pointless. Thinking about Mom's sex life was beyond my capabilities.

It was a restless night. I marked the passing of each hour on my travel alarm before I finally gave up shortly before six. If my stay was going to be over in the next few hours my inner diva stomped her prissy little foot and demanded that I end it looking, if not smoking hot, at least semi-hot. And who am I to ignore my inner diva? I showered and took extra time applying make-up. I finished by using the flat iron and smooshing a big glop of gel on my hair. I gave myself a mental two thumbs up. I opened the door quietly and held my breath as I edged into the bedroom. I didn't want to wake Chrissie.

I needn't have bothered. She was propped up in bed –- a romance novel balanced on her knee. "Nice." She peered at me over her reading glasses. "You'll look awesome on the slab in the morgue."

I stalked over, pulled the pillow from behind her head and pummeled her with it.

"Stop," she said when she caught her breath. "You look gorgeous. Let the scumbags sit up and take notice."

I smacked her one final time with the pillow and tossed it aside. "I was thinking more of how I'd look on the news when we capture those scumbags."

"You think?" She hopped out of bed and vanished into the bathroom.

"And," I called to the closed door, "Hot is the look I had in mind."

My hand shook as I picked up my mug and coffee slopped on the table. I mopped it up with a wad of napkins while Chrissie gnawed on a fingernail. She peered under the table for at least the tenth time in the same number of minutes.

"Still there?" I asked.

She gulped and nodded.

I stared suspiciously at each passer-by. "Where are they? They're late."

"No. We're early." Chrissie picked at a croissant. "Oh, there they are."

"About time," I said grumpily as we watched Casey and Tessa and Mom file out of the hotel and trot across the street toward our table at *Le Bonne Crumbe*.

Dressed all in black Casey and Tessa were apparently taking our sting operation seriously. "They look like cat burglars," Chrissie murmured as they reached us.

Casey loomed over us --- her eyes darting from me to Chrissie. "Where's the money?"

I slid sideways in my chair to reveal the two *J'aime Paris* tote bags full of marked bills tucked securely between our feet under the table.

"Whew." Casey exhaled and sank into a chair. "This is crazy."

"Let's go," Tessa said, hand on hip. "Let's get this over with."

"Too early, dear," Mom said. "They said ten and it's barely seven. We should eat so we keep up our strength."

Tessa's blue eyes filled with tears and she scrubbed at them with her fists. She bit her lower lip and then said, "Okay, you're probably right, Nonny. I'll go get you some coffee and croissants. But I, personally, couldn't eat a crumb."

She marched away --- girl on a mission.

Casey broke off a piece of croissant and examined it. "You can tell Tessa's tense when she won't eat." She dropped the croissant without taking a bite. "Or shop."

"We're all uptight," I said. "Casey's right. This is insane. Where's the inspector? He said he'd be keeping an eye on us. I don't see him. Do you?"

"That was kind of the point," Chrissie said. "No one could pick him out of a crowd. Not us. Or them."

We checked out people around us on the street. A drunk sleeping it off on the sidewalk under a sheet of plastic. A man selecting fruit from a sidewalk stand. Another man running for a taxi.

"I guess he could be anywhere," I whispered. "Anywhere at all."

"Or nowhere," Casey said.

Tessa returned with another basket of croissants and a carafe of coffee. She plunked them on the table in front of her grandmother and slumped into a chair. "There. Let them eat croissants."

"*Merci*, darling," Mom said. "Don't worry it will be fine. Bobby's watching out for us."

"Ah," Tessa said. "Your outfit says you're more interested in catching a baron than catching a thief."

Mom merely smiled and took a sip of coffee. Then she stood up and smoothed her navy slacks and straightened the hem of her powder blue suede jacket. "The early bird catches whatever she might be after. It's time to go."

Casey and I walked together down the street toward the Metro station. She gave me a sideways look and said, "So how are these guys going to recognize us, Mom?"

"Maybe by the tote bags." I tipped my chin at the bright red *J'aime Paris* tote bag I had tucked securely under my arm.

"I don't think so, Mom. Look." Casey made a sweeping gesture at the crowds on the sidewalk.

Bags. Coming. Going. A family came around the corner — mom, dad, two little girls. The mom swung a red bag identical to mine in one hand.

Ooh. Another. This one blue. An elderly woman leaning on a cane carried it --- a baguette poking out the top.

A white one filled with school books across the chest of a curly-headed teen in a school uniform.

"Must have been a sale on these tote bags."

"Dunno," Casey said. "But it creeps me out to think the bad dudes know exactly who and where we are."

I shivered.

By nine-thirty the five of us clustered at the base of the steps leading up the "mountain" to *Montmartre* and *Sacre Couer*. I shaded my eyes with my hand and squinted. The *Basilique du Sacre Coeur* gleamed at the top of hill --- the morning sun reflecting off its white stone exterior. Beside me Chrissie gazed upward. "Now that's a lot of steps," she murmured.

"Seriously. Do you honestly expect us to climb all those steps?" Tessa crossed her arms over her chest. "There must be a million.

"Are you telling me that pole dancing doesn't keep you in shape to climb a few measly steps?" Casey said.

I glanced at my mother. She looked doubtful. "Mom?"

"I agree. That's a lot of steps."

Casey took her grandmother's arm. "You don't have to walk up the steps, Nonny. You and wimpy Tessa can take the funicular." She pointed to the little cable car that ran up the hill next to the steps. "I'm sure Tessa would love to go with you."

Tessa scowled at Casey. "You go with Nonny, Casey. I'll walk. These steps are nothing."

Mom stepped between her granddaughters. "Neither of you will use me as an excuse to not walk the steps. I'm walking them." And she began the climb without a backward glance.

The rest of us shrugged and followed her. I bounded upward for a while before I got a stitch in my side and stopped to catch my breath. Chrissie huffed to a halt next to me. "Whew. And I thought Super Step Class was tough."

"If Mom can do it, we can do it."

Tessa clomped by us muttering under her breath. "Fifty. Fifty-one. Fifty-two."

Chrissie and I pulled off our jackets, resumed the climb and caught up to Mom who had paused to take in the view. "This is beautiful," she said as we stopped on either side of her, "but I feel kind of vulnerable."

I peered upward at the church and downward to the street. I didn't like being caught in between. "Onward and upward," I said and we tackled the remaining steps with as much energy as we could muster.

Tessa and Casey were waiting for us at the top. "Two-hundred and sixty-three and a quarter," Tessa crowed triumphantly.

Sweaty, a bit disheveled and definitely jittery, we moved en masse toward the steps to *Sacre Couer*. Casey took out her camera and posed us with the venerable church in the background and then with Paris as the backdrop. To the casual observer we were five American sightseers. Carefree and happy. We hoped.

Still no sign of Inspector Bouchard or any of his men. I looked around wondering where and who he could be. A trench coat clad tourist? A street vendor? A man strolling by with a baguette in hand? What was his disguise today?

By shortly after 10 o'clock Casey had tired of shooting photos and sat down on a step jiggling one foot. "How long do we play this game? I don't have all day."

Chrissie paced back and forth the strap of her tote clenched in her hand. A motorcycle backfired and we all jumped as if bullets were being fired. At 10:15 I was about to suggest abandoning the mission when a small boy of about nine peddled his bright red bike in our direction. He wore jeans, ragged sneakers and a baseball cap on backwards. Cute kid — dark hair and eyes and an intense look of concentration on his face. A red rose clutched in one grubby fist. He skidded to a stop in front of us, threw his bike down on the cobblestones and held the rose out to Chrissie.

She shook her head. "*Non, Merci*. Not today." She turned away scanning the steps for our tardy thugs.

The boy tugged at her sleeve. "Madame. The rose is for you. The man paid me and he said for me to bring it to you."

Chrissie took a step back so she could examine his face and then dug into her purse for a Euro to tip him and extended her hand. The boy gave her a gap-toothed grin as he pressed the rose into her hand. Then he hopped on his bike and peddled away calling over his shoulder, "*Merci beaucoup*."

The rose looked harmless enough. No ticking bombs. No hidden gas spray. Chrissie picked at the stem with her fingernail and pried loose a piece of lined paper wrapped around it. She unrolled it. "This is it," she said. "A message from them."

Scrawled on a scrap of notebook paper in the same masculine handwriting as the previous note were the words, "*In Place du Terte you will find an artist drawing crayfish.*"

"Crayfish?" Tessa exclaimed.

"Who draws crayfish in *Place du Terte* on *Montmartre*?" Casey said.

"Let's find out," Chrissie said and, stuffing the note into her pocket, led the way to *Place du Terte* just a few steps away.

On another day it would have been fascinating to explore the *Place* — an old town square that is basically the heart of Montmartre — with its restaurants and cafés and artists crowding the space with easels and a multitude of paintings. Today art took a back seat.

Within seconds we were surrounded by caricature artists who trailed after us offering the opportunity of a lifetime. "*Mademoiselles, Madames.* You are so beautiful. Let me create for you a masterpiece."

Casey gave them an airy wave of her hand. "Not today, *Merci.*"

We elbowed our way through the crowd to the center of the square. "So many artists," Mom said. "How are we ever going to find the crayfish?"

Paintings. So many. It was overwhelming.

Suddenly Chrissie grabbed my arm and pointed. "Crayfish. Over there."

Silently we gathered around the painting Chrissie had spotted. Not particularly good. Primary colors --- red, yellow, green — smeared on the canvas like a child's finger-painting.

"Ugh," Casey said. "It's gross."

"Shh," I said. "We're not here to critique the artwork."

The artist — a small man in paint-stained smock and baggy pants, a beret tilted rakishly over one eye --- smiled at us revealing a gold front tooth. "You like fish? I have more." He shuffled through a stack of paintings and withdrew another one --- clownish neon green fish swam in a muddy brown pond. He handed it to Chrissie. "Look it over, Madame. I think you will find it is what you want."

Chrissie turned the painting over and then passed it to me. A piece of lined notebook paper was taped to the back. I showed it to Casey, Tessa and Mom. Chrissie nudged Casey, "Talk French to him, Case. Find out what we need to do to get the note."

Casey negotiated with the artist and then explained, "He says he will sell it to us for 50 Euros. Take it or leave it. Personally, I'd leave it. That's one ugly painting."

"Ask him if he'll take 25."

Casey spoke to him. "Aunt Chrissie, he won't go lower than 35. Do you really want to give money for that nasty fish?"

"As you said earlier, we're not looking for beauty, we're looking for crayfish. This is it. We don't have a choice."

"Of course, we do," I said. "Why are we supposed to buy a painting so we can find out where to hand over a pile of money to some crooks? They should pay us."

Casey quizzed the artist and then told us, "Pierre, here, says he was promised a sale if he agreed to put a note on the painting. He's not really involved. Just a guy trying to make a living."

"What do you say, Kate?"

I shrugged. "Give him the money."

Chrissie pulled out her wallet and counted 35 Euros into Pierre's hand. He handed her the rolled up painting and we found a quiet spot under a nearby tree to unroll it and peel the note from the back. *Go buy a drink at Le Café Montmartre.*

"What is this? A treasure hunt?" Tessa asked.

"One that's costing me a lot of money," Chrissie said.

We had passed *Le Café Montmarte* as we entered *Place du Terte*. It was a bustling establishment occupying the lower floor of a 17th century building on the corner of the square. A bright blue and white awning shaded the tables in the front. The tall windows on the upper floors were framed by weather-beaten shutters, the white paint peeling from them in long strips. Black wrought iron railings protected the tiny balconies outside the windows.

"Charming in a shabby way," Chrissie murmured to me as the maître d' showed us to a large table in the rear of the second of two rooms. The interior of the café was homey with wood paneled walls and a large stone fireplace in the center. Large paintings of Paris scenes hung on the walls and vases of flowers sat in the middle of each table.

Our table was a heavy wooden trestle table tucked into the corner of the room and just outside the double swinging doors to the kitchen. It was pushed up against the wall on one side making it difficult to slide into the chairs. Chrissie and I took seats opposite each other at the center of the table --- she was against the wall and I faced the dusty window above her head. Casey sat to my left, Mom to my right with Tessa across from Casey.

Chrissie and I carefully stowed our tote bags between our feet under the table and hung our jackets on the back of our chairs. It was a relief to be sitting in the restaurant.

"Our goons are obviously playing some kind of demented game of hide and seek," Casey said.

"Time to call Bobby and get them to meet us here," Mom said. She held out her hand and Casey handed her the phone. Mom made the call. She closed the phone and returned it to Casey. "Bobby and his grandsons will be here shortly."

I am certain I didn't imagine it --- Casey and Tess immediately sat up and engaged in copious hair fluffing and lip gloss applying. Then apparently satisfied with her appearance, Casey signaled the waiter and ordered drinks for all of us. "I got us a carafe of water and a *pichet* of house white and house red. Is that okay?"

"Casey, honey," Mom said, "I think it's too early for wine."

"Nonny, it's five o'clock somewhere. And I think we deserve it after the morning we've had. I'll order you a coke if you want."

"No, I guess I can drink wine if you all are having it."

"Just not two bottles," I said to her under my breath.

The waiter served our drinks just as the three MacTavish men stalked into the room and pushed through the noon lunch crowd to reach our table. Bobby kissed my mother on the cheek and took the chair opposite her and next to Chrissie. Robert claimed the seat adjoining Casey's and Mac slid into the chair beside Tessa. The men ordered beers and sipped them as we described our morning. They didn't interrupt until we were finished.

"Hmm," Robert said. "So the thieves didn't show up?"

"Uh, uh, not officially," Casey said. "But I'm sure they're around."

All business, Bobby said, "So let's see the painting. And the note."

Casey and Tessa made gagging noises as Chrissie unrolled the crayfish and held it up.

"Now that's one gnarly lobster," Robert said.

"Nah, it's not a lobster, ya gowk," Mac corrected him. "That's a crayfish."

"It's one gnarly crayfish, then."

Mom looked up at Bobby. "So, Bobby. What do you think we should do?"

Bobby's gaze lingered on Mom for a second before he said, "I think we should have some lunch and see if they try to contact you again."

"They won't," I protested. "Not with you guys here. But we might as well get something to eat. This treasure hunt has made me hungry."

Lunch turned out to be a welcome diversion. I had to smile as I watched Casey flirt with Robert. He acted like someone who had won the lottery and couldn't believe his luck. He kept his arm around Casey and fingered a lock of her auburn hair. She, in turn, leaned into his shoulder and grinned up at him --- sharing a private joke. I rejoiced that at last she was over the weasel, I mean, Lester. Mac and Tessa were enjoying a flirtation of their own, while Mom and

132

Bobby were so absorbed in each other they barely noticed anyone else. Or so I thought.

At a table near ours two men wearing blue work shirts and dusty pants played some kind of energetic card game involving a lot of laughter and chugging of beer. Local color.

It was loud. Laughter. Music from a strolling accordionist. Patrons trying to talk over the noise. My head was beginning to ache when Chrissie said, "I'm not waiting around anymore. I'm sure the goons will find us when they want us. And I'd like to see Paris. Not the inside of this café. Charming though it might be."

"Totally," I said and the rest murmured agreement.

Bobby handed his credit card to the waiter and as we waited for him to return, I licked my lips. "Hey, Chris, it's really dry in here. My lips feel like the Sahara. Can I borrow some lip gloss?"

She rummaged through her purse, pulled out a tube of lip gloss and tossed it to me across the table. I tried to catch it but the tube slithered through my fingers, bounced off my plate onto the floor and rolled under the table.

"Damn." I shoved my chair back and dropped to my knees to peer under the table. Ick. I felt around with my fingers on the sticky floor and then crawled beneath the table. In the dark I couldn't see the tube or find it with my hand. I pushed the tote bags aside to see if it had rolled between them. Wait. The bags were light. Way too light. I straightened up quickly, banged my head on the underside of the table and, dragging the bags with me, wriggled out. "It's gone."

Immediately Mom began foraging in her purse. "I think I've got another..."

"No, not lip gloss." I rubbed my sore head.

"What then?" Chrissie said.

"The money. These bags are empty. The money is gone."

Chrissie wormed under the table to verify my report. Maybe the money was under there somewhere and I had just missed it. Seconds later she popped back up. "No way. It is not possible."

One by one everyone scrambled under the table and one by one concluded that the money we had been guarding so carefully was no longer in our possession. We stared at each blankly, shocked into silence.

"But how?" Chrissie asked. "How on earth did someone get under that table without one of us noticing? And when? I do not believe this."

Bobby dialed his cell phone. "I'm calling Inspector…Yes. Bouchard? This is MacTavish. I'm with the lassies and there has been an unforeseen problem. It seems that the cash has disappeared."

Within seconds of Bobby concluding his story and closing his cell phone, the two card-playing workmen jumped to their feet toppling one of their chairs. Then badges in hand they closed in on our table. Undercover cops. I should have guessed.

"Did you see anything?"

"What happened?"

"Are you sure the money is gone?"

They fired questions at us but we had no answers for them. The men dove under our table and turned the now empty tote bags inside out. Nothing. One of them called our waiter over and began to grill him and Casey moved closer to eavesdrop. She flicked a lock of hair out of her eyes and said to us, "Our waiter didn't notice anyone crawling on the floor. Not that I would expect him to."

Suddenly a street artist exploded through the door and dashed toward us. His paint-stained shirt was unbuttoned and his beret askew. I jumped back to avoid being run down and Tessa squeaked in alarm as he brushed by her. "Whoa," I said. "What the …"

The street artist conferred with the two badge-wielding workers and then faced us. It was none other than Inspector Bouchard --- Master of disguise. "They have escaped once again. This time it is more amazing than ever before though. I would have sworn they could not escape. The table against the wall. My men close by. I was outside watching."

Bouchard interrogated us for a few minutes. Then he shrugged. "No one saw anything. No one felt anything. No one heard anything. No one noticed anything out of the ordinary. It's almost as if the money disappeared by magic."

I gulped. Mom and Chrissie made identical bug-eyes. Suddenly we had a hunch about what happened. The inspector had given us the answer. "Magic."

"Fifi and Georges," Mom breathed. "*Le Grande Laurent.*" She turned to the inspector and quickly explained our suspicions.

He narrowed his eyes and his expression became grim as he listened. When she finished he ran a hand through his hair and sighed. "I'll take it from here."

With much gesturing Bobby and Inspector Bouchard consulted with the two beer-drinking cops. They were joined in their huddle by a variety of other street types who rushed in from the street. A musician toting a worn guitar. A businessman. A mime. The inspector's men had, indeed, surrounded us. And yet the money was gone. It didn't exactly put my mind at ease.

While the inspector and Bobby and the cops-in-disguise flitted around doing cop things, Chrissie, Mom and I sat back down at our table to wait. No way we were leaving until we found out exactly what was going on.

Mom did the pursed lip look I remembered from breaking curfew in high school. "I'm just so disappointed in Fifi and Georges. I really did believe they were just in over their heads. Now I don't know what to think."

"I think they flat out lied to us," I said.

Chrissie gnawed her lip. "Well, at least neither of you gave that deceitful little wench your brand new hot pink suede jacket."

At the other end of the table our daughters were flirting with the MacTavish brothers. I didn't think they were paying a bit of attention to us, but Tessa obviously was. She bounced to our end of the table and gave her mother a disgusted look. "You did what?"

Chrissie ignored her and rooted around in her purse --- totally absorbed in that task.

Tessa tapped Chrissie's shoulder. "Mother. You aren't answering my question. Did you or did you not give this Fifi person your precious jacket?" Tessa clenched her hands on her hips --- five feet six inches of indignation.

Chrissie finally met her daughter's eyes. "Well, what if I did? I thought they got a crummy deal and I felt sorry for them. I was just being nice."

Tessa harrumphed. "Oh, Mom, you are too gullible. You need to get out more." She whirled and flounced back to Mac.

"She's right you know," I said. "You're a big softy."

"Am not."

"Are too."

"Girls," Mom said. And we stopped bickering.

Eventually Inspector Bouchard completed his investigation. He and his men scoured every square inch of the café, interviewed the other patrons and searched outside for a single piece of evidence that could lead them to the thieves. No one had seen or heard anything out of the usual. The thieves managed to steal the money right out from under our table. A magic trick worthy of a David Copperfield.

"*Merde*," Bouchard said. He sank into a chair and accepted a cup of very black coffee from the waiter. He took several sips and tugged on an earlobe before he spoke again. "It would appear that your friend Georges is quite the *illusioniste* if he pulled this off. Too bad he had to use his talents to break the law."

"Maybe he had no choice," I suggested. "Maybe he has an explanation. Or maybe he wasn't even involved."

"Perhaps. If we can find him, we will ask. But we aren't having much luck finding him." The inspector blew out a huge sigh. "*Merde*."

When the inspector offered no further enlightenment about the men he was seeking or the nature of their crimes, I decide to pursue it. "Pardon, Inspector, can you please tell us about these criminals?"

He deliberated a moment and then shrugged his little shrug. "*Oui*, Madame. I will try. We have been chasing these fellows for months. All over Paris. Every time we think we will capture them ... poof ... they vanish." He waved his hand in front of his face as if shooing away mosquitoes. "We think they are part of --- how do you Americans say it --- a gang?"

Bobby slouched in his chair — hands stuffed in the pockets of his leather jacket --- an impassive look on his face. I doubted that any of this was a surprise to him. The four young people ceased flirting and listened intently.

"So," Chrissie broke in. "What is it that this gang does? Drug runners, bank robbers, threats to national security, murderers?"

"They are counterfeiters of the French bread?"

"Bread? You mean money? Euros?"

"*Non*. Bread."

Bobby's lip twitched and he gave a snort of laughter. "Go on, Claude. Why don't you tell the lassies about the bread gang?"

The Inspector leaned forward and fingered his mustache. "*Oui*. Perhaps you have heard of the famous French bakery, *Bonne Palate*?"

We shook our heads.

"Oh. Well it is the number one bakery of French bread. And perhaps you know the French winery called *Chateau de Maman Cherie*? Or the famous chocolatier, *Tout Suite*?"

"Not specifically," I said.

Bouchard's face fell. "*Non*? *C'est la vie*. These are some of the better known purveyors of French gourmet goods. They are known around the world as the best quality. It displeasures us greatly to have this --- gang, is it? — selling copies. Fakes of these things."

He swigged his cooling coffee. "What we know at the moment is that an internet company has been formed that sells these goods to the unenlightened. Especially to the Americans."

Tessa coughed and covered her mouth with her hand. "Because we Americans can't tell a fake from the real deal, of course."

Bouchard pleated a napkin in his fingers. Folding and refolding it. "*Pardon.* I am sorry if I have offended you."

"Shh," I said to Tessa. And turned back to the inspector. "Go on, please."

"*Oui.* The company sells to internet customers and charge *beaucoup* dollars for the fake goods. No one is the wiser. The wine is a cheap variety with not so good grapes. The chocolate is not made by hand. The bread is made from a recipe stolen from *Bonne Palate* and then they substitute cheap ingredients for high quality ones."

"Wow, that's really a 'rye' twist," Casey broke in. She nudged Tessa. "Get it, Tess?"

"Oh, man, Case, that's just sour---" She waited a beat. "dough." She sucked in her cheeks as she tried not to laugh, but her shoulders shook.

"Ooh, I'll toast to that," my sister added.

"We're really on a roll now," Mom said.

The five of us doubled over with laughter.

"I think the police must have been loafing," I said.

"That would sure leave us in a jam," Chrissie finished.

The men watched impassively. The inspector concentrated on twisting his napkin in his hand while the others looked around in embarrassment. Probably hoping the other customers were not focusing on us.

Finally, we ran out of bread puns and wound down. I fished a tissue from my bag and wiped my eyes. "I think that's enough of this humor."

Robert flicked a lock of hair off his forehead and pulled Casey into his arms. "Muffin, you are too much."

She giggled and I beamed at him. The anti-Lester.

Inspector Bouchard cleared his throat loudly. "Ah hem. May we continue?" He sped through the rest of his account, suddenly anxious to escape. He swept his beret from the table and clapped it on his head haphazardly as he stood, shook hands all around, and dashed out the door cell phone in hand.

"Whoa, what lit a fire under him?" I asked.

"Something sure did." Chrissie polished her sunglasses on her sleeve. "We don't have the full story yet, I am pretty sure."

"Maybe we offended him with our insanity," Tessa said.

I glanced at Bobby. The odd way he was following Bouchard's departure with his eyes suggested that he knew something he wasn't sharing. Or was I just channeling my inner Stephanie Plum again?

Chapter 13

I checked my watch for the tenth time. Seven o'clock. Where was everybody? I sat alone at a table set for nine in the restaurant where we had agreed to meet for dinner --- an invisible cloak of annoyance wrapped tightly around my shoulders. I fumed. Was I the only one who had the courtesy to be on time? Apparently.

Casey had recommended the restaurant, *Thanksgiving*, located on the quaint cobblestoned *Rue St. Paul*. Her friends Judith and Frederick owned the place and I mentally congratulated her on her selection. It was her choice so why wasn't she here?

I swiveled in my chair to check the door and I took in the eclectic collection of art hung on the whitewashed cement walls. Pots of flowers hung in curtained windows. A heavy wooden bar guarded the entrance to the kitchen. I felt as if I had been transported into the 18th Century before the advent of modern conveniences. Like watches.

I drummed my fingers on the white tablecloth covering the wooden table --- a tin bucket of flowers and glowing candles in the center. I ordered a glass of white wine and studied the menu. Hmm. A blend of Cajun and French cuisine --- Crabcakes soufflé, crayfish boil with Cajun spices and a nice French Cabernet. Yum. I couldn't wait to try it. That is, if anyone else bothered to show up.

I was debating another glass of wine, or maybe an entire bottle, when I spotted Casey and Robert at the door. Casey hugged the woman who greeted her and the three of them talked animatedly for a few minutes before Casey dragged the woman over to my table. "Mom, this is my friend, Judith. Judith, my mom."

I listened with half my attention while Casey and Judith reminisced. The other half I used to inspect young Robert MacTavish. He was as tall as his grandfather, Baron Bobby and he shared the same gene pool that had distributed movie star good looks. His light brown hair hung over his ears –- he needed a haircut --- and he kept tossing his head in an attempt to keep the hair out of his eyes. And, oh, those eyes. Onyx colored under dark brows. Finish the picture with a smile showcasing orthodontically straight white teeth and you had one sexy Scot. No wonder Casey was entranced.

When Judith excused herself to return to the kitchen, Casey and Robert sat down across the table. "I'm sorry we're so late, Mom, but I wanted to show Robert where I used to live. Then we kind of took a mini-tour and well…I'm sorry. I see you have wine already. What kind? Let me see the menu. Oh, they still have crabcakes. They make the best crabcakes."

Casey and Robert chatted amiably as they settled in. As I listened to them talk, I was intrigued by Robert's accent. I couldn't quite place it. I knew he was born in Scotland and grew up there and had studied in the United States. Finally nosiness won out. "Robert, where did you go to college?"

"Duke, ma'am."

Ah, that explained it — kind of Sean Connery meets Billy Bob Thornton.

I drifted back into my oblivious state only half hearing the conversation until Robert said, "Yeah, Grandpa Robbie's (it sounded like Grampa Rabbie) old barony is not much more than a pile of rocks. Do you know? (I heard 'do ye know')"

I tuned in. This was fascinating.

Casey did a "hmm" indicating interest.

"He's been here in Paris looking for fresh money to invest in the place. It's a regular money pit. Do you know?"

Robert had piqued my interest. "What's he trying to do to the barony? Keep it in good repair?"

"Not exactly," Robert said. "He and my grandma, before she died, wanted to turn it into one of those bed and breakfast places. He has invested everything

141

he has in it and borrowed up to the hilt and it still needs a bigger investment to get it up and running."

My antennae shot up. I knew it would be impolite to ask, but I couldn't help but wonder if Bobby was broke. If so, how was he affording expensive restaurants and bottles of wine to woo my mother? My suspicious nature reared its ugly head and I would have questioned Robert more, but just then Chrissie and Tessa breezed in flaunting bags bearing the label of an elegant *Ile Saint Louis* shop. They were followed almost immediately by Mac who produced a bouquet of spring flowers from behind his back and presented it to Tessa with a flourish. Tessa and Mac were still in the doorway laughing when we heard the roar of a motorcycle outside. And in blew Mom and Bobby --- eyes sparkling and twin heads of white hair tousled by the ride.

I rolled my eyes at Chrissie. And she shrugged.

"Nice of you to join me," I said to her.

"Tessa and I had to make a quick trip to that cool store on *Ile Saint Louis* to get that stone necklace she's been lusting after."

Tessa displayed a turquoise stone necklace and matching bracelet. "Awesome, huh?"

"Why didn't you get one for me?" Casey asked and poked her cousin in the ribs.

While the girls oohed and ahed over the necklace, Bobby studied the wine list and then ordered wine for all of us. Expensive wine. I pondered again the state of his finances, but commanded myself, like Scarlett O'Hara, to think about it tomorrow. "I can't believe this is our last night in Paris." I sighed. "It went so fast."

Chrissie toyed with one of her gold hoop earrings and tucked a strand of hair behind her ear. "Time flies when you're chasing crooks?"

"Yep," I answered her. "This has been like an episode of Nancy Drew Does Paris."

Everyone laughed. It sounded forced to me.

Our waitress poured the wine and after much debate we agreed to order eight different selections to share. We had a feast of Gumbo, Filet Mignon de Porc New Orleans, Barbeque Shrimp, Jambalaya and Blackened Rib Steak. Of course, Casey chose the Crabcakes a la Paris that she said were "to die for". And Tessa insisted her mother have a dish named Bubba Comes Home --- a crawfish boil --- in honor of her new painting.

Everyone was in good spirits — anxious to forget, at least for a little while, the stress and excitement of the past few days. Fueled by copious amounts of wine and excellent food there was a lot of laughing and passing around of plates.

"Try this."

"You haven't ever tasted anything like this."

"Oh-my-god, this is so amazing. You have to have a bite."

Judith and Frederick checked on us frequently and our little blonde waitress was attentive — anticipating our needs before we had to ask. Finally, after we scraped every morsel of cheesecake and the specialty of the house, Mississippi Mud Pie, off our plates, we settled back in our chairs and groaned with pleasure.

"I don't think I'll ever eat again," Chrissie moaned, holding her stomach. "I'm so stuffed I can't move."

I plunked my coffee cup on the table with a thud. "Well, I'm going to the restroom."

As I lurched to my feet, the floor tilted under me and I realized that perhaps that last glass of wine was one more than I needed. I leaned toward Chrissie and whispered, "Order me another cup of coffee, would you?"

She looked me up and down. "One cup won't do it. I'll get you a pot."

I minced toward the stairway that led to the second floor restroom. The room rolled gently around me. I navigated the stairs in a fog, clinging to the railing as if it was a lifeline. At the top of the steps I tried the door to the restroom. Locked. I leaned against the wall to wait and idly surveyed the top floor. Most of the tables were occupied. A couple in the corner caught my attention. There was something vaguely familiar about them. On another night I might have approached their table, but in my current somewhat befuddled condition, I just looked away, distracted by Casey climbing the steps.

"Hey," she huffed. "You okay?"

"Never better. *Thanksgiving* is great."

"I knew you'd like it."

"You and Robert seem to be getting along well."

"Yeah. I really like him." She might have said more but the restroom door opened and she shoved me inside. "Age before beauty."

"Brat."

I took my time in the restroom --- splashing water on my face and fixing my make-up. I felt much better when I came out. As I waited outside the restroom for Casey, I gazed once again at the couple in the corner. One had unfolded a large tourist map and it obscured their faces. Since both wore khaki trench coats I wasn't positive of their genders. Odd.

When Casey rejoined me I grasped her arm and held her back. "Casey, sweetie, will you do me a favor?"

"Sure. Name it."

"I'm curious about Baron Hot Legs. Nonny seems quite smitten with him and I'd like to know a little more about him. And, more importantly, his finances."

"What you're really asking is for me to find out if Bobby wants to be Nonny's gigolo?"

I nodded. "The gigolo thing might be a family joke but I don't want her to get hurt."

Casey patted my cheek. "I'm on it."

The party was breaking up by the time we got back to our table. I sank into my chair and poured myself a cup of coffee from the pot sitting at my place. "Thanks," I said to my sister.

"No problem."

"What do I owe for dinner?"

"Not a thing. Everything is handled. I took care of it."

"You did? Everything? What about…." I jerked my head toward Bobby.

"Yes, *I* did," Chrissie said. "*Bobby* misplaced his credit card."

Bobby overheard her and apologized --- obviously not for the first time. "I am so embarrassed. I wanted to buy you lassies dinner, but I must have left my card in the pocket of my leather jacket after lunch."

"Don't worry about it," Chrissie said. "After all you've done for us and the girls, I am happy to do something for you and the – er – laddies."

I rolled my eyes.

I nudged my daughter and gave her a pointed look. I knew that my mother wouldn't be happy about us trying to dig up dirt about Bobby, but my instincts were screaming that something was not the way it appeared. If Bobby had secrets, I wanted to find out what they were. I was certain I could count on Casey to unearth them.

After dinner Casey and Tessa planned to check out a new club in *Place Pigalle* with Robert and Mac while Bobby and Mom headed for a romantic boat ride on the *bateaux mouche* on the Seine.

Before we split up, I said, "Our train leaves Gare Lyon at eight tomorrow morning, so I think we should meet in the lobby by six. I asked Madame Reno to arrange for a taxi. That way we'll have plenty of time."

Chrissie added, "We've planned a nice, leisurely train trip through the French countryside."

I envisioned green hills, quaint villages and long conversations.

"And," Chrissie continued. "Aunt Kate and I have bought stuff for an exquisite train picnic."

"Wine, brie, baguettes, strawberries and chocolates," I said. "We will not be happy if someone messes up our plan by being late."

"Mom! Chill! We'll be ready," Casey said.

"No problem," Tessa echoed as the four of them strolled away.

Robert looped his arm over Casey's shoulder as she looked up at him. Her laugh drifted back to us.

Bobby's red motorcycle was parked at the curb in front of *Thanksgiving.* He handed Mom a helmet and she tugged it on. As she started to get on, Chrissie caught her arm. "Whoa. Just a minute."

Startled, Mom stopped. "What's the matter?"

"You can't get on that thing." She pointed at Bobby. "He's been drinking. It's not safe."

Mom looked concerned — her brow furrowed and her eyes serious. "She has a point, Bobby. Maybe we should take a taxi."

Bobby shook his head. "Laura, love, I take my responsibilities as your chauffeur very seriously. I am --- how is it you Americans say it --- the distracted driver. I didn't have any wine. Just a coke."

Mom chuckled. "That would be designated driver, Bobby."

We hugged Mom and watched as she and Bobby mounted the motorbike and roared off, veering around parked cars and wayward pedestrians.

Chrissie slapped a hand to her forehead. "I hope he really does know how to drive that thing."

I had a sudden thought. "You know, Chrissie. In all the days we've hung out with him, I've barely seen Bobby do more than sip at a beer. Why do you suppose that is?"

Chrissie shrugged. "He takes his responsibilities as Mom's chauffeur seriously?"

"Or something."

Chapter 14

At 6:15 the next morning I paced the tiny lobby of *Le Hotel Mignon*. We had settled the bill and, surrounded by a haphazard pile of luggage, a couple of shopping bags and our picnic basket, we were waiting for Casey, Tessa and Mom. I checked my watch for at least the tenth time and blew out a sigh.

"The taxi is due any second. We're going to miss the train, I know it. Where are they anyway?"

Chrissie wore a mantle of Zen-like calm. "Take a breath, Kate. They'll be down any second. We won't miss the train, but there are other trains all day if we do."

Her complacency annoyed me. "True. But we have reservations. We paid extra for a private compartment. I hate being late. It's so rude. Casey knows…"

Fortunately, the elevator door slid open at that moment and interrupted my diatribe. Out spilled our sleep-deprived and grumpy daughters. Yawning, they stumbled over to us, complaining about the time and what on earth we had been thinking when we made the train reservations. In no mood to dispense comfort, I groused, "It's about time. We are going to miss our train."

I looked toward the elevator, expecting to see my mother's white curls peeking out. A couple of seconds passed and I realized that the elevator was empty. No Mom.

"Casey, where's your grandmother? Is she having trouble with her bags? Why didn't the two of you stay and help her?" I gave an impatient harrumph.

Chrissie, still enveloped in her mystical calm, said in a patronizing tone, "Chill, Kate. I'll go up and get her. Relax, you'll have a stroke. The taxi isn't even here yet." She started for the elevator.

"Mom. Wait," Tessa called.

Chrissie stopped and whirled to face Tessa. "What?"

Casey and Tessa exchanged looks.

"Um, Mom. Aunt Chrissie," Casey began.

"Nonny's not coming," Tessa finished.

"She's not what?" Chrissie and I exclaimed.

Casey handed me an envelope with the hotel letterhead. I ripped it open, unfolded the page and scanned the note hurriedly. Then I read it aloud.

"Dear Kathleen and Christine, Bobby has invited me to spend the weekend with him in Troon inspecting his barony. I know you and the girls will have a wonderful time in Nice. I'll catch up with you at the hotel in Barcelona. Casey has Bobby's cell phone number if you need to reach me. Don't worry. I'll be fine. Bobby has arranged everything. Lots and lots of love, Mom."

I handed the note to Chrissie. She read it, stuffed it in her pocket and marched toward the elevator. "I'll just have a word with Nonny. I'm sure we can convince her that this isn't a good idea."

"Um…Mom," Tessa said. "Wait. Nonny's not in the room."

"She's not? Where is she then?"

But we knew.

Casey confirmed it. "She left about an hour ago with Bobby."

"Oh. My. God." Twin cries of alarm.

"Well, we'll just have to find her and bring her back," Chrissie said.

"Damn straight," I agreed.

The voice of reason and sanity intervened — Casey. "Mom, Nonny's a big girl. She's going to Troon with Baron Robert MacTavish, not on a tramp steamer with her gigolo."

I took a deep, cleansing breath the way I learned in Yoga long ago. I tried to visualize cool, calm waters and beautiful flowers swaying in the breeze. I attempted to release my anguish by breathing through my nose. Nope. Not happening. I gave in to the panic threatening to overwhelm me. "But that's not what we planned," I wailed.

"Duh," Tessa said. "But Aunt Kate, this is cool. Think of the stories. And

Nonny wouldn't have liked Nice as much as we will. It's not her thing."

"And Troon is?"

"Well, Bobby is, at least." Chrissie conceded the point.

I might have argued more but the long-awaited taxi pulled up outside and tooted.

"Well, what's it gonna be?" Casey asked. "Stay and try to find Nonny and Bobby or go to the train station and on to Nice? Beaches. Sunshine. Shopping."

The three of them looked at me expectantly and I relented. "Oh, okay. We probably couldn't stop them at this point anyway. And Nonny can take care of herself. I'm sure she can." I could only hope.

We hauled everything to the curb, threw our things into the taxi and piled in. "*Gare Lyon*," I said to the driver.

I needn't have worried. In spite of the drama over Mom's defection, we made it to *Gare Lyon* with plenty of time to spare. The lobby was crowded but we managed to navigate the steps and security checkpoints leading to the train platforms with no delays.

We arrived at Platform Four at 7:15. Where was the train to *Nice Ville*? I checked and double-checked our tickets to be certain we were in the right place. Yes. Platform Four. But there was no train. No other passengers. It was dim, deserted and faintly creepy.

"Are we in the right place?" Chrissie scanned the empty platform nervously.

I handed her the tickets. "That's what it says."

"Relax, Mom," Casey said. "We're really early. The train isn't scheduled to leave until eight."

"I'm going to find someone to ask," I said. "You guys stay here and don't leave without me."

The helpful man in the information booth reassured me. "The train isn't due in until 7:45. Then they will unload the passengers and you will board. *Pas de problem."*

I made my way back to Platform Four through a growing crowd of passengers. I edged past a young couple locked in each other's arms. A family walked past --- two blonde toddlers pushed doll carriages. I passed a blind man wrapped in a voluminous trench coat over baggy slacks being led by his seeing-eye dog. Big dark sunglasses covered most of his face and a battered fedora was pulled low on his forehead. *"Pardon,"* I said as I stepped out of his way.

At precisely 7:45 a long, silver passenger train chugged into the station and slowed to a stop. Other passengers began to gather their possessions.

"We're in Car 21, a no smoking car," I said. "Compartment G." We walked along the platform until we spotted our car. I pointed. "There it is."

We waited for the departing passengers to get off and then the conductor gestured for us to board. Staggering under the weight of our bags, we started to climb the steep steps when the blind man approached from behind. We stepped aside to let him and his dog get on the train. *"Merci,"* he murmured as he hurried past and disappeared down the aisle.

Huffing and puffing the four of us dragged our stuff up the steps and onto the train. We lurched down the corridor looking for our compartment. Tessa and Casey led the way counting off compartments. "E. F. G. Here it is."

The private compartments were designed for four people comfortably or six squeezed in like sardines. Each opened off the aisle with a pneumatic door that required a great deal of effort to open. Tessa dropped her bags, grabbed the door handle and gave it a giant heave. Reluctantly the latch released and, with Casey at her heels, Tessa fell into our compartment. And froze. "There are already two people in here," she called over her shoulder. "I thought you said it would just be the four of us."

"Dammit. It's supposed to be," I snapped. "I can't believe it. Nothing is going right today."

Behind me, Chrissie said, "We'll straighten it out. They're probably in the wrong compartment or wrong car."

Hot, sweaty and furious, I pushed past Tessa and stepped into the compartment. Tessa was right. There was a couple occupying our space. They were sound asleep in the window seats, propped against the side of the car.

"I'll take care of this," I said and tapped the sleeping man on the shoulder. "*Pardon, Monsieur.*"

He didn't move. I tapped a bit harder. Still no response. At the end of my patience, I grabbed his shoulder and gave it a healthy shake. "Wake up, *Monsieur.*"

To my shock, the man slithered limply to the floor where he lay in a heap --- a bright red blotch stained the front of his jacket. Blood? Unable to move, I stared at him. Behind me I could hear the others breathing heavily.

"Oh, no. Oh, no. Oh, no," I chanted. "Not again. Oh, not again."

"Mom." Tessa's cry was piercing. "Isn't that your jacket?"

My stomach lurched. I tore my horrified gaze away from the body on the floor of the train compartment to focus on his companion. She was, indeed, wearing a hot pink suede jacket. Chrissie reached out --- her hand shaking --- and touched her. The woman's head flopped forward spilling blonde frizzy curls over her face as she slowly toppled out of the seat and belly-flopped onto her companion. My heart stopped. Fifi. The woman in the jacket was Fifi. Which meant that the man in the bloodstained jacket was --- I stared at him --- Georges! Oh, no. Fifi and Georges. What on earth were they doing in our train car? And who had hurt them? My thoughts raced like Indy cars careening around the track.

There was a moment of unnatural silence in the car before the four of us began to shriek.

"They're dead."

"Are they dead?"

"Is it Fifi?"

"Oh, God. It is Fifi."

"And Georges."

"What're they doing here?"

"What happened? Are they shot?"

"Is there blood?"

"There is blood. Oh no."

I'm not sure what I thought I would discover, but I knelt and put my fingers on Fifi's neck. All I felt was damp, clammy skin. That was more than enough. I yanked my hand away as if I had touched a red-hot burner and stared at the red, sticky smudges on my fingers.

"Oh, God. Oh, no-o-o. It's blo-od. F-f-f-i-f-f-f-i's blood." I waved my hand frantically in the air.

A conductor heard our cries and rushed into our compartment. One look and he vanished, only to return seconds later with the blind man who, it turned out, was no blinder than I am. He removed his dark glasses and threw them aside. Then he knelt on the floor next to Fifi and Georges. He did the fingers to neck thing and then spoke in a harsh voice in French to the conductor who disappeared once again. Then the "blind" man stood up and faced us. We were stunned to see that it was Inspector Claude Bouchard.

"Inspector Bouchard? You aren't blind. What are you doing here?" I was babbling but couldn't help myself.

He held up his index finger and spoke rapidly into his cell phone. When he disconnected he fixed us with a grim look --- his dark eyes stony and unblinking. "You insisted on leaving Paris, Madame, so I followed you to protect you from danger." He frowned. "Do you see now that you are not safe?"

"B..but..." I obviously was a blithering idiot. "Are t-they d-dead?"

"Not yet," he said ominously, "but those bullet wounds look serious."

He turned back to Fifi and Georges. "Let's get them up on the seat. I've called for an ambulance. It should be here at any moment."

I sucked in a deep cleansing breath to calm my nerves. It didn't work. My hands shook as I helped Chrissie and the inspector lift Fifi and stretch her out on the seat. The inspector then hooked his hands under Georges' armpits and hoisted him onto the seat across from Fifi. Then he strode back to the door to organize the inspection of the crime scene. Chrissie perched on the edge of the seat and smoothed Fifi's hair back from her forehead. One of Fifi's arms dangled over the edge of the seat and Chrissie gently picked it up and placed it on her chest. Suddenly, Chrissie took a sharp breath. "Kate," she whispered. "Look."

"I don't see…" I began and stopped.

We stared at the silver charm bracelet on Fifi's slim wrist --- dangling from it was a skull and crossbones charm. Identical to the one Mom found in her ice cream.

"Is it the same?" My lips felt like they had been injected with collagen.

"It looks like it," she whispered back.

"What does it mean?"

"Someone is trying to warn us?"

"About what?"

I looked down at Fifi's pale face and was startled to see her eyelids flutter. She gave a little moan and her eyes opened and then slid closed.

"Chrissie," I said. "Look. She's awake. Tell the inspector."

Fifi licked her lips and rasped a barely audible, "No. Not him. Don't."

I reached blindly into my bag and pulled out a bottle of water and held it to her lips. She took a tiny sip and her eyes drifted closed. Just when I thought she had lapsed into unconsciousness again, she clasped my wrist with freezing fingers. The skull and crossbones charm brushed against my skin and I shivered. I leaned closer as she struggled to speak. Finally, she whispered, "Hurt. Can't trust. Careful. So sorry…" Her eyes closed --- her breathing labored.

Chrissie stared at me, fear in her eyes. "Did she mean?" She flicked a glance in Inspector Bouchard's direction.

I gulped. "I think she did."

"Shush," Chrissie said as we heard the sing song sound of an ambulance and then paramedics stormed into the compartment carrying medical bags, oxygen and stretchers. The tiny compartment suddenly swarmed with burly men administering aid to Fifi and Georges. The airless compartment was hot and claustrophobic. We watched in horror and tried to disappear into the background, but we weren't invisible and Bouchard focused on us. "You ladies must leave. You will only be in the way here. You will be escorted to another compartment until I can speak with you." We didn't want to leave Fifi and Georges, but he wasn't giving us a choice.

One of the uniformed policemen escorted us to an adjoining compartment. "Stay here," he said with a stern look. "The inspector will talk to you when he is finished in there." He brought us stale packaged croissants and cold coffee the consistency of an oil spill. Then he left us alone.

Casey huddled next to me and buried her head on my shoulder. Her voice was muffled. "This is all my fault, isn't it?"

I tilted her chin so I could see her face. Tears glistened on her eyelashes and her lower lip trembled.

"No," I said, "It's not your fault. Fifi and Georges were involved in something dangerous and illegal before you tried to help."

She sniffled. "T-that's true, but…"

"But you got us involved," Tessa finished helpfully.

"Tessa!" Chrissie's voice was sharp. "Don't pick on Casey. She's upset enough as it is. Let's wait to see what the inspector has to say."

"If anything," I added, thinking of Fifi's warning.

Time passed excruciatingly slowly. We waited. And waited. And waited some more. Occasionally one of us would pace to the door and peer out. But neither Bouchard nor any other policeman came to clue us in on what was going on.

After what seemed like an eternity we heard the chime of the ambulance and, assuming that it was transporting Fifi and Georges to a hospital, Chrissie and I leapt to our feet and stared out the window to watch it speeding away.

"Do you think they're dead?" Chrissie pressed her open hand against the windowpane.

I traced the outline of her hand in the condensation on the window. "I hope not," I said. "I pray they aren't."

"What are we going to do?"

We didn't really need to discuss it --- the twin thing again. We agreed without a single word that we had enough. Paris was too dangerous. When Inspector Bouchard finally took a break from the investigation and came to our compartment, we were frantic to leave. Things were getting way too scary.

"We're going to Nice as planned," I told the inspector. "We aren't waiting around to end up like Fifi and Georges."

His eyebrows shot up. "You know them? By name?"

"We told you about Fifi and Georges. Casey helped them bring in their suitcase."

He scowled. "Why did you not tell me that you knew them? That would be important for me to know."

"I suppose," Chrissie said, "but we haven't had a chance for discussion, have we? And it's not like they are our best friends or anything."

"*Merde*," I said. A perfect time to demonstrate my ability to curse in five languages -- if you count sign language.

The inspector's lips twitched. An odd look crossed his face and his eyelid crinkled. Was that a wink?

"*Merde*, indeed," he said.

"How are Fifi and Georges doing?" I knew we couldn't leave without knowing.

"Well, Georges --- you say his name is. He --- we are not sure will make it. The doctors at the hospital will keep me informed. And the woman...?" He shrugged. "I do not know. It is not good."

I swallowed a lump the size of the Eiffel Tower. The cabin lights spiraled. "That would be murder."

Chrissie gasped. "Who," she asked, "do you think did this to them?"

Bouchard did the shrug thing again. "*Je ne sais pas.* You know them. Who do you think? We'll find out but it will take time."

"We've told you everything we know," I said. Almost.

"We are taking the girls and getting out of harm's way," Chrissie added. "You can't keep us here."

Bouchard fingered the lapel of his trench coat. Was he going to pull out a gun to stop us? "Actually," he said, "you are correct. I cannot hold you, *Madame*, or your sister. But I could hold *Mademoiselle* Casey if I chose to do so. And *Mademoiselle* Tessa as well."

My breath caught in my throat --- his words formed a stranglehold around my neck. Would he really arrest Casey? I began to pray silently.

"*S'il vous plait, Monsieur.* Casey may be impulsive but she is no criminal. Let us take the girls to Nice before the person who hurt Fifi and Georges finds us and does the same to one of us."

The inspector closed his eyes and said nothing. I counted the months of my life before he finally opened them and said, "At least let me notify the gendarmes in Nice. They can watch out for you."

I met Chrissie's eyes. Then I nodded. "Okay. We agree."

After that it didn't take long for the long-delayed train to get underway. A drawn-out to-oot echoed through the station as our train chugged toward the French countryside.

Au revoir, Paris.

Chapter 15

"Thank you, Jesus," Tessa said as the cab from the train station pulled up at the pink canopied entrance to *L'Hotel Belle de Nice*.

"Tess-a," Chrissie objected automatically.

"Seriously, Mom," Tessa protested, "we've lived an entire season of Law and Order in a single day. Personally, I think it would be damned ungrateful not to thank Jesus. Just look at this place. The answer to my prayers."

"It is adorable," Casey agreed. "Look at the palm trees."

After our long, stressful and scary day we were nearly brain-dead with fatigue by the time we arrived. But just looking at the charming facade of our hotel --- located on a quiet side street but near a bustling shopping area --- was enough to revive our enthusiasm.

"Let's hurry and get checked in," Casey said. "Mom and I can show you our favorite places. You guys will love it here."

The lobby of the hotel was just large enough to hold an overstuffed couch and several chairs covered in some sort of faded chintz fabric. A myriad of brochures for various tourist venues was displayed on a wooden table in front of the white curtained window. Casey and Tessa scooped up a stack of pamphlets while Chrissie and I approached the clerk --- a large 50ish man sporting a scruffy mustache and a full head of equally scruffy salt and pepper hair.

"*Bonjour, Madames*," he greeted us with a welcoming smile.

"*Parlez vous Anglais?*" I asked.

"*Oui. Un petit peu.* Just a little," he replied with a self-deprecating shrug.

I think I might have been exercising my independent streak but I confidently breached the language barrier and asked Monsieur Durac --- his name was posted on a nameplate on the counter --- for two adjoining rooms on the quiet side of the building. We had a lovely conversation, I thought, as I did a lot of nodding to indicate I understood when I really had no idea what he was saying.

Finally he said, "*Oui. Vous comprends?*"

I nodded again and he handed me the keys to two first floor rooms. "*Merci, Monsieur.*"

Monsieur Durac directed us to the stairs and since our rooms were up only one flight, we decided to walk. Easier said than done. We hauled our motley collection of suitcases, shopping bags and picnic basket up the steps and looked around breathlessly. Our two rooms were side by side in the front of the building overlooking the street. Quiet? Maybe not. Should have been my first clue.

I handed one set of keys to Tessa and unlocked the door to the other room. It wasn't large, but much bigger than our postage stamp-sized room in Paris. The double beds were neatly made up with fluffy pale green comforters. A large desk stretched across the entire wall. A huge closet and an antique armoire housing the television set completed the decor. The room was spotless. The artwork on the walls vaguely Impressionistic and the view out the window enticing.

I high-fived Chrissie.

"Now this is what I'm talkin' about." She beamed.

I dumped the luggage inside the door and sank down on one of the beds.

"Very nice." I congratulated myself. Cute hotel. Charming room.

Suddenly there was frantic banging on the door and Tessa's voice. "Open up right this minute. I mean it."

Chrissie and I exchanged "what now" looks and she yanked open the door. Tessa was standing there, hands on hips.

"Tessa," Chrissie said. "What on earth has you so upset?"

Tessa did the eye roll thing and huffed. "Mother. Aunt Kate." She bit off each word and spat it at us. "We. Have. To. Share. A. Bathroom."

I quickly surveyed our room and realized that, sure enough, the bathroom was missing. Oops. Maybe my skill in the French language was not what I thought.

Casey lounged against the doorframe, an amused smile playing across her lips. To Casey essential creature comforts include a roof and a bed --- and even those aren't mandatory. Tessa, though, demanded more.

"I do not do communal bathrooms," she said. "Uh-uh. No way."

"Good job, Mom," Casey said with a grin. "You've unleashed her inner high maintenance girl."

Tessa glared at her cousin. "Case. Go down and fix this. Talk to someone. Get us a room with a bathroom."

"Not my job. My mother got us these rooms. She can get us out." Casey was enjoying herself.

"Oh, for heaven's sake," I said. "These rooms are fine. So we have to share a bathroom. Big deal." I wasn't going to admit that the idea of trudging across the hall in the middle of the night wasn't thrilling me either. I wouldn't give Tessa the satisfaction.

Tessa minced over to the door across the hall on which "*La Toilette*" was written in gold script. Using only two fingers she opened it and peered inside. "Yuck."

Casey smirked. "Tessa, you're being a spoiled brat. Get over it."

Chrissie patted Tessa on the head. "If you think it's so yucky, you can do what we always did when we went camping --- wear shower shoes.

Tessa tossed her hair, pirouetted haughtily, and flounced toward her room. At the door she stopped and looked back. "The only shoes I intend to wear when I'm naked are my stilettos." And she stomped into her room, slamming the door behind her.

"*Au revoir*, Tessa," Casey said and the three of us burst out laughing.

A short time later we heard a meek tap on our door. Chrissie put her eye to the peephole and then, grinning, pulled it open. "Why, Kate, look who's here.

It's Tessa."

Tessa squirmed, shifting her weight from one platformed sandal to the other. Chrissie tugged her into the room and waited. Tessa took a deep breath. "Um. I'm really sorry. I acted like a big baby. I guess I can suck it up and use the bathroom." She muttered under her breath. "Gross as it is."

"That's okay, sweetie," I began while Chrissie fished around in her bag.

Having found what she wanted, she presented her daughter with a pair of low-heeled but still dressy red sandals. "Will these do? I don't have stilettos."

Tessa giggled. "Mother! You are so mean!"

A few seconds later Casey poked her ahead around the door. "Hey gang. Let's rock and roll. It will be dark soon and Nice is right outside waiting for us."

I looked out the window and was surprised to see that she was right. We needed to try to put crime and all the frightening events of the day behind us --- if that was possible --- and let Nice's magic work on us.

"Casey's right," I said. "Places to go. Sights to see."

In a few minutes we were pushing through the hotel doors and onto the sidewalk outside. It had been a sunny day in the south of France and the day's warmth still lingered in the air. It promised to be a perfect evening for exploring Nice.

Casey, who had visited Nice many times, checked her tourist map and said, "Follow me *mes amis*."

The hotel was located on a quiet side street. We strolled past a quaint wine shop/market and peered through the grimy windows at dusty displays of bottles of fancy wine and cheeses. The door to the shop was propped open and we could see racks of wine and snacks. The proprietor --- a gnarled elderly woman with neatly groomed hair pulled into a tidy bun --- smiled at us and beckoned, but we were anxious to see more of Nice before darkness descended, so we simply waved and continued.

"She's going to be my new best friend," Chrissie said. "French wine and snacks at our doorstep."

"I hear you," I replied.

Casey snorted. "You two and your wine. There is no shortage of that in Nice or anywhere else in France for that matter."

"I can't believe we're actually here," Tessa bubbled. "On the French Riviera. This is so awesome."

"Just wait," Casey told her, "you ain't seen nothin' yet." She turned to me. "What do you say, Mom? Should we head for the walking street?"

Casey was referring to *Avenue Jean Medecin*, Nice's pedestrian --- or as Casey said --- walking street. Several blocks long and lined with a seemingly infinite array of restaurants, cafes, bistros, shops, street performers and people. Vendors spread their wares --- purses, jewelry, quirky clothing --- on the sidewalk forcing the crowds to pick their way around them. One of my guilty pleasures.

"The walking street is a perfect intro to Nice," I said. "Especially for these material girls."

The street where the hotel stood was lined with attractive apartment buildings featuring wrought iron enclosed balconies and tall windows. It was peaceful but when we turned the corner we were on a bustling street with shops and tiny cafes.

Tessa pointed. "Is that what I think it is? A grocery store? Where I can buy shampoo and conditioner? I'm in heaven."

"All this history and quaintness and she is excited about a *supermarche*. Seriously, Tess."

"A girl's gotta look good is all I can say. Besides I'm almost out of shampoo." Tessa swung her hair.

Chrissie tucked a lock of blonde hair behind Tessa's ear. "We'll attend to your personal hygiene needs later. Right now I want to see Nice before it's too dark."

Tessa batted her mother's hand away and pulled the lock of hair from behind her ear, letting it fall over her face. She grinned and bounced up and down. "Bring it on."

Camera in hand, Casey led us down tree-lined streets and through a quiet park surrounding a church. An older couple sat together on a bench and tossed crumbs toward greedy pigeons circling them. Casey aimed her camera in their direction and I flashed back to a years' old memory.

"Hey, Case," I said. "I think this is the very same park where your Dad and I sat right after we learned we were pregnant with you. In fact, that might be the exact same bench."

Casey let her camera swing on its strap around her neck. Her brown eyes sparkled with mischief. "Really? That's cool. We need a picture."

The pigeon-feeding couple stood up, crumpled a paper bag, tossed it in a waste bin and wandered away. Casey motioned me toward the bench.

"Sit, Mom," she said. "I am recording history here."

I perched on the edge of the seat. "We were so young and so excited." I sighed. "Seems like an eternity ago."

Casey snapped my picture from several angles while I reminisced. Finally, I said, "Hey, we need a shot of both of us. Before and after."

Casey laughed. "Before you didn't know what you were getting and now you do. I'm so sorry."

She handed her camera to Tessa and dropped onto the bench next to me. I put my arm around her and we posed for Tessa. "We got the best daughter in the world. Wouldn't trade her for all the popcorn at the circus."

"Aw, thanks, Mom." Casey beamed.

"Enough of this trip down memory lane. Mushy, mushy," Tessa said. "Let's move."

We wandered past a toddler with chocolate ice cream dripping from the cone and down her arm and a statue of some dignitary with a bird perched on his bronzed head. Casey shot photo after photo filling memory cards with a Casey's eye view of Nice.

Finally we reached *Avenue Jean Medecin*. Chrissie paused by a vendor who had "designer" purses displayed on a tattered quilt spread on the sidewalk. "This is so tacky and cheesy," she gushed. "But I love it. I absolutely have to have one of these purses."

"What I absolutely have to have," I said, "is food and a place to crash and absorb the ambiance. It's been a long day. We can shop later."

The others agreed. So after checking out the menu posted in front, we selected a bistro and were soon seated at an outdoor table next to the sidewalk.

I sighed. "Now this is perfect."

The waiter came over to take our orders and when we learned he spoke very little English, Tessa said, "Let's let Casey do the ordering. I don't think I can take any more of Aunt Kate's surprises today. God knows what we might get. Roasted rat?"

"You don't like surprises?" I said. "Life would be so boring with no surprises."

Tessa wrinkled her nose in mock distaste. "Next time surprise me with a diamond bracelet not a community *toilette*."

"Don't hold your breath."

"Ah, but I might have to in that *toilette*," Tessa said.

Just then the waiter served us our dinner. I breathed in the aroma of the steaming cheese omelets and French fries as he put my plate in front of me. I sighed with pleasure. "Ah, heaven. Nothing soothes the soul like a good French fry."

Casey nodded. "Mom, you think anytime you can have *pommes frites* you are in heaven."

"Absolutely," I said and waved a fry in her direction. "Want one?"

"*Non, Merci*," she said. "I've got my pizza."

"And *Merci* to you," Tessa said. "This pizza is awesome."

Chrissie poured wine for all of us and took a bite of her omelette. "Umm. I needed that." She chewed thoughtfully and then said, "I hate to bring it up, but I'm thinking about Fifi and Georges."

"Me, too," I said. "Food is a great distraction, but we can't avoid thinking about it forever. I wonder...." I slapped my forehead with my hand. "Oh, no. I forgot that I wanted to call Mom to make sure she and Bobby got to Scotland all right. Casey, do you have your cell with you? Call Bobby. I want to talk to Nonny."

Casey dug her phone out of her bag and punched in the numbers. We waited while the call went through and then Casey shook her head. "Voicemail."

"Leave a message. Have her call us."

Casey left the message and disconnected. "Chill, Mom. Nonny's fine."

I knew she was probably right, but I would have liked to talk with her to be sure and I was certain Chrissie felt the same.

"I don't have a good feeling about this," Chrissie said.

I turned to my daughter. "Casey, honey, what did you find out from Robert?"

"He told me that his grandparents --- that would be Bobby and his now dead wife --- owned this pile of rocks in Troon that they believed would make a successful bed and breakfast. The barony. Remember?"

I nodded. "Go on."

"Since golf is a big deal and the British Open is there sometimes, they figured that it would be an ideal location for an inn. Tourists and golfers would love it. A real moneymaker."

"According to Robert, they put every bit of money they had into the place, mortgaged their home to the hilt and borrowed until their credit ran out. Then Robert's grandma died and Bobby gave up on the idea. He grieved for his wife for a long time. He almost went bankrupt just living on a stipend from the government for his parliamentary duties."

"Lately, though," Casey told us, "Robert says Bobby's been trying to dredge up some interest in the old place. Hunting for backers again. Robert guesses Bobby is expecting to get some money --- an inheritance maybe --- soon. He wasn't really sure."

Chrissie's eyes were wide and horrified. "Are you thinking what I'm thinking?"

"Probably. What are you thinking?"

"That Bobby intends to scam some money from Mom."

"Yeah, but her money is all tied up. It's not like she's carrying it around in her purse. It would take some doing to get it. In fact, no one can touch it unless..."

"She gets remarried," Chrissie and I cried together our voices high and shreiky.

"She couldn't."

"She wouldn't."

"You don't think..."

"Mom, Aunt Kate." Tessa interrupted our babbling. "Get a grip. Do you honest to God think Nonny would marry Bobby? As she likes to say, she didn't just fall off the turnip truck."

"But she's so smitten," I said. "She might get carried away with the romance of it all and elope. If Bobby's desperate, he might be pretty convincing."

I pictured Mom and Bobby riding away from a small village church on Bobby's motorbike --- their twin heads of white hair blowing in the wind and Mom tossing a bouquet of flowers to the gathered *cows*?

"Get real," Casey said in a no-nonsense voice. "Nonny wouldn't elope. She would want her family with her on her wedding day." She paused and giggled. "But engaged? Maybe."

"I guess we're being silly," I said. "She's fine. Bobby's showing her the sights."

"I suppose," Chrissie said but she didn't look convinced. "As long as that's all he shows her."

I pictured Mom and Bobby in the tower room of a secluded castle surrounded by a moat. She wore a flowing white gown and he nothing but kilts. I shook my head to erase the vision.

We paid the bill and gathered up our suspicions and our purses and stumbled into the thickening dark. As the stars began to twinkle insanely over our heads we wandered down the *Promenade des Anglais,* a five mile-long walkway bordering the Mediterranean Sea. During the day the *Promenade* bustles with bikers, roller-bladers, joggers and strollers of all shapes and sizes, but at night it is a much mellower spot. The moon rose over the sea casting a sparkling beam of light across the sea. Couples strolled hand in hand while families trudged by urging weary toddlers toward their beds. We joined the parade. I took a huge breath of salt air and tried to push my wild fantasies aside.

Casey and Tessa, arm in arm, sauntered along chattering and gawking at the hotels, the beach and other pedestrians. On one side of us the waves lapped against the rocky beach. On the other cars whizzed by leaving a cloud of fumes in their wake.

I peered into the fumes looking for the policeman that Inspector Bouchard had promised would be looking out for us. I didn't see him. Nor did I see a mad gunman ready to shoot us like he did Fifi and Georges. Thank you, Jesus. We passed a couple huddled in the shadows, lips locked in a passionate kiss. I stared at them.

"Stop that, Kate," Chrissie said. "You're being rude."

I tore my glance away with difficulty. "Um. Sorry. *Pardon,*" I murmured in their direction.

"I know what you're doing and you can quit anytime."

"And what precisely am I doing?"

Chrissie shook her head and did an eye roll. "Exactly what I've been doing.

Checking out the landscape for suspicious characters. Friend or foe."

We fell silent as we passed an elderly couple sitting on a bench hand in hand.

Chrissie stuck an elbow in my ribs. "Cops?"

"The geezer patrol," I answered.

And we laughed uneasily.

"I guess I'm not as good a detective as I'd like to be," I said.

We strolled along, each of us sunk in her own gloomy thoughts. Where was Mom? Was Bobby a con man who would swindle her out of her money? And where was that police protection? And the two "perps" who were still after the money? Were they lurking in the shadows waiting to pounce?

I abandoned my bleak speculations when we caught up to Tessa and Casey who were standing facing the sea, the ocean breeze ruffling their hair. Tessa pointed at a cruise ship steaming by. "Is that awesome or what? We're on the actual Riviera. How cool is that?"

"Totally," Casey said.

We found a bench and watched the ocean for a while. Finally, Chrissie stretched and said, "Well, this has been delightful, but I, for one, am ready for bed?"

"Not exactly the word I'd use," I said, "But I am too. What about you girls? Clubbing tonight?"

Casey shook her head. "It's been a weird and creepy day. Not a day to celebrate with a party." She paused to stare out to sea. "And we don't know much about the club scene. What do you say, Tess, shall we join the ancient twins at the hotel?"

Tessa dusted off her jeans and stood up. "Lead me to *la chambre*."

As the four of us crossed the busy thoroughfare and headed toward our hotel, I glanced back. A man wearing jeans and a dark windbreaker got lazily up from the bench he had been sitting on. He pulled his ball cap low over his forehead and stood hands on hips watching us. When he noticed me looking at him, he tipped his cap and turned away.

I shivered in spite of the balmy night.

Chapter 16

Fifi dangled the skull and crossbones charm in my face and I felt her breath hot on my cheek as she leaned close and whispered in my ear, "He is bad. Very, very bad."

I reached for the bracelet but Fifi backed away from me still murmuring, "Bad man. Beware."

She inched away from me --- the charm bracelet dangling from one manicured finger. I stretched a hand out to snag her sleeve. "Wait, Fifi," I said. "Wait." But she faded into the fog that suddenly surrounded me.

Before I could catch her I heard loud banging and I sat up straight with my heart pounding and sweat streaking my forehead. I jerked my head around trying to get my bearings. Where had Fifi gone? And where on earth was I?

"Wha?" I mumbled. "Who?"

"Brilliant, Kate," Chrissie said as she stumbled over to the door to our hotel room and yanked it open. Casey and Tessa bounded in fully dressed and ready for action.

Casey bounced on my bed. "Mom, you're not up," she said, disgust dripping from her words. "And you look awful."

Slowly I recognized my surroundings, peered groggily at my travel alarm and moaned. "Seven o'clock? It's too early to be that cheerful."

"Kate, what on earth is your problem? You're acting like something out of Dawn of the Dead." Chrissie dove back under the covers of her bed. "Go away, you two. Can't you see we're sleeping?"

Ignoring me, Tessa plopped onto her mother's bed and pulled the blanket from over Chrissie's head. "See," she said, "I'm wearing the shoes you gave me."

I dragged myself into focus and saw that Tessa, indeed, had on Chrissie's red, heeled sandals.

"Shower shoes," Tessa explained. "I took a shower."

Her blonde hair swung from side to side as she shook her head and the aroma of coconut shampoo wafted in the air. "Aren't you proud of me?"

"Oh, for sure," Chrissie said and sat up --- running a hand through her own disheveled locks. "Second only to the time you got accepted to law school."

Tessa laughed. "Mother! Now you're just being mean."

Casey leapt off my bed, marched over to the windows and raised the blinds with a snap. Daylight streamed into the room. "Time to get up and move out," Casey said.

"What's the big hurry?" I grumbled still trying to shake off my nightmare. I staggered to my feet and started pulling clothes out of the dresser drawer. "I have to tell you about this dream..."

Casey interrupted me. "Over breakfast, okay? We got cheated out of a lot of time here by the whole Fifi/Georges disaster. And there is so much to see."

"When Casey says see, she means shop," Tessa added.

"Damn straight," Casey said. "So move it, you two. There's a cute little café around the corner. Next to the big *supermarche*. Tess and I will be there drinking café and eating croissants. And we won't wait forever."

The two of them checked out their reflections in the mirror, did identical hair fluffs and flounced out of the room.

"What was that?" Chrissie asked.

"I have no idea. I don't suppose you want to hear about my dream."

"Later, baby," Chrissie said. She tripped and fell out of bed --- the sheets tangled around her feet. She sprawled on the floor and giggled as she sniffed. "I think I need a shower. No, I definitely need one. I listen better when I'm clean."

Chrissie extricated herself from her bedding, gathered up her shower things and staggered out of the room.

Still haunted by my vision of Fifi, I wandered to the window and stared out at the street in time to see Casey and Tessa emerge from the hotel and bounce down the street --- the early morning sunlight glinted off one eggplant head and one blonde one.

I sighed again, sank onto my bed and reached for the cell phone Casey left behind. Suddenly I felt the need to hear my husband Scott's voice. I didn't really want to touch off his over-protective gene, but I could at least give him an edited version of our latest adventures. Did he really need to know all about Fifi and Georges? No.

"Hi, Honey," I said when he answered the phone.

"Kate?" Scott's voice was muffled. "Is everything okay? Do you realize what time it is?"

I did a quick mental calculation. It would be --- what --- one a.m. his time. I had kicked off his over-protective gene after all.

"I'm sorry. I totally forgot the time change. I just missed you."

His familiar laugh was reassuring.

"Hurry, Kate," Chrissie said as we rounded the corner. "The girls will have given up on us."

"I know," I said, "but Casey will kill me if I don't have her cell phone. Life would be impossible." I had my head down and was digging through my bag. "I'm sure I put it in here somewhere."

"I don't think she's worrying about her phone," Chrissie said as she grabbed my arm.

"You don't?"

Chrissie jerked her head in the direction of the outdoor cafe a half block away. "Look."

Ah, it was obvious that our tardiness was not presenting a problem. In fact, I suspected that Casey, at least, had totally forgotten our existence. The girls were camped at an outdoor table at *Café Annabelle*. Tessa, her feet propped on a chair, had her nose in her guidebook but Casey --- my formerly heartbroken daughter --- was deep in conversation with an extraordinarily handsome dark-haired man and two adorable little girls at an adjoining table. She looked up as we approached and broke off her conversation to introduce us. "Mom, Aunt Chris, this is Luc." She waved a hand toward the curly-headed blonde children who I guessed to be about four and two. "And his daughters, Noelle and Clarice."

They gazed at us solemnly and trilled in tiny voices, "*Bonjour Madames. Enchante.*" And then went back to smearing strawberry jam first on their croissants and then on their faces.

Their father --- Luc, was it? --- flashed us a Crest white-strip smile. I noticed that one of his front teeth had a tiny chip, but somehow this made his smile even more enchanting than pearly perfection would have. "Excuse please, *Madames*, their mess. I am pleased to meet you," he said.

Chrissie shoved Tessa's feet off the chair and plopped down in it while I sank into one at the opposite side of the table. I gave Casey a questioning look before turning my attention to Noelle and Clarice. I couldn't resist those blonde curls and smudged faces. "*Ca va?*" I said to them as Casey continued to chat with their father.

Even with my limited vocabulary and horrible accent I managed to make small talk with the two little girls. I was disappointed when Luc wiped their faces with a napkin, stood up and took them by the hand. He and Casey exchanged phone numbers and the dreamy look on her face told me how much she had enjoyed this encounter.

"*Au revoir,*" Luc said as he sauntered away. He paused to lean down to listen to something Noelle said and then threw back his head and laughed. The three of them turned to wave at us and then hand-in-hand disappeared around the corner.

Casey sighed as she dragged her attention back to us. Tessa cackled as she said, "And that, ladies and gentleman, was the sight of Lester's tail lights vanishing once and for all into the mist never to be seen or heard from again."

"Lester who?" Casey asked.

"Exactly," her cousin said.

"Is Luc married?" I asked. He was definitely eye candy but I needed to know that he was not part of a matched set.

"No," Casey said. "His wife died a year ago."

Tessa started to giggled again. "Just how did you ferret this out in the few minutes you had to talk to him?"

"I have my ways."

"Are you seeing him again?"

"You bet I am if I get the chance."

Our waitress appeared with two mugs and a pot of coffee and another of steamed milk. She took our order and hurried inside while we poured coffee and milk and settled back to enjoy the activity on the busy street. Groups of elementary school-aged children wearing backpacks streamed by on their way to school. They shared sidewalk space with elderly ladies pulling carts filled with fresh produce from the farmers' market down the street and suit-clad businessmen racing by with baguettes tucked under their arms. A fascinating scene.

As the river of pedestrians eddied around us, we sipped coffee and nibbled croissants. It was a sparkling morning --- sun glinted off the sidewalk and the temperature edged up. I shrugged out of my denim jacket and hung it on the back of my chair --- the sun on my arms warm and inviting.

"So," Chrissie said. "What's our plan for today?"

"I vote for Old Town," Tessa said.

"I second that," Casey said.

Old Town, or *Vieux Nice*, is a maze of winding cobblestoned streets surrounding a central plaza. It offers everything any self-respecting tourist could want. Shops display a variety of goods from wine and gourmet goodies to trendy clothing to jewelry to cheese and olive oil. Captivated we lost ourselves in the twisty maze of streets shaded from the sun by the ancient buildings. Attractive cafés and bars line the congested walkways where tourists and locals mingle. It took some serious head swiveling on our parts in order not to miss a single bit of the action.

Tessa consulted her guidebook and then led us to the *Cours Saleya* where a food and flower market was in progress. We wandered through the plaza stopping to check out various stalls featuring sausages or bread or olive oil or chocolate. Huge arrangements of brightly colored flowers were available at other stalls and the faint aroma of lavender floated in the air.

We spent the entire morning exploring Old Nice. No matter which direction we turned there was yet another shop or stall too inviting to miss. Finally, laden with bags and packages, we stopped to rest in one of the many open plazas. Perched on the edge of a water fountain, we compared bargains.

Tessa stuffed a swirling skirt in shades of orange back into its bag and stretched. "This has been awesome, but I think I've had enough retail therapy for the moment."

Casey looked up from pawing through her own bags. "Any suggestions, then, Tess?"

"I think we should go back to the *Promenade* and eat lunch at one of those cute places right on the beach. I love Old Town, but I feel sand and sea luring me. I hear the waves calling my name. Tess--a. Oh, Tess--a, come to me."

"Right," Casey said, "and when Tessa is called, the rest of us must follow."

As we emerged from the shadows of Old Town I was momentarily blinded by the glare of the sun and stumbled into a crowd of tourists heading in the opposite direction. One super-sized woman knocked my bags out of my hand and we both scrambled to retrieve my scattered purchases. "*Merci,*" I said as she handed me a bag and then hurried after her friends.

I started to say more, but she disappeared around the corner before I could do so. I shrugged and rejoined my family as the growling in our stomachs urged us down the cobblestones toward a rendezvous with lunch. Before we reached the *Promenade*, though, we were waylaid by the view of the Marina spread out below us. Yachts of all sizes bobbed on the swells and sunlight sparkled across the water. A big cruise ship was preparing to leave port and trucks and vans lined up to load supplies. We watched the activity in silence for a few minutes. Tessa waved her arm --- a sweeping gesture that took in the entire waterfront. "Now, that's what I'm talking about," she exclaimed.

When we started to melt in the hot sun, we dragged ourselves away from the fascinating scene and moseyed down the walkway. We vetoed several beachfront restaurants before settling on *Café de la Mer* and descending the white-painted cement steps to the entrance. The maitre d' showed us to a glass-topped table at the edge of the sand protected by a green and white striped umbrella. We sank into our chairs and sighed with contentment as we studied the panorama spread before us. The sun was bright against a cloudless blue sky melding into an aquamarine sea. The cruise ship we had seen earlier steamed past and a few power boats flirted in its wake. A silver airplane split the sky with a roar and we stared until it disappeared into the atmosphere.

I kicked off my flip flops and leaned back in my chair. I could feel myself relaxing. I glanced around to see if there were any suspicious types lurking but everyone seemed perfectly unthreatening. Whew. The waiter who poured water and brought us a basket of sliced baguettes was amicable and the few other patrons paid us no attention.

"Okay, gang," Tessa said. "Is this perfect or what?"

No argument there. It was perfect. We ordered lunch --- fresh tomato, basil and mozzarella salad and *omelettes* with *pommes frites*. Chrissie looked over at me and I nodded. "Definitely," I said to her. And she ordered a *pichet of vin blanc*. It was a wine kind of a day. But then, I guess, every day is a wine kind of a day when you're on vacation in Nice.

As we waited for the waiter to bring our wine, three of us discussed our plans for the afternoon. "I'd like to check out some of the galleries," Casey said. "I hear there's a great one for photography."

"Fantastic," I agreed.

"Is that okay with you, Tessa?" Chrissie asked and Tessa, who was crunching on a crusty baguette and staring dreamily at the beach, glanced up. "I have a better idea. Let's go to the beach."

Casey followed Tessa's gaze and started shaking her head. "You're insane, Tessa. You just want to practice for your new profession. Stripping."

I turned to see what the girls were looking at. A group of four women had staked out space on the rocky beach a few yards from our table. A blonde of indeterminate age had removed her top and stood, back arched and hands on her hips, her perky breasts pointing confidently at the cruise ship passing by. The others spread their towels under the shade of a red, white and yellow striped umbrella. All were topless. Two were about Chrissie's and my age and apparently unconcerned about revealing their "ancient" breasts.

"I'm not stripping," Tessa objected. "But that looks like fun."

"Nope, no way," Casey said.

"Aw, come on, Case. Girls just wanna have fun."

"My girls are perfectly happy appropriately covered," Casey said, "but I'll come to the beach with you to keep an eye on *your* assets."

"What about you?" Chrissie said to me.

"I wouldn't miss this for all the opals in Australia," I answered.

An hour later the four of us minced single file across the rocky expanse of beach not far from the *Café de la Mer*. We found the perfect spot close to the water and the girls wasted no time in spreading out the straw beach mats they bought from a seaside vendor. Chrissie and I settled nearby under an umbrella we rented from a tanned beach boy.

As I spread sunblock over my arms and chest I noticed a pair of deeply tanned and very toned men of about 40 stretched out in beach chairs a few yards away. The pair wore huge dark sunglasses and not much more. Both sported those Speedo-type suits that are little more than a nylon loin-cloth --- one in red and the other in a bright yellow. I ogled them for a moment before I tore my gaze away --- my cheeks hot with embarrassment. Had I turned into a middle-aged voyeur? Oh, God.

Just then the one in yellow tipped his sunglasses up on his forehead and grinned in my direction and I was struck by a bolt of recognition. The man from the beach the night before --- the one who had tipped his hat to me. He must be our bodyguard. I looked over at Tessa who was at that moment unclasping her bikini top. She pulled it off and tossed it onto the sand. Yellow loin-cloth winked at me. If he was our bodyguard he was obviously putting way too much emphasis on the *body* part of bodyguard. And enjoying it way too much.

I scowled at him.

Tessa stood over Casey and stared down at her while Casey stared back.

Finally Tessa said, "I dare you, Casey."

In our family challenges are made to be met and Casey was genetically unable to refuse this one. The gauntlet, or in this case, the bikini top, had been thrown down.

"Oh, what the hell," Casey said. She unclasped her top and flipped it in the general direction of her beach bag. "Now are you satisfied, Tessa?"

Casey turned over on her stomach and buried her face in her hands. The two loin cloth clad bodyguards watched unapologetically --- admiration etched on their faces. I glared at them. This was too much.

A short time later I had drifted into a half dose when Chrissie poked me with a fingernail. I tried to ignore her, but she poked me more insistently. "Yes," I drawled without moving a muscle.

"You need to see that woman over there. I'll bet she's Mom's age."

I lifted my head and shaded my eyes to see the woman Chrissie was indicating. She wasn't quite Mom's age, but close. She was sitting on her straw mat facing the sea, her knees bent and her arms looped around them and carrying on a conversation with a gentleman in a baggy swimsuit --- gesturing and laughing. But what Chrissie wanted me to see was that the woman was topless and, obviously, completely unselfconscious about it. What confidence.

I rolled over to lie on my back. "I think she's really bold."

Chrissie didn't say anything --- her eyes glued to the waves washing onto the beach. Minutes passed and then she removed her sunglasses and faced me. "Kate," she began.

I didn't have to hear the words. I knew. "Don't say it," I said. "Please don't."

Chrissie studied me solemnly for a few seconds. Then she grinned. Smugly, I thought. "I dare you."

Live by the dare, die by the dare. I didn't have a choice. A lifetime of accepting her challenges kicked in. Like Casey before me, I said, "What the hell."

We sat up and exchanged lingering looks. Then we pulled our tops over our heads and threw caution, as well as our swimsuit tops, to the wind. Half-naked we grinned at each other in triumph. The breeze felt wonderful on my bare breasts. I have never felt as liberated as I did at that moment. Which was a good thing, because I have never felt as embarrassed as I did a few seconds later. Suddenly I wished a random tsunami would wash me out to sea and I flopped onto my stomach to hide my nudity. Too late. Yellow loin cloth had witnessed the entire display. I moaned. Then before I could bury my head in the sand --- literally --- he once again removed his mirrored glasses, winked and gave me two thumbs up. Seriously. What kind bodyguards were these guys? Or were they guarding us at all? Maybe they were bad guys. Leering bad guys.

"I think I'm going to die," I said to my sister.

Chapter 17

"Let's do scissors, stone or paper for the first shower," I said to Chrissie as I tossed my beach bag onto my bed.

I did scissors. She did stone. And she grabbed her shower stuff and vanished into the bathroom across the hall.

I shoved aside my beach bag and the accumulated plastic bags from our morning shopping spree to make space and sank onto my bed. I kicked off my flip flops and fell backwards against the pillows. Sweaty and sticky with the remnants of sunblock and sand, I craved a shower the way a depressed woman craves chocolate. Patience, Kate, I counseled myself.

While I waited for my turn in the shower I upended the shopping bags onto the bed and began to sift through my bounty. I held up a frothy white top edged with glitzy rhinestones. Definitely a bargain. A pair of sparkly flip flops. Couldn't pass those up. A denim skirt for only five Euros? Who could say no to that? I folded a scarf in shades of ocean blues and put it aside. Then I fingered my final prize --- another scarf, this one in shades of hot pink and orange. I looped it around my neck and then hopped up so I could admire myself in the mirror. Perfect. I twirled around to scoop up the white top and --- froze. I blinked and then rubbed my eyes. It couldn't be. Too much sun. I must be having sunstroke. Or hallucinating. For --- in the center of the bed, just peeking out from under the blue scarf was --- I must be imagining it --- *Fifi's skull and crossbones charm bracelet.*

I couldn't move. I was paralyzed. I couldn't take my eyes off the bracelet. How did it get there? Was it Fifi? It couldn't have been. She was in a hospital bed in Paris. Wasn't she? Who put it on my bed? Why? When? I was so mesmerized by the bracelet that I didn't hear Chrissie return from her shower until she tapped me on the arm.

"Kate?" she said. "What are you looking at?"

I jumped and let out a tiny scream. I pointed at the bracelet.

"I know," Chrissie said, "I wish I had gotten one of those scarves...."

I shook my head. "Not the scarf. That...." My finger trembled as I pointed at the bracelet.

"This?" Chrissie reached around me and snatched the bracelet off the bed and held it up to examine it. "You put Mom's charm on a bracelet. That's a unique gift."

I shook my head and backed away from Chrissie's hand. I was having a hard time forcing words through my frozen lips. "No. I didn't. Do it."

Chrissie's gaze swung from me to the bracelet and back. "You didn't what?"

"Put the bracelet there. Or the charm."

Chrissie stared at me. "Explain your over-the-top freakiness, please. You look like you've seen a ghost."

"Maybe. I found that bracelet lying on my bed. I don't know how it got there." I paused. "Or why."

Chrissie's confusion morphed into comprehension as it dawned on her what I was saying. "It magically appeared?"

I nodded. "I don't know if it was on the bed already or in one of my bags. I'm not sure which is a scarier thought. Either someone has been in our room or someone has been following me and dropping things in my bags."

"But why?"

"As a warning?"

"I suppose. But a warning about what? Over-indulgent shopping habits?" Chrissie shrugged. "Of which we are guilty."

"Don't be stupid. Of course, not. Think about this. First a skull and crossbones charm shows up in Mom's ice cream. Then we find Fifi bleeding all over your precious jacket and what is she wearing?"

Chrissie turned white. "A bracelet just like this one."

"She warned me to beware."

"And now this?"

"It wasn't some random thing," I said. "Someone is trying to tell us something. But what?"

"What did Mom do with that charm she found?" Chrissie asked.

"I'm not sure," I said. "I think she kept it. Why?"

"Because," Chrissie said and her lips trembled, "we haven't talked to her since we left Paris."

My heart started to beat faster and I lunged for the door. "Mom. I'm calling her right now. I'll get Casey's cell phone."

We had been trying to reach her all afternoon with no luck. Where on earth could she and Bobby be? I pounded on the door to the girls' room. "Casey," I called, "I need your cell."

Casey popped open the door and silently handed me the phone. With it in hand, I rushed back to Chrissie who hadn't moved. The girls followed me.

I punched in the number I had by now committed to memory. I listened to it ring and was about to disconnect when I was startled to hear Bobby's deep baritone. "Hello?"

"Bobby?"

"Ach, yes, this is Bobby. Who is calling?" Bobby sounded gruff and impatient --- quite unlike the genial man who had been our companion in Paris.

"This is Kate Kelly. I'm Laura Stevens daughter. Remember?"

"Oh, of course I remember you, Kate," Bobby said in a tone only marginally more friendly than before. "What can I do for you?"

"Well, we haven't heard from either of you since we left Paris and we wanted to find out how things are going and how Mom is."

"Your mother is just super," Bobby said. "Now if that's all I'll just be getting on..."

"Bobby," I interrupted before he could hang up on me. "I'd like to speak to my mother."

There was a long silence and I thought he had hung up. Finally, he said, "Your mother is in the shower, I believe. She can't come to the phone right now."

"Oh. Well, would you please have her call Casey's cell when she's available? We'd like to hear from her."

Bobby cleared his throat and then he (reluctantly, I thought) said, "I'll tell her you called. Maybe she can call back when she gets a minute. She and Agnes have gone out for the day, so I don't know when she might be free."

"But," I began.

Bobby cut in. "Not to worry." And severed the connection.

"That was odd," I said.

I related Bobby's end of the conversation to them and concluded, "He said she was in the shower and then he said she was out with Agnes. Something weird is going on. Bobby didn't sound like himself at all."

Chrissie looked as concerned as I felt. "But he said she was okay, didn't he? And that she was just out with Agnes?"

"Who's Agnes?" Casey wanted to know.

"Good question," I said. "A very good question."

I fought the growing unease that began in my stomach and radiated outward. Everything is good, I scolded myself.

Casey patted my hand. "I'm sure Nonny is fine."

Tessa nodded vigorously --- blonde hair swinging. "Nonny is just out with Agnes." A beat of silence. "Whoever she might be."

"Yeah," Chrissie added in the doomsday tone of a newscaster announcing an impending disaster. "She's either out with the mysterious Agnes or taking the longest shower known to woman. We'll have to keep calling until we reach her."

I dragged myself to my feet. "I don't know what we can do right this minute. How about getting some dinner?"

"I suppose," Chrissie said. "It's not very productive to sit here obsessing about her."

After a subdued meal at an outdoor table in the courtyard of an Old Nice café, Casey and Tessa excused themselves. The gorgeous Luc, the young father Casey had chatted up at breakfast, had called earlier and asked if Casey and Tessa would like to go out for a drink and a bit of gambling. Casey quickly accepted and Tessa, not wanting to miss a party, decided to tag along.

"Luc is bringing a friend," Casey winked. "He can be your date, Tess."

"Because I can't get one on my own?"

"Did I say that?"

"You didn't have to."

"Go. Don't worry about us. Have fun." Chrissie and I hugged each of them.

"Be careful," I added, "you don't know these guys at all."

They laughed, gave us the hand on hip accompanied by the flip of the hair. "Don't worry, Mom," each said. "We'll be fine."

As we watched our daughters hurry down the street, I turned to my sister. "Why is it that everyone is partying but us? It's our birthday."

"Don't whine. It's unattractive," Chrissie chided me. "Actually, this is what I had in mind when we decided to take this trip. The two of us hanging out at cute cafés, soaking up atmosphere."

"Finding suitcases of money and stumbling over bodies." I stretched and let my gaze take in the cobblestoned street, the ancient buildings, the charming shops. "You're right. What was I thinking? This is fabulous."

We clinked our coffee cups together.

"To us," I toasted.

"To the big ..."

"Do not say it." I glared at her. "Don't we have enough to worry about without bringing up our ages?"

We high-fived each other sedately --- befitting our advanced years.

We paid the bill and wandered through the streets of Old Nice before we emerged onto the *Promenade.* It was another beautiful evening --- balmy with a soft breeze ruffling the umbrellas on the vendors' carts. Most of the tourists and half the population of Nice were out enjoying it. I would have been enjoying it too but I couldn't quell the rising panic I felt when I thought of my sweet --- maybe not so innocent --- mother in the clutches of scheming Baron Bobby Hot Legs. My thoughts kept returning to my nightmares.

I led the way with Chrissie limping in my wake and suddenly she collapsed onto one of the benches facing the sea. She kicked off her shoes and rubbed her feet. "I swear to God that the next time I go anywhere I'm bringing only sensible shoes. To heck with style. Look at these blisters."

I dropped onto the bench next to her and sank deeper into my gloomy meditation.

For a few minutes neither of us said anything. Chrissie massaged her damaged feet and I watched the waves curl onto the shore. Finally, she said, "Kate, I've been thinking."

"Whoa. That could be dangerous."

"No. I mean it. Do you remember the day we had drinks with Fifi and Georges and he explained how they got into the whole bag exchange fiasco?"

"Sure. What about it?"

"Do you happen to remember the name of his manager? The one who booked them on their ill-fated tour of the U.S. and hooked them up with the guys who paid them to smuggle in a bag of money?"

"I haven't a clue. Why?"

"I'm thinking..." Chrissie hesitated, wrinkling her nose. "No, I'm sure Georges said his name was Luc."

"So?"

"So, what was the name of the young father that Casey picked up at breakfast? The one she's out with tonight. Wasn't it Luc?"

The name smacked me --- a fist to my stomach. I sucked in a deep breath and let it out with a whoosh. I stared at Chrissie. She stared back. I closed my eyes and pictured the gorgeous Frenchman with close-cropped dark hair and easy smile --- bookended by a pair of blonde cherubs. Were they even his daughters? Or loaner children he borrowed to lure my innocent (oh, okay, maybe not so innocent) daughter into the clutches of the villains? Don't be stupid. I gave myself a mental slap.

"Must be a coincidence. I mean Luc is a fairly common name in France. I'll bet there are a million Lucs."

"Take your head out of the Seine, sweetie."

"But he seemed perfectly nice," I said.

"Uh, huh," Chrissie said. "Too convenient if you ask me."

"So, what are you proposing we do? Tessa and Casey are out with this guy. Should we try to find them? Call the police? Inspector Bouchard claimed we have police protection while we're here."

Chrissie continued to knead her feet. "Let's not panic. There's probably nothing to worry about. Before we call the gendarmes let's go to the casino and see if we can 'accidentally' run into them?"

I bounced to my feet. "Let's go."

Chrissie gingerly stuffed her feet into her shoes. "I don't suppose you have a band-aid."

I rummaged in my bag, pulled out my emergency supply kit and handed one to her. "At your service. Problem solved."

"I sure hope the rest of our problems are solved as easily," she said as she stuck the band-aid to her foot.

The *Casino de la Mer*, across from the *Promenade des Anglais*, was lit up as if for a movie premier. Spotlights swept over the white facade and illuminated the sidewalk and palm trees lining it. Limos pulled up in front to disperse bejeweled women in evening gowns escorted by tuxedo-clad men. Only the red carpet was missing.

Inside the high-ceilinged foyer, elegant ladies and gentlemen mingled with tourists wearing jeans or shorts and flip flops. An eclectic crowd. Little old ladies clutching huge handbags brushed elbows with greasy-haired men in tight pants. Chrissie and I peered into the large room beyond the foyer. Beneath a hanging fog of cigarette smoke we could see the gaming tables --- an odd assortment of gamblers crowded around each one.

"Are you sure this is the casino they were planning to visit?" I asked.

Chrissie swiveled her head in every direction. "This is the one Tessa mentioned."

"Even if the girls are here, I don't think we have much chance of finding them."

The crowd shifted and moved under the cloud of smoke and we circled the room, stopping to watch the action at the craps tables, the roulette wheels, the poker and dice games. I halted in front of a bank of slot machines.

"Slots," I said. "I love to play the slots. How much do they take do you think?"

"Looks like a Euro, but we're not here to lose our money."

"Who says we can't profit from the experience?" I said and headed for the change window to buy tokens for the greedy machines.

I found a machine that gave off lucky vibes to me and began to feed tokens into it while Chrissie watched over my shoulder. A cocktail waitress offered us free glasses of champagne and we happily accepted. I managed to run up a small profit and was in the process of losing it again when Chrissie nudged me. "Over there."

I dragged my attention away from the hungry machine and looked in the direction Chrissie indicated. Casey. Striding toward us.

"Mother, Aunt Chris," Casey called. "What are you two doing here?

"Losing your inheritance, of course," Chrissie said. "Your mother is addicted to slots."

"Uh, huh," Casey said in a voice laced with skepticism.

I ran out of tokens to plug into the machine and abandoned it. I hugged my daughter. "We didn't have anything else to do, so we decided to check out the casino scene."

"Right. You just happened to show up at the very casino where Tessa and I are with Luc and his friend? Are you sure you aren't checking on us not the casino?"

Chrissie and I exchanged looks. Busted.

"I saw that look," Casey said. "You two are so obvious."

Before I could attempt a feeble explanation we were interrupted by Tessa leading the gorgeous Luc and his equally attractive friend toward us.

"Well," Casey said. "As long as you're here, I might as well introduce you. You remember Luc from the café this morning. And this is his friend, Jean Paul. And these two..." She paused and grinned at us. "Are my mother, Kate Kelly, and her twin, Tessa's mom, Christine Montgomery. Who just happened, oddly enough, to come to this particular casino."

Tessa laughed. "Amazing coincidence."

Both young men said, and with proper deference, "*Enchante Madames.*" The gorgeous Luc kissed each of our hands in turn. He certainly had a corner on the charm market.

"We were just going to the bar for drinks," Luc said. "We would be so pleased if you would join us."

"I'm sure they have better things to do, Luc. They can't..." Casey began.

But I interrupted her. "We'd love to." The better to uncover your secrets, my dear.

The bar was located in a separate room adjacent to the foyer. Six stools were tucked under the huge gleaming mahogany bar --- three small tables were scattered across the room with a couple of chairs pulled up to each. Limited seating, I deduced, to discourage patrons from loitering in the bar when they could be losing money gambling. The room was almost deserted so we snared stools at the bar, making small talk as we settled ourselves. We ordered drinks and then exchanged "now what?" looks.

"Jean Paul is a lawyer," Tessa said to Chrissie. "Isn't that ironic?"

"Oh, very," Chrissie said. She put her elbows on the bar and leaned closer to Tessa and Jean Paul. The better to interrogate him. "What type of law do you practice, Jean Paul?"

The three of them quickly became immersed in an animated discussion, presumably about law and lawyers. I toyed with my wine glass and gazed around at the huge crystal chandeliers overhead and the massive pieces of artwork adorning the walls. I watched the gorgeous Luc as he chatted with Casey. No alarm bells sounded in my overprotective brain. Luc laughed easily and often --- seemingly enjoying his conversation with Casey. They conversed in French so it was impossible for me to eavesdrop as much as I wanted. I caught a word here and there, but not enough to be helpful. Finally Luc excused himself to call the babysitter watching his daughters. Seriously. Daughters? Casey hopped off her perch. "I'm going to the restroom, Mom. Come with me." It was an order not a request.

As soon as the restroom door closed behind us, Casey put her hands on her hips. "So, what's really going on? I've been on my own for years and you haven't felt it necessary to check up on me. What aren't you telling me?"

"You're right," I said. And I launched into an explanation of our suspicions that the Luc who was Fifi and George's agent and the gorgeous Luc who had introduced himself to Casey at the café were one and the same. That perhaps his motives were not pure and innocent. That perhaps he was the one who was hunting for the bag of cash Inspector Bouchard confiscated from us.

"But," I concluded, "he seems perfectly nice. There must be millions of Lucs in France. I'm sure it's a huge coincidence."

Casey had remained silent throughout my account. She leaned over the sink --- took out her make-up bag and began to apply mascara. She carefully reapplied her lip gloss, taking an inordinate amount of time. That done, she checked her reflection one last time and faced me. "Maybe it's not."

"Not what?"

"A coincidence. Luc does manage groups. He told me that. His sister usually babysits the girls when he's on the road --- which is a lot. You and Aunt Chrissie failed to mention that Georges' manager was named Luc."

"Didn't seem important at the time. I had completely forgotten it until Chrissie mentioned it tonight."

Casey stroked her chin. "Well, then, I'll just have to see what I can find out from him. I'm totally up for being Mata Hari."

"Oh, no, you aren't," I protested. "If he's after the money, it's too dangerous. I don't want you to hang out with a criminal. Especially one who might be a murderer."

"I'm a big girl. Don't worry."

I tried to talk her out of it, but I've never had much luck stopping Casey when she's determined. So, I gave in. "I was going to ask for your cell phone, but now I don't want you to be without it. If there's trouble you can call for help. But maybe I'll borrow it for a second to call Bobby's phone again."

While Casey returned to the bar to begin her covert spying operation, I took her phone outside to make one last attempt to reach Mom. The continued silence from Scotland made me nervous. I shifted from one foot to the other as I stood on the sidewalk in front of the casino and dialed Bobby's cell phone number for what seemed like the millionth time. The beautiful people milled around me. I listened to the ringing. Where could Mom be? What was Bobby up to? Still no answer. Just voicemail. I left a terse message. "We are extremely worried. Have my mother call us. If we don't hear from her by tomorrow, I'm going to be forced to call the police." Maybe that would get some action.

When I returned to the bar, Luc was paying the bill and the four young people were preparing their assault on the gaming tables. Tessa and Jean Paul were obviously enjoying each other's company and Luc had a possessive hand on Casey's shoulder. "Well, have fun, you two," Chrissie said in a phony chipper voice.

"Are you sure you don't want to come back to the hotel with us?" I asked. "It's late."

"Mom, it's nine-thirty. Only old people retire at this time of night. We'll be fine," Casey said.

I shrugged and with one final worried look over my shoulder at my daughter and the gorgeous Luc, I marched out of the casino with my sister trailing me.

As soon as we stepped outside, Chrissie stopped. "Nice try. But really? It's late? Couldn't you have thought of something more clever?"

"My brain is fried. And I don't like leaving them with those guys." I repeated the conversation I had with Casey in the restroom.

"Oh. My. God." Chrissie looked ready to storm back inside to drag the girls out.

"Chrissie. Stop. You know Casey. We'd have a huge battle if we tried to stop them. I'm telling myself to have faith that they can take care of themselves."

"Good luck with that."

The two of us shuffled back to the hotel, each mired in dismal thoughts of murder, mayhem and possible abduction. Was Luc a dangerous felon? Had our mother fallen prey to a scheming Scot and hustled into a hasty marriage? Who was behind the bag switch? Would we ever have answers and be safe again?

191

Chapter 18

I spent the night like a turkey burger on the grill --- flipping from one side to another with heat searing my backside. Between bouts of flipping I lay on my back --- eyes wide open staring at the ceiling, listening futilely for the sound of Casey and Tessa returning from their dates. I heard laughter and talking coming from the sidewalk beneath our windows, the roar of a motorcycle, distant church bells chiming each hour. I drifted off from sheer exhaustion a couple of times only to be startled into wakefulness by a sneeze from the room across the hall or a breeze rattling the window blinds. At each noise my eyes flew open and I sat bolt upright holding my breath. And each time I was disappointed. Where were they? I glanced at Chrissie who had her back to me. I sighed noisily hoping she would turn over and we could hash this out, but she remained silent. Finally, at just past five-thirty in the morning, I gave up and tossed aside the bedcovers that were in total disarray from all my thrashing. I crept across the room to gather up my shower things and tiptoed toward the door. Just inside the door my toes crinkled a piece of folded hotel stationery. I snatched it up and unfolded, to my huge relief, a note in Casey's loopy handwriting. I felt my lips turn up into a grin before I even read the note. They were safe. Thank God.

"Mom ... I was right. Luc does manage groups. I didn't mention Georges, but it's possible they have a connection. Luc has tickets to a movie premier in Cannes at the Film Festival this afternoon. Tess and I are going. You guys are invited too. Meet us at 'our' café at eight. Je t'aime. Casey."

Clutching the note I flew across the room and bounced on Chrissie's bed. She immediately sat up. "What's wrong?"

"I knew you were awake," I said.

"Like I could sleep knowing the girls were out with God knows what kind of people."

I waved the note under her nose. "They're fine. But we still don't know Luc's relationship to Georges and Fifi."

She read the note and then winked. "You know what this means, don't you?"

"Cannes Film Festival?"

She nodded.

"Sleuthing at the Cannes Film Festival?"

She nodded again.

"Oh, my God, what will we wear?"

By eight o'clock we had considered and rejected dozens of possibilities from our travel-worn and rumpled wardrobes. Finally, hoping we had achieved just the right note of understated class we poised near the door in pencil skirts, loose sleeveless tops and our new Paris leather jackets. Chrissie bent to fasten the buckle on her low-heeled sandal. "Are you ready to mingle with celebrities?"

"I am," I said and swung open the door to the hall. "*Bonjour*, Hollywood stars."

"And hello to you." Tessa and Casey were poised to knock on our door. "You two look fantastic," Tessa said as she looked us up and down.

"Totally," Casey agreed.

With the double daughter stamp of approval, Chrissie and I felt ready to tackle anything. At least our outfits didn't scream tacky tourist. Casey and Tessa looked especially beautiful, I thought --- both similarly attired in short skirts, loose halter tops and cropped sweaters. Maybe it was motherly pride, but I couldn't help thinking they would attract attention and admiration from the celebrity types in Cannes.

Luc was already at the café with his daughters --- or perhaps faux daughters --- when we arrived. He stood as we approached. "My sister is ill and I couldn't find a babysitter. I hope you don't mind that I brought the girls."

The two little girls were seated at the round table sipping orange juice through straws. They stared at us with unblinking blue eyes. "*Bonjour, Madames,*" the older one said politely. The younger girl just watched us solemnly.

"Of course, not," I said to Luc. "It was so kind of you to include my sister and me in your plans. The girls are a bonus."

Casey knelt so that she was on the same level as the children and drew them into a conversation. Luc smiled and seemed to relax.

"*Merci,*" he said. "I hope they won't be any bother."

By the time we finished breakfast, Casey and the little girls were fast friends. The older one, Noelle, paraded her dolls for Casey's approval and the little one, Clarice, fed her bits of croissant smeared with jam. With the girls occupied, Luc leaned back and chatted easily with the rest of us. I couldn't find anything threatening about him. Maybe the name and the job were a coincidence after all.

I slipped into sleuth-mode --- channeling Stephanie Plum. Welcome to my parlor said the spider to the fly. "So, Luc," I said, "what do you do for a living?"

He was happy to elaborate. "My job of managing entertainers, Madame Kelly, gives me much traveling. I am so fortunate that after Annalise died, my sister was able to take charge of my girls." A shadow passed over his face at the mention of his dead wife. "I don't know what I would do without her."

I caught Chrissie's eye. I knew she was thinking the same thing I was. What a pleasant young man. He couldn't possibly be involved in anything illegal. I liked Luc. I didn't want him to be a criminal.

Luc paid the bill over our protests and Casey wiped the girls' faces and clasped their hands to escort them to the *toilette*. Casey and Luc almost looked like a couple which gave me a pang of concern. A French husband was not something I had envisioned for my daughter. But then, I figured, it's way too soon to be worrying about that.

Casey returned with the girls and Luc bent down to speak to them. Noelle tugged on his hand and he smoothed her blonde curls. "The girls were disappointed to miss the picnic my sister had planned for them so I promised we could stop in Antibes at Marineland. It's on the way to Cannes and the showing isn't until later this afternoon. I hope you won't mind."

"I've always loved dolphins," Casey said. Clarice tugged on her skirt and she grinned down at her. "I can't think of a better way to start our day."

The rest of us agreed. Luc appeared relieved at our acceptance and led the way to his mini-van parked around the corner.

The Marineland Park in Antibes was large, but not especially well-kept. The wood benches were smoothed from years of use and weeds poked up in the numerous cracks in the asphalt walkways. The ticket agent gave us maps of the park but they weren't necessary. Noelle and Clarice knew exactly where they wanted to go and skipped toward the dolphin pool. Holding hands with Casey and Tessa, the little girls pointed at various landmarks and chattered non-stop. Chrissie and I trailed behind with Luc.

The dolphin arena was empty since it was nearly 25 minutes until showtime. We easily found good seats in the front row on the tiered cement steps.

"I know it's early," Luc said, "but we always come to the dolphins first. They won't have it any other way."

"Don't worry," I said. "We're enjoying ourselves."

A clown in baggy pants and jacket set up in front of the pool and entertained the early comers by making balloon animals. Casey turned to Luc. "Do you mind if we take the girls down to see the balloon guy?"

"*Si'l te plait, Papa*," Noelle begged.

Luc shook his head. "I don't think....," he began and Clarice wrapped herself around his leg and stared at him with pleading blue eyes. "Oh, all right." He relented and Casey and Tessa and the little girls picked their way down the steps toward the clown. Luc started to follow them and then sank back onto the bench. "I have a hard time letting them go."

"They'll be fine," I assured him. "Casey and Tessa will look after them."

"It's not that," Luc said. He hesitated before he spoke again. "Perhaps I should explain. Otherwise you will think I am the overprotective father."

Chrissie and I waited while he gathered his thoughts.

"I have spent the last year fighting not to lose my daughters as well as Annalise. My wife," he said. "She was killed by a drunk driver just over a year ago. She had just dropped the girls off at her parents' home and was on her way to the school where she was a teacher."

He swiped at his eyes with the back of his hand and continued in a shaky voice. "I was in the *Etats-Unis* ... the states ... for my job when the accident happened. My in-laws tried for hours to reach me. By the time they found me Annalise was dead. They have never forgiven me for that."

I patted his arm --- unable to think of anything to say.

"So, by the time I am able to get back to France, Annalise's parents have found a lawyer and started to fight for custody of the girls. They claimed that if I had not been traveling, Annalise would not have been on the road that morning. They claimed I was not a fit parent since my job takes me out of France so often. They said they could provide a more stable and comfortable home for my daughters.

"I had to hire a lawyer. Jean Paul. Do you remember him from last night?"

We nodded.

"The judge is much impressed with the argument of my in-laws. He was becoming convinced I could not be a father. Not with the job I do. So I did what I must. I told him I would quit my job. I would not travel. I would stay in Nice and be a full time parent to Noelle and Clarice.

"Finally after many months I was awarded custody. The girls' grandparents have much visitation, but my daughters live with me. I am still afraid that

Annalise's parents will --- how do you say it --- kidnap? --- the girls. I am not trusting where they are concerned."

During this discourse Luc had not taken his eyes from his daughters who were giggling as the balloon man twisted animal shapes for them. I'm always a sucker for a sad story and unshed tears clogged my throat as I thought about Luc's ordeal.

"Do you know what is *ironique*?" he asked. "Annalise always wanted me to quit the traveling. She wanted me to stay home with her and our daughters. Now I am finally doing that and she is not here."

Chrissie sniffed and I fished two tissues out of my bag and handed her one. The three of us sat in mournful silence until the little girls and Casey and Tessa clambered back to our seats. The girls climbed into Luc's lap and pummeled him with the balloon animals.

"*Regarde, Papa*," Noelle chimed. "*Un chien.*"

Luc hugged her and laughed. "*Tres bien, ma petite.*"

The show began and diverted our attention from any lingering sad thoughts. The dolphins were cute and funny and performed adorably. The girls giggled and squealed with delight. Three dolphins somersaulted into the air and dove into the pool with a huge splash that sent water cascading over us. Those front row seats didn't seem so enviable at that moment. But the girls thought this was hysterical and didn't mind a bit being drenched.

Still dripping we followed the girls to the killer whale performance and from there to the penguin pool. We tagged after them until Luc glanced at his watch and said, "We'd better head for Cannes. We don't want to miss the premier."

As we passed a vendor's cart on our way out of the park, Noelle tugged on Luc's hand. "Hot dog?"

"The girls always want hot dogs when we come here," he said. "But if you prefer a more elegant luncheon we can eat in Cannes."

The girls pleading looks decided us. "I'd love to eat here," Casey said. "But I'll have a crepe."

A short time later we perched at a picnic table shaded by a rainbow striped umbrella and devoured crepes while the girls gobbled hot dogs, *pommes frites* and fruit juice. The sun shone on our heads and, at that moment, I couldn't think of a place I would rather be. The girls were precious and I believed Luc's story. I was convinced that he was exactly what he appeared to be --- a charming young father who had suffered an appalling tragedy.

Chapter 19

"I can't believe I'm in Cannes," Tessa said as we gazed up and down the busy street lined with hotels, shops and casinos, "during the Film Festival. Is that George Clooney? I think it is. Oh-my-god."

"I think you're right, Tess," Casey said. "Go ask for his autograph."

Luc put a restraining hand on Casey's arm. "Ground rules here, ladies. No asking for autographs. No taking photos. No bothering anyone. It is not permitted."

"Of course, not," I said. "We would never...." But I knew that we could and would if given half a chance.

On the beach across the street from us waves curled onto the sugary sand. It was amazing. Cannes.

Luc pulled an envelope from his pocket and handed it to Casey. "Here are the tickets to the premier. I will watch Noelle and Clarice while the four of you go to the movie."

"Oh, no," I objected. "We can't take the tickets. Luc, you need to go."

"*Non, Madame*," he argued. "I cannot leave my daughters and the tickets must not be wasted. You must go."

"We would love to babysit the girls," Chrissie said.

"And Luc you might meet someone who can help you find a job."

"Oh, you are right. *Merci*. It is too kind of you."

He appeared to be reconsidering when Noelle pointed to the beach and whispered in his ear. "They want to go to the beach," Luc explained. "And you obviously aren't dressed for that." He gave us an appraising look.

Our pencil skirts and leather jackets while classy and chic were definitely not beach attire. There was an easy answer. Shopping.

Chrissie and I left Tessa and Casey and Luc and his little girls relaxing on one of the benches lining the sidewalk while we ducked into a shop to buy something more appropriate for the beach. In the back of the shop we found two large round racks filled with swimsuits in a variety of colors and fabrics. As I combed through the merchandise, though, I realized there was a problem. I pulled out a suit supposedly in my size and held it up to examine it. I don't think there was enough fabric in it to make a decent potholder.

"Chrissie," I said, clutching the hanger, "I'm in the wrong section. Where do I find the sensible suits?"

Chrissie held up a suit that was *almost* large enough to make a headband. "You are in the sensible department, my dear. I'm in the more revealing department."

"Oh, no," I cried. "What are we going to do? These suits aren't big enough to cover our bare assets, if you don't mind my saying so. I can't go outside in one of these."

"When in Cannes," Chrissie said, "do as the French do. Let it all hang out."

"Are there any one-piece suits?"

"Don't be ridiculous. Just pick one and let's get on with it. The kids are waiting."

I rummaged through the suits and finally selected a black bikini that offered as much coverage as I was going to find. Chrissie picked out a green one and we hurried over to a rack of cover-ups. We grabbed t-shirt style cover-ups that unfortunately only reached the top of our thighs. Our assets would indeed be barely covered.

I saw Luc pacing on the sidewalk through the shop window and knew our time was up. We snatched sun hats and flip flops to complete our beach attire, handed over our credit cards and, purchases in hand, rejoined the group on the bench.

Luc heaved a sigh of relief, checked his watch again and handed us a beach bag containing the girls' beach things. "We have to run if we are going to catch the opening credits," he said. "Are you sure you will be all right?"

"Go," I said.

"We can certainly handle two little girls," Chrissie added as Luc, Casey and Tessa scurried down the sidewalk.

We discovered a beach changing room nearby and went inside to put on our swimsuits. I took Clarice into the cubicle with me and struggled to stuff her diaper-clad bottom into her pink, ruffled suit. But that struggle was nothing compared to the one I had trying to stuff my bottom into the skimpy black bikini. Finally, I accomplished the deed and squinched my eyes shut so I wouldn't have to look at myself in the mirror. Curiosity won out, though, and I ventured a peek. Horrified, I stared at my reflection.

"Chrissie," I called to her over the partition. "You're on your own. I'm not coming out."

The only sound from adjoining cubicle was Noelle chattering in French. At last, Chrissie said, "I'm not feeling real confident myself."

"I think going topless was way better," I said. "I look like something out of a Rubens painting."

"Better than I look," Chrissie answered. "I have a striking resemblance to the Pillsbury doughboy should he ever wear a green bikini."

I was trying to dredge up the nerve to leave the security of the changing room when the matter was taken out of my hands. Clarice, out of patience with me, burst out of the room and padded barefooted toward the door to the beach. Her rear end waddling she almost reached the door before I caught her and swept her into my arms. I yanked the cover-up over my head, stuffed my straw hat on, stuck my feet into my flip flops and shoved our clothes into the beach bag Luc had provided.

Chrissie and Noelle joined us and we slathered on enough sunblock to grease an entire fleet of cars. And headed for the beach. We took only a few steps onto the sand before the girls raced for the water. Giggling, they dashed into the surf and plopped down into the water.

We spread blankets a few feet away and settled ourselves for an afternoon of chasing the energetic girls into the waves. After hearing Luc's story, we didn't dare take our eyes off them as they splashed and laughed.

Luc had included pails and shovels and soon Clarice and Noelle were building elaborate sand castles. Chrissie and I were commandeered into acting as architects and designers. Just as we were running out of energy and inclination, two little girls approximately the same ages as Luc's daughters edged toward our towels. They watched Clarice and Noelle cautiously for a bit before they struck up a tentative friendship. Soon the children were giggling and splashing each other as if they had been friends for years.

"Thank heavens," Chrissie murmured. "I need a break."

"I dug into the beach bag, pulled out a juice box and offered it to her. "Best I can do for now. But later margaritas are on me."

I looked up the beach. "It's getting late. Maybe we should think about getting these two dressed. The movie should be over soon."

"I wonder where the parents are," she said indicating the two little girls playing with our two. "I haven't seen anyone who seemed to be watching them."

She was right. I walked over to the four girls and knelt beside them in the sand. "*Maman*?" I said to the older of the two. "*Papa*?"

Her face lit up and she pointed to a red umbrella only a few yards away. Beneath the umbrella were two beach chairs. Parked next to it was one of those twin baby carriages with hoods pulled over them to shade the babies inside.

"*Papa*," she said and ran toward the umbrella.

Her sister dug her feet deeper into the sand and refused to budge. I was thinking of taking her hand and leading her toward the umbrella when I noticed the dad unwinding himself from his chair and struggling to his feet. He stretched his arms over his head and shoved his aviator sunglasses up on his nose. And I began to hyperventilate.

"Chrissie," I croaked. "That's. That's. I mean, that's..."

"What *do* you mean?" she demanded. "I don't know what you're trying to say." She turned to see what had me stammering gibberish.

"Oh, Lord. It is."

"I know. I was pretty sure."

"It's..." I began.

"Brad Pitt," she finished.

"Not only that," I said, "he's coming this way."

Sure enough, Brad Pitt was sauntering toward us. When he reached the edge of our blanket I'm sure he didn't miss the fact that we were staring at him like a pair of idiots. He spoke to us in French and we stood rooted to the sand, unable to muster a coherent response. He tried again with the same result. Yes, we were a pair of half-witted mute dolts.

By this time he was grinning at us. "I gather you aren't French," he said.

I found my voice and succeeded in stammering, "No. We're American."

"The girls are French, though," Chrissie added pointing to Noelle and Clarice who were pouring water over Brad's daughter's head. "They are the daughters of a friend of ours. Luc Marin."

"Oh, Luc," Brad said. "He's a good guy. One of the best. Tell him I said hello."

Brad patted his little girl on the head and spoke to her in French. "Oh, I'm Brad," he added --- unnecessarily.

"Kate."

"Chrissie."

"Glad to meet you. Always good to find Americans here."

He turned to his daughter. "Shiloh, it's time to go. *Maman* is waiting for us."

Chrissie and I whipped around. Yes, it was Angelina. Wearing big sunglasses and a straw hat. She bent over the baby carriage and then stood up, faced us and waved. We waved back.

Chrissie and I were sitting on a bench nibbling ice cream cones with Noelle and Clarice when we spotted Casey and Tessa bouncing down the sidewalk toward us. Luc and his attorney friend, Jean Paul, trailed behind. They all were enveloped in an invisible cloud of laughter and high spirits as they approached.

Clarice spotted her papa and raced into his arms and offered him her dripping cone. Luc plucked the cone from her sticky fingers and licked the chocolate trickle from the side. He planted a kiss on her cheek and Clarice burst into high-pitched giggles.

"It looks like you had a good time," I said.

"Did you meet any celebrities?" Chrissie asked.

"Oh, you guys, it was so cool," Tessa said. "We saw Bradley Cooper and Nicole Kidman...."

"And Meryl Streep and George Clooney," Casey added. "And we met the director of the film and ..."

They bubbled on until they ran out of energy.

"What about you?" Casey asked finally. "How was the beach?"

"The beach was great," I said.

Luc polished off the last bit of Clarice's cone. "Did you have any problems? Did the girls behave?"

"They were perfect," I said. "Made a couple of new friends too."

"They did?"

"Yes, they did. Their father asked us to say hello to you."

"Really? Who was that?"

"Brad Pitt," Chrissie and I said in unison and watched our daughters' mouths drop open.

"Get out of town," Tessa said. "No way."

"Yep. Way."

Casey spun around to face Luc. "You know Brad Pitt?" Her tone was accusing. "You never said you knew Brad Pitt."

Luc shrugged. "I didn't think it was important."

"Men," fumed Casey. "He didn't think it was important. I wonder what he would consider important enough to mention."

Luc looked confused. He ran a hand through his hair and opened his mouth to explain, but was spared by the chiming of Casey's cell phone. She gave him one last disgusted look and dug in her bag for her phone. She glanced at the number displayed, mouthed the word "Bobby" and slapped the phone to her ear.

"Bobby?" she said.

A big grin split Casey's face. "Nonny," she cried. "Is it really you? I can't believe..."

I grabbed the phone out of her hand before she could finish her sentence.

"Mom? Where have you been? We've been so worried about you."

I heard muffled voices in the background and then my mother's voice. "Chrissie, darling. I'm so glad to hear your voice."

"It's me, Mom. Kate."

Chrissie squeezed next to me and pressed her ear against the edge of the phone. I waved her away and fumbled with buttons trying to activate the speaker. I nearly dropped it as I stabbed ineffectually. Finally I gave up and put the phone back to my ear and heard only the end of Mom's sentence. "... tell Kate what I said."

"Mom. This *is* Kate. What did you say again? I dropped the phone."

"I said, Chrissie, that you should tell Kate and the girls that Bobby and I are fine and having a wonderful time."

I gave up. Obviously, she couldn't tell the difference between us with the poor reception. "When are you getting to Barcelona?" I asked.

"Late tomorrow," she said. "Remember how Dad and I loved Spain when we were there. I can't wait."

"But Mom," I said. "You and Dad never..."

"That's right, Chrissie. You do remember."

I heard Mom whispering, probably with her hand over the phone. "Okay, okay," she said breathlessly. "Well, darling I must run. Kiss Katie and Melissa for me."

"What? Who? Kiss who? Casey and Tessa?"

"Right," she said. "Katie and Melissa. Bye, darling. I love you so..."

And she was gone.

"Mom? Mom?" I said into the empty airwaves, but there was only silence.

I stared at the phone and then turned to face my sister. "That was weird."

"What do you mean?" Chrissie asked.

"You didn't hear?"

"Not everything. You were hogging the phone. What exactly are you talking about?"

"Well, first, she kept calling me Chrissie. Then she said to kiss Katie and Melissa for her."

Chrissie frowned. "Bad connection? Casey and Tessa sounds a lot like Katie and Melissa."

"I guess. But there was all this whispering and shushing and I don't know. Something wasn't right."

Chrissie gave me a stern look. "Kate Kelly, you are making too much out of this. You know what everyone says about your imagination."

I shook my head. "Not this time. She was trying to tell me something. Maybe a cry for help."

Chrissie eyed me warily but our debate was cut short by the little girls who were tired and cranky. Clarice was asleep, thumb in her mouth, leaning against Luc's arm. Noelle tugged at his leg and whined.

"Time to go home," Luc said. He hoisted Clarice onto his shoulder and Casey took Noelle's hand and they led the way to the car.

It was a quiet trip back to *L'Hotel Belle de Nice*. Tessa decided to drive back with Jean Paul and the little girls were sound asleep in their car seats before five minutes passed. Casey and Luc murmured softly in the front seat and Chrissie stared out the window at the passing scenery. I replayed the conversation with my mother over and over as fear nibbled at my spine like a plague of ants. What were we going to do?

As soon as our hotel door closed behind us I collapsed onto my bed. With her back to me, Chrissie unzipped her pencil skirt and let it fall to the floor, puddling around her ankles. She stepped out of it and kicked it aside and then rummaged in a drawer to find her jeans. She tugged them on and then turned so that I could see her grim, tightlipped face.

"Talk to me, Kate." She twirled a lock of hair around her finger --- a sure sign of nerves. "I'm scared to death."

"Me too. I almost feel like we should go to Troon and find this mysterious Agnes and grill her for information."

Chrissie sank onto her bed and buried her head in the pillows. Her voice muffled she said, "We need to call someone. Police or whatever. We can't handle this alone."

"Or," I added, "we could go on to Barcelona and hope that Mom shows up the way she said she would."

Suddenly I sat up as if I had been launched. "That's it. That's what Mom said."

Chrissie stared me. "What are you talking about?"

I paced to the window and peered out and then paced back to the bed. "Mom said she loved Barcelona when she and Daddy were there."

Chrissie looked at me as if I had lost my mind. "So?"

"She and Daddy never went to Barcelona. Or anywhere in Spain for that matter."

"Are you sure?"

"Positive. You remember. They had a trip to Spain planned but that was the year that all four of us came down with chicken pox. One at a time. By the time we were all healthy again, it had been nearly two months and Dad had that conference in Turkey he had to attend. They never made the Spain trip. Mom used to tease us about spoiling her second honeymoon."

Chrissie's eyebrows shot up into her hairline. "Oh, my God. I had completely forgotten." She paused, her brow furrowed. "Obviously, she was trying to tell us something. I wish I knew what."

"I think she was telling us to be careful. That something isn't right. She said to kiss Katie and Melissa. Maybe she meant call Inspector Bouchard."

I started toward the door, but Chrissie caught the hem of my skirt and stopped me. "I'm not sure we should call him. Fifi made some sort of cryptic remark about him. Should we trust him?"

I pulled away from her. "We don't have a choice." I opened the door. "I'm going to get Casey's cell and call him. Mom is in danger and maybe he can help."

Chapter 20

When I returned to our room Chrissie's suitcase was lying open on her bed and she was hastily stuffing her clothes into it. She air-folded a tank top with a snap and dropped it onto the pile of garments. She didn't look up from her packing until I let the door slam. Then she jumped and jerked around.

"Did you talk to Inspector Bouchard?" she asked.

"I did."

"And?"

"Well, first I tried Bobby again. I hoped he would answer and explain all the craziness and we could stop worrying about nothing. But it went right to voicemail. So I called the inspector."

"Go on." Chrissie didn't miss a beat in her packing.

"He didn't seem overly concerned. Said Bobby and Mom were probably busy and distracted. He implied that Mom was a bit of an airhead."

Chrissie stopped at that. "He what? He barely knows us. How could he call Mom an airhead?"

"I know. I thought the same thing. I kind of liked him too. Now I'm not so sure. He said he'd call someone in Scotland and have them check on Mom and Bobby, but I think he was just trying to pacify me."

"Are you pacified?"

"Not really. I keep telling myself that Mom is off on a romantic adventure with Baron Bobby Hot Legs. As the inspector said --- distracted."

"By Bobby's sexy legs, no doubt."

"Doesn't sound like Mom to me. But what can we do? Inspector Bouchard thinks we should go on to Barcelona as planned and if she doesn't show up there then we can call the police," I said.

"This is the same guy who tried to keep us in Paris to protect us? Now he's ignoring what we think is Mom's cry for help?" Chrissie dropped onto the bed and put her head in her hands.

"It gets worse." I twisted my wedding ring around and around. Sweat trickled down my sides. "He said. He said. He told me..."

"You're killing me here," Chrissie said.

I forced the words out. "He said that both Fifi and Georges are dead. Didn't survive their wounds. Gunshot wounds."

Chrissie turned white. "Oh, no. That's horrible. Do the girls know?"

"Yes, I told..." I began when I was interrupted by pounding on our door.

"Mom," Casey called, "let us in. You need to hear this."

I yanked the door open. Casey and Tessa white-faced and vibrating with anxiety hovered on the doorstep.

"What on earth?" I said as they pushed past me.

"Go ahead. Tell them, Case," Tessa said.

Chrissie and I exchanged apprehensive looks and waited.

"Okay, okay," Casey said. "Don't rush me. I need to tell this right." She paused and peered out the window.

"What do we need to know, Casey?" I wasn't sure I wanted to know.

Casey ran her fingers through her already disheveled hair. "Okay here goes. When Inspector Bouchard didn't seem that concerned about Nonny and Bobby, I figured I'd call Robert to see if he had heard from his grandpa. Then I could pass that information on to you two and you'd feel better."

"Good idea," I said. "So where did Robert say they are? Off to visit some ancient castle or ruins?"

"Not exactly. Apparently no one has heard from Bobby in the last two days. His housekeeper, the mysterious Agnes, said he and Nonny never returned to the barony after they went to explore the flea market. She expected them but..."

"Oh, my God, Casey," I interrupted her. "Where can they be? What did Robert think?"

Casey shook her head. "He didn't know, but his idea was that they were

210

hiding out at some romantic hotel. Maybe..." She wrinkled her nose.

"No way." Chrissie's voice shot up like a firecracker. "Mom wouldn't do that. She's. She's..."

"Mom," I finished. "She calls to tell us when she's going out to dinner with her girlfriends. She would never just disappear."

"No matter how sexy Bobby is," Chrissie concluded.

The four of us digested this in silence. Chrissie chipped away at her nail polish while I paced across the room. I considered our options for a moment and then said, "Well, I hope Robert is right. The inspector wasn't worried. Maybe we should go on to Barcelona. I'm sure she'll be there waiting for us."

"I guess," Chrissie said. "I wouldn't know where to go in Troon anyway and Inspector Bouchard said he'd check on them."

Tessa poked Casey in the ribs. "Finish it, Casey. Or I will."

Chrissie and I stopped stuffing clothes into our bags and turned to stare at Casey. Casey bit her lip. "Robert also passed on some other information that was kind of unsettling."

"Unsettling? I'd call it downright scary," Tessa said.

By now Chrissie and I were clutching each other's hands. "Tell us," I said. "Now."

"Well, I kind of got talking with Robert about where they might have gone. And he was telling me about this really quaint little hotel where his grandpa liked to take his grandma before she died. And I said something about how sad it must have been for her to die so young and was it a long illness? And he said, well no it wasn't an illness at all."

Casey refused to look at me. "Actually, he said she died in an accident."

"An accident?" Suddenly I was terrified to hear what she was going to say. "A car accident?"

"Um, no. It was a rock climbing accident. She and Bobby were staying at the romantic little hotel and went climbing. On the rocks. She kind of fell off

211

the mountain and died."

Dead silence. Finally, Chrissie managed a feeble croak. "Please tell me there were a dozen witnesses to this fall. Tell me that she and Bobby weren't alone when she fell to her death."

"I wish I could," Casey said, "but, according to Robert, they had gone for a little walk after lunch and didn't want to wait for the tour group. No witnesses."

"Oh, no," I breathed. "Mom is off to god-knows-where with a kilt-wearing murderer who needs money. What if he married her and then decided to kill her on the honeymoon?"

"Then he'd inherit the money Daddy left her and there wouldn't be anything we could do," Chrissie said.

"First," Tessa said, "you don't know that Bobby killed his wife. And second, you don't know that Bobby and Nonny got married. And third, you certainly can't assume he offed her for her money."

"Mom, stop jumping to conclusions," Casey said. "Maintain calm. Get real."

"We are," I said. "Real worried. As in panicked. Freaking out."

"Girls," Chrissie ordered. "Go pack. We'll be at the airport first thing tomorrow morning. Two of us can go to Scotland and the other two can go on to Barcelona."

Casey had no more than reached for the doorknob than her cell phone began to chime. We froze and waited while Casey dug her phone out of her pocket and glanced at the display.

"Is it Bobby?" I asked with a surge of hope.

Casey shook her head. "Inspector Bouchard." She dropped onto the edge of my bed and spoke to him in rapid French.

I struggled to figure out what was being said, but I only caught a word or two. Finally after a nearly unbearable few minutes, Casey hung up. The air in our hotel room was stagnant with fear.

"What did he say?"

Casey twisted her bracelet around and around. "He said we shouldn't worry. He said the police tracked down Bobby at some little inn and he and Mom are fine. He said Bobby apparently left his cell phone on a train and that's why we can't reach him."

"Casey, did you tell him what Robert said about Bobby's wife?"

"He knew all about it. Called it *l'tragedie* not a crime."

"Very convenient, if you ask me," Tessa said.

"Shush, Tess."

No one said a word as we waited for Casey to finish.

"He said that everything was fine. We shouldn't worry. We should go to Barcelona and Nonny would be there. He promised to contact them when he got off the phone with me to tell them the news about Fifi and Georges."

Chrissie stuffed another pile of clothes into her bag and zipped it shut. "Do you trust him?" she asked.

"Do we have a choice?" I answered.

PART FOUR
LA VIDA LOCA
Chapter 21

The taxi ride from the Barcelona airport to the *Montecarlo Hotel* was tense. Butterflies flapped maniacally in my stomach and I squeezed Chrissie's hand for support. We stared blankly out the windows each enveloped in her own thoughts. We spoke only to reply to our driver's cheerful attempt to interest us in local landmarks. I'm sure he thought he'd landed the biggest bunch of party poopers to ever arrive in his fair city, but we were focused on the moment we would reach our hotel and find Mom waiting for us in the lobby. Or that our worst fears were realized and she was being held hostage by an evil baron with hot legs.

Our hotel was located on *La Rambla*, a busy street crowded with shops, restaurants and tons of pedestrians. I wanted to scream as the taxi driver made his way slowly through the clogged traffic. Come on. Come on. Get out of our way. We needed to get there. Now.

When we pulled up in front of the hotel, Chrissie and I leapt out and ran up the steps leaving our daughters to deal with the bags and the bemused taxi driver.

"She's not here," I said.

The cool marble lobby of the *Montecarlo* was empty except for the two young men behind the reception desk. Since Spanish is Chrissie's domain she took charge and marched over to them. "*Hola*," she began, "*me llama Señora Montgomery.*" Then she gave up and switched to English. "We have a reservation. *Señora Kelly y Señora Montgomery.*"

"Ah, yes," the clerk said, "we have been expecting you." He reached beneath the desk and pulled out an envelope and handed it to Chrissie. "This came for you."

"Is it from Mom?" I asked.

Chrissie snatched the envelope from the clerk's hand and stared at it as if it might explode. Her hands trembled as she clutched the envelope and I peered over her shoulder.

"It's not from Mom," Chrissie said.

"How do you know?"

She showed me. An ordinary business sized envelope and on the front, in a masculine scrawl, the words *Las Señoras Montgomery y Kelly*.

"What do you think?" she asked finally.

"I don't know what to think. We have to read it."

At this point Tessa and Casey straggled into the lobby dragging our bags. They dumped their burden at the top of the steps and hurried over to the reception desk.

Chrissie held up envelope. "We got a note." She waved it.

"Oh, good," Casey said. "From Nonny? What does it say?"

"It's not from Nonny. That's a man's writing," I told them.

"Maybe it's from Bobby," Casey said.

"Maybe," Chrissie said. "Let's not stand here in the lobby and carry on this discussion. Let's go up to our rooms. We can open it there."

We had adjoining rooms on the fourth floor. The decor was sleek and modern. The polished hardwood floors gleamed. Sunlight streamed in from the windows overlooking the busy street below.

We dumped the luggage in the larger of the two rooms and slumped on the beds. For a few minutes the only sounds were street noise and Casey methodically clicking the clasp on her silver bracelet open and then shut. Finally I snapped at her. "Cut that out. You're driving me crazy."

Casey looked offended but didn't bother to reply. She pulled off the bracelet and plunked it onto the bedside table with more force than necessary. She heaved a sigh. "Now what?"

"Now your aunt will open that envelope."

"We can't put it off indefinitely," Tessa interjected. "Open it, Mom."

Chrissie continued to stare at the envelope as if it might contain one of Mom's ears. Gently I pried her damp fingers open and took it from her. "No," she protested in a shaky voice.

"We have to," I said. "We need to know what it says."

I ripped open the envelope and gingerly pulled out a single sheet of lined paper. I held it cautiously between my thumb and my index finger. "Fingerprints," I explained. "There might be fingerprints."

The others nodded. I held up the paper, took a deep breath and read, "*Señoras, we have your mama. Do not notify the policia or you will not see her alive again. Stay in your room and wait for further instructions.*"

A wave of nausea swept over me and I collapsed onto the bed. Tears rolled down Chrissie's cheeks.

"Someone has Nonny," Tessa said. "What are we going to do?"

"We have to call Inspector Bouchard," Casey said. "He'll know what to do."

"He's the one who told us they were safe. He said he would talk to them," I said. "He could be involved."

"We can't call the police," Chrissie added. "The note says not to."

I thought for a moment. "It's always a bad idea to try to handle things like this on our own. We need to call someone. Even if it's not the inspector."

"No," Chrissie protested weakly. "We can't."

"Well, we can't just sit here like helpless ninnies and wait for a phone call that might never come," I said. "Let's go down to the desk and see if the clerk knows who delivered the message. Then we can decide."

Chrissie agreed reluctantly. While we went downstairs to question the clerk, Casey and Tessa would stay in our room in case we did get a call.

As Chrissie and I stepped off the elevator, she grabbed my arm. "Let me do the talking. Okay?"

"Fine," I said. "Whatever you want."

Shoulder to shoulder we crossed the lobby and approached the reception desk. The friendly young man who had checked us in looked up. "Is there something I can do for you, *señoras*?"

"*Si, señor*," Chrissie and said and displayed the sweat stained envelope which had contained the note. "Who delivered this?" she asked in halting Spanish. "Can you describe him or her?"

"*No problema*," the clerk said and gave us a description that could have fit half the male population of Barcelona. Dark hair and eyes. About five feet ten. His co-worker interrupted to add that he was wearing a dark leather jacket and jeans.

"That narrows it down," I said. "This is useless. We have to call the police."

Chrissie held up her hand. "No. Wait a minute, Kate." She turned back to the clerk and smiled grimly. "You see, *señor*, this person might be a person of interest in a police investigation. We need to find him."

As she continued to grill the poor clerk, I gazed idly at the pedestrians on the street and found myself caught up in a scene being played out in front of the hotel. A battered car pulled up and the driver hopped out and strode around the rear of the car. He opened the rear door and leaned into the back seat. Then he stood with one hand on the open door and gesticulated wildly with his other hand. He certainly seemed excited. I wondered about the still unseen passengers. Finally the driver threw his hands in the air in an "I give up" gesture and stepped back to allow a small figure wearing camouflage fatigues to emerge. The passenger stood facing the car and I couldn't see his face. As I continued to watch, however, it dawned on me that the figure was a woman, not a man. And there was something about that back. Something familiar.

"Chrissie." I poked a finger into her ribs. "Chrissie, look."

She brushed my hand away and continued her cross-examination of the clerk.

I poked her again. Harder. "Chrissie."

Impatiently, she said, "What?"

At that moment the small figure pivoted to gaze at the hotel. I gasped. "Mom." Chrissie and I sprinted for the doors.

We reached the sidewalk at the same moment that a navy blue knee-sock emerged from the back seat --- followed by a hairy knee cap. And then kilt-clad Baron Bobby Hot Legs stepped out onto the street. Chrissie and I stood rooted to the steamy pavement as Bobby and Mom spoke to the driver.

Suddenly the front passenger door popped open and a man the size of a small apartment building clambered out. He stalked to the trunk, released the lid, pulled out some luggage and tossed it onto the curb with a mere flick of his meaty hand. A fearful sight. That is, until Mom stood on her tiptoes to give him a hug.

We edged closer and heard Mom say, "Now, Guillermo, don't be sad. You did a good job. It's not your fault. And Julio..." She faced the driver. "...straighten up. Stop slumping."

To our amazement the driver straightened his spine. Then he, too, hugged Mom. Both men piled back into the car and slammed the doors. Mom and Bobby, arm in arm, watched as the dusty car pulled into the street and careened away.

"What on earth is going on?" Chrissie said.

"Let's find out," I said.

As Mom and Bobby retrieved their scattered luggage, Chrissie and I closed the gap between us and snatched her into a group hug. Our three way embrace went on until Mom broke away laughing and said, "Girls, girls. Stop. You're suffocating me."

"Are you okay?" I asked.

"Did they hurt you?" Chrissie demanded. She jerked her head in Bobby's direction. "What's he doing here?"

"I'm fine," Mom said. "You knew I was with Bobby in Scotland."

"But," I said, "we got a note. From kidnappers." I pointed at the taillights of the disappearing car. "Was that the kidnappers?"

"I can explain everything," Mom said. She stared at the hotel and a concerned look crossed her face. "Where are Casey and Tessa? They aren't out on their own are they?"

"Oh, God," I said. "Casey and Tessa. We have to let them know you're okay. They're in our room waiting for the kidnappers to call. Worried sick."

Chrissie grabbed Mom's small carry-on bag and I wheeled the other the few feet to the hotel entrance and manhandled it up the steps while keeping one hand firmly on Mom's arm. I wasn't about to have her snatched away again. Bobby followed us --- his expression somber. Was he friend or foe? I was anxious to find out.

The television in our room was tuned to some noisy soap opera *telenovela* and Casey and Tessa stared at the screen --- seemingly wrapped up in the drama. But when we opened the door and pushed Mom into the room in front of us, they leaped from the bed where they had been lying and pounced on her.

"Nonny, you're here," Casey cried. "Thank God."

"We were so scared," Tessa said. "Where have you been?"

They released their grandmother as Bobby maneuvered the pile of luggage into the room and stood by the door unsmiling. Sudden silence descended as the girls tried to absorb what was happening. One moment they were waiting for a call from Nonny's kidnappers and now the kidnappee had miraculously reappeared.

Casey recovered first. "Answers, Nonny, we want answers. We haven't been able to talk to you for days and now you're here? How did you get here?" She gave Bobby a cold glare. "And what part did he play?"

Mom bobbed her head sending her white curls bouncing. "It's a long story. But I can explain."

SCOT ON THE ROCKS

Laura Stevens knew that she had been included on Kate and Chrissie's birthday trip as an afterthought. They felt guilty about excluding her --- particularly after her granddaughters, Casey and Tessa, were invited to go along. Laura had protested that she would be a burden --- although she really didn't believe that. She thought she was much more fun than most women half her age. Still she didn't want the girls dragging her along out of some ridiculous sense of responsibility. But when they insisted, Laura examined her options. Stay at home and play endless games of bridge and golf with the same boring women she'd been playing with for decades or go on a European adventure with her family. When she looked at her choice that way, it was easy. She'd tag along.

She was even happier about her decision when she met Baron Bobby MacTavish on the flight over to Paris. She smiled smugly when she remembered how her skillful maneuvering netted her a seat next to the handsome, sexy Scot. And a baron to boot! Amazing.

She and Bobby hit it off right away. At first it was his accent that intrigued her, but before the flight ended, she was more intrigued with the man. Honestly, she hadn't been as drawn to any man since Bill, her beloved husband of more than 40 years, died. Since his death she had dated a little, but no man had been more than an interesting distraction. Until Bobby.

Laura had certainly enjoyed her time in Paris with Bobby. It was fun, romantic and just the slightest bit dangerous. Zipping around Paris on the back of his motorbike was the most excitement Laura had in years. She had to admit that horrifying her daughters and granddaughters added something to the affair.

Well, affair was probably the wrong word. They hadn't done -- you know -- but if she was entirely truthful, she wouldn't rule it out. Bill died four years ago. That was a long time. And Laura wasn't dead yet. So, who knows?

So when Bobby asked her to come with him to his barony in Troon, Scotland, she jumped at the chance. Scotland? Who turns that down? And with Baron Bobby? No way she was missing this. She knew the girls would squash her plans somehow if she told them, so she simply left a note and flew off with Bobby. Kate and Chrissie could just deal with it. Laura trusted Bobby. Even if her family didn't.

Bobby arranged for a car to meet them at the Glascow airport and drive them to the barony in Troon.

"I thought you'd enjoy a bit of a tour," Bobby said as they climbed into the backseat. "I know you love golf. Would ye like to see a golf course? Scottish courses are among the most beautiful in the world."

Laura sucked in a breath. "Oh, my, Bobby, I want to see it all."

They drove through the countryside and Laura marveled at the beauty. But it was the golf course that really took her breath away.

"It's so green," she said. "Bill …er…my husband would have loved this. He always wanted…."

Bobby squeezed her hand and wisely didn't interrupt her reverie with words.

By the time they reached the MacTavish Barony Laura was in love with Scotland and well on her way to being in love with Bobby.

Bobby's housekeeper, Agnes, greeted them at the door. "Welcome Miss Laura. I've prepared some tea and cakes if you'd like them. Or you can go right on up to your room."

Laura snuck a quick look at Bobby and then said, "Oh, Agnes, this is wonderful, but I'd love a tour of the barony first if that's all right."

Bobby grinned at her. "And I'd love to show you."

He led the way through the rundown barony and Laura was entranced by the charm of the ancient place.

"Bobby," she said when he finished the tour. "It's falling apart a bit, but this could be a showplace. If you do it right, people will flock from miles away to the MacTavish Barony. It could be amazing."

Bobby studied his hands for a few moments and then linked his fingers through Laura's. "Would ye like to be part of this?"

Laura's heart stopped. What was he saying? Confused, she mumbled, "I don't know. We've only just met and...."

Bobby burst out laughing. "I meant. Would you like to be a consultant on the restoration?"

Laura let out her breath and laughed. But she had to confess that she was a bit disappointed. For just a second she thought. Oh, well. That doesn't matter.

"I'd love that," she said. "The girls will have other ideas, of course, but I'm not going to let that spoil anything."

And she hadn't. The first day in Scotland she and Bobby explored the harbour and did some shopping for souvenirs. And she accompanied Agnes on her daily grocery shopping in Troon. Agnes was perhaps a few years older than Laura but appeared much older with her steel-grey bun and plain housedress. She had a quirky sense of humor and Laura found herself enjoying her company far more than she expected.

At breakfast on their second morning in Troon, Laura said to Bobby, "Agnes tells me that there's a huge flea market not far from the village. Could we go and see if we can find some rugs or paintings or furnishings for the barony?"

Bobby frowned. "Well, um, it's just a huge dusty place. I'm not sure it's such a good idea."

"Please."

"Well, I can't have you going by yourself then can I?"

The Troon Flea Market sprawled over a large, packed dirt parking area. Dozens of booths were crammed next to each other and Laura scoured through them eagerly. She unearthed so many treasures that Bobby left her to take them back to the car.

She lost track of time in her quest for buried treasure and was surprised to find that nearly an hour had passed since she'd seen Bobby. She was scanning the area when two dark-haired men approached her.

"Are you Laura Stevens?" the smaller of the two men asked. He spoke with an accent she couldn't quite place.

"Yes."

"Baron Bobby MacTavish's friend?"

Concerned now, Laura said, "Has something happened to him?"

The larger of the two men said, "He has had an accident. They are taking him to the hospital to check out his injuries. He asked us to take you to him."

Laura studied the two men suspiciously before she answered. They were well-dressed and there were plenty of people around. She was safe and Bobby was hurt?

"Fine," she said. "Has he had a heart attack or been hit by a car?"

Neither spoke as they led the way behind some buildings. Suddenly it was very quiet. The people had vanished. Laura was isolated. Frightened now, she turned to go back to the busier part of the market and the smaller of the two men pulled a gun from his pocket and pointed it at her.

"Don't make any noise," he said and nudged her back with the gun. "You are coming with us."

Something in his tone made Laura angry. She had no intention of going anywhere with these two. Not without a fight. She started to scream and scratched at the face of the larger man. Startled the smaller man dropped the gun and tried to wrestle Laura into a car parked nearby. Laura fought --- twisting and kicking at his … um … vulnerable parts --- and might have gotten away, but Bobby came around the corner at that moment. He raced over and lunged at the man holding Laura's arms. The other man unearthed his gun and slammed it down on Bobby's head. Bobby dropped to the ground in a heap.

The larger man scooped up Bobby's unmoving body and dumped him into the backseat of the car. Laura stopped struggling and let the smaller man push her in behind Bobby and slam the door. She couldn't abandon Bobby. Although later she questioned her actions, at that moment it seemed the only course of action.

The smaller of the two men slid behind the wheel and the larger man slipped into the passenger seat and trained his gun on Laura. They sped out of the parking lot and headed away from the village. Laura could only hang on and pray.

Bobby's eyes remained closed and his breathing labored for what seemed like an eternity to Laura. Then he moaned and his eyelids flickered and then he opened his eyes.

"Where are we? What happened? Are you hurt, Laura?" he mumbled through stiff lips.

"Apparently, we've been kidnapped," Laura told him. "I don't know why."

A look of horror crossed Bobby's face and he struggled to sit up. "That was dumb of me. I should never have let them take us like this. What kind of dolt am I?"

"Shhh," Laura said. "You were only trying to rescue me." She patted his hand and stared out the window at the passing scenery. Trees, rocks, a stream tumbling down the side of a wall of stone.

They rode for a while in silence and then the driver pulled into a long isolated dirt road that wound uphill through rocks and scruffy underbrush. At the top, barely visible from the road, was a tiny stone cottage. The driver stopped and the two thugs pulled Laura and Bobby from the car and marched them into the house.

"Make yourselves comfortable," the smaller man said. "You will be staying here with us for a while."

"But why? What do you want?" Laura asked.

"Who are you working for?" Bobby wanted to know.

The two men said nothing. Only shrugged and led them to a tiny bedroom in the back. Twin beds and a tiny dresser the only furnishings. The smaller thug pushed them into the room and closed the door. Laura and Bobby heard the key turn in the lock. Then silence.

Laura circled the room slowly, inspecting the surroundings. She peered into the dresser drawers and opened the closet door. No boogie men leaped out at her. The room seemed perfectly ordinary to her. She bounced on the corner of one of the beds, testing the mattress and looked up to find Bobby grinning at her.

"Ah, twin beds, my dear," he said. "Under the circumstances, I might have hoped for something more intimate."

She narrowed her eyes at him. And he grinned. "I'm joking, love."

"Odd time to joke, if you ask me," Laura said biting off each word.

"Sorry," Bobby said. "Old habit. Make jokes when things get rough."

"I'm being silly," Laura said. "What's going on? Who are these guys and what do they want with us?"

"I wish I knew."

"They speak Spanish, you know," Laura said. "I heard them before you woke up. And they look Spanish."

"Good work. Anything else."

Laura smiled. "The little one is Julio and the big one is Guillermo."

"Clever girl. Can you think of anything else?"

Laura shook her head. "What do we do now?"

"Wait and see, I suppose," Bobby said. Then his glum look brightened and he patted the pockets of his jeans and his jacket. His face darkened again when he found nothing. "My cell phone is gone. I hoped maybe they'd missed it."

"Guess we have to make the best of things," Laura said.

It wasn't too long before the smaller man, --- Julio was it? --- unlocked the

225

door and brought in a tray of sandwiches and two bottles of water. He set it on the dresser and turned to leave, but Laura caught the edge of his sleeve and he stopped.

"Julio?" she said.

He froze one hand on the doorknob and very slowly turned so that he could see Laura. "*Como*?" he said. "How do you know my name?" Shock and disbelief were written on his face.

"Oh, Julio," she purred. "I have my ways."

And that was the beginning. At first the kidnappers acted stern and foreboding --- waving their guns and shouting at Laura and Bobby is Spanish. But Laura's intuition told her that they weren't bad types --- or maybe she was just hopeful --- and she made it her mission to win them over. After the first meal of stale sandwiches and bottled water, Laura cautiously offered to take over as cook. Initially the two thugs refused, but eventually hunger won out. Apparently the way to a man's --- or a thug's --- heart is, after all, through his stomach. Laura's biscuits turned the tide and the men allowed her free reign of the kitchen which, it turned out, was exceptionally well-provisioned.

The three men began hanging out in the kitchen while Laura cooked. She plied them with biscuits and peppered them with questions. Her Spanish wasn't great and their English was not much better, but they managed to communicate and became if not actual friends at least not enemies.

Early on their second day of captivity Laura caught Julio mooning over a photo of a beautiful dark-haired young woman and three adorable dark-haired little girls.

"*Muy bonita*," Laura said. "*Su familia*?"

Julio beamed with obvious pride. "*Si, señora. Mi esposa, Consuela y mi hijas, Carmelita, Juanita, y Teresa.*"

Julio appeared eager to talk about his family and Laura skillfully wormed information out of him. His three daughters ages six, four and two were his joy. But the little one, Teresa, has a serious heart problem. Julio told Laura that the baby is very sick and gets tired so easily she can't play with her sisters. The doctors told him that she needs surgery.

"*Muy grande y muy caro,*" Julio said --- his voice breaking.

Laura pressed him further and Julio confessed that a man approached him and offered him money if Julio could do him some favors. Julio leaped at the opportunity to make some cash to pay for surgery for the baby.

"And, *mi amigo*, Guillermo, he need money also so he agrees to help me," Julio said.

One of the jobs they did for this mysterious benefactor, Julio told her, was to hire innocent travelers to smuggle in cash from the US.

"Ah," Bobby said when Laura related the conversation, "Small world. Or is it? It seems too convenient. I'm rather afraid this all might be about me. I might have made someone angry and they sent the thugs after me."

"They aren't thugs, Bobby," she chided him.

"Be careful, my dear. I know that you like bringing out your inner granny and bonding with these men, but keep in mind, they kidnapped us. And they are dangerous."

Laura swatted Bobby's arm. "Inner granny, indeed! Makes me sound like someone you'd find on a box of pancake mix. I'm a nonny. Not a granny."

Solemnly Bobby studied her face for a moment. "Excuse me," he said with a tiny smile. "Nonny."

"Besides, I'm a nonny not a ninny." She smirked. "I have heard of the Stockholm Syndrome, thank you very much."

Suddenly Laura stopped and stared at Bobby. "Wait a second. What do you mean you made someone angry?"

"It's a long story."

"We have time." Laura stretched out on her bed and propped pillows behind her back. "We aren't going anywhere. I think you'd better explain."

Bobby sank onto the edge of the other bed and stared at the floor for a few minutes. Finally, he looked up. "Well," he said drawing out the word. "It seems that I have something that some fellows want very badly. When I refused to sell it to them, they have become extremely persistent. I thought I had discouraged them, but now? I don't know."

"What is it that they want?"

"The barony."

"Why?" Laura said. "I mean, it's not in the best shape, is it? Is it so attractive that someone would have us kidnapped to force you to sell it?"

"I wouldn't have thought so. And maybe it is all about the bag switch in Paris, but somehow I don't think so. There must be something in the barony or on the property that these fellows need."

"Have you looked for a hidden bag or money or jewelry or anything?"

"Agnes and I have torn the place apart searching for a clue and found nothing suspicious."

"Isn't kidnapping kind of extreme?" she asked. "Who are these men anyway?"

"I'm not sure. I got an offer for the barony through a local barrister who represents the potential buyers. When I asked him who they were he said he didn't know. The offer was made by an anonymous source and he was advised that further inquiry would be frowned upon. He took that as a threat."

He stared glumly at his feet. "So do I. But I won't be bullied."

Laura reached across the gap between the beds and took Bobby's hand. "I won't be bullied either. We need to get Julio and Guillermo to trust us and then maybe we can figure a way out of this."

"Doubtful," Bobby said. "This isn't a game."

Laura never had the chance to test her theory. The kidnapping was over as quickly as it had begun. She was in the kitchen heating soup for lunch when Julio's cell phone rang. He took one look at the caller ID and hurried outside. Laura watched him through the window as he paced with the phone clasped to his ear. He vanished from her sight and then reappeared with Guillermo by his side. They had a hurried consultation and then Guillermo strode away and Julio came back to the kitchen.

Laura started to put a dish of soup in front of him, but he pushed it aside. "*Lo siento mucho, Señora*," he said, "but it is time for us to go."

She thought she had misunderstood him. Go? Did he mean leave the cottage? And go where? Was this a good sign or a very bad one?

Guillermo and Bobby joined them --- Guillermo pointing his gun at Bobby's back. Oddly, Bobby had changed into his kilt. What was going on? Guillermo tossed a bundle of clothing at Laura. "Put this on, *Señora*. We are leaving."

With the men watching her, Laura struggled into the camouflage suit that Guillermo gave her. What was going on?

Julio and Guillermo hustled them into the car and drove them to the airport in nearby Prestwick where a private plane was waiting. Julio escorted them up the stairway and into the plane where they were greeted by a pilot and a young woman in a flight attendant's uniform. Wide-eyed Laura looked around. This was no second class means of transportation. Leather seats and copious food were available to them.

Bobby and Laura buckled themselves into comfortable seats opposite Julio and Guillermo and held hands as the plane raced down the runway and into the air.

Finally, Laura, said, "Where are we going?"

"Do not worry," Julio said, not unkindly. "It will be fine."

Chapter 22

Mom talked for a long time --- tolerating Bobby's interruptions with a roll of her eyes or a scrunch of her nose. Finally, she leaned back in her chair and squeezed his hand.

"Now here we are," she concluded.

"Oh, my God," I exclaimed. "That's scary."

"Are you sure you're all right?" Chrissie asked.

Mom fiddled with the hem or her camouflage shirt, pleating and unpleating it over and over. She glanced up at Bobby and he shook his head. Was there something they weren't sharing with us?

I caught Chrissie's eye and tried to convey my thoughts. Dark-haired Spanish men? The ones who paid Georges to smuggle in their suitcase? Chrissie shot me a quick look before returning her attention to Mom and Bobby.

"Did they hurt you?" Chrissie asked. "What did they want? Why did they let you go? And did you know that we got a note from the kidnappers?"

I broke in. "Have you talked to Inspector Bouchard? He said he talked to you and that you were okay. Or maybe he said one of his men did. I don't remember."

Bobby frowned. "That's odd. I certainly never spoke with him. How could I? I lost my cell phone or they took it."

"But the inspector said..." Was I confused?

"Who sent this then?" Casey handed the now crinkled note to Bobby. "It was here when we checked in."

A car horn sounded outside our window and the breeze ruffled the sheer white curtains. No one spoke as Bobby read the note and then passed it to Mom. His eyes darkened and he pursed his lips into a scowl. Mom cut her eyes to him and sucked in a breath.

"Bobby?" she said.

"Very strange," he said. "I'll get to the bottom of it, you know. Something is not as it seems."

My mind whirled as I tried to fit all the pieces into the puzzle. I could almost make connections, but not quite. Answers danced just out of reach. Definitely needed more information.

"So," I said, "they never mentioned who they worked for? You said this Julio and Guillermo were Spanish, but it all began in Paris. Do you think they were hired by a French guy? Or Spanish?"

Bobby stroked the stubble on his chin. "Good questions. I will ring Claude… I mean Inspector Bouchard and see what I can find out from him. I rather think I should let him know that Laura, your mum, and I are safe here in Barcelona."

He cut his eyes to Mom and I had the feeling, again, that they were hiding something. Oh, jeez, I thought, I'm doing it again. Trying to make a big mystery out of nothing. Well, a kidnapping is not exactly nothing, now is it? Oh, damn.

"So what about this Guillermo?" I asked. "What's his tale of woe?"

"Kathleen," Mom said. Her tone had warning signs posted all over it. "Don't be sarcastic."

"Me? Sarcastic?"

Mom flashed me "the look" and I snapped my mouth shut.

She sighed. "Guillermo was tougher. He didn't want to talk much. I thought he didn't speak English for the longest time."

"Probably trying to protect himself," Bobby suggested.

Mom glared at him. "Robert," she said her eyes flashing.

"From what did he need to be protected?" Casey asked.

Bobby grinned. "From your Nonny and her prying questions and her infernal grammar."

"Ah," I said. "She can be a bit of a grammar policewoman."

"That's putting it mildly," Bobby said.

231

Mom looked offended. "Where was I before I was so rudely interrupted? Oh, yes. Guillermo. Well, long story short he just wanted to provide for his dear mama in her golden years. An admirable goal, if you ask me."

We laughed and some of the tension seeped out of the room.

"Not to worry," Chrissie said, "we'll provide for you in your declining years. But not until you are doddering and helpless and can't find your way home from the golf course without a GPS."

"GPS?"

"Never mind. So bottom line is that Julio and Guillermo were down on their luck and got involved in this kidnapping to earn money for their families," I said.

"And don't forget the bag switch scheme," Chrissie added.

Mom and Bobby nodded.

"But they let you call us," Casey said. "You kept saying things that made no sense. Katie and Melissa?"

Mom fidgeted again with the hem of her shirt. "I don't know why they let me talk to you. Yes, I was trying to warn you, but then all of a sudden they let us go."

"Why?"

Bobby took over the narrative. "Not exactly sure, but I promise you I will get to the bottom of this. For starters I will check the N number on the tail of the plane. I'd bet it's been painted over and changed, but it's a place to begin. Then I'll contact the police in Troon and have them check out the cottage for any trace of evidence there. Please leave it to me."

There didn't seem to be much choice. We wanted to believe that Bobby would track down the kidnappers and the murderers. Wait, did he even know about that?

"Bobby," I said suddenly panicked. "Did you know that Fifi and Georges --- the ones who switched their bag for Chrissie's --- are dead?"

All the color drained from Bobby's face. His eyes widened in shock. I was positive he couldn't have faked his reaction. He wrapped an arm around Mom's shoulders and said in a shaky voice, "No, I didna know that. That puts things in a different light, I think."

He stood up and put a hand on the door. "I'll leave you now. I have some calls I'd best make." And he slipped out the door leaving us gaping.

Chrissie's eyes were wide and frightened. "This sure isn't what we planned is it?"

"Definitely not," I said. Goosebumps tiptoed across my arms and down my spine like tiny pattering feet. I shuddered as a vision of Fifi and George drenched in blood floated behind my eyes. The hotel room had suddenly become too claustrophobic to bear. "Let's get out of here. We need to try to celebrate Mom's return. Besides it's the last day we qualify for senior discounts."

"When everything goes to hell, we'll at least have that," my sister said and grabbed her trendy new leather jacket and headed for the door. "Never let the bad guys catch you in frumpy clothes."

We left our hotel room as if we were being chased. And for all we knew, we probably were.

Chapter 23

On the morning of the birthday that we had come to Europe to celebrate, I cautiously cracked open one eye and peered at the travel alarm next to my head. Yep, it was morning all right. Which meant... Yikes. I was officially and unequivocally old. The handwriting was on the wall. I was headed down the path toward senility. I foresaw a future of arthritis and hip replacements, knee surgery and wrinkle creams, dentures, and, oh my God, hemorrhoids. Stop it, I told myself, and I repeated the party line. Age is just a number. It's better than the alternative. You are only as old as you feel. Ha.

I stretched out one leg and wiggled my toes. Arthritis hadn't set in overnight. I ran my tongue over my front teeth. Still there. I sat up carefully and yawned. I didn't feel any different than I felt yesterday, but nonetheless, I knew something had changed. At the very least, I would have to check a different box when a survey wanted to know into which age group I fell. Or in this case, into which age group I staggered and collapsed. There was a solution, of course. Lying. If I didn't look my age, I could fudge a little. Scrape off a few years. Then my gaze fell on Chrissie huddled under a mound of covers on the adjoining twin bed. Blabbermouth Chrissie. I never tell a lie Chrissie. The truth will set you free Chrissie. My twin sister exactly seven minutes and 23 seconds younger than I. Evil thoughts swirled and I tossed my pillow at her.

"Hey, wake up. It's arrived. We have crossed the line. Kiss your youth goodbye."

Chrissie groaned and pulled the covers over her head.

"No more shopping in the junior department. Time for sensible shoes. Prune juice. Metamucil, " I said.

Nothing from the other bed. Frustrated, I stomped over and yanked her covers back. "Wake up. I need to commiserate. I need you to join my pity party."

Slowly she emerged from her cocoon. "What you need is help. Serious help.

A shrink."

I sighed. "I know. But I never thought I'd actually ever be this old."

"What did you think? That you could live in Never-Never Land forever? You aren't Peter Pan and I am, for sure, not Tinkerbelle."

"I know that." I huffed. "I'm just old." I threw myself down beside her. "And so are you."

We lay in silent but companionable misery for a few minutes. Finally, I scooched myself into a sitting position and said, "I'm really sorry about that wallet, you know."

Chrissie flopped onto her stomach and pulled her pillow over her head. "Not the wallet again."

"It's tradition. And I *am* really sorry."

Her voice muffled by the pillow, she said, "Kate, I am so over it. Drop it."

"But," I began and Chrissie flung back the covers and pounced on me. She pummeled me with the pillow and chanted, "No more. No more. No more. About the stupid, stupid, stupid wallet."

I should explain that the wallet to which we were referring had appeared miraculously on the table between our two powder pink twin beds on the morning of our eighth birthday. It was pink and bejeweled and obviously, to my eight-year-old eyes, filled with bounty meant solely for me. Chrissie was still sound asleep as I reached out and snagged the treasure and secreted it under the covers. I burrowed under and counted out the bills hidden in it. Eight crisp new one dollar bills. One for each year of my life.

Greedily, I removed the bills and hid them under my pillow and returned the wallet to the table. At that point I spotted an identical wallet except that it was purple. I was certain that it held the exact amount of birthday bounty as the pink one had. One wallet for each of us.

Suddenly I swiped the purple wallet and counted out the bills. Sure enough, eight brand new ones. Quickly I removed four of the bills and stuffed them into the pink wallet and put both on the bedside table. My sneaky little fingers felt under my pillow to make sure the original bills were safely hidden and then I turned over with my back to the table to wait for Chrissie to wake up. What she didn't know, I told myself, wouldn't hurt her.

My petty thievery remained my guilty secret for years. I'm not sure if Mom figured it out or not, but she never uttered a word. I never spent a single penny of my ill-gotten treasure. I transferred it from one hiding place to another until I couldn't take it anymore and confessed my crime to my twin when we were about 13. She didn't get angry; she didn't yell; she just smiled sadly and put out her hand while I counted the bills into it. That was punishment enough, but somehow I felt obliged to bring it up every birthday and to apologize yet again.

"The statute of limitations on that whole wallet thing has expired," Chrissie told me as she sat up and pushed her hair out of her eyes. "Do not mention it again. Ever."

She grinned at me. I grinned back.

"So," I said, "how do we celebrate now that this infamous day has finally arrived?"

Chrissie arranged some pillows behind her and leaned back. I tugged the blankets over our knees and squirmed into a more comfortable position. The travel alarm ticked off the seconds. Older, it said, older, older, older.

"We have that dinner tonight that Bobby is arranging to pay us back for not having his credit card at *Thanksgiving*," she said.

"Uh, huh," I agreed. "But we have an entire day to celebrate. Dinner isn't until nine o'clock."

"Shopping?" she suggested. "And lunch someplace fun with Mom and the girls?"

I considered for a moment. "I was thinking of going to Montjuic."

"Where? Mont ju-what?"

"Montjuic. It's a kind of mountain park. The 1992 Olympics were there. I read that it's beautiful with tons of gardens and outdoor restaurants and museums and things."

Chrissie slipped from under the covers, tiptoed across the chilly tile floor to the window and peeked out. "It looks like it's going to be gorgeous today. Perfect for your mountain. It works for me."

"Do you think Casey and Tessa will agree? And Mom? And Bobby?"

"They have to. It's our birthday."

"I do have another idea," I said.

"Hmm?"

"Let's have a picnic. Like when we were little."

Chrissie beamed at me. "Kate and Chrissie's traditional birthday picnic. I love it."

Every year when we were kids we would have a birthday picnic and the two of us were allowed to select the venue. One year it was Lake Michigan. Another the zoo. Still another in our backyard. But our birthday was always an outdoor event. We drifted away from the birthday picnics as we got older, but today seemed a perfect time to reinstate the tradition.

We high-fived each other. "Where should go to buy picnic stuff? Is there a grocery store around here?" Chrissie asked.

"Wait a second." I snatched my purse from the desk and pawed through it, throwing things on the bed as I searched.

"Ah, ha," I said and held up white business card. "This could be the answer."

Chrissie took the card and read. "*Le Picnic Francais.* Gourmet Feasts the World Over. Where did you get this?"

"Oddly enough from Luc. When we babysat the girls I stuffed all our things into their beach bag. This got in with my stuff. And I saved it."

Chrissie turned the card over. "There's an address in Paris and in Nice and in Barcelona, too. Why would the Spanish people want a French picnic?"

"The French think they are in charge of all things gourmet. Not just in France, but everywhere. Seriously I can't say they're wrong. Think of the brie."

"With raspberries," she added.

"French baguettes."

"Wine," we said together.

"Serendipity."

"If there is such a thing. What do we have to lose by checking it out?"

We showered, spent an inordinate amount of time on hair and make-up and selected our outfits with more thought than usual. Today, of all days, was not the day to present ourselves to the world in a slapdash fashion. We needed to put our best, albeit old, faces forward.

Finally, having left no eyebrow unplucked, no lip unglossed, no lash unmascaraed, we were ready to brave the streets of Barcelona secure in the knowledge that we looked as good as humanly possible for twins rapidly approaching residence in the nursing home.

As I slid my arm into the sleeve of my cherry red leather jacket and dumped my sunglasses, make-up bag and guidebook into my tote bag, Chrissie scavenged through her carry-on bag. Finally she pulled out a small, beautifully wrapped package.

"Thank heavens I didn't pack this or Fifi would have stolen it," she said. "Something told me to keep it with me in my carry-on." And she handed it to me. "Happy Birthday, Kate."

"Shouldn't we wait?"

"No," she insisted. "I want it to be just the two of us. This is a twin thing. A birthday like this should have some purely 'us' time. And it's now."

I fingered the package and shook it. Then I dropped it on my bed and dug through my own carry-on to find the package I had hidden there for this occasion. I handed it to my twin.

"Ahh," she said as she examined the small, golden foil-wrapped package.

"You go first."

"No, you," I said.

"You're older."

"Rub it in, why don't you?"

Smiling at each other we slumped onto our beds. With one fingernail I carefully loosened the tape and wrapping paper to uncover a box with the name of a familiar jeweler embossed on it. "*The Perfect Gem*" was the store in our Michigan hometown where each of our husbands purchased our engagement rings; where we bought silver charms to mark the birth of each of our children; where we shopped for those really special occasions.

"What did you..." I began as I lifted the top to reveal the earrings inside. My mouth dropped open. The earrings were double gold intertwining hoops set with alternating tiny diamonds and emeralds, our birthstone. We had admired them together months ago, but neither of us felt we could afford them. I stared at the earrings too astonished to speak. As the silence dragged on the look of excited anticipation of my sister's face changed to one of disappointment. Her lip trembled the tiniest bit and I knew she was on the verge of tears.

"You don't like them."

"I love them. You know I do. Thank you so much." I hugged her. "Open yours."

She looked at me with dawning realization. And she ripped off the wrapping paper to reveal a box identical to the one I had just opened. Her eyes widened and her cheeks were flushed. "No way."

"Open it."

She took off the lid to reveal a pair of earrings nestled in soft protective velvet. A pair of diamond and emerald earrings identical to the ones I clasped in my hand. Her mouth was a perfect "O" of wonder. "No way," she said again.

"Yep. Way."

"I can't believe this."

"How did you?"

"When did you?"

"I love them."

"Obviously. So do I."

We burbled nonsensically at each other for a few more seconds and then burst out laughing. We scrambled off the bed and stood in front of the mirror over the dresser to put them on. Then we faced each other and nodded our mutual approval.

"When did you buy them?" I asked.

"Right after we saw them when we were home for the family reunion last summer. I went back the very next day."

"I sent Mom to *The Perfect Gem* after I got back to Ohio."

Chrissie shook her head. "They told me they were designer pieces. One of a kind."

"Me, too."

"Ironic," she said. "Just like twins."

We giggled as we admired each other again and then I looked at my watch. "Oops. We should have been downstairs to meet Mom and Bobby and the girls ten minutes ago."

"Let's go," she said.

Arm in arm. Earring to matching earring we marched down the hall to the elevator.

"There they are," Tessa exclaimed as we paused at the entrance to the sunny breakfast room a few minutes later.

"It's about time," Casey cried.

Both girls leaped up from their chairs and darted across the room to envelope us in hugs. "Happy Birthday, Twins," they chorused and dragged us over to the round table where Mom and Bobby sat observing us with goofy smiles on their faces.

Laughing, I protested, "Stop. You're making a scene."

"It's embarrassing," Chrissie added.

"You know you love it," Mom said as she embraced each of us in turn. "Birthdays are a very big deal and you should be in the spotlight."

"Perhaps not this much of a spotlight, though," I said as Chrissie and I sank into the two vacant chairs. But I wasn't really uncomfortable at being the center of attention. Today was not a day for hiding in the shadows. Old and proud, that's us.

Bobby rose from his chair to circle the table and peck each of us on the cheek. "Happy Birthday to ye both."

We accepted mugs of steaming *café con leche* from the hovering waiter and looked around the crowded room. No one seemed to be taking any special notice of our little group.

It took Tessa, our little fashionista, about 15 seconds to notice the identical earrings sparkling in our ears. She aimed a finger at us and said, "I don't believe it."

"What don't you believe?" Casey asked.

"Them."

Four heads turned our way. Four pairs of eyes scrutinized us. Then Casey spotted the earrings. "Wow. They're gorgeous. I suppose you two planned this."

"Not really," I said and rapidly told them the story.

Mom beamed when we divulged her role.

"You knew all along?" I asked her.

"Of course."

"And you kept it a secret?" Casey pretended to be incredulous. "I'm amazed."

Mom patted her older granddaughter's cheek. "You couldn't have dragged it out of me if I was kidnapped and tortured."

Oh, no. We fell silent as her words slammed us back to reality. I took a sip of coffee to calm myself before I turned to Bobby. "You said you were going to make some calls last night, Bobby. What did you find out?"

"Did you talk to Inspector Bouchard?" Chrissie asked. "What did he say?"

He toyed with his napkin and tugged on his mustache. Finally, he said, "I didn't talk to him. The lad I spoke to at the station said he was taking a bit of vacation time. Wasn't sure when he'd be back on duty."

Bobby and Mom exchanged a long look. He continued, "The lad did confirm that Georges and Fifi didn't survive their injuries. And he said the police had a couple of lads in custody who they suspect as the perpetrators."

"Could it have been Julio and Guillermo?"

"Not unless they could be in two places at once," he said. "They were holding us hostage in Troon when Georges and Fifi were murdered."

"So who are these perps anyway?" Chrissie asked.

"Since it's an ongoing investigation, the lad couldn't reveal much. He did tell me that they are well known for armed robbery and other crimes."

"Swell," I said. "Georges and Fifi were in our train compartment. Were they after us?" I choked off impending hysteria. "Was...? Was it the suitcase they were after, do you think?"

I looked around the table at the ashen faces. "Should we go home?"

Slowly Bobby shook his head. "Let me do some more checking before you abandon your birthday celebration and rush home. I know some lads who can find out more than I perhaps."

Suddenly it was all too much and the words were out before I could stop them. "It seems to me that for a lowly Scottish baron you know an awful lot of people in a lot of places." I know I sounded hostile, but I was seriously stressed and somehow Bobby's calm got on my nerves.

Mom was more offended than Bobby. "Kate. How rude. You know nothing of Bobby's affairs. He's just trying to help us."

242

"Are you sure about that? With all the people he knows or says he knows, it wouldn't be that tough for him to arrange a kidnapping." I scowled at him. "Or a murder for that matter."

Apparently unperturbed by my outburst, he patted Mom's hand. "Now, Laura. I don't mind. I do have many friends around the world. Europe is just a small town when you get down to it. And between government business and the barony, I have numerous contacts."

With Mom's eyes boring holes into my forehead, I gave a tiny shrug of defeat. "I owe you an apology. This whole thing is making me a crazy person."

"No apology needed, lassie. I can see how I might seem a bit suspicious."

Silence shrouded the table as we brooded over my accusations and the situation we found ourselves in until Tessa shoved her chair back and sprang to her feet. "Enough of this moping," she said. "It's the twins' big day. I say we dig into that delicious looking buffet and try to have some fun."

Chrissie squeezed my hand under the table. "I agree with Tessa. Come on, Kate."

I heaved a huge sigh and let her pull me to my feet. "Oh, okay. You're right. I'm being a jerk. Let's forget about the bad stuff for a little while."

We attacked the spread like locusts after a seven-year fast. When we couldn't eat another bite we leaned back in our chairs and looked questions at each other.

"Now what?" Casey asked. "Are we celebrating this long-awaited day or are we going to hole up in our rooms like a bunch of scaredy cats?"

"Don't be silly. Of course, we're celebrating. And keeping our eyes open for clues. We didn't come all this way to hide," I said. "Let's channel our inner Stephanie Plum."

"Nancy Drew," Chrissie said.

"Agatha Christie," Mom added.

"Cagney and Lacey," Chrissie said. She elbowed Tessa and winked.

"Cagney and who?" Tessa asked.

"Lacey," Chrissie told her. "Famous television detectives. You're so young, baby girl."

Casey fished around in her bag and pulled out a tube of lip gloss. She checked out her reflection in a spoon as she applied it and handed it to Tessa. "Apply your armor," she said. "Twins on the loose."

Tessa giggled. She ran the tube over her lips and smooshed them together. "Let's roll."

"We'll be fine," I said. "Bobby says the two thugs who attacked Fifi and Georges are in custody so they can't hurt us."

"And," Tessa added, "Nonny has soothed the savage Spaniards. Made them into pussycats. Let the celebration begin."

"We have the whole day before the dinner Bobby's organizing," I said.

"So we thought we might resurrect an old tradition. Take a picnic lunch up to Montjuic," Chrissie concluded.

Mom clapped her hands and grinned. "Perfect." She turned to Bobby. "Of course you'll join us."

Oh, of course.

Bobby shoved aside a crumb castle he had been building and put both hands flat on the table. He leaned forward and tapped his front teeth with a finger.

"Oh, dear," Bobby said. "I think I must beg off. I know you lassies won't miss me and you need to spend some time alone. Besides I have some business to attend to. Give me a few minutes and I'll organize some fellows to go with you."

"That won't be necessary, Robert," Mom said in a don't-argue-with-me tone. "As Kate said, we can channel our inner tough cookies."

"Tough cookie?" Bobby looked confused.

"Never mind. I'll walk you outside."

She took Bobby by the hand and the two of them strolled across the breakfast room. At the door Mom stood on tiptoe and whispered in his ear and the two of them pivoted and gazed at us. Then Mom waggled her fingers in our direction and they vanished into the hallway.

Chrissie refilled our coffee mugs from the carafe on the table. She sank into a chair and took a long swig. "Did you see the look on Bobby's face? He doesn't know what to make of us?"

"And vice versa," I said.

"Aunt Kate, do you seriously think Bobby arranged to have Nonny and himself kidnapped?" Tessa asked.

"I don't know," I said, "but it is sure an amazing coincidence that he's been around for every single weird event on this trip."

"Not to mention," Chrissie added, "that Mom met him on the plane and told him all our plans before we even touched the ground at *Charles DeGaulle*. If he was involved in smuggling he certainly could have used us to help pull it off. He knew where we were staying and a lot more."

"Very true," I said, "but I guess we have to trust Mom's instincts on this. She really likes the guy. And trusts him."

"Maybe she's distracted by those legs," Tessa suggested. The look on her face was so comical that we couldn't help laughing.

Chrissie flashed me a wicked grin. "Maybe it's the knees."

"Too tempting for Mom to..." I began and belatedly realized that she was lurking behind me.

"For Mom to do what?" she asked. "What am I missing?"

Chrissie waited a few beats and then slowly looked Mom up and down. "Maybe," she said, "you found those knees of Bobby's so irresistible..."

"...that you couldn't help yourself," I added. "And then we all know what happens."

245

"Ha," Mom said. "Stop that giggling." She scowled. "The four of you. I'll have you know that Bobby and I are just friends. Your Dad would have been happy for me." She swiped at a nonexistent tear and slumped into a chair.

"Oh, man, Chrissie," I said. "She played the Dad card."

"Mom wins," Chrissie said. "I can't trump the Dad card."

The Dad card, however, brought us to our senses and we wiped our eyes and sobered up. Our birthday lay before us. As we headed for our rooms to get ready for the day, Mom fell in beside me. "Admit it, sweetheart, Bobby does have the cutest legs, doesn't he?"

I could only roll my eyes in response.

Chapter 24

"Are you sure we're in the right place?" I asked. The sunlight was blinding as we emerged from the dimly lit subway station.

Casey waved the business card from *Le Picnic Francais*. "It says one-seven-eight-eight *La Avenida de los tres Burros*." She gestured at the street sign a few feet away. "And this is *La Avenida de los tres Burros*. So we walk a few blocks and we'll be there."

I squinted up and down the street and saw nothing even vaguely resembling a grocery store or market. We were surrounded by tall grey buildings and dilapidated warehouse-type structures. Not the kind of area where you would expect to buy an upscale picnic lunch. Or, for that matter, any lunch at all. The surroundings were ominous.

"It's creepy around here," Tessa said with a dramatic shiver of distaste. Her blonde hair swung from side to side as she scanned the street. "I don't know about three burros, but I see five, no make that *cinco*, jackasses standing around a skeevy neighborhood waiting to be mugged."

"Tessa," my mother scolded. "Language." But there was no conviction in her tone.

"I'm just saying," Tessa grumbled and lapsed into moody silence.

"Casey, we appreciate your leading us to this picturesque spot, but why don't we find someplace else to buy a picnic? This doesn't seem very promising."

The others nodded agreement, but the set of Casey's jaw told me her stubborn gene had kicked in. "I'm sure this is the right place. All we have to do is find Number One Seven Eight Eight. It's not that tough."

"Oh, okay," I said and we grudgingly trotted after Casey as she hurried along the desolate sidewalk.

After trudging about eight blocks we passed a dingy coffee shop. The gold lettering on the windows was nearly obscured by grime. *La Casa de Café* . The

House of Coffee. The name almost as uninspired as the shop itself. I saw no one entering or leaving the place and couldn't tell if it was even open for business. It was depressingly quiet.

A few doors away we reached our destination --- a two-story structure on the corner. It looked like a warehouse with a small glass entry door on *La Avenida de Los Tres Burros* and wider garage-type doors opening around the corner on a side street. "*Le Picnic Francais*" was spelled out in gold lettering with the number 1788 below. '

"This doesn't look right," Tessa complained for the hundredth time. "This can't be a place to buy lunch."

Casey gave her cousin a disgusted look. "Why don't we go in and see, Grouchy?" She tried the large brass doorknob, but it refused to yield. "Damn. It's locked."

I pushed the doorbell next to the door and we could hear a buzzer echoing inside as we peered through the glass door. It appeared as deserted as the street.

"Okay," Casey said. "I give up. Obviously no one is here."

"Let's go," I said and started down the steps. "Let's find someplace else to buy stuff for our picnic."

Before I could take a second step we were startled by a bell tinkling to announce the door opening and a girl regarded us curiously from the doorstep. Dark-haired and dark-eyed and totally gorgeous. Out of breath and slightly flushed, she pushed a strand of hair off her face. "*Lo siento mucho. No oigo el timbre.*"

"She didn't hear the bell," Chrissie said. Then she addressed the young woman. "*Habla usted ingles? Estan Americanas.*"

The girl stared at us for a few seconds before deciding that we were harmless. "*Si.* I speak a little English. *Por favor* to come in. How can I help you?"

We followed her into the building. The office was small but tidy, lined with filing cabinets and shelves. A large desk occupied most of the room. The desktop was covered with papers and a computer sat to one side. Typical office space. Nothing remarkable.

Clearly baffled by our appearance on her doorstep, she repeated her question. "How can I help you?"

"Is this *Le Picnic Francais*?" Chrissie asked.

"*Si.*"

"We came to buy a picnic lunch," Chrissie explained. "We have one of your cards."

The girl seemed perplexed but whether from her lack of understanding of English or from something else wasn't clear. But Chrissie persevered. "Lunch. You know. *La comida?*"

A small plaque on the desk spelled out a name, "Marielle Sanchez." Chrissie pointed at the plaque. "*Su nombre?*"

Marielle nodded, still looking confused.

I was beginning to think that Marielle was not the crispest chip in the basket. It couldn't have been just her inadequate language skills that caused her continued bewilderment. Finally, when I thought we should just leave the poor girl to whatever dimwitted pursuits she had been involved in, she shook off her lethargy and plucked the business card from Chrissie's hand. She examined it at some length. She chewed her lip. "But we don't sell the picnic baskets to ... how do you say it? ... people from the street."

"Well, then to whom do you sell them?"

Marielle's face brightened as she realized what Chrissie was asking. "Ah, *señora*, I see the *problema*. You want to buy a picnic to eat."

Exasperated, Chrissie said, "Well, what else would we do with it?"

"*Lo siento, Señora.* I will explain. *Le Picnic*...how do I say it?...ships the baskets to *Los Estados Unidos.* We *solamente* sell to *clientes* in big numbers. Many basket to each *cliente en los Estados Unidos.*"

Finally we understood. *Le Picnic* was not a retailer but a wholesaler shipping picnic baskets out of the country. We couldn't buy a single basket.

"*Lo entiendo,*" Chrissie said. "We didn't realize that. It's just that it's our birthday..." She waved a hand in my direction. "...and we are planning to take a picnic to Montjuic and..." Her voice trailed off.

Casey and Tessa slung their bag straps over their shoulders and turned toward the door. "We're outa here," Casey said.

"I told you so," Tessa said. "No one ever listens to me."

Murmuring apologies we edged toward the door, but Marielle put a hand on Chrissie's arm. "*Momentito.* Don't go yet. I have the idea."

She heaved open the heavy metal door at the rear of the office and disappeared, leaving us staring after her. A few moments later she struggled back through the door with a large cardboard box cradled in her arms. Red-faced and breathing heavily she dumped the obviously heavy box at our feet.

"I have the solution," she said.

We eyeballed Marielle and the box skeptically. "What...." Chrissie began, but Marielle was already slicing open the box with a pair of scissors. She ripped back the flaps on the top of the box and pulled out handfuls of shredded straw-like packing, throwing them in the general direction of the wastebasket. Finally, she unearthed the contents and reached in to hoist out a picnic basket. But not an ordinary picnic basket. No. This was the most exquisite basket I had ever seen. It was woven of the palest golden willow and seemed to shimmer under the fluorescent office lights. A band of deep green encircled the top of the basket and on it dark burgundy *fleur de lis* were scattered. The basket was huge. Big enough to hold a picnic for a small army.

Marielle flashed us a smile --- all white teeth and red lips. Her dark eyes sparkled. "Is for your *cumpleaños*. I give it to you."

"Oh, no," Chrissie protested. "We couldn't. *Es demasiado.* Too much."

Marielle grinned and turned the box around so that we could see the back. A large tire print ran over a slightly crushed corner. "You see. It is damage. We can't send to customers. We must put in ...how you say it? ...trash."

"It's not damaged," I protested. "It's beautiful. *Muy bonita.*"

Marielle stripped off the cellophane wrapping and tapped one red manicured fingernail on a minute scuff mark. "*Mira.* Look. Is damage." She gave us a conspiratorial smile. "I give to you."

We tried to refuse but Marielle wouldn't budge. Finally it seemed rude not to accept the gift she was so eagerly pressing upon us. "*Muchas gracias,*" Chrissie said. "We really should give you something for it."

Marielle looked offended for a moment before she grinned. "No way. Is gift from Marielle."

"Awesome," Casey said.

"*Gracias,*" Tessa added, "but we still need to buy some picnic food to put in it."

"Oh, no, *señorita,*" Marielle said. She bent and flipped open the double lids to reveal that the basket was crammed full. I saw plates, wine glasses and silverware secured to the top lid and a box of chocolates rested on what I was sure was a treasure trove of goodies. "The basket *está preparado.* Everything you need *estan aqui.* Is here."

Thinking we would look greedy if we started pawing through the contents, I closed the lids. I reached for the handle and tried to lift it. "Whoa," I said, "it's really heavy. I'm not sure we can carry this all the way up to Montjuic."

"*No es problema, señora,*" Marielle said. She tilted the basket up on one end to expose two wheels tucked into the bottom. Then she pushed a button under the handle and another handle exactly like one on a wheeled suitcase popped up. A rolling picnic basket.

"Amazing," I said.

We surrounded Marielle and the basket while she demonstrated its features. We were so engrossed that the sound of the heavy door in the back of the office scraping open took us by surprise. I whipped around and caught a glimpse of a smallish dark-haired man with an olive complexion wearing a workman's jumpsuit. "*Adios*, Marielle," he began and then realized that she wasn't alone. For a heartbeat no one moved and then the man disappeared through the door as quickly as he had appeared.

"Who was..." I began but I stopped when I saw Mom's face. Her eyes were wide with surprise and something else. Recognition? Suddenly she shook off her paralysis and bolted for the door. She tugged on it unsuccessfully for a few seconds before she managed to get it open and lunged across the threshold into the space beyond. The door slammed shut behind her. It took me a second to recover and then I whirled and raced after her.

I found Mom rooted to the floor, a perplexed look on her face. "Mom?" I called, but she seemed not to hear me. I tiptoed closer and tapped her arm gently. "Mom?"

She turned toward me and looked right through me.

"Mom?" I said again. "What's going on?"

We were in what appeared to be a large warehouse lined with shelves neatly stacked with a variety of cardboard boxes. On one side of the space an enormous metal desk was pushed against the wall. A computer occupied most of the top of the desk. Filing cabinets filled the wall behind it. A tractor with an extendable arm was parked on another wall. A series of garage doors presumably opened to the street. The cement floor was whitewashed and free of any litter or grease. I supposed I could, as the saying goes, eat off that floor.

Finally Mom shook her head and turned slowly in a circle. She shrugged. "Kate?"

"What's the matter? Are you okay?"

As if waking from a trance she stretched and looked at me. "You won't believe this."

"What won't I believe? Now you're scaring me?"

"Oh, sorry. I didn't mean to scare you. But that was Julio. If it hadn't been for that stupid door I would have caught him."

"Julio? Kidnapper Julio?" I flashed to the street scene not many hours before where Mom and Bobby had been arguing and then hugging the man. "But what was he doing here at *Le Picnic*?"

Mom rolled her eyes. "One would wonder wouldn't one? Let's go find out what Marielle knows about him. This is no coincidence."

Chrissie and the three girls were exactly as we'd left them and they jumped to their feet when we reentered the office. Chrissie dashed to Mom's side. "What's going on? Were you chasing that man?"

"Take a breath, Chris," I said. "That was Julio."

"Julio? Kidnapper Julio? Are you sure?"

"I didn't get a good look at him, but Mom says it was Julio in the flesh."

Chrissie chewed thoughtfully on her lower lip. "Why would he be here?"

"Let's hear what Marielle has to say about it." Mom looked Marielle in the eye. "Marielle, dear, does that man work here? Is his name Julio?"

Marielle shook her head. "*Si*. He worked today but is not regular. He is... how do you say...a temporary?"

Mom continued her inquisition. "Do you know his name?"

"*Si*. He has work before. When we have much work. He and his *compadre*. His name is Julio. Good worker. Hard worker. *No problema*. Do you know this man, *señora*?"

"It's a long story," Mom said. "Do you know his friend's name?"

"*Si, es Guillermo*."

"Ah," Mom sighed. "Julio and Guillermo. The kidnappers."

"The plot thickens," Casey said to no one in particular.

"Indeed," Mom agreed. She fired more questions at Marielle, but the girl either knew nothing or wasn't going to share the information with us. She shrank into her desk chair and regarded us with wide eyes, undoubtedly wishing she hadn't opened the door to this pack of raving lunatics.

I squeezed Mom's arm. "Stop. You're scaring her to death. She's told us all she's going to."

Mom relented. "Oh, my. I am so sorry, my dear. It's just that...well, never mind."

"My mother had a frightening experience a few days ago," Chrissie explained. "She thought she recognized that workman."

"I did," Mom began. "It was...."

Now that Mom wasn't grilling her, Marielle's worried expression cleared. "Oh, *Señora, lo siento mucho.* Julio and his friend seem *simpaticos.*"

I had a thought. If Marielle didn't have more information for us, perhaps someone else did. "Do you work here by yourself?" I asked.

Marielle slouched deeper into her chair and hastily checked out the ceiling --- wide-eyed and apparently terrified. Her hand shook as she arranged a stack of papers on her desk. Finally, she stammered, "Oh. No. My boss is on trip. Out of office."

"Your boss?"

"*Si. Señor Obregon.*"

"Is he the owner?"

"Oh, no. This is only one small office. Main office is in Paris."

"Maybe," I suggested, "we could come back when Señor Obregon is here and ask him about the two workers." Channeling my inner Stephanie Plum yet again.

"Oh, no, you can't!" Marielle shoved back her chair and leaped to her feet knocking the stack of papers to the floor. Then she dropped to her knees and scrabbled around on the floor trying to corral the scattered pages. When she straightened up clutching the papers, she was slightly more composed. "No, no," she said. "*No es posible.* Do not come back. If he find I talk to you, I am in trouble. No. No. No."

Marielle started to usher us toward the door --- our presence no longer welcome. Then she stopped and yanked open the bottom drawer of her desk. She pulled out something and handed it to Mom. "I am sorry I am bad manners."

Mom gave her an assessing look and then unfolded a picnic blanket. As Mom examined the beautifully woven and probably handcrafted blanket, Marielle exclaimed, "You need a blanket for picnic. Ground is damp." She smiled proudly.

"No, no," Mom protested and tried to hand the blanket back to Marielle. "We can't take this. It looks expensive."

"*Si*," Marielle insisted. "You must accept. It is apology. I will be dishonored if you don't take it."

That closed the deal. After our insane interruption of the poor girl's quiet day, the last thing we wanted was to "dishonor" her in any way. Mom tucked the blanket into her bag and hugged Marielle. And as Marielle stood in the doorway waving good-bye, I saw her breathe a deep sigh of relief. *Las locas* were finally leaving. *Adios.*

Chapter 25

It was a glorious blue-sky day with the temperature edging up into the 80's and the sun beat down on us mercilessly. Muscling the heavy picnic basket through the crowded streets was exhausting so by the time we exited the funicular at the top of Monjuic we were sweaty and winded. We dug out Marielle's blanket and spread it in a grassy spot shaded by huge, old trees.

Gratefully I collapsed onto the blanket and pulled my cotton sweater over my head. "Whew," I moaned, "that was drudgery."

Chrissie flopped down next to me. "But totally worth it." She pointed at Barcelona spread below us --- a breathtaking panorama of red-tiled roofs and taller skyscrapers set against the aquamarine sea. "That's so awesome."

We scooched over to make room for Mom on the blanket while Tessa and Casey sat cross-legged in the grass. After a few minutes I recovered enough to ask, "So, what do you think was going on at *Le Picnic*?"

"Let's not discuss this until we have a glass of wine," Mom said.

"Never argue with Nonny," I said. I rooted around the picnic basket until I came up with a bottle of red wine, five plastic wine glasses and a corkscrew.

I handed the bottle and the corkscrew to Chrissie who made a small fanfare over opening the bottle and pouring each of us a glass. Solemnly we clinked our glasses together.

"Cheers."

"Happy Birthday, Kate and Christine," Mom said and took a sip of wine.

Casey and Tessa echoed their best wishes and we sipped silently for a few minutes while we contemplated the grandeur of Barcelona below. Finally I couldn't stand it another second. "That was weird, right?" I said. "Mom's kidnappers working at *Le Picnic Francais*. What's the connection?"

No one offered an answer so I continued, "What occurs to me is that this pretty much connects Luc as well."

Casey slopped wine on her hand as bolted upright. "My Luc? How is that possible?"

"First of all," I said, "I didn't know he was your Luc."

"Mo-om," she said, "what are you saying?"

"Don't you remember where I got that *Le Picnic* business card?"

"Not exactly."

"From the beach bag Luc gave us in Cannes. The one that had the little girls beach things in it."

"That doesn't prove anything," Casey said. "So what if he had some stupid card?"

Tessa frowned. "Think about it, Case. Even if Luc is only associated with *Le Picnic* as a customer, it's kind a huge coincidence that the pair who kidnapped Nonny and Bobby would just happen to find temporary work there. Unbelievable."

"Luc being associated with any lowlife criminals is what is unbelievable. Those two precious little girls..." Casey's voice trailed off.

"Maybe he's doing it for those two precious little girls," I said.

Casey picked up her now empty wine glass and tossed it on the grass. "I am so not having this conversation," she said. "I'm starving."

And she turned her back and began ransacking the picnic basket in search of lunch. She unearthed a feast of gourmet goodies, tossing each item on the blanket as she dug for more. Soon we had a second bottle of French wine, a loaf of bread, a selection of cheeses wrapped in cellophane --- brie and a variety of white and orange types, a pair of foil-wrapped sausages, a jar of Spanish olives, *pâte de fois gras.* a selection of jams and jellies, a tin of cookies and a box of chocolates. Casey sat back on her heels and, good mood restored, let out a whoop. "*Gracias,* Marielle. Now that's what I call a picnic."

We needed a distraction. And what better than food to push aside dire thoughts of villains? So we fell upon the basket with gusto. We sliced and ripped and twisted and unwrapped until we had a banquet displayed. We filled our plates and chomped away happily.

"Perfect," I said.

"Exactly," Chrissie agreed.

I snagged the container of *pâte de fois gras* and examined it. "*Pâte* always reminds me of Dad."

Mom smiled. "If he'd just said no thank you the first time the Devereaux's offered it, they would have taken the hint. But no. He was polite and they served it to him every time he was in Paris."

"Poor Dad," Chrissie said, "he was a good sport."

"Oh, no he wasn't," Mom said. "He never stopped complaining about it."

I stuck my nose in the jar and sniffed. Then I dipped my finger into it and scooped out a dab of *pâte*. I licked my finger. Not bad. I smeared a hunk of bread with the *pâte* and gingerly nibbled. I smacked my lips. "It's kind of good."

I broke off a larger piece of bread and slathered a healthy dollop of *pâte* on it. I eyed it for a moment and then took a bite --- and shot straight into the air as I bit down on something solid. "Yow," I howled. "I think I broke a tooth. What on earth did I bite?"

I felt around in my mouth with my tongue and found something small and hard. A tooth?

"Oh, no," I moaned. "I did break a tooth."

Cautiously I worked the hard thing to the front of my mouth and spat it into my hand. I rocked back and forth with tears in my eyes envisioning Spanish speaking dentists and root canals. Gently Casey took my hand and uncurled my clenched fingers and began to laugh.

"It's not funny," I said. "I'll have to find a dentist and ..."

Casey snorted and opened her hand. "This isn't your tooth, Mom. Not unless you have some serious mold issues going on."

I peered at the tiny bit resting in her palm. It wasn't the white enamel of a tooth, but rather a glimmering green.

"Is that...?" Tessa said.

"I think it might be," Chrissie agreed.

"What?" I asked. "Might be what?"

Mom plucked the hard thing from Casey's palm, wiped it on her napkin and pinched it between her thumb and forefinger. "It looks," she said, "like an emerald."

"No way. Why would there be an emerald in the *pâte*?"

We passed the green tidbit from hand to hand and each of us inspected it --- turning it over and holding it up to the light. Finally we turned to Mom for her opinion. Our resident jewelry expert cleared her throat. "Ah, hem. I'd say it was real."

"But what," Casey repeated, "would an emerald be doing in the *pâte*?"

"Someone dropped it accidentally?" Tessa suggested.

"Or it fell out of a necklace or earring," Chrissie added.

"That must be it," I said.

We went back to eating our lunch a bit more slowly and a bit more carefully. As we chewed and sipped the robust red wine, I relaxed and allowed myself to believe that there was nothing inherently suspect about an emerald in the *pâte*. Happens all the time. What do I know about *pâte* anyway? And this self-delusion continued until Tessa cried, "Well, now what's this?" as she extricated a bit of red "glass" from her jam sandwich.

"That could not be a ruby," I said. "Could it?"

But after a careful examination of the red bit we unanimously concluded that it was indeed a ruby. Or a darn good imitation.

"What on earth is going on?" Chrissie asked. "Jewels in the jam?"

"And in the *pâte*," I said. "Do you suppose there are more jewels hidden in the picnic food?"

We fell upon the basket as if were pirates excavating buried treasure or the

Forty-Niners panning for gold. Using fingers and knives and teeth we picked and patted and squashed and nibbled. And like the Forty-Niners before us, we uncovered more "jewels." A "diamond" in a chocolate. An "amethyst" in a pot of jelly. A "pearl" instead of a pit in an olive. In all we exposed a handful of what appeared, and I stress appeared, to be genuine gemstones. Not to mention that we consumed about a million calories in our quest.

Stuffed and puzzled I poured the last of the wine into our glasses and leaned back on one elbow on the blanket. I propped my head in my hand and fingered the gems. I cleared my throat. "This is beyond bizarre."

DIAMONDS ARE A GIRL'S BEST FRIEND
(NONNY'S STORY)

Laura Stevens had never spied a piece of jewelry she didn't lust after. It didn't matter if it was a $5 bauble from a street fair in New York City or a $50,000 ruby pendant. She didn't discriminate. She adored it all. In a very discreet sort of a way, of course. After Bill died so unexpectedly her secret forays to various jewelry stores were her guilty pleasure. In those dark days after his death, her shopping trips were a pleasant diversion and spirit lifter. Shopping for gold and silver brought back those golden days with Bill. Hours spent wandering through shops and markets on their travels all over the world debating this piece or that while Bill, grumpily, of course, followed her --- complaining all the while. And then buying her some tidbit and presenting it to her with that mischievous grin of his. Her addiction to jewelry was harmless and even came in handy at times like now.

Laura's eyes gleamed as she watched her daughter, Kate, sift the cache of gems through her fingers. They sparkled in the sunlight and Laura felt that familiar tug in her stomach. She gingerly picked up a single "diamond" from the pile and held it up to examine it. Real? Maybe. At the very least, darn good fakes. The bigger question, of course, was why in heaven's name jewels, fake or otherwise, would be hidden in a picnic lunch?

No one spoke for a moment and then Kate guzzled the last of her wine and cleared her throat. "This is beyond bizarre."

"Weirder and weirder," Chrissie agreed.

"Can it all be a coincidence?" Kate asked.

Laura slowly shook her head. "Too many coincidences. It all has to be connected somehow."

The others nodded and Laura fingered the gems piled in front of Kate. Sunlight reflected off the stones casting colored beams of light. Mesmerized

Laura drifted into a half daydream where she was strolling through an obscure flea market and discovered the most amazing amethyst broach hidden among the cheap imitation stuff. When was that anyway? Years ago. Before she could pin down that vague memory, she was brought back to reality by Kate's voice.

"Mom, hey, Mom," Kate said. "Where did you go? I asked you what you thought was going on."

With an effort Laura shook off that foggy image of the long ago market. "I don't know if it really matters if they're real or not."

"Go on," Kate said.

"Well, real or not we have this pile of gems we dug out of our picnic lunch. What are they doing there?"

"That's easy," Kate said. "Smuggling."

"Okay," her twin, Chrissie, agreed. "By whom?"

"Again, easy. Where did we get this exquisite picnic?"

"From *Le Picnic Francais*," Laura said. "And Marielle said the picnics were shipped overseas. Mostly to the US. I'd assume someone was smuggling jewels to the US."

Suddenly everyone tried to talk at once.

"What happens next?" Laura's granddaughter, Casey asked.

"Duh," her other granddaughter, Tessa, scoffed. "Someone in the loop exhumes them from the picnic and sells them."

"Sells them to whom?" Casey interrupted.

"I'd guess there are plenty of criminal types who would buy stolen goods," Kate said. "And for a nice piece of change."

Tessa's eyes lit up. "Then the person who sold the jewels has to get the money back to the original source in Europe. Say Paris or Barcelona. And that person takes his or her cut first." She beamed with pride at her deductive prowess.

"Okay," Chrissie said, "so how do they do that?"

"Reverse smuggling," Kate suggested. She paused a moment with her brow furrowed. "Suppose, for the sake of argument, that they hire couriers to smuggle the cash back to Europe."

"Georges," Casey exclaimed. "Fifi and Georges."

Laura sat up and dropped a ruby she'd been admiring. "Of course. That does fit. Georges told us he was set up. His manager arranged for him to meet two men --- Fifi said they spoke Spanish --- who offered him cash, which he desperately needed, to take the suitcase back to France."

"And who," Kate added, "was George's manager?"

"Luc," Laura, Chrissie and Kate exclaimed.

Casey glowered. "Not Luc. He wouldn't associate with criminals. He's not a crook. He can't be."

Kate put an arm around Casey's shoulder. "Maybe not, babes, but he did have a serious money problem when he had to fight his in-laws for custody of the girls. Maybe he was just desperate enough to get involved."

"And," Tessa added, "here's another strange coincidence. Case, you and I accidentally met Luc and his little girls at that café in Nice. Right after we arrived from Paris. Also right after we found Georges and Fifi shot in our train car. How convenient is that? Maybe Luc was sent to keep tabs on us."

"Absolutely, no way," Casey insisted, but the look on her face suggested that she was wavering.

Laura had been listening to the interchange quietly but now she spoke up. "There is another tiny detail that you seem to have forgotten."

"And that is?"

"Julio and Guillermo. My kidnappers. Julio was working at *Le Picnic*. We saw him there. That's no coincidence if you ask me."

"Oh, my gosh," Kate said, "that does make a connection between them and this so-called smuggling operation."

"Hah," Casey said. "And doesn't that implicate Bobby?"

Laura froze. One hand clutched the picnic remains she'd been stowing in the basket. Bobby? She'd almost forgotten him in her absorption in solving this mystery. Things were moving too quickly. She'd have to bring him back into the picture. After all, he'd been a part of the entire trip since the very beginning. But before she could say a word Casey broke in.

She studied her grandmother's face for a moment, considering her words before she spoke. "Nonny. Even you aren't that naive. Robert told me that Bobby's wife died under very suspicious circumstances. I'll bet you didn't know that."

Laura sighed and fluttered her fingers in the air. "Oh, that. Bobby told me all about that. We don't have secrets from each other."

"Oh, right," Tessa said. "You've known each other for like five minutes. Maybe you don't keep secrets but I'll bet Bobby has some doosies."

How much should she tell them? His story wasn't hers to tell. Was it? Laura buried her nose in the picnic basket. When she spoke her voice was muffled. "Ummf. Don't underestimate me, young ladies. I'm not the gullible little old lady you obviously think I am."

"Oh, no, Nonny," Tessa said. "We don't think that. Do we, Casey?"

"Of course, not," Casey said, "we just...."

Good. She'd managed to divert them from Bobby for the moment. Laura knew she'd have to confide in them eventually. Just not quite yet. She was kind of enjoying keeping it to herself.

Chrissie dusted off her pants and stood up. "I say it's time to call Inspector Bouchard. He'll know what to do."

Laura dropped the plate in her hand and jumped to her feet to face her daughter. "Oh, no. You can't do that."

"Why not?"

"Let's wait until we talk to Bobby."

"What can Bobby have to say?"

"If he's not involved," Kate concluded.

Stall. Laura needed a bit more time. She drew in a huge breath and stared at her twin daughters --- so alike in their determination to figure things out. Well, they could just wait.

"I can't tell you," Laura insisted, "but Bobby will explain if you can give him a chance. Then if you still feel you have to call the inspector, I won't stop you. Please. As a favor to me."

Laura knew she'd played the "Mom card" and now she waited to see if it trumped their inner Nancy Drew.

"Oh, okay," Chrissie said. "If you put it that way, I guess we can wait."

Laura breathed a sigh of relief as they swept up the picnic debris and stuffed the leftovers into the basket. Kate scooped the alleged gems into her make-up bag and tucked it into the zippered pocket of her purse --- patting it protectively as they finished the clean-up. When Kate's back was turned, Laura snagged a few gems and secreted them in her own bag. Never know when they might come in handy.

"Okay, gang," Tessa said, "what now?"

"I feel almost guilty suggesting it," Casey said, "but I want to see some of Barcelona before we have to leave. Can the twin detectives take a break for a little while?"

Laura hastily agreed. "We have tons of time before Bobby's dinner."

"When is that?" Kate asked.

"A nice civilized ten o'clock tonight."

"Ten?" Tessa grumbled. "I'll die of starvation before then."

"How can you even think about food after that lunch? Casey asked. "Besides I really want to see the famous church, *La Sagrada Familia*. I heard it's gorgeous."

And the five women quickly packed up the rest of the picnic and headed for the funicular that would return them to sea level.

"There's the subway entrance over there." The silver bracelets on Casey's arm gleamed in the sunlight as she pointed.

The five women stood on the corner watching traffic speed by as they waited for the light to change. When it turned green, Casey and Tessa stepped off the curb and hurried into the crosswalk with the leggy, loose-limbed strides of the young and athletic. Laura followed them --- fumbling in her purse to make sure she still had her secret cache of gems as she did so. Her head was down so she didn't see the large out-of-date vehicle which came barreling down the street much too fast for the midday traffic congestion.

Kate and Chrissie, who had hung back skirmishing over who could drag the cumbersome picnic basket, watched with horror as the car raced through the red light and headed for Laura. Her head still buried in her purse she didn't see it coming until Chrissie screeched, "Mom, look out." And Laura looked up and froze.

As the car accelerated, Kate launched herself at Laura and with a flying leap shoved her out of danger. They landed in a heap on the street --- Laura sprawled under Kate. And the car sped away and vanished into traffic.

Laura wiggled out from under Kate and cautiously scrambled to her feet --- her heart pounding. She peered mindlessly at a large rip in her formerly pristine white capris as she was struck by the realization that she had missed possible death and certain injury by a mere fraction. She opened her mouth to speak but no words came out. She could only stare at Kate as other pedestrians surrounded them and bombarded them with concern.

"Mom, are you okay?" Kate asked. "Didn't you see that car?"

Casey and Tessa on the other side of the street turned to see the commotion and when they saw their mothers and grandmother picking themselves up from the street flew to their sides.

"Girls," Laura said finally --- her voice quavering just a bit. "I'm fine. Let's not make a scene." Staunchly she marched to the curb shooing away the remaining crowd of Good Samaritans. She sank onto the curb and groaned. "Oh, my poor pants."

"What the hell was that?" Kate said. "That car nearly killed you."

Laura had regained her equilibrium enough to murmur, "Crazy Spanish drivers."

"He didn't even slow down for the red light," Kate said. "Too much vino for lunch?"

Chrissie looked thoughtful. "There was something about that car...." She hesitated. "I'm not sure what. Something."

After a few more minutes Kate said, "Thank God, we're all in one piece. Let's get out of this sun and find the subway."

With Casey leading, the women stepped into the dim subway station and found their way to the proper platform where a crowd was waiting for the train to arrive. All the benches were occupied so they claimed a spot to stand near the tracks. It was sweltering and sweat dripped down Laura's back. Hadn't these people heard of air-conditioning?

It seemed like forever as they stood shifting their weight from one foot to another. The girls pored over the guide map while Kate and Chrissie maneuvered the heavy picnic basket into position, ready to leap aboard the train the moment it appeared. Laura slouched next to them, still trying to catch her breath. A mass of people closed in behind them as they heard the roar of the approaching train. Suddenly there was a commotion in the back of the crowd and it surged forward. Laura was caught by surprise, stumbled and lost her balance. Had she been a step closer to the edge of the platform she probably would have tumbled onto the tracks just as the train arrived. Fortunately, Chrissie saw her trip, grabbed her shirt and pulled her backwards as the train rumbled into the station and braked noisily. The doors rasped open and the five stunned women lurched into the car. Kate shoved Laura into the single vacant seat as the doors screeched shut and the train pulled away picking up speed as it entered the dark tunnel ahead.

The five exchanged horrified looks. Laura put her head in her hands and moaned. "I must be the clumsiest woman on earth."

"Or the unluckiest," Kate said. "That's twice in 15 minutes that you've almost been killed."

Her hand shook as Laura picked at the ragged hole in the knee of her pants. "I need a drink," she whispered. "Make that a double."

"We all do," Tessa said.

"This is just crazy," Casey said. "Stuff like that doesn't just happen. Not to Nonny."

"It was an accident," Laura said. "I'm fine."

"To be more precise," Casey told her, "it was two accidents. If they actually were accidents."

"Do you want to go back to the hotel and rest?" Kate asked. "That was pretty damn scary."

Laura considered it for a moment. A nice cool hotel room sounded lovely, but she wasn't a wimp. "Absolutely not," she said. "I keep telling you that I'm not a fragile little old lady. It was an accident and I'm fine. I want to see *La Sagrada Familia*."

The debate was cut short as the train arrived at their stop and they exited the station onto the steaming, crowded sidewalk.

"This way," Casey said and strode off down the street.

Laura and the rest of the family trailed wearily behind.

Tessa, the official Keeper of the Guidebook, made a sweeping gesture at the church behind her. "*La Sagrada Familia*," she read from her book. "Or the Church of the Holy Family was designed by Gaudi. It was begun in 1882 and is still not complete today."

Chrissie shaded her eyes with her hand and peered up. "It reminds me of one of those sand drip castles we made at Lake Michigan when we were kids. Remember, Kate?"

"Very observant, Mom," Tessa said with an approving nod at her mother. *"La Sagrada* has indeed been referred to as 'the sand castle church.'"

Impatient with Tessa and her tour guide mode, Casey announced. "Well, let's go inside already not just stand on the street and gawk."

"This is amazing," Laura said as she stepped into the cool, dim interior of the church. It was a relief to be inside after the blazing heat on the sidewalk. Laura looked around taking in brilliantly colored stained glass windows and soaring arches.

As Tessa had informed them, the church was unfinished. Signs in Spanish, which Chrissie translated for them, announced that the completion might not occur until the middle of the 21st Century. Indeed, Laura thought it did resemble a construction site. Workers perched on scaffolding far above them and the noise of hammers and saws echoed throughout. Various drawings depicted what the finished church might look like.

Laura thought of how impressed her friends at the club would be if they could see this gorgeous church. Why that Elmira Morton would be absolutely green with envy. She thinks she's some big authority on cathedrals. Ha. Wait until she sees this. "I need pictures," Laura said. "Lots of pictures."

She snapped a series of shots of a particularly intricate drawing. Then she turned to her family. "People. I need people in the pictures. Your father always said photos were more interesting with people in them. Girls, get over there by that drawing and I'll take your picture.

Laura positioned them around the drawing and focused her attention on the digital screen on the back of her camera. Frowning, she edged backwards to get everyone in the shot. She was so preoccupied that she didn't notice that she ended up directly under one of the scaffolds. Far above her workmen labored. And as Laura called out, "One last picture, girls," a brick plummeted from above and crashed onto the floor mere inches from her --- a corner of red brick broke off and landed on her tennis shoe.

Too stunned to react, Laura froze, her camera dangling by its cord from her stiff fingers. Her family sprinted the short distance toward her and Kate yanked her unceremoniously from under the scaffolding. The five of them peered upward. Where a few moments before workmen hustled, it was now silent. No one was in sight.

Casey picked up the brick with one hand and with the other grabbed Laura's arm as the five women hurried to find one of the many security guards in the church. But the guard just gave her a confused look as Chrissie explained in halting Spanish what had happened.

"Maybe he doesn't understand you, Chrissie," Kate said.

"No, no," the guard protested. "I understand what she says to me, but no one has been working in that section for many days now. Perhaps you can show me the spot."

He followed them back to the spot under the now deserted scaffolding from where the brick had fallen. "There," Kate said. "The brick fell from up there."

"*No es posible,*" he said. "No work here today."

"But we saw workmen," Chrissie objected.

"*Lo siento mucho.* You are mistake." And he walked away muttering, "*Pobrecitas.* Poor little things."

"But we did," Chrissie began.

Kate put her hand on her twins' arm. "Let's get out of here. I don't feel especially safe."

Laura shook her head and peered up at the empty scaffolding. "I think we all need a drink now."

They trudged down the street until they found a sidewalk restaurant with tables shaded by cheerful red umbrellas. They sank into chairs surrounding the round table and eyed each other warily. Too dazed to attempt even rudimentary conversation, Laura stared mutely at a scrawny waiter who wiped down the table with a grimy, stained cloth and then plunked coasters in front of them. Normally Laura would have lectured the young man on the appalling lack of hygiene involved in using the filthy rag and sent him back to the kitchen for a clean one, but at the moment she couldn't even summon a grimace of distaste.

They ordered a bottle of red wine and Casey mumbled under her breath, "One bottle will not be nearly enough." As the waiter scurried toward the bar, she reached under the table and revealed the brick she had been clutching all this time. She plunked it in the center of the table and the women gaped at it as if it was a ticking time bomb.

Tessa tapped the brick with her fingernail. "I can not believe you took this, Case. Isn't there some law about stealing artifacts from monuments?"

"Like I care. This artifact nearly killed Nonny. Tess, you need to stop thinking like the lawyer you don't want to be and try to channel your inner pole dancer."

"Now, now, girls. Don't bicker," Laura said. "Casey can take the brick back to the church." She put a soothing hand on Casey's arm. "It was just an accident, dear."

"Like hell it was," Casey exploded.

Laura blanched. This she didn't need to hear. She was frightened enough already.

Kate interrupted them. "Casey's right, Mom. Once is an accident. Twice is bad luck. But three times is something more sinister."

"I think," Chrissie said, "that someone is trying to kill you."

"Me? Why me?" Laura's voice was a squeak pitched high enough to startle dogs for blocks around.

"Think about it," Chrissie said. "Obviously you know something or saw something that someone (her tone suggested someone evil) doesn't want spread around."

Laura's mind raced over the events of last few days. Kidnapped. Nearly run down by a car. Almost squashed by the subway. And now a brick dropped almost on her head? Who would do that? She had her suspicions, but seriously things like this don't happen to petite white-haired Republicans from the Midwest. Do they? She'd need some convincing before she believed it. And Bobby? It was probably time to call him. Before she could say anything, Kate, as usual, took charge. "I think it's all connected with the kidnappers. Maybe someone doesn't want the connection between them and *Le Picnic* made. And if you are out of the picture..." She didn't finish the thought. She didn't need to. Laura shivered in spite of the heat.

The waiter reappeared with the bottle of wine and performed the ritual of opening the bottle and pouring a small amount for Chrissie who had ordered it. She sipped, nodded her approval and waited for him to pour each of them a glass. No one spoke until he went inside. The noise of traffic and the laughter of children at a nearby playground were the only sounds as they sipped the red wine. It could have been nail polish for all anyone tasted it.

Kate plunked her glass on the table and leaned back in her chair. She stretched out her hand. "Casey, give me your cell phone. Now it's time to call for help. I'm calling Inspector Bouchard."

Casey scrounged in her purse, pulled out the phone and slapped it into Kate's hand. But before she could make the call, Laura snatched the phone and dropped it into her purse. "You promised to call Bobby first."

"That was before someone tried to kill you," Kate said.

"Three times," Chrissie added.

Laura slumped in her chair. They were right, of course. They needed help. But not from Inspector Bouchard, Definitely not. "You don't think I'm just having a spell of bad karma then, do you?"

"No way," Tessa said. "Call the inspector, Aunt Kate."

"No," Laura protested, but even she heard how meek she sounded. "Call Bobby."

Casey swiveled her head to make sure no one was within earshot before she said, "The thing is, Nonny, and I know you don't want to believe it, but maybe Bobby is involved. You know his first wife was in a horrible accident. Robert said she fell off a cliff under very suspicious circumstances. Maybe Bobby killed her for her money or something."

Laura burst out laughing. "I've never heard anything so ridiculous. Bobby didn't kill her. It's hard to explain. I'll let Bobby do it."

She fished in her purse for Casey's cell phone and squinted at it as she punched the number. "I'm calling Bobby. He can meet us here and if, after you talk to him, you still want to call the inspector, I won't say another word."

With her family's eyes glued to her face and hanging on every nuance of every word, Laura spoke to Bobby. She didn't want to unleash his inner Sir Galahad so she glossed over the more dire aspects of the day and blithely related the events as if she was giving a rundown of a garden party she'd attended. He was obviously concerned. After all, she'd never called him before.

"It's been an unsettling day," she said.

"Unsettling?" Chrissie interrupted. "Tell him about the car."

"And the train," Kate added.

Casey waved the brick under her nose. "And this, Nonny. Tell him you were nearly decapitated."

Laura put her hand over the phone. "Shush, everyone. No, not you Bobby. I was talking to the girls. Really it would be better to discuss this in person."

She listened with the phone pressed against her ear and finally, ended the conversation with a soft laugh. "Oh, no, dear," she into the phone. "I'm right as rain, but the girls are a bit worried, you see. They want to call Inspector Bouchard." She pressed the phone closer to her ear. "I know. I told them, but I think they'll want to hear it from you." She listened again. "Oh, okay." She put her hand over the phone and whispered, "What's the address here?" Casey handed her the bar napkin and she read off the address, disconnected and handed the phone to Casey. "Bobby will be here soon. I told him we'd wait."

Casey flinched. "Oh, sure, Nonny. Why don't we stay right here and be sitting ducks while Bobby sends one of his stooges to off you?"

Laura patted Casey's hand. "Aren't you being a bit of a drama queen, dear? I'd expect it of Tessa but not you."

"Hey." Tessa tossed her blonde bob. "I am so not dramatic."

Her family smiled tensely and Laura said, "Really. Bobby is not a crime lord or a murderer. Do they even have them in Scotland?"

"Murderers, yes," Kate said. "Crime lords? I don't know."

"Enough of this murder talk," Laura said. "I'm sitting right here to wait for Bobby." She motioned to the waiter and indicated that another bottle of wine was required. "We can sit here peacefully and enjoy the wine." She folded her arms in front of her and sat back in her chair to wait for the appearance of Baron Bobby.

"We're going to be so drunk we won't understand a word that Bobby says," Kate muttered as the waiter opened the bottle. "The way things are going, though, a drunken stupor might be an improvement."

Chapter 26

We settled back to wait for Bobby. Well, more precisely four of us did. Casey, on the other hand, perched on the edge of her chair as if she expected to dive under the table to escape the hail of bullets aimed at us by the guns of a marauding gang of murderous thugs. She scrutinized each passerby, each vehicle, and every potential restaurant patron with suspicion. So much so that one woman took one look at Casey and faltered as she was about to sit at the table next to ours and turned on her heel and scurried out of the restaurant without looking back.

"Casey," Tessa rebuked her, "what did you expect that poor woman to do? Pull a Uzi out of her crocheted handbag and mow us down?"

Casey was watching a city bus that was slowing to pick up passengers and she didn't reply.

"Or," Tessa continued, "do you think a gang of rifle toting goons is going to leap out of that bus and open fire?"

As the bus pulled back into the traffic, Casey turned to Tessa. "You never know. Bobby knows exactly where we are, doesn't he? If he wanted he could send some of his minions to wipe us out."

"Minions? You're being ridiculous," Mom began.

"I'll handle this," I said to my mother. "Casey, darling, you're blowing things a bit out of proportion. I can't explain what's happened but I doubt we are about to be attacked by a band of snipers."

"Better safe than sorry," Casey said. "We're so totally exposed out here. Maybe we should go inside."

"Exposed?" Tessa asked. "We are?"

Casey heaved an aggrieved sigh. "Get your mind off the dance pole, my little exotic dancer." She gave Tessa's skimpy halter top a pointed glance.

Tessa huffed in mock offense. "You're mean. I'm offended." But she was smiling. "And you told me to channel my inner pole dancer, didn't you?"

Casey had to laugh in spite of herself. "I did and you don't do offended."

"Besides," Chrissie suggested mildly, "I think Tessa's more in danger from him..." She pointed at our waiter who was ogling Tessa, his teenaged hormones obviously raging out of control. "...than from sniper fire."

Her eyes narrowed, Casey scrutinized the sidewalk in front of the restaurant and, finding nothing to alarm her, slouched in her chair and fingered her wine glass. "Okay," she said and raised her glass, "I'll drink to Tessa's boy toy."

Tessa winked. "He is kind of cute."

"If you're into cradle robbing," Casey said.

We lapsed into an uneasy silence and sipped our wine until finally we spotted Bobby striding down the street, his white hair tousled and his navy windbreaker blowing open. When he spied us he increased his pace and covered the final few yards at a trot. He dropped to one knee in front of Mom and took both her hands in his. For one mad moment I thought he was going to propose to her and that insane idea rendered me deaf and dumb for a few seconds before I regained my grip on reality and realized that he was only inquiring after her health.

"Laura, my dear," he said, his breathing a bit labored, "are you quite all right? You said you'd had several accidents? What is this all about?"

Casey slammed the infamous brick down on the table. "It's about this. What do you have to say about it, Bobby?"

Startled, we jumped as the table shuddered under the impact and Bobby appeared genuinely perplexed as he stared at the brick. "A brick? What does that have to do with your grandmother's health?"

Casey studied his face for a long moment and fixed him with a steely gaze. "Perhaps you can explain it to us," she said.

"Casey," my mother cautioned, "I don't think..."

Bobby put a hand on Mom's arm and she bit her lip and fell silent.

"Let her talk," he said. "She's obviously upset."

"Upset? I'm upset, am I?" Casey appeared ready to launch herself across the table at Bobby. "That's an understatement. Three times today someone tried to kill Nonny. Three times! This brick was just the last attempt. Tell me why I shouldn't be upset."

"Take it easy, Case," Tessa said. "Let the man talk."

Bobby shook his head and scrubbed a hand across his forehead. "Before we go any further will one of you please tell me what in the name of all that's holy has gone on today. Laura's phone call was a bit unclear, don't you know?"

Mom's somewhat distracted phone call had made it sound as if some reckless pranksters had been toying with her not as if there had been three quite legitimate near-death experiences. Bobby could be excused for being confused so I jumped in and related in as much detail as I could recall the tale of the careening car, the push from behind in the crowded subway and the plunging brick in *La Sagrada*.

When I finished Bobby signaled the waiter who hurried over with a fresh wine glass in his hand. Bobby shook his head sharply and spoke rapidly in Spanish. Within seconds the boy made a quick trip to the bar and returned with a shot glass filled with amber liquid. Bobby tipped the glass up, downed its contents in one quick swallow and signaled for another. Not until the second glass of --- Scotch was it? --- had been placed in front of him did he speak.

"Casey, I completely understand why you, all of you, are so upset. Believe me I'm not taking any of this lightly. But I assure you that I had nothing, absolutely nothing, to do with it. I truly value your grandmother's life more than I can tell you."

Uh, oh. That sounded serious. But it wasn't the time to fret over a potential suitor for my mother. That could wait until later.

"Well," Casey said, only partially mollified, "why wouldn't Nonny let us call Inspector Bouchard? Why did she make us call you first?"

Mom and Bobby exchanged what could only be termed conspiratorial looks. "Tell them, Robert," Mom said. "It's time they knew."

Bobby bobbed his head and smiled at her, but before he could tell us whatever it was we needed to know Casey exploded. "Enough of all this secrecy. Tell us what's going on. Right now."

Bobby sucked in a breath and blew it out. "It's simply that I work for the International Criminal Police Organization."

"The International Criminal Police? Wait a damn minute," Casey said. "You work for Interpol? You're a cop?" Her voice rose several octaves. "No way. No freaking way."

"Yes, it's true," her grandmother interjected mildly. "Show them your ID, Robert."

"That won't be necessary," Chrissie said. "We believe..."

"Like hell it won't," Casey interrupted her. "I, for one, absolutely do need to see it."

Mom shook her head in warning. "Language, dear."

Casey gave her an exasperated look, but Bobby was already digging in his pocket to pull out his wallet. He flipped it open to display a gold badge and an identity card. "Robert MacTavish, Lieutenant First Class, International Criminal Police Organization."

Casey was struck dumb as she stared at the badge.

"Is it real?" Chrissie looked at me. "What do you think, Kate?"

I had no idea.

"So," I said to Bobby, "you seriously work for Interpol?"

Bobby nodded. "I do."

"Doing what?"

"Investigating..."he began.

Casey, her tone dripping with sarcasm, broke in. "Obviously."

"Don't be snarky, Case," Tessa said. "Listen to what he has to say."

With an obvious effort, Casey pursed her lips and sat back in her chair, her arms folded in front of her. We waited for him to continue.

Mom patted his arm softly. "Tough crowd," she murmured.

Bobby shifted in his chair and eyed us cautiously as he took a sip of his drink. The atmosphere at our little table was strained and tense. "Um. Err. Now where was I?" He looked at Casey. He paused to collect his thoughts and then hurried on. "I'm employed in the Smuggling Response Unit."

"Smuggling?" I said. Finally it was all beginning to make sense.

"As in suitcases full of money?" Chrissie asked.

Obviously relieved not to have to elaborate further, Bobby inclined his head. He watched us over the rim of his glass as the connection clicked. Bobby worked for Interpol trying to catch international smugglers? And we had, inadvertently as it had been, done exactly that. Smuggled. Chrissie's bag had been used to smuggle money illegally into France. Was Bobby working that case? Had he been working us, and Mom, the entire time we'd known him? He was using us? That really hurt. So how was it that Mom was still gazing at him all mushy-eyed like the stupid cat that swallowed the idiot canary?

Apparently I wasn't the only one who felt betrayed. Tessa leaned forward and said in a voice laced with acid, "You've been using us this entire time. That sucks."

The accusation from sweet Tessa took Bobby aback. He stammered, "Well, not, not the entire time. I mean. What I mean is it didn't start that way." He looked helplessly at Mom who offered no help. He blundered on. "It wasn't on purpose. Really."

He was drowning in our hostility when Mom took pity on him. "Girls, listen to what he has to say. Then you can judge whether or not to believe him." She turned to Bobby. "Go on, Robert. Tell them the whole story." She hesitated. "Or I will."

Bobby cast a longing look at the waiter but didn't order a third drink. Good thing. Far better to face our cold stares sober and not addled by alcohol. He needed to be at the top of his game to convince us --- as he apparently had Mom --- that he hadn't reeled us in with his sweet Scottish brogue and his abundant charm. He fiddled with his empty glass and tension mounted. I wanted to reach over and grab his lapels and shake him until his teeth rattled. Before I could leap into action, though, he cleared his throat and spoke.

"Well, as I said, I've worked for Interpol for more than thirty years. As you can imagine the baron business isn't terribly lucrative and to support my family, I accepted an offer to join Interpol. Over the years I've held a number of positions, but for the last few years I've been involved in Smuggling Prevention. I head up a team tracking a certain smuggling ring operating in France and Spain."

"How very James Bond," Tessa whispered to Casey.

Chrissie shot Tessa the "mom look" and Tessa sank back into her chair with her teeth clenched so tightly I thought she might fuse them together.

"Go on, Bobby," Chrissie said.

"Hm. Yes. So I was in the States visiting the boys, Robert and Mac, in school. Robert was graduating from Duke and I was determined to be there so I took a leave of absence from my post. I was enjoying some much-needed family time with my grandsons and their mother, my daughter-in-law, Elinor, when I got a call from my superior. He said they'd received information that a member of the ring I was investigating was going to be on a certain flight out of New York going to Paris. Would I, my superior asked, be willing to take that flight and keep an eye on the suspect?"

"I had been in the States for a couple of weeks and Robert and Mac were eager to get back to Europe anyway, so I told him I'd be willing to take the flight. I really can't tell you all the details. Police confidentiality, you know. I can assure you that I had no intention of meeting a beautiful American and her lovely granddaughters. That was never part of any plan."

"I should hope not," Mom said.

"When we struck up our first conversation," he said to her, "I thought it would just be a pleasant diversion during the long flight. I never expected to see you again once we landed in Paris."

"Nice," Tessa commented. "I suppose Robert and Mac were working with you. Were they supposed to hook up with Casey and me and lead us on?"

Bobby frowned. "Of course not. Robert and Mac have no idea what I do at Interpol. They assume I am some sort of glorified clerk. Not an actual operative in the field. I do know for sure that they met you and Casey and liked both of you very much. They are certainly not immune to the charms of beautiful women."

"When I saw Georges, our suspect, at Baggage Claim and he switched the two bags, I planned to follow him. Then I saw the person who claimed the bag that Georges had tampered with."

"Chrissie," I exclaimed.

"Indeed," Bobby continued, "and I knew that she was traveling with Laura and the two lasses. So, I changed my plan. I decided to make sure that I didn't lose track of you all. I'd already made a kind of a date with Miss Laura and I realized that I could kill two birds with one stone."

"Interesting way to put it," I said.

Bobby coughed and cleared his throat and then looked apologetically at Mom. "I just meant…"

"It's okay, Robert," Mom said. "I understand. I really do. We were a means to an end."

"A lovely means, though," he said. "I guess you can finish the rest of the story yourselves."

"Not entirely," Chrissie said. "I'll accept your word that you weren't trying to seduce Mom to get closer to me, but what about Inspector Bouchard? And that whole money exchange fiasco at Montmartre?"

Bobby shrugged. "Perhaps bad judgment, but I knew he could help sort out the mess that Miss Casey created for you. You never would have been involved if she hadn't tried to help her friend, Fifi."

Casey's face fell and her brown eyes glistened with unshed tears. "Oh, God, I'm so sorry. I didn't mean to drag us all into this."

I gave her a quick hug and then said, "There's something you aren't telling us. Inspector Bouchard is the key, I think. Why wouldn't Mom let us call him? He's involved somehow isn't he?"

Mom smiled weakly at Bobby. "I told you they were clever, didn't I? Tell them what you told me."

Bobby sighed. "I don't suppose you could let it go?"

We shook our heads.

He sighed again. If he thought he could get off easy he was mistaken.

"Okay," he continued. "As I told you we've been investigating this particular ring for some time and we have evidence that puts the mastermind in Paris. More precisely, in the police department. We knew someone fairly high up in the department and with access to classified information was involved. I can't reveal our source, of course, but let's just say it came from a very reliable person. I thought if we let Bouchard know we had a clue to the identity of one of the alleged smugglers that someone might get nervous and tip his, or her, hand."

"And did that happen?" Chrissie asked

"In a manner of speaking," Bobby said. "After I brought Bouchard into the picture, a number of strange things transpired. The muffed suitcase exchange. The odd kidnapping of Miss Laura and myself in Scotland and then being returned to Barcelona. Georges and Fifi being shot and left in your train compartment. And finally, the attempts on your mother's life this afternoon."

I glanced around the restaurant. No one appeared to be paying any special attention to us, but I still felt appallingly vulnerable. "So," I said, "you admit it's all connected?"

Bobby shrugged. "Indeed, I think we have stirred up a very nasty nest of hornets. Whose sting could be quite deadly."

Casey shivered and tears rolled silently down her cheeks. "Oh, my god." Which I think about summed it up.

No one uttered a sound. Even breathing seemed like too much effort. A question fluttered to the top of my stunned brain and I opened my mouth to speak. Nothing came out. I swallowed and tried again. Finally, I blurted, "I thought Inspector Bouchard was your friend. Do you actually think he's a crook?"

Bobby laced his fingers together, rested his chin on them and stared into space. The look on his face announced that he was considering the possibility. After a few seconds he said, "No. I honestly don't think Claude is a crook. I've known him for a great number of years and I cannot imagine him descending into a life of crime. The Claude I know would never do anything even remotely dishonest."

"Maybe you don't know him all that well," I suggested. "Maybe he has a secret life that you know nothing about."

Bobby laughed briefly, but his blue eyes were icy. "That's absurd. I've known Claude since university in the states. We were two lads from the other side of the pond. We played soccer together. We were mates. We were in the same club."

"That was then," I said. "Things change."

Bobby shook his head. "No. We've kept in touch all these years and I've never been even remotely suspicious of him. After we graduated, I went home to Scotland and the rundown barony. Claude returned to Paris to the darling French girl ... her name was Desiree ... who had been waiting for him. He might have been a bit of a party boy at Yale but he settled down after he married Desiree. We visited occasionally and about the time I joined Interpol, Claude signed on with the Paris police. He's had a distinguished career. Many awards. I can't fathom him engaging in illegal activities."

"Well, okay, then," I said, "you went to Yale?" Somehow that was reassuring. The inspector had been nothing but kind and solicitous and helpful to us and to the girls. Why was I so suspicious? Was it Fifi and her mysterious "warning" or something else? A sixth sense maybe? I didn't know.

"But," Chrissie added, "he certainly did help Casey and Tessa. Without him they might be occupying a cell in the Paris jail and not a table in Barcelona."

Casey and Tessa exchanged sheepish looks and nodded.

"True," Tessa said. "I see your point."

"I contacted him for two reasons. To help you with your dilemma with the added bonus of maybe getting some information which could lead me to the bloke I was looking for."

"Does he, the inspector, even know what you really do?" Chrissie asked.

"He knows I work for Interpol, but he thinks I have a desk job. Most of us who work undercover, as you yanks say, have other 'official' jobs. My title is Commissioner of International Affairs. A paper pusher and a drone." He smiled a self-deprecating smile. "I'm quite good at it."

"No one suspects otherwise?" Chrissie persisted.

"Not until ..." he hesitated and made a wry face, "...now. My cover is blown."

At that Mom drew in a sharp breath and jerked upright. "Oh, Bobby," she said. "I didn't think. I mean, I'm so sorry. Will you lose your job?"

Bobby took her hand and linked his fingers through hers. "Ach, most likely I will lose my undercover position when all this comes to light. But don't worry, my dear, I had to retire sometime now didn't I?"

"But Bobby..."

"Tsk. Tsk. I'll still have my desk job and this will leave more time for the barony, don't you know?"

"I'm so sorry." Mom looked as if she might break into tears at any moment.

Bobby gave her hand a consoling pat. "Not another word about it, Laura. My first concern is the safety of you and your family. And," he added with a glance around, "perhaps finding the men who have caused all this trouble for you." He cut his eyes to my mother. "And me."

He turned to look Tessa in the eye. "Contrary to what you might believe, Miss Tessa, no one would mistake me for James Bond. However, my official job has given me the opportunity to travel to many places where I can work undercover quite successfully."

"I'll just bet," Casey said. "Like on airplanes."

Now Mom stepped in. "Okay, girls, I've think we've taken quite enough of Bobby's time. He's explained his actions sufficiently. I believe him." She favored Bobby with one of those mushy-eyed gazes. "So now you know why we can't call Inspector Bouchard."

Bobby tunneled his fingers through his shock of white hair, leaving tufts standing up straight like peacock feathers. He ran one hand over the white stubble on his chin while he chewed his lower lip. "No, Laura, I think that's exactly what you should do."

"What?" Mom asked. "Call the inspector? Why?"

"Because we might just shake something loose that way. One of you calls and tells him about the accidents today. And how worried you all are. You can also lay out all the other information. Our kidnapping. The mysterious return. Your suspicions about *Le Picnic Francais*. Your seeing the kidnapper there. All of it. He shouldn't suspect a thing and he also, particularly if he's the man I think he is, will be concerned enough to do some checking himself. I'm hoping he might lead me directly to the mastermind. If you can get him to Barcelona, I'll take it from there."

"Won't that just make us targets for the bad guys?" Tessa asked.

"Perhaps," Bobby said, "but I'll have one of my lads watching you at all times."

"Right," I said. "They've done a bang up job of protecting us so far."

"To be fair," Mom interjected, "that hasn't been their job until now."

Bobby was quiet for a few beats and then he focused on my mother. "Laura, I think maybe you're at too much risk. I'll arrange to have you fly home. At least you'll be safe and I'll feel better about all of this."

Mom glared at him. "I am not leaving my family here, Robert. You might feel better, but I most definitely won't. I'll take my chances."

"Mom, he's right," I said. "It's too dangerous."

She cast a withering look at me. "Kate. There will be no discussion about this. I'm staying."

"Stubborn," Chrissie said with a frown.

Mom turned her withering look on Chrissie. "Darn right. Now, Robert, what's next?"

Bobby tugged on one end of his white mustache. "Well," he said. "I think one of you should make the call to Claude ... err ... Inspector Bouchard and get the ball rolling."

"No time like the present," Chrissie said and held her hand out for the cell phone.

She and Casey scuffled over possession before Chrissie won the battle. She looked inquiringly at Casey who said, "Speed dial 13."

Chrissie punched in the number and waited for the inspector to answer. I drummed my fingers on the table while Casey and Tessa leaned forward so they wouldn't miss a word. Mom, the victim of so much madness and mayhem, was the calmest of us all. Her casual posture suggested nothing more sinister than a call to an old friend. Bobby, on the other hand, twirled the end of his mustache, his body coiled and ready to spring into action. Of what type I wasn't sure.

It seemed like an eternity before Chrissie straightened and said, "Oh, Inspector Bouchard, what a relief to reach you. You won't believe the awful things that have happened."

Chrissie sounded frantic and frightened. And why, for heaven's sake, shouldn't she be? Her voice quavered a bit as she recounted in great detail the scary events of the last few days. She left nothing out, finally concluding, "And so Inspector, we don't know what to do. This is all so awful. It's our birthday and it was supposed to be fu-un." A single sob escaped her.

She was certainly doing a fantastic job of conveying how terrified we were. Maybe she overdid it a bit, but, in the end, she said, "We really didn't know who else to call. You've been so wonderful with the girls and..."

She listened for a few seconds. And then said, "Yes, uh huh. Certainly. That would be fantastic. I can't tell you how much better I feel knowing you are on the way."

She gave us a thumbs up. "Yes, the *Hotel Montecarlo*. Tomorrow? That's wonderful. I can't thank you enough. *Merci. Au revoir.*"

She disconnected and reached across the table to exchange a high five with me and then with Tessa, Casey and Mom. "He'll be in Barcelona tomorrow."

"Let the games begin," I said.

Chapter 27

With the conclusion of our discussion Bobby caught our waiter's eye and signaled for the check. "I need to get back to my laptop," he said. "I'll walk you ladies back to the hotel." He shoved back his chair and stood up.

Mom leaped to her feet and confronted him. Where previously she had been mushy-eyed, her eyes were now steely weapons flashing at Bobby. "No, you won't. The girls and I aren't going back. We have other plans."

"We do?" Chrissie and I exclaimed together.

"We do," Mom said firmly. "So you see, Robert, we won't be needing an escort."

Ooh. Way to go, Mom!

Not to be dismissed lightly, Bobby said, "Laura, I must insist. I simply cannot allow you to go off on your own."

Oops. When will men learn that the "a" word is a red flag to most of us self-respecting 21st Century women? Men don't "allow" us to do anything. We make our own decisions, thank you very much. My feisty mother was no different.

She fixed Bobby with an indignant stare. "Robert. I won't be bullied. Not by you or by any alleged thugs. The girls and I will be just fine."

Bobby was taken aback by this new attitude from my formerly docile and agreeable mother. He slumped into his chair. "I was only concerned for your safety, my dear."

He appeared so woebegone --- his professional manner slipping a bit --- that Mom took pity on him. "All right, Robert. What do you suggest?"

"Well, if you won't let me escort you back to the hotel, at least allow me to assign a lad to follow you."

Mom heaved a huge sigh. "Oh, okay. If it will make you feel better."

"Much better," Bobby told her. "Thank you."

The matter settled to Bobby's, if not Mom's, satisfaction, Mom hoisted her purse onto her shoulder and marched off in the direction of the ladies room without a backward glance. Chrissie and I exchanged amused looks and followed her.

When we returned Bobby stood to hold a chair for Mom. She shook her head and stomped around the table to stand behind Tessa and peer over her shoulder at the guidebook Tessa had open in front of her. Obviously she was still peeved at Bobby.

"Tessa? Casey? Do you want to come with your mothers and me? Or do you have other plans?" Mom asked totally ignoring Bobby.

"Do you want to go back to *La Sagrada*?" Casey said. "We didn't see much of it."

Tessa stabbed her finger on the open page. "The only familia I want to see is this one."

I leaned over her shoulder and read aloud, "*La Boutique Familia.* World Famous boutique in Barcelona. Designer clothing and handcrafted items from all over Spain."

"Yep, Aunt Kate," Tessa said. "I'm ready to exchange culture for retail. Right, Casey?"

"Absolutely," Casey agreed. "Culture will kill you if you're not careful."

As Casey and Tessa jumped to their feet and started gathering their stuff, Chrissie snagged Tessa's arm to restrain her and turned to address Bobby. "Wait a second here. I'm no more comfortable sending these two out on their own than you are letting Mom go. They need protection as much as we do."

Bobby nodded and gestured toward the sidewalk. "I've got that covered."

We all turned to look where he was pointing.

"Robert," Casey crowed.

"Mac," Tessa echoed.

And they sprinted toward Bobby's two grandsons who we were astounded to see hurrying toward the café. The two young men swept our daughters into hugs that suggested they were far more than mere friends. Soldiers returning from war might not be greeted with more enthusiasm than that with which Casey and Tessa welcomed the MacTavish grandsons.

"I thought," I said to Bobby, "that Robert and Mac didn't know anything about your undercover activities?"

"They don't," he answered.

"Then why?" I began.

"Love or something like it," Bobby said. "They came to Barcelona to surprise the girls at dinner tonight. I simply called the hotel to get them here a bit sooner."

"Inspired idea," I agreed as the two couples strolled toward us hand in hand.

Casey's fingers were entwined with Robert's as she announced, "I say we abandon retail therapy for some serious recreational therapy." She smiled up at him and he pulled her closer. "You know what I mean?"

Tessa poked Mac in the ribs. "I couldn't agree more."

With the four young people engrossed in each other, I pulled Bobby aside and whispered. "I gather you don't want to boys to know the exact nature of your job."

"Not at the moment," he replied. "I'll have to fill them in later."

"And you think the girls will be safe with your grandsons?'

"Safe from the criminal element, yes. I don't know about my grandsons." He grinned.

"Ha ha," I said.

"Seriously," Bobby said, "I wouldn't send them off if I thought they were in danger."

"Now what?" Chrissie asked.

"We should be all set," Bobby said as he dropped Euros on the table. "The girls and my grandsons can do some exploring and you two and your mother can enjoy the rest of your birthday. There's plenty of time before the limo picks you up for dinner."

Dinner. I had almost forgotten the elaborate dinner Bobby had planned. And he'd arranged for a limo to pick us up at the hotel.

"What time will the limo be at the hotel?"

"Nine-thirty. "You have plenty of time. I'll say goodbye and see you later."

"Wait, Bobby," I said. "Where is our bodyguard?" I surveyed the restaurant and the sidewalk in front. "I don't see anyone."

Chrissie rolled her eyes. "That's kind of the point, isn't it?"

"I suppose," I said, "but I'd feel better if I saw a great big former Marine toting a machine gun following me."

Chrissie did a slow turn, clutched my arm and then whispered. "Maybe there is."

Over Mom's objections Bobby called a cab for us and she was still grumbling as it pulled up in front of the restaurant and she climbed into the backseat. "This really isn't necessary. We shouldn't spend the money."

"On the contrary," Chrissie said as she climbed in behind her, "my feet are grateful to be riding and not striding."

I had one foot in the cab and then stopped as I made a decision I probably should have made long before. After all I had to trust in someone. I reversed direction and stepped back onto the curb. "Bobby," I called, "there is one more thing."

He looked at me quizzically. "Yes?"

He waited patiently while I rooted around in my purse until I unearthed my make-up bag. I unzipped it and handed it to him. "I should have given this to you earlier."

Bobby peered curiously into the bag and then reached inside. Brandishing a tube of lipstick in his large hand, he quirked an eyebrow at me. "Not quite my usual shade."

Ah, so he did have a sense of humor. Good to know.

"Don't be dense," I said and dumped the contents into his hands.

The pile of gems sparkled among the used tissues and gum-wrappers and tubes of lip gloss.

"Ah," Bobby said. "I wondered when you were going to let me see these."

"Sorry," I said. "I don't know why I didn't show you sooner."

Bobby looked at me and smiled. "You do know you can trust me, don't you, Kate? I'll see what I can find out about these. I have my sources, don't you know?"

I nodded and climbed into the cab. "Thank you, Bobby."

I looked out the window and waved at Casey and Tessa as they hurried away with their respective MacTavishes. Bobby was still standing on the curb watching us as our cab pulled away and was swallowed by traffic.

I turned my attention to the conversation between Chrissie and Mom. "So where are going?"

"Shopping," Mom said. "We told him..." she nodded at the driver "... to take us to the best shopping district in Barcelona"

"Just because the girls are giving up the wonderful world of material goods doesn't mean we have to," Chrissie added. "Let's shop 'til we drop."

"My sentiments precisely," Mom said as she searched in her purse.

"What on earth are you looking for?" I asked.

"Hmm. What? Oh, nothing darling. Just seeing if I'll have enough money to buy you birthday presents after the outrageous cab fare we're going to have to pay."

I didn't believe she was telling the complete truth, but I didn't think it was worth the effort to try to ferret more information from her. She'd tell us when she wanted to share. Until then --- let the shopping begin.

The cab driver let us out in front of a two-story mall on *Avenida Diagonal*. The sign over the entrance read *"L'illa Diagonal"* and I knew from my reading in Tessa's guidebook that this mall promoted primarily luxury items as well as many upscale bars and cafes. A bigger mall, the *Centre Comercial Barcelona Glories*, was just down the street.

"Perfect," Chrissie said as she looked around. "Everything that could possibly tempt us in one glorious place."

"Lead on," I said.

We paid the cab driver and I scanned the street before I followed my mother and sister into the mall.

"Don't worry," my twin said looking over her shoulder, "he's got our back."

"That's kind of what I was worried about," I said. "Who might have our backs."

We spent the next hour wandering in and out of a variety of shops, but nothing spoke to us. Until, that is, Mom paused in front of a small shop with the seductive name, *"La Gema Perfecta."*

"Oh, girls, look," Mom breathed with her nose practically pressed against the glass.

A smorgasbord of brightly colored gemstones intertwined intricately with silver and gold --- each piece different from the piece next to it --- presented a tempting display.

"Let's go in," Mom said and without waiting for our reply, slipped inside. Chrissie and I exchanged knowing looks and followed her.

The two of us were at opposite sides of the shop when Mom called us over to the counter where she was examining a tray of rings --- each featured different gems in a twisted maze of silver and gold. "Just look at these," she said. "Aren't they gorgeous? You know what would be fun?"

"I have no idea," Chrissie said as she picked up one ring after another.

"Tell us what would be fun," I said.

"I haven't done a thing for your birthday," Mom said. Her eyes gleamed with excitement. "I'd love to buy a ring for each of you."

She fingered one of the rings. "I have the best idea. We should get rings that have not only your birthstone in it, but also the birthstone of your daughter. That way you'll have something of your daughter wrapped around your finger. Not the other way around."

It was a brilliant idea --- sentimental and sweet --- but impractical. "We aren't going to find the exact stones we'd need," I said. "It's a lovely idea, though."

Mom approached the clerk, who it turned out, was the shop owner as well the designer of the jewelry. They conferred in quiet tones while Chrissie and I tried on rings. The owner disappeared into the back of the store and returned bearing a display tray.

"I believe you might like these," he said and beamed at Mom.

Two rings --- not identical but obviously from the same designer --- just like Chrissie and me --- nestled together on a bed of black velvet. One ring featured a setting of tiny emeralds and opals, Casey's birthstone. The other was set with emeralds and sapphires, Tessa's birthstone. Tiny diamond chips sparkled on them.

"Well, how about that?" Mom said. "These are perfect."

I looked at Chrissie. She looked at me.

"We've been had," I said.

"Aren't you the devious little thing?" Chrissie added. "You planned this."

"Me?" Mom asked all innocence. "I have no idea what you're talking about."

Chrissie and I crushed her between us as we hugged her and planted noisy kisses on her cheek. Mom laughed and pretended to try to extricate herself but she was delighted that her surprise had gone off so well.

"Nice touch with the diamonds," I said.

Mom smiled. "You got that, did you?"

Chrissie blinked at us, a puzzled expression on her face. "What about the diamonds?"

"Think about it," I explained. "We've got emeralds, our birthstone, our daughters' birthstones and the diamonds are for Mom because..."

"Diamonds are her birthstone," Chrissie finished with a laugh. "Three generations on a single finger. Cool."

I held up my hand and turned it so that the ring caught the light and gave off a rainbow reflection. "I love it. How did you ever find this place?"

Proud of her success Mom grinned. "I have my ways. And a little help from Mr. Google."

"You're amazing," Chrissie said as she twisted her ring on her finger.

As Mom handed her credit card to the smiling shop owner, I glanced at my watch. "Oh, my gosh," I said. "I can't believe how late it is. We need to get back to the hotel to get ready for dinner."

Mom folded the credit slip and stuck it in her billfold. "I just have one more thing I need to do." And she hurried out of the shop and into the crowded mall.

"We don't have time..." I began.

"It won't take long," she said. "I'm just going over there." She pointed.

"Where?" I asked.

"There," she said. "That jewelry store."

"But we were just in..."

"Trust me," she said and led the way to the jewelry store --- much larger and more elegant than the one we'd been in. Indeed, the price tags on the items were substantially higher than at *La Gema Perfecta*.

She dug into her purse.

"What are you looking for?" I asked. "Buried treasure?"

"Hmm," she said. "What? Oh, wait a second. Here it is." She pulled out a small baggie and waggled it in the air.

I squinted at the bag in her hand and sucked in a breath. "Mom, are those..."

"...gemstones?" Chrissie finished.

Mom grinned a Cheshire cat grin and said nothing.

"I know where she got them," I said. "They're from the lunch stash. I even see crumbs clinging to the inside of the bag."

Chrissie grabbed Mom's arm. "I thought Kate gave the bag of gems to Bobby. Where did these come from?"

"I kept a few so I could find out for myself what they're worth. What Bobby doesn't know won't hurt him."

"Why you sneaky little devil," Chrissie said.

"My great aunt Clara died recently here in Barcelona and I found these going through her things," Mom explained to the jeweler behind the counter as she shook the baggie like a tambourine.

Chrissie and I exchanged amused looks.

"Clara was quite eccentric and squirreled away valuable things in odd places. I found these in an old urn. I'd like to know if they're genuine gemstones," Mom continued.

The jeweler's dark greased-back hairstyle and large handlebar mustache made him look like a villain in a 20's silent movie. His eyes were black and shining with curiosity --- or was it greed? He slicked his long, pointy tongue over his lips as he looked my mother --- and her baggie --- up and down. "I can't tell you how much they are worth unless you commission a complete appraisal, but I'd be happy to examine them. I feel certain I can assure you one way or another about their authenticity."

Mom relinquished the bag of gems. "*Gracias, Señor.*"

The man dumped the gems onto the counter and flicked the crumbs aside with evident distaste. Then he affixed his jeweler's loupe to his eye and inspected the sparkling gems. When he finished he pulled the loupe away and regarded

Mom with a serious look. "*Si, señora*, these appear to be genuine."

Mom nodded as if she had expected to hear nothing else. "So, could you make a guess as to their worth." She flashed him a dazzling smile. Was she flirting with this sleazy guy? Amazing. I underestimated her all these years.

Surprisingly, he blushed and smiled back, revealing a gold front tooth. Ugh.

"I could make a guess. But I would prefer you left them for an appraisal."

I'll just bet.

Mom shook her head. "No, that isn't possible at the moment. If you can just give me your best estimate, I would be grateful."

Mom batted her eyes at him and he stammered, "We-ll, it..it is not our policy to make guesses, but, but for you *una señora hermosa*, I will make the exception."

Double ugh. Now he was flirting back.

"*Gracias, señor.* You are too kind."

His blush deepened. "Well, then. There are ten stones here. Diamonds, rubies and emeralds. Uncut. Fine quality. Perhaps a value of 20,000 Euros. Maybe more."

He scooped up the stones and reached under the counter to secure a velvet jewelry bag and dropped them into it. He handed the bag to Mom who tucked it into her purse as if it contained nothing more than cheap knock-off baubles from a street fair. "*Muchas gracias, Señor...*" She read his name tag. "*Feliciano.* You have been very helpful. I appreciate your taking the time to inspect my little find." She chuckled and added, "I'll put them back in that urn so that my sneaky brother, Howard, won't suspect I have had them appraised."

Having completed her mission, she turned and glided airily out of the store with Chrissie and me close behind. She didn't stop until we reached a tall column well out of view of anyone who might have watched us in the store. Then she reached into her purse, removed the velvet bag and tucked it into her bra. She patted her chest and Chrissie and I burst into nervous laughter.

"She missed her calling," I said to Chrissie.

"Should have been a private eye," Chrissie agreed. "She has skills I wouldn't have believed possible."

Mom snorted. "Let's get a cab. I'm going to have a nervous breakdown. I have 20,000 Euros worth of gems hidden in my bra."

"More than you usually fit into a 34A," I commented and ducked as Mom took a swing at me.

Chapter 28

As we waited for the elevator at the *Hotel MonteCarlo*, Mom brushed her chest for the zillionth time, reassuring herself that the jewels were safely secured in her bra.

"Not to worry, Mom," I said, "the family jewels are still there."

"Very funny."

She stabbed repeatedly at the up button and tapped her foot. No one said a word for a few minutes until, unable to stand the silence, I said, "Mom, are you mad at me?"

She continued to punch the button without turning around. "Of course." Jab. "Not." Jab. "Don't..." Jab. "...be..." Jab. "...ridiculous." Jab.

I bit my lip and kept my eyes focused on my shoes. I didn't have to look at my twin to know what she was thinking.

"Stop that," Mom said.

"Stop what? I'm not doing anything."

"Oh, yes, you are. I can feel it. The twin thing," she said without taking her eyes from the elevator door. "And I do not appreciate being thought about behind my back."

I couldn't help it. I chanced a glance at Chrissie. She did an eye roll and her lips twitched. I bit my lip more forcefully, nearly drawing blood, but I couldn't stop the giggles. It was contagious. Chrissie and I burst into laughter. Mom whirled to face us and her scowl crumpled into a tiny smile, followed by a grin and then she cracked up as well. When she caught her breath, she said, "It's been a long day. What's taking the stupid elevator so long?"

At that moment I heard familiar voices and laughter and stepped back to peek around the corner. I saw Casey, Tessa and the MacTavish grandsons sprawled on a large brocade couch in the lounge engrossed in a raucous card game. It was obvious that they had put aside, at least for the moment, any worries about our screwy day. Suddenly, Casey looked up and spotted me. "Yo, Mom," she bellowed, "about time you got back. The limo will be here in less than an hour."

I checked my watch. How had it gotten so late? "Tell it to wait," I called across the lobby. "You can't celebrate without the honored guests." And I wheeled around as the elevator doors slid open and Mom, Chrissie and I crowded inside. We stood like three statues facing the door as we ascended to our floor. No one said a word and I focused on a framed poster of a happy couple toasting each other with champagne in the hotel restaurant. A pang of longing swept over me. I missed Scott. Why wasn't he here drinking champagne with me on my birthday? Then the elevator door opened. I sighed and followed my mother and my twin down the hall.

At the door to our room, Mom said, "Do you mind if I come in for a minute? The girls are busy downstairs." Without waiting for an answer, she brushed past us and flopped down on the nearest bed. "Whew," she said as she dislodged the now-sweaty velvet jewelry bag from her bra. "I thought I'd have a heart attack before we got back here."

I met Chrissie's eyes and she lifted one shoulder in a half-shrug. I mimicked her gesture as we followed Mom into the room. While we might have liked a little twin time, which of us, under these circumstances, was going to tell our mother that two's company and three's a crowd? Not I, for sure.

"You're safe," I said to Mom. "No one will mug you now. Guess you like to live life on the edge --- stashing a horde of contraband in your lingerie."

Mom emptied the bag and was carefully counting the gems. She gazed at me from under her lashes. "Call me Mata Hari, dear." She settled back against the pillows and, now that she wasn't in any imminent danger, smiled serenely and closed her eyes.

"Scissors, stone or paper for the first shower?" I said to Chrissie.

She nodded and, as I expected, topped my scissors with her rock and headed for the bathroom. I heard the shower start and I exhaled a long breath and stretched out on the other bed. I glanced at Mom whose eyes were still closed and decided to clear up something that had been nagging at me all day.

"Um, Mom. It came up a couple of times today. About how Bobby's first wife died. You didn't seem surprised or upset. What's the story?"

"Ahh." She rolled over and propped her head on her hand. "Bobby blames himself for Emmaline's --- that's his wife --- death. That much is true. But he didn't kill her like Casey wanted us to believe."

"Well," I said, "so what did happen?"

Mom pulled herself up and sat on the edge of the bed. She ran a hand through her hair and stared into space for so long that it was all I could do not to reach over and poke her. Finally, she said, "It's a sad story."

"Go on."

She wrinkled her nose and seemed to be debating the wisdom of going on before she gave me a grave look. "I guess it won't hurt for me to tell you all of this. I'm sure Bobby wouldn't mind."

"Uh, huh."

She took a deep breath. "So, you know Bobby works for Interpol? Well, Emmaline did too. She was his secretary when he first started. Then they fell in love and got married. It was all perfect at first. They had children and a happy life."

"Then it happened that Bobby had a case involving some really crafty smugglers. His team couldn't seem to get enough evidence to arrest them. And then they managed to track their operations to a hotel in Switzerland."

"It was Emmaline who came up with the plan. She proposed that she and Bobby take a vacation at the hotel in question. She said it was an ideal cover. No one would suspect an ordinary Scots couple of being undercover agents. Bobby says she even joked about killing two birds with one stone. That it was the only way she'd ever get him to take her on a vacation."

"Unfortunately, there was a leak of some kind and the bad guys found out that they were cops. One day Emmaline went hiking with a group of tourists while Bobby stayed at the hotel. She never returned. Bobby sent his men out to find her, but days went by before they found her body at the bottom of a rocky cliff."

"Bobby was devastated. Still blames himself to this day."

"Oh," I said. "That's horrible."

"What's horrible?" Chrissie poked her head out of the bathroom.

"I'll tell you later," I said. "Are you finished in there yet?"

"Just about. Would you look in my suitcase and find my pink bra and panties and bring them to me?"

Mom hoisted herself to her feet, tucked the jewelry bag back in her bra and gathered her purse and shopping bags. "I'm going to go shower. We can talk more about Bobby and Emmaline later if you want, but right now I need to get ready for dinner."

Mom threaded her way through the clutter, and letting the door slam behind her, disappeared into the hallway. I dropped to one knee beside Chrissie's suitcase and began rifling through it in search of the underwear she wanted. I finally unearthed it at the very bottom of the bag. As I tugged on the bra, a pile of clothes fell out of the suitcase. I snatched them up and was about to stuff them back in the bag when I noticed a small rip in the lining. "Hey, Chris," I called, "did you know there's a rip in your bag?"

She couldn't hear me above the noise of the hairdryer so curiosity won out and I tossed her underwear on the floor and stuck my finger in the tiny tear. As I did, an SD memory card for a digital camera fell into my hand. That's odd, I thought. Why is she storing her memory card in the bottom of her bag?

The racket from the hairdryer quit and Chrissie stuck her head out the bathroom door again. "Hey, Kate. Have you forgotten that I'm naked in here? I need my undies and then the bathroom is all yours."

I knew she wasn't going to be pleased to see that I'd made a shambles out of her things so I crammed the SD card into my pocket and tried quickly to repair the lining rip and repack her crumpled clothes. As I stuck the frayed ends in the hole, I felt what seemed to be a hard package under the lining. She was so sneaky. Probably another gift for me. Well, I wouldn't let on that I'd found it and spoil her surprise. I scrambled to my feet with her undies in my hand and shoved them at her as I stripped and ducked into the shower.

"Remind me again why we're going out for dinner at this ungodly hour?" I grumbled as we stepped into the elevator.

"Because," Chrissie said with exaggerated patience, "well-bred Spaniards never dine before ten o'clock."

"I'm neither Spanish nor well bred. What I am is starving to death. I'm going to keel over from hunger."

My mother gave me a stern look. "You're ungrateful as well, Kate. Bobby is saving you from having your birthday dinner at a greasy Spanish equivalent of MacDonald's."

Okay. So she had me there. When we were planning this birthday trip the one thing that my friend Mary Linda left to me was the venue for our birthday dinner. She had presented me with a list of possible restaurants, but it was my job to select one and arrange for dinner. Alas, typically I suppose, I had procrastinated about doing it until we arrived in Barcelona. And then, due to a major convention of some sort, I found that every place on my list was booked. Not a single one of the snooty people at the reservation desks was willing to squeeze us in.

I complained at breakfast about the condescending way I'd been treated and Bobby stepped in. He offered, diffidently and not wanting to intrude, to arrange our birthday dinner. I objected, at first, that our dinner shouldn't be organized by a nearly perfect stranger, but relented when I realized that, literally, beggars don't get to be choosers. In spite of his generosity, though, I was hungry, tired and feeling hostile toward our benefactor. Not one of my better moments. I bit my lip and choked back any further whining as the elevator doors glided open and we were face to face with Casey and Tessa and the grandsons.

"So, there you are finally," Casey said --- hand on hip. "The limo's been here for ages. We were coming up to see what was keeping you."

"Relax, darlin'," I said. "Party won't be a party without us."

"True," Casey said. Then she stepped back and checked us out. "Whoa, you two look smokin'."

Chrissie and I had, indeed, expended a great deal of effort to make ourselves, as Casey so kindly put it, smokin'. As the guests of honor we wanted to turn heads and earn compliments about how much younger than that dreaded number of years we appeared. Apparently we'd been successful.

I winked at Chrissie and she winked back.

"Smokin'," I said.

"Hot," she answered.

When the limo driver parked in front of the restaurant Bobby had chosen, I looked out the window in dismay. It was in the *Barceloneta* neighborhood near the waterfront. *La Barceloneta*, formerly a fishing district, still maintains a slightly seedy ambiance with quaint seafood restaurants lining the narrow streets. Our destination was a dilapidated building with a magnificent view of the harbor to the rear. A sign hanging lopsidedly from the weathered beam above the entrance welcomed us to *El Pescadero Barcelona*. From the rundown exterior, I feared that the interior would be grimy and depressing.

I hesitated before I got out of the limo and Chrissie gave me a gentle nudge from behind. "Too late to back out now," she said.

I needn't have worried. Once we crossed the threshold we found ourselves in a warm, cozy, if somewhat rustic, tavern. A cheerful fire burned in a huge stone fireplace to our right while a long wooden bar stretched along the entire wall to our left. The tuxedo-clad maitre d' greeted us effusively and escorted us through the bar to a more secluded dining area behind it. Another fire burned in a smaller fireplace and tall windows opened onto a breathtaking view of the marina and the harbor beyond. Fishing boats as well as pleasure craft bobbed at the dock and harbor lights reflected off the water in the distance. A terrace dotted with tables ran along the entire back of the building.

"Oh, wow," Chrissie said as she gazed out the window. "I guess Bobby knows what he's doing."

"I'm impressed," I said.

We were still gazing in awe at the waterfront when Bobby appeared. He bowed to us and then kissed Mom's cheek. In honor of the occasion, and with the perhaps unanticipated effect of titillating our mother, Bobby was again attired in his kilt. Tessa and Casey exchanged knowing smirks and gave Bobby's knobby knees a lascivious once over while Robert and Mac pretended to ignore their silliness. Mom and Bobby remained oblivious to all of us as they gazed at each other.

"Welcome, Kate. Welcome, Christine," Bobby said when he could tear his eyes away from Mom. "I hope that *El Pescadero* doesn't disappoint. The food here is the best in Barcelona."

"The view is outstanding, Gramps," Robert said.

"Depends on what it is you're viewing." Casey jerked her head at Bobby's stocking-clad legs.

Tessa covered her mouth with her hand to hide her giggles.

A large round table covered with a pristine white tablecloth and decorated with red candles in glass lanterns sat in front of the windows. Each place was set with silver table service and crystal wine glasses and a cut glass bud vase containing a single red rose. Bobby guided Chrissie and me to the places of honor side by side with the best view of the waterfront beyond.

"Bobby," I said, "this is amazing. Everything is gorgeous. This place wasn't even on my list."

Bobby beamed with pleasure. "I know your mother told you, but I felt terrible about all the messing about that has taken place on your birthday trip. I hoped that I could make it up to you in some small way by hosting your dinner."

I ran a finger over the tablecloth. "You didn't have to go to so much trouble."

"But we're glad you did," Chrissie added. "Thank you."

"Just have a good time tonight," Bobby said. "That's all the thanks I need." He turned to speak to the headwaiter lurking at his shoulder.

"Wait a second. Bobby?" I tugged on his sleeve to get his attention.

He held up a finger to the headwaiter and raised his eyebrows at me. "Yes?"

"I believe there are eight of us. Five of us and three MacTavishes. But I noticed the table is set for nine."

"Oh." An odd expression crossed his face. "I hope you won't mind, but I invited a friend to join us."

"Of course, we wouldn't ..."

"There he is now," Bobby said and began to edge toward the entrance.

Casey and Tess had joined us and we all peered curiously across the room at Bobby's friend, a tall dark-haired man in a black leather jacket talking to the maitre d'.

"I wonder who he is," Chrissie whispered.

Then the maitre d' gestured toward our dining room and black leather jacket turned around. At first he was hidden in the shadows, but as he strode through the bar firelight flickered across his face.

"Small world," I murmured as I saw his face.

Casey, who had her back to the door, looked over her shoulder to see the newcomer and her mouth dropped open. She took a single step toward the door then stopped and sank into a chair. Her eyes filled with tears and she said in a shaky voice, "Luc?"

Tessa whirled around and stared at him. "Casey? Are you okay?"

Casey ignored her and stormed across the room to confront him. She swiped a hand across her eyes and glared at Luc until he lowered his head to avoid her hostile gaze. "What," she demanded, "are you doing here? Did Bouchard send you to find us?"

Luc jerked his head up and met her eyes. "Bouchard? Why would he send me?"

Casey glared at him, her fists clenched at her sides. "Ah, ha," she said. "Then you do know him. They kept telling me not to trust you. You two-faced, double-dealing faithless fraud! I suppose those two adorable little girls are actresses too."

"Do you mean Noelle and Clarice? My daughters? What are you talking about? Actresses? *Mon dieu.*"

Luc's face grew flushed with indignation as he realized that Casey was accusing him of using the little girls. A single vein throbbed in his temple and he ground out his words through clenched teeth. "Noelle and Clarice are my daughters. I would never do anything to harm them. Never. *Sacre bleu.*"

He lifted one shoulder in disgust and scowled at Casey who looked nonplussed for a moment before she stood her ground. The pair glowered at each other while the rest of the room grew hushed.

"Uh, oh," Chrissie breathed over my shoulder. "Trouble in paradise."

I crossed the room in two quick strides to reach Casey's side. Bobby stepped between them at the same moment. "I invited Luc," he said, but Casey remained oblivious to Bobby, her eyes narrowed with contempt.

I seized Casey's arm and dragged her toward the ladies room leaving nothing but stunned silence in our wake. I shoved the door open with my foot and pushed her gently down on the worn brocade couch just inside. I stood over her and waited. Then as the silence stretched out, I said, "Casey Kelly, what on earth was that about?"

Casey scowled at me and then her lower lip trembled and her face turned upside down and she burst into tears. I dropped onto the couch next to her. "Oh, sweetie," I said as I put my arm around her. Casey leaned on my shoulder and sobbed.

Finally she scrubbed the heels of her hands into her eyes and said in a strangled tone, "Oh, Mom, I'm ruining your new jacket."

"Don't be silly," I said as I continued to hold her. "Daughter trumps jacket every time." But I confess I did sneak a peek at my shoulder to assess the damage that her waterworks might be causing. Then I did a mental "*c'est la vie*" and rubbed my daughter's back while she wept.

At last she stopped crying and sniffed loudly. Her eyes were red-rimmed and black rivers of mascara meandered down her damp cheeks. She hiccoughed and said ruefully, "I don't know what came over me."

I took a paper cup from the dispenser by the sink, filled it with water and snatched the tissue box from the counter. I handed both to her and she gulped down the water, blew her nose, and wiped her eyes.

"I didn't think you were that serious about Luc," I said.

"I'm not."

"I think, and feel free to deny it, that this isn't about Luc at all."

Casey looked at me mournfully and twisted the tissue into shreds. When she didn't speak, I forged ahead. "It's my humble opinion that this is more about Lester than anything else. Maybe you aren't really over him after all."

She shook her head. "No. I am. Over him. Really." She took a tiny sip of water. "At least I thought I was."

"Then what was that scene with Luc all about? I thought you were going to gouge his eyes out."

Casey grinned in spite of herself. "I was kind of fierce, wasn't I?"

"Scary is the word I'd use."

"I know. I think it's just everything, Mom. They tell you you're the only one for them and convince you to give up everything and move to California." Her voice cracked. "And then they want space to find themselves. What's that about?" Tears rolled silently down her cheeks. "Men lie."

"Ah," I said. "Now I get it. Lester lied. And then Luc didn't tell you everything you think you should have known."

She nodded unhappily. "I guess so."

"But sweetie pie, Luc just met you. He can't really be expected to confide all his secrets. Not yet."

"I suppose."

I sagged onto the couch next to her and closed my eyes. Neither of us could think of anything to add to our discussion so we sat in affectionate silence until Casey blew out a huge sigh and said, "I guess I should go out and apologize to Luc. And to everyone else."

I opened my eyes and studied her woebegone face. "That would be a beginning. And stop trying to prove how okay you are about Lester and that whole fiasco and let us in. We can help. I promise."

Casey wrapped her arms around me and gave me a hug. For just a moment as she rested her head on my shoulder, I remembered her as a little girl. Then she sat up and ran her hands through her hair. "I'm a mess."

Before I could offer another word of encouragement, there was a timid knock on the door and Tessa poked her head around it. "Are you okay, Case?" she asked.

"Just peachy," Casey answered. "Right as rain. Just love it when I can make a scene."

"Come on in, Tessa," I said.

Tessa slipped through the door and examined the wreckage of her cousin's make-up with a critical eye. "You need to let me repair your face and then you need to get back out there. You won't believe it."

"What?"

"I'm pretty sure that Luc and Robert are about to do battle over you. They're looking daggers at each other and I think a duel is going to break out at any moment."

Casey perked up considerably at this news. "They are? Seriously?"

Tessa bobbed her head. "You'd better believe it. Now let's do a quick reclamation project and get you out there to poor olive oil on troubled suitors ... so to speak."

I started for the door. "Tessa, you help Casey and I'll go out and do damage control. Poor Bobby is probably distraught."

"Oh, no," Casey cried, "I've ruined your party. And your jacket. I'm a bad person."

"You're being silly. The party isn't ruined..." I brushed at the tearstained shoulder of my jacket, "...and neither is this dumb jacket. That's why we have dry cleaners. Don't worry your pretty little head about it."

Casey drooped into the corner of the couch and watched me with a contrite look. "I'm sorry, Mom. I love you."

Moms are suckers for that kind of stuff. I couldn't hold a ruined jacket against her. "I love you too, Casey K. All there is and more."

Not to be left out, Tessa caught me up in a bear hug and planted a noisy kiss on my cheek. "I love you, Auntie Katie."

I laughed. "And I love you, too, you goofy girl."

Chapter 29

I had no sooner returned to the dining room than Chrissie and Mom converged on me and bombarded me with questions and concern.

"Is Casey okay?" my twin asked.

"Is there anything we can do?" Mom wanted to know.

"I think she's fine," I told them. "Just your basic meltdown."

When Bobby spotted me he hustled over. "I'm so sorry, Kate. I should have told you I was inviting Luc. I didn't realize...."

I cut him off. "It's not your fault. Casey has some issues she needs to work on. She's embarrassed she made a scene."

The worried look on Bobby's face turned to relief and he heaved a huge sigh. "Lassies are so different from lads." He jerked his head toward Robert and Mac who were engaged in some sort of wild conversation involving much waving of hands. Robert kept darting suspicious looks at Luc who lounged against the opposite wall staring moodily into his wine glass. I feared Bobby's relief might be a tad premature.

"Shall we call off dinner then?" Bobby asked. "I would understand if you just want to go back to the hotel."

"Absolutely not," I said. "You've gone to all this trouble and we've been looking forward to it."

"The prodigal daughter hath returned," Chrissie whispered in my ear. I turned to see Casey sailing into the room, head held high, as if she hadn't a care in the world. Tessa trailed after her, a Mona Lisa smile on her face.

Casey and Tessa breezed up to us. "I apologize for my behavior, Bobby," Casey said. "I hope I haven't wrecked the evening."

"Not at all," Bobby said. "I hope you've recovered." He smiled a fond smile at Casey who blushed.

"Me too," Tessa interjected with a wicked grin. "Too much drama spoils the broth."

"I should have told you I invited Luc," Bobby said. "I wasn't aware that you and he..."

"No need to say anything else. I was totally out of line. Let's get back to the celebration of the twins' advanced years." Casey whirled around to face the room.

"Hey," I said and caught her arm. "Maybe you ought to say something to the guys." Indeed, Robert, Mac, and especially, Luc were eyeing our little group warily. "I really think they deserve some explanation."

Casey looked dubious but, nonetheless, she nodded and floated toward Luc. Robert and Mac edged closer to the pair so they could hear the conversation while the rest of us held our breath. Casey looked up at Luc and murmured, "*Desole*. I think I kind of overreacted."

Luc mustered a faint smile. "*Pas de problem*," he said.

Casey laughed --- a sound full of pony tails and jingle bells that promised wonderful things to come. She linked her arm first through Luc's and then through Robert's and beamed at each of them in turn. "I don't believe you all have been introduced. Luc, this is Robert... " She glanced over her shoulder to include Mac. "... and Mac. Bobby's grandsons. And, MacTavishes, this is Luc Marin. Tessa and I met him in Nice with his daughters."

Tessa added helpfully, "He knows Brad Pitt."

"I don't truly know him all that well," Luc began and then realized that Tessa was teasing. He chuckled. "But I do know a few other stars."

"Such as?" Tessa demanded.

The five of them drifted over to stand by the tall windows, laughing and chatting --- the tense situation defused for the time being.

"I'll tell the waiters to begin serving in a moment," Bobby said, "but since everyone here knows my precise position with Interpol except my grandsons, perhaps I should fill them in before they hear it from someone else."

312

We nodded and Bobby strode over to corral Robert and Mac. "A word with you lads," he said and steered them into a corner.

Chapter 30

I slipped a morsel of seafood into my mouth, placed my fork on my plate and leaned back with my eyes closed to savor the flavor of the sauce --- a perfect marriage of spiciness and salt.

"Mmm," I said. "Bobby was so right about the food here. It's awesome."

"And the wine..." Chrissie sighed as she sipped the fine Spanish rioja poured for her by the white-gloved waiter. "What can I say? Except, I'll have more, *por favor.*"

Unfortunately, the atmosphere didn't match the food. Yes, we ate and drank and the sounds of glasses clinking and conversation filled the room, but underneath the camaraderie an aura of apprehension lurked. Secrets and mysteries eddied in the air and the ghosts of Fifi and Georges hovered over our table.

Casey and Luc exchanged smoldering looks while pretending to ignore each other. And Robert watched the pair as if he expected them to leap up and race out the door heading for a remote French vineyard where they would raise grapes and babies in equal numbers. Suddenly, looking at them, I had had enough. I was weary of all the drama and the mystery and dead men and crooked policemen and all of it. This was our birthday, for crying out loud, not some cheap paperback tale of crime and corruption. I didn't have to even see Chrissie's face to know that she felt the same way.

I tapped her on the arm and raised my wine glass. She clinked her glass against mine. "To us," she said.

"To us," I echoed and with complete unanimity we decided to rise above it all and enjoy the elegant dinner.

Casey and Tessa disappeared with Bobby and returned carrying an elaborately decorated cake on which flickered a huge --- in my estimation --- number of candles. After we blew out the conflagration representing our

314

advanced years, the girls presented us with twin silver bracelets. A single heart charm engraved with our initials dangled from each bracelet and inside the charm was a small photo of the five of us taken one day in Paris. I blinked back tears when I saw the five smiling faces and I was not surprised to see a single tear rolling down Chrissie's cheek.

"That's so sweet," I said to Casey. "How did you manage it?"

"I love it," Chrissie agreed. "You two are amazing."

We hugged our daughters and then Mom and then we all began to cry --- tears of happiness, sadness, confusion. You name it, we were crying about it. The four men looked on as if we were an alien species who had wandered into their previously ordered lives.

Finally, Luc said in a teasing voice. "*Mon dieu*. You are all just like Clarice and Noelle. Do you women cry over everything?"

"After tonight," Casey said, "do you really have to ask that?"

We laughed, a bit tentatively at first, but when the men joined in, the tension that had enveloped us all evening eased and the real revelry began. By the time I scraped up the last bite of chocolate cake and licked it off my fork, it was no longer our birthday. The evening ended far better than it began. After consuming mountains of traditional Barcelona dishes and copious amounts of fine Spanish wine, we all felt mellow. Even Luc and Robert had achieved a tentative detente. Casey perched between them flirting with first one and then the other while they vied for her attention. Mac and Tessa were too preoccupied with their own private conversation to take much note of the rest of us. Mom and Bobby wandered over to the tall windows and hand-in-hand gazed out at the harbor lights. Chrissie and I slumped side by side, empty coffee cups and liquor glasses in front of us, and let the chatter swirl over our heads.

"Hey, birthday girl," Chrissie said, "this has certainly been an unforgettable day."

"Definitely," I agreed. "Although not exactly as I pictured it ahead of time."

She blew out a breath. "I'm so exhausted I can't think straight. Do you suppose anyone would miss us if we snuck out?"

I did a quick survey of our group and shook my head. "We're superfluous. I'm ready to escape if you are."

Before we could make our getaway, though, Bobby tore himself away from the view, and our mother as well, and dragged a chair over, wedged it between our two chairs and sat backward on it, his elbows propped on the chair's back.

"Did you enjoy the evening?"

"It was lovely," I said. "Thank you again for planning it. I'm sorry if things got off to a rocky start."

"Don't apologize," Bobby protested. "I really wasn't aware of Casey's friendship with Luc."

"So, how is it that you know Luc anyway?" I asked, channeling Nancy Drew. "He's quite a bit younger than you."

"Kate," Chrissie scolded. "Don't be rude."

"It's fine," Bobby said to her. "Kate's right. Luc is young. And, well, it's complicated."

He scratched his head and stared blankly into space.

I bit the inside of my cheek to keep myself from demanding more answers than he was ready to provide and my uncharacteristic patience was finally rewarded.

"It's complicated," Bobby said again. "I'm not really at liberty to explain, but...." His voice trailed off and he looked around to see if anyone else was listening to our conversation. Apparently reassured that the young people were too absorbed in their flirting to eavesdrop, he said, "Luc is more of a colleague."

"A colleague? As in working together?" Chrissie asked.

Bobby cut his eyes to Casey and Luc, put a finger to his lips and nodded. "Precisely."

"Interpol?" I asked.

Bobby gave me a vague look and shook his head.

"It's Interpol," I insisted. "I know it is. But Casey and the rest of us are convinced he knows Inspector Bouchard. Is that possible?"

"I can't say," Bobby said, but I was certain I was on the right track.

"And Interpol, too?" Chrissie asked.

Bobby rolled his eyes. "I really can't say another word."

"Oh, good Lord," I exclaimed. "Luc's a double agent. Cool."

If Luc worked for Bouchard and also for Interpol, did the inspector know? And if he did, how did that impact the entire Paris/Georges/Fifi situation? Thousands of questions sprang to mind, but I couldn't wangle another word out of Bobby. He had told us as much as he intended to --- probably more --- and he wouldn't budge. I glanced at Chrissie. I knew she must be as anxious as I to get back to our hotel room to dissect this latest tidbit of information.

Chrissie and I weren't the only ones eager to return to the hotel. It had been a tumultuous day and everyone appeared ready to have it end. Even Casey and Tessa, usually primed to party all night, were droopy and listless. As the others gathered up their things and said their goodbyes, I decided to make a quick trip to the ladies room. I trudged across the dining room and as I rounded the corner, I spotted Casey and Luc. He had his back to the wall and was leaning toward her as she tilted her head back to gaze up at him. I stopped, thinking I should give them their privacy, but nature took over from nurture and the need to pee won out. I tiptoed toward the door, but Luc glanced up and met my eye as I approached. Casey followed his gaze and when she saw me she held up one hand to Luc. "*Un moment.*"

She grabbed my elbow and propelled me into the ladies room. "Is everything all right?" I asked as the door closed behind us.

Casey laughed. "*Oui, Maman. C'est bonne.*" Before she could say more I was shifting from one foot to the other as the urgency of my situation grew more pressing. She laughed again and pushed me toward the stalls. "Go, Mom. I don't want to be the cause of you wetting your pants."

I disappeared into the stall while Casey stood outside. "I'm going back to the hotel with Luc," she said. "We need to talk without an audience. Besides, I'm my mother's daughter and I intend to do a little detective work."

"Casey, wait and we can..." But I heard the restroom door open and I was in no position, literally, to stop her. When I came out of the stall, the room was empty.

As I stood at the sink with hot water running over my hands, I studied my reflection in the mirror. The woman who stared back at me looked haggard... lines which had been laugh lines only a few hours before had turned into craters. I shuddered and stuck my tongue out at her. At this rate the glue factory was just around the corner. Unfortunately, I couldn't stand there brooding all night so I finished up and limped wearily back to join the others waiting for our limo.

By the time we stumbled out of the elevator on our floor of the hotel, though, we had revived somewhat. Or maybe it was just a sugar high from all the food and drink. Either way no one, it seemed, was quite ready to climb into bed. So Chrissie and I found ourselves hosting an impromptu rehash of the evening's events. Only Casey --- still out with Luc --- was missing from our little conclave.

I kicked off my shoes, tossed my bag on the desk and sank into the single upholstered chair. "Whew, what a day."

More food or alcohol seemed ill-advised so Mom busied herself making hot tea from the collection of tea bags on the dresser. As she handed each of us a cup of steaming tea, I eyed my family ---Tessa and Chrissie sprawled on one of the twin beds and Mom puttering with the tea bags. "I've been thinking ..." I began.

"I've warned you about that," Chrissie said.

I gave her my best, most practiced big sister look. "I've been thinking," I repeated, "maybe we should reconsider the rest of the trip."

"Meaning?" Chrissie asked.

"Meaning maybe we should just go to Madrid tomorrow and eliminate the whole Ronda side trip. We could relax in Madrid. Do the Prado Museum. Kick back." I stole a look at Chrissie and added, "Skip the bulls."

"Much as I would love to say *adios* to the bulls," Chrissie said, "Ronda was your idea and I was kind of looking forward to it. In an odd sort of a way."

Ronda had, indeed, been my idea, but the *Parador Ronda* was not the most logistically convenient of our hotels. To get there and back to Madrid where we were catching our flight home involved at least two, and possibly three, train trips. The first train, booked for the following night, was an overnight trip of about nine hours. I looked at my family calculatingly. Suddenly it all seemed a bit much.

"I thought the overnight train sounded cool," Tessa protested.

"And we reserved that five course dinner on the train," Mom added. "I was really excited about it."

Before I could slip in a single word of explanation there was an impatient rapping on the door. Casey? "Mom, Aunt Chrissie," my daughter stage whispered, "are you still up? We need to talk. I have ..."

Tessa vaulted to her feet and yanked the door open as Casey fell inside one fist raised to knock again.

"Hey, Casey," Tessa said. "Your mom thinks we should cancel Ronda. What do you think?"

"What? Ronda? I don't know. But wait until you all hear what I found out from Luc."

Casey had our attention. She made a production out of unwinding her scarf from around her neck and with excruciating precision slowly unzipped her jacket, clearly enjoying our growing agitation. Finally, I couldn't stand the suspense and blurted, "All right, Casey. You're making me crazy. What did you find out that's so earth-shattering?"

She plopped down on the bed, elbowing Tessa aside to make room, and sucked in a huge breath. "Well, it seems that Luc met our friend Inspector Bouchard under very interesting circumstances. Unreal."

Tessa stuck a finger in Casey's ribs. "If you don't talk right now, I'm going to smother you." She waggled a pillow under Casey's nose.

"Okay, okay. Here goes. We know that Luc's wife was killed by a drunk driver a couple of years ago. He says he had a tough time dealing with both her death and taking care of two little girls on his own. So he found help by joining one of those grief support groups."

"And?" I considered strangling her but rejected the idea as impractical.

"And that's where he met the inspector."

"At a grief support group? Why was the inspector there?" Tessa demanded.

Casey heaved a jaded sigh. "Because my dear little law student, he was grieving. Duh. It seems that his wife, daughter and two little granddaughters were in a horrible automobile accident. And his wife died."

"What about the daughter and the two little girls?" I asked.

"Luc says they were in the hospital for a long time. Their injuries were severe, but they survived."

"Where was this support group located? In Nice? Doesn't the inspector live in Paris?"

"According to Luc, Bouchard's wife was from Nice and they were vacationing there when the accident happened. Inspector Bouchard was so devastated by his wife's death and the injuries to the rest of the family, that he took a leave of absence from his job in Paris and stayed in Nice to be close. When they finally recovered enough to leave the hospital, he moved back to Paris and resumed his duties."

When Casey paused to take a breath, Chrissie broke in. "Did Luc maybe say that he worked for Bouchard? Or someone else?"

Casey shook her head. "Nope. Why? Do you know something I should know?"

Unable to sit still I paced --- perhaps more of a mince than a pace in the confined space --- across the room. Finally Casey grabbed my arm and pulled me down next to her. "Mom! Stop! You're making me dizzy. Tell me what you two found out."

I caught Chrissie's eye and raised a questioning eyebrow. She nodded and I said, "Chrissie and I had a long conversation with Bobby and he told us that Luc works for Interpol."

Casey's head jerked up and her mouth dropped open. "Interpol?" she squeaked. "Seriously?"

Mom clapped her hands together and we stopped talking to look at her. "Bobby would never," she said, "have told you two that."

"Well-l-l," I said. "Maybe he didn't actually say it in so many words, but that's what he meant. Right, Chrissie?"

"Absolutely, positively," Chrissie said. "Besides..." She stared at our mother. "...what do you know about what Bobby might or might not have said?"

Mom tipped her head back and closed her eyes for a second. Then she said, "I can't tell you. I've been sworn to secrecy."

We all started speaking at once. "By Bobby?" "What did he tell you?" "Why can't you tell us?"

"Honestly, Mom," Chrissie said, "what's the big deal? It's not like you haven't blabbed secrets before, now is it?"

Mom grinned sheepishly. "This is different."

"Uh huh," Chrissie said. "I've heard that before."

"Right," I interjected. "I believe this is the same woman who leaked the news that Betty White was paying a top secret visit to a dear college friend in our little community to her entire bridge club."

"Causing," Chrissie continued, "a mob scene at the airport when Betty arrived. A hysterical band of cane-wielding octogenarians nearly beat her to death in their zeal to get her autograph."

"And," I concluded, "in Betty's attempt to escape she tripped over Millie Utterback's walker and sprained her ankle."

"So she had to cancel a planned photo shoot for a commercial as well as an interview with the newspaper that Dad had set up," Chrissie said.

"Well, there was that once," Mom said, "but I didn't...."

"And then," I went on, "there was the time that you spilled the beans to Mayor Morton that the DAR was planning a parade down Main Street complete with marching bands and fire trucks to surprise him for his 50th birthday. And he skipped town and didn't show up."

Mom looked embarrassed but valiantly explained, "Morty thanked me for that. He hates parades. And surprises. And he said it was the best spur of the moment vacation he and Sadie ever had in nearly 30 years of marriage."

"That's great," Chrissie said, "but I don't think that Millie Steubenside and the gals at the DAR felt the same way about it. They'd been planning that parade for over a year."

"Besides," Mom said, "it was a wonderful parade even without Morty."

"Then, oh great secret keeper," I said, "there was the time that you revealed to your buddies at the country club that your successes on the golf course --- the club championships, the hole-in-one --- were primarily due to prodigious consumption of raisins soaked in gin."

"Which caused," Chrissie added, "a run on the very best gin at Al's Knock-One-Back Liquor Store."

"Al's supplies were so depleted that the Men's Club was forced to cancel their annual Martini Night festivities," I said.

Mom squirmed. "Your dad wasn't too happy with me about that one, I have to admit."

"I'll bet that Althea Zulpo wasn't real pleased either. While under the influence of gin-soaked raisins she ran her golf cart over the edge of the ravine on the thirteenth hole and landed face down in a bed of poison ivy."

Mom snorted. "Althea's allergic to raisins so she just drank the gin. Not my fault she doesn't know when to quit."

"She still isn't speaking to you, Mom," I said. "Her image was seriously tarnished by the whole affair."

"She's just jealous because I clobbered her in the final round of the club championship," Mom said. "Poor loser."

By now we all were convulsed with giggles. I'm sure the late hour and the alcohol didn't help, but finally we managed to squelch the silliness.

"Enough of this humor," Casey said as she wiped her eyes with the back of her hand. "What do you mean Luc works for Interpol?"

"Tell us, Nonny," Tessa said.

Mom hesitated. "I honestly can't tell you. However, if you just happened to make a good guess I might not be able to stop myself from nodding a bit. I do that, you know."

"Okay," Tessa said, "keep an eye on our secret agent over there and let's figure this out."

"Go on, Tess," Casey said.

"Remember I told you that we studied Interpol last semester. I remember a lot of so-called agents were undercover. That could be Luc. I mean, think about it, he claims to manage entertainment groups and arranges their tours."

Casey grabbed her cousin's arm. "You think that Luc...?"

Tessa shook off Casey's hand. "Let me finish, Case. I think Luc's job is a perfect cover. What better excuse to travel outside of France?"

"So," I said. "We have Luc working as a tour manager and perhaps Interpol as well. Am I good so far?"

323

We looked at Mom who sipped her tea and nodded happily "to herself".

"What if Luc worked for Bouchard as well as Interpol? If Bobby suspects Bouchard of being involved in the smuggling ring he could use Luc to get closer to him. Be a double-agent of sorts."

"Luc? A double agent? But, but, he knows Brad Pitt." Casey jiggled one foot up and down, up and down.

"Does that disqualify him?" Tessa asked. "It might make it even more logical. You've heard the expression --- it's not what you know but who you know."

"So, the inspector meets Luc at grief counseling. Finds out that Luc travels a lot in his role as a manager. I'm sure that the inspector could have discovered quite easily that Luc needed money desperately and offered him a job as a courier."

"If, in fact, Bouchard was involved in the smuggling ring," Casey added.

Mom was nodding vigorously now. All attempts at subterfuge thrust aside in her eagerness to figure out the mystery. "I'm confused about one thing, though," she said. "Bobby didn't want to believe that his old friend was involved in smuggling. Could he really be the one in charge?"

"What better way to find out," I said. "We know for a fact that Luc arranged Georges' American tour and, more than likely, put Georges in contact with the two Spanish men who wanted him to bring a suitcase full of money back to France. For the sake of argument, let's say that if Luc was working for Bobby at Interpol he could have tipped him off so that Bobby could follow Georges once he had the bag in France. The idea being that Georges might lead them to the bad guys. But when Georges switched the bag for Chrissie's, the plan evaporated."

"Whoa," Casey said. "This is really confusing."

Mom nodded more vigorously than before --- her white curls bobbing. "Truth is stranger than fiction."

I moaned. "Sad but true. I think we need to sleep on this. I'm going to bed. My brain is mush." I started toward the bathroom, but Chrissie stopped me.

"One more thing," she said. "Is Ronda a go or a no go?"

I surveyed the cast of characters in the birthday adventure. "Mom?"

"I say go."

"Casey?"

"Well, why wouldn't we?"

"Tessa?"

"One hundred percent yes."

"That leaves you, Chrissie."

"I say we go and bulls be damned."

"Okay, then," I said, "Ronda it is. So we check out in the morning and catch the overnight train at nine-thirty tomorrow night. Agreed?"

Nods all around and Mom and the girls left for their room. It took only a few minutes to strip off our clothes and fall into bed. As Chrissie pulled up the covers she said, "I've been wondering. What if Luc isn't a double-agent? What if he's the one heading up the smuggling ring? He has motive --- needs the money --- and opportunity --- travel with his clients outside France."

"It's crossed my mind too," I whispered into the shadows.

"Of course."

"I'll think about it in the morning, Scarlett," I said.

And within mere seconds both of us were asleep.

Chapter 31

I was buried under the covers when the sound of shuffling in the hallway and then scratching on the door woke me. I was groggy and disoriented. Where was I? Why was the maid knocking on our door in the middle of the night? We just turned out the lights a few minutes ago. I stuck my head out and squinted with gritty eyes at my travel alarm. Six-thirty? What on earth? And then I heard my mother calling softly. "Girls? Girls, it's your mother. Are you awake?" Scratch, scratch, scratch. More loudly. "Girls! Time to get up. Girls?"

I reached across the gap between our beds and poked Chrissie's blanket-covered rear end. "Chrissie. Hey. It's Mom. She's at the door."

Chrissie groaned and pulled the covers over her head. Her voice was muffled as she said, "Ignore her. Maybe she'll go away."

"Oh, for heaven's sake," I said and threw back the tangled sheets. "Big help you are." I struggled to my feet and lurched to the door. I fumbled with the lock and then yanked the door open. There stood Mom. Her white hair was perfectly coiffed and she was dressed as if for a ladies' luncheon at the country club in her powder blue suede jacket and spanking white slacks.

She beamed at me. "There you are."

"Where else would I be at this hour?" I did a quick sweep of the hall to check for any activity and then hauled her into our room.

Mom spied the mound of bedding that was Chrissie and said, "Christine. Get up, darling. The morning awaits us."

"Mom," Chrissie protested, "you're so perky I might have to smack you. Why're you up and dressed and ready to go at this ungodly hour?" She peered at her alarm clock. "We've only been asleep three hours. I'm not getting up yet. Go play with someone else."

"Can't," Mom said.

"What do you mean? Where are the girls?"

"Gone out," Mom said, "with Robert and Mac."

"At six-thirty? Casey thinks anything before ten is the crack of dawn," I said. "Where in heaven's name have they gone?"

"Don't know."

"Well, then what about Bobby? Can't you go play with him?" I asked and immediately regretted my poor choice of words.

"Bobby's working. He's meeting his friend, Claude. You two are the only ones not up." She smiled at us. "So get up." And then in a helpful tone. "I'll make coffee."

Chrissie managed to emerge from the tangle of blankets and struggled to a sitting position on the edge of the bed. Her hair stuck up in all directions and she had raccoon eyes from leftover eye make-up. "I guess she isn't going away," she said to me.

"Reminds me of when she used to drag us out of bed for school," I answered.

"But," Mom chimed in, "I'm making coffee. At least you could be a little appreciative." She puttered with the coffee maker --- filling the carafe with water and putting in the coffee pack. "I could use a cup myself."

"Besides," she said as the coffee began to perk and she turned to confront her grumpy daughters, "we have to check out of the hotel this morning." She looked disapprovingly around our room. "You're not even packed!"

"Relax," I said. "We have plenty of time."

Chrissie staggered to her feet, trailing bedclothes onto the floor behind her. She wobbled toward the bathroom. "If you can't beat 'em, join 'em," she muttered. She paused at the bathroom door and shot us an irritated look. "And there had better be coffee left when I come out."

The door swung shut behind her and the only sound was the dripping of coffee into the pot. Neither Mom nor I said a word as I tossed things randomly at my suitcase and Mom focused her attention on the hissing coffeemaker. Finally, when the coffee completed its brewing cycle, Mom lined up three cups on the dresser and filled them. Holding her cup in her hand she faced me. "She always was cranky in the morning," she said, her lips twitching.

"I heard that," Chrissie called from behind the closed door. "I wasn't the cranky one."

"She's right. Perfect middle children are never cranky."

Mom sat on the bed sipping coffee and watching me as I haphazardly stuffed things in my bag until she couldn't stand it any longer. "Kate," she said, "do you want some help? At the rate you're going we'll still be here when the train pulls out tonight."

"Help yourself," I said as I pulled things out of the dresser drawer.

She set her cup down and began to fold the mound of clothes I had dumped on the bed. Near the bottom of the pile she unearthed the capri pants I had worn on our birthday picnic the day before. She attempted to smooth out the wrinkles and, failing that, picked them up and shook them. An object was ejected from the pocket, shot across the room and clipped my shin.

"Oops," Mom said mildly.

"Ouch," I said. I stooped to pick up the missile and realized it was the SD card I had found in Chrissie's suitcase. She emerged from the bathroom and snatched the remaining cup of coffee as I handed the card to her. "This is yours."

She turned it over in her hand and then put it down. "Not mine."

"Are you sure? I found it in your suitcase last night."

"In my suitcase? That's crazy." She picked up her camera from the dresser. "Mine's right here. Must be yours."

"Not mine either. Whose can it be?"

"Tessa's? Or Casey's?"

"Let's find out," I said. "Hand me my camera, Mom."

I slipped the SD card into my camera, turned it on and began to scroll through the pictures. Chrissie and Mom peered over my shoulder. I stopped after scanning about ten photos. "Who are these people anyway?" I asked.

Chrissie shrugged. "Keep going."

I scrolled through a dozen more pictures. A group of men huddled around what appeared to be a briefcase. The figures were tiny and blurry and appeared to have been photographed from a distance.

"There's something...." Mom reached over and took the camera out of my hand and scanned through a few more. "Wait. There. Isn't that...." Her forehead wrinkled in concentration she looked at us and then back at the camera. "Julio and Guillermo?"

"Are you sure?" I gently slipped the camera out of her hand and fiddled with the controls until I had a photo that was sharper and enlarged it as much as possible.

The three of us concentrated on the tiny screen for a few more seconds. Then we stared at each other. "It's them," Mom said. "I'd know them anywhere, but who else is in these pictures? Who's that guy in the weird hat?"

"You haven't seen him before?" I asked Mom. "On the plane maybe?"

"I think I'd remember someone wearing a plaid bucket hat that nearly covers his face," she said. "Not terribly fashion forward."

I had to admit that it was an unattractive hat, but style wasn't really the issue. Was it?

I scrolled through a few more photos before I hit pay dirt. "Look at this!" I said. I'd noted a familiar looking figure with his back to the camera in most of the pictures, but in this shot he was looking over his shoulder. His expression was furious and you could almost hear him yelling at the unknown photographer. "Turn that damn thing off." The picture was kind of fuzzy, but clear enough for the three of us to identify him instantly.

"Oh, my god," I exclaimed.

"What is Inspector Bouchard doing with those two thugs?" Chrissie asked as she focused on the screen.

"Looks like he's handing over the briefcase," I said.

"Or receiving it," Chrissie suggested.

"This clearly links my kidnappers with the inspector," Mom said. "He and Julio and Guillermo are engaged --- along with weird hat guy --- in something criminal, I'd guess."

"Unfortunately," Chrissie said, "we don't have any real evidence. We need more than some fuzzy photos on an SD card. I'm sure there could be a million perfectly innocent reasons why they were meeting."

"Name one," I said.

Chrissie shrugged. I idly scrolled through the remaining photos while she and Mom tossed around ideas about why the inspector could be in cahoots with these criminals. Then I got to a photo that made beads of sweat hatch on my forehead and my hands start shaking. "Look." I pushed the words past the lump in my throat. "Look at this." A close up shot of the briefcase --- open to reveal its contents. A stack of bills. Next to the bills was a Wall Street Journal dated a few days before we left on our birthday adventure.

"Now that's more like it," Chrissie said.

"I'm guessing that the inspector was giving the briefcase to Julio and Guillermo. And that it had money in it to be transported back to Paris," Mom said.

"And they in turn gave it to Fifi and Georges," I added, "who put it in the suitcase which happened to be a twin to yours, Chrissie."

"Georges and Fifi told us about meeting two Spanish guys," Mom said. "Must have been Julio and Guillermo."

"Then who took this picture of the money and the paper?" I asked. "And why?"

"The why is obvious," Chrissie said. "The who is more difficult."

"All we're doing is making guesses about what's really going on. We need more concrete evidence to indict Bouchard. Like actual documents," I said.

"Oh, sure, let's do that," Chrissie scoffed. "Just where do you suggest searching for these incriminating documents?"

I thought for a second. "Maybe where I found the SD card. It's worth a try."

"I'm on it," Chrissie said as she snatched her suitcase and upended its contents on the bed. She tossed her neatly folded clothing aside to expose the ripped seam in the lining. It had been crudely repaired with brown thread and the frayed ends were visible. She stuck a finger in the hole and wiggled until the seam gave way. Then she stuck her hand into the hole. "Ta da."

She pulled out a vinyl document holder a little larger than a business-sized envelope. We stared at it for a few seconds before we pounced. Chrissie unwound the string from around the clasp that secured the folder and started to remove the folded contents. Mom grabbed her wrist. "Stop."

Chrissie froze. "Why?"

"Because," Mom "it's evidence. And there might be fingerprints that we shouldn't mess up."

"So what should we do?" I asked.

Mom looked at me as I was not terribly bright and said in a tone of exaggerated patience. "Wait and watch." She hurried to the dresser and scooped up a pair of tweezers and some unused tissues. Then using the tweezers she pried the papers loose and dropped them on the bed. She wrapped tissue around her fingers before she carefully spread the papers out so we could see them.

"She's done this before," I said to Chrissie.

"A woman of many hidden talents," she agreed.

We cautiously, using tweezers and tissues, began to examine each page with as much reverence as if it might hold the secret to eternal youth. The papers appeared to be photocopies of the originals --- the print pale and in some places illegible. It appeared to be a stack of bank statements. A list of dates ran down the left-hand side of the page and each date was followed by an amount. Another page was a list of numbers followed by a "code" of letters and numbers. At the top of one page we read the words "The International Bank of the Cayman Islands." We scrutinized each page and finally I dropped the tweezers and arched my back to relieve the tension. "Looks like bank statements from one of those offshore accounts."

"Where crooks stash money they've obtained illegally. Or don't want anyone to find," Chrissie added.

"And copies of other financial documents," Mom said. "It must all be connected to the inspector --- the kidnapping, the smuggling, *Le Picnic.*"

"Definitely," I agreed. "But who put the papers and the memory card in Chrissie's bag? And why?"

"It's proof that the inspector was in it up to his eyeballs," Chrissie said. "Maybe Georges hid the evidence my bag."

"Georges isn't clever enough. He really wasn't the hottest croissant in the *patisserie*. What about Fifi? She was the brains of that pair," I suggested as I paced around the room.

"Kate. Sit," Mom said. "You're making me dizzy."

I dropped into the chair next to the desk and gave my head a quick shake. "This situation is making me dizzy. I wish I could talk to Fifi and Georges, but they're dead."

"Before she died, though, she warned us about the inspector. Remember, Chrissie? In the train compartment?"

Chrissie sat cross-legged on the bed amid the scattered papers, painstakingly avoiding touching them. She tapped a finger against her lip. "She was in rough shape, I'm not sure she knew what she was saying."

Mom tugged on a single white curl. She stared into space for a moment and then said, "Personally, I think the good inspector is involved up to his cute French butt."

"Cute butt?" Chrissie said.

"A girl can look can't she?" Mom asked blandly. "I'm not quite ready for the glue factory, you know."

"Okay, okay," I said. "How exactly do you two think he's involved? Is he investigating the smuggling ring or ringleader?"

"I vote for ringleader," Mom said. "Our evidence casts suspicion at the very least."

"And his motive would be?"

"Money. Pure and simple. After his wife died in that accident his daughter and granddaughters were hospitalized for a long time. I'd say that would make a man jaded and bitter. The hospital bills had to be huge. He must have been desperate for money to pay them."

"But Bobby said he was a stand-up guy. A good cop. Lots of awards," I objected.

"Grief does weird things to a person," Mom said.

"Speaking from experience?" Chrissie asked.

"Well, I haven't exactly turned to a life of crime, but yes, I'm speaking from experience," Mom admitted. "But we aren't talking about me, we're talking about Claude Bouchard. You heard Bobby say he was a party boy in college. Liked fancy cars and fast living. Until he met Desiree and settled down. Maybe he reverted to type."

I considered that. "Maybe. You have a point. How do we, as they say in crime novels, get the goods on him?"

"I have an idea," Mom said.

"Of course, you do," Chrissie said. "When didn't you?"

Mom shot a laser look at my twin. "If you'll stop being such a comedian, Christine, I'll tell you."

Chrissie groaned and clapped a hand over her mouth.

"As I was saying…I think we should pay a purely social call on Marielle at *Le Picnic Francais*. She was so kind to loan us her blanket. It would be rude of us not to return it."

Chrissie and I exchanged amused looks.

"By george, I think she's got it," I said.

"And if we happen to pick Marielle's brain while we're there...why so much the better," Chrissie added and stretched across the bed to hug Mom. "Brilliant, my dear Watson."

"Thank you very much, Sherlock," Mom said and hopped off the bed and started collecting the clothes strewn around the room.

Chapter 32

"Now what?" I asked as we loitered on the corner across the street from *Le Picnic Francais*. We had been there for several minutes and were, as we wannabe detectives say, conducting surveillance. If we had expected anything out of the ordinary, though, we were disappointed. *La Avenida de los Tres Burros* was as quiet as it had been the last time...no traffic and only a few pedestrians to disturb the eerie silence. A man in a dark suit emerged from *La Casa de Café* carrying a cup of coffee and melted into the gloomy side street. No one came or went from *Le Picnic*. As detective work goes, this was a dud.

Mom adjusted her sunglasses on her nose and tucked Marielle's blanket more securely under her arm. She stuffed her street map into her purse and said, "I'm going in."

"Wait." I grasped her arm. "What did Bobby say about this mission?"

"Bobby?" she said in a vague tone as if she'd never heard the name before.

"Yes, Bobby. You know, the white-haired guy with a sexy Scots accent and hot legs. Bobby. Your kilt-wearing boyfriend."

"Don't be ridiculous. Bobby isn't my boyfriend."

"I think," I stage-whispered to Chrissie, "that our dear mother is avoiding the question."

"Wild guess says she didn't tell him anything."

Mom whirled to face us. "Well, what if I didn't mention anything to him? If I told him about our *purely social* visit to *Le Picnic*, he'd have tried to stop me. Or even worse, he'd have sent one of his flunkeys along to protect us. So I didn't tell him. As it is, he gave me one of his business cell phones to use if we had any trouble." She unzipped her purse to reveal the phone nestled inside and then quickly closed it.

"What does he think we're doing all day?" I asked.

"Well, I kind of led him to believe we were going to the chocolate museum."

"Chocolate museum?" Chrissie licked her lips "Why is this the first I'm hearing about a chocolate museum? That sounds like something I could really get into."

"Focus, Christine," Mom ordered. "This is an investigation. We don't have time for frivolity. Like chocolate."

"Ha." Chrissie huffed. "There's always time for chocolate."

"After we talk to Marielle, I'll let you have chocolate for dessert," Mom said as she started to cross the street.

"I think we've created a monster." I hurried after my mother with Chrissie a step behind.

Mom marched across the street and up to the door. She stabbed impatiently at the doorbell and then stepped back to wait. Nothing. The three of us exchanged questioning looks and Mom punched the button again. Then she thumped the heavy brass doorknocker against the door. Still no answer.

"I guess no one's here," I said. "Let's go."

"Not yet, Kate." Mom reached for the brass doorknob, gave it a twist and then stepped back in surprise. "It's not locked."

"Are you really going inside?" Chrissie whispered.

"I am," Mom said and then stopped with her hand frozen in midair. "Wait a second. I hear voices. Someone's inside after all."

Barely breathing we put our ears up to the door. Mom was right. I heard voices too. Loud voices. A masculine voice. Yelling. Threatening.

"Call the police," I said. "Something bad is going on." My legs trembled.

Mom frowned and hovered indecisively for a second and then took a step back. Then a woman screamed. With no hesitation whatsoever --- who'd have thought my petite mom was such a tiger? --- Mom wrenched the heavy knob and thrust open the door. Calling "Marielle, dear, it's *Señora* Laura," she burst into the foyer, and, with Chrissie and me close behind, headed for the office.

We had only taken a step or two when a wild-eyed and obviously terrified

Marielle erupted from the inner office and nearly bowled us over in her panic. She took one look at us, broke into hysterical sobs and collapsed into my mother's arms.

"*Señoras*," she sobbed. "*Vamos*. Inside. He is *muy mal*. He want to kill Marielle. Run." And she bolted out the door. It didn't take a genius to figure out that if a killer was inside, it was not the place for us to linger. We dashed after Marielle, leaving the door to *Le Picnic* standing wide open. I took one frantic look back over my shoulder and was astonished to see weird hat guy glowering at me from the doorway. How many hats in that odd combination of orange, lilac and brown could there be? It had to be the same man as the one wearing the plaid bucket hat in the photos on the SD card. The unidentified fourth man with Bouchard and Julio and Guillermo. The missing connection. Heart pounding with fear and excitement, I raced after my family and Marielle.

Mom caught up to Marielle --- who knew my mother was such a sprinter? --- and seized her arm and dragged her into *La Casa de Café*. It seemed unlikely that weird hat guy, no matter how irate he was, would follow us into the shop --- too many witnesses. So we felt safe --- at least for the moment. Still, if the man who had terrorized Marielle had a gun, maybe he wouldn't hesitate after all.

We grabbed a table in the very back and ignored the curious stares of the few patrons who didn't seem all that interested in our drama. But as Marielle continued to sob hysterically the lone waiter in the place edged our way. He patted Marielle's shoulder and spoke quietly to her. Finally she drew a ragged breath and quit crying. "*Gracias, Juan*," she said to him. "*Estoy bien. No es problema*."

Marielle sniffed loudly and Mom handed her a tissue. The girl blew her nose and her hand trembled as she wiped at her teary eyes. At that moment I was distracted by two dark-haired men in blue jumpsuits who clattered through the door and shattered the peaceful silence with their loud bantering and raucous laughter. They grabbed two chairs at a table near the entrance and motioned to the waiter.

My mouth grew dry as I observed the pair. Were they Bobby's lads here to protect us after all? Or did they have a more sinister motive? I was so consumed watching them that I jumped when Chrissie punched me in the arm --- hard.

"Kate," she said. "Pay attention. I'm trying to tell you something."

I jerked my attention back to our table with some effort. "What?"

She tipped her chin in Marielle's direction. "Do you see what she's wearing?"

I turned to check out Marielle's outfit. Navy blue --- was it silk? --- blouse. Ivory pencil skirt. Navy stilettos. Sophisticated. Classy. Perhaps expensive. I nodded my approval. "Looking good."

"No, no, no. Look at her wrist."

Dangling from her wrist was a silver charm bracelet featuring a single charm. A skull and crossbones. It had to have some meaning. But what?

Mom was beginning to question Marielle when I broke in. "Marielle! Where did you get that bracelet?"

Bewildered by my interruption, Marielle stared at her arm. "This one? Señor Obregon, he give it to me as first month bonus. Is scary, *si*? But he say wear it always, so I do."

Mom lifted Marielle's wrist so she could see the bracelet too and she examined it silently. Then she said, "Looks like the charm I found in the ice cream."

"And the one on Fifi's wrist when we found her in the train compartment," Chrissie said.

"And the one I found on my bed in Nice," I added. "Too many to be an odd coincidence. It's all connected. I know it."

Marielle unclasped her bracelet and dropped it onto the table where the gleaming eyes of the skull stared up at us. "I no wear."

Reluctantly I scooped the bracelet off the table and dangled it from my index finger. There was something about those eyes that gave me the shivers. A vague feeling of familiarity. I turned to my mother. "Do you have your charm?"

She shook her head. "No. I gave it to Bobby? What about yours?"

"Left it in my bag at the hotel."

I fingered the skull. "There's something about the eyes." I scratched a nail over the stones. "Do you think these could be real stones?"

Our jewelry expert lifted the bracelet and held it up to the light. "Could be diamonds," she said. "Tiny ones."

"I wish I knew more about these bracelets," I said. "Maybe they are the answer."

"But what's the question?" Chrissie said.

"Let's see what Marielle can tell us," Mom said. She turned so she was facing Marielle. "Marielle, dear. *Que pasa? Quien es el hombre?*"

The girl looked around anxiously before she spoke. "He is one of the big bosses. From Paris. He comes in this morning and finds me. He is in a terrible temper. He threaten me. He tear my *blusa*." Indeed, one sleeve of her blouse was ripped and hanging lopsidedly from her shoulder.

"What did he want?" Mom asked.

"I am not sure. He was angry because..." She wiped her eyes with a shaking hand. "...because I give away the basket to you. He say I do not have --- how do I say it?--- oh-tority?"

"Authority," I interjected. "He say...er, *says*...you don't have the authority to give away a basket?"

"*Si.*" Marielle shrugged. "I do not think it is such a big thing. It is only one basket. And it is damage." She appeared bewildered by the confrontation. "He say it is one of the special baskets. I can never give those away. *Nunca mas.*"

"Special baskets? What's a special basket?" Mom asked.

"We ship only a few of the special ones to customers. They are the ones with *las floras* design. I did not know this thing. I am not working there for long. I did not know." Tears leaked from her eyes. "I am losing my job. *El hombre* want to hurt me. He rip my *blusa*. *Es muy malo.*"

The waiter brought over a pot of tea and then retreated a few paces to keep an eye on us and, I supposed, to make sure we didn't upset Marielle any more than she already was. Mom poured tea into our cups and I took a tentative sip. "I'm thinking," I said, "that the baskets are special because they're the ones that contain the gems they're smuggling. Not all the baskets have them. Of course, the boss might be a little upset."

"Upset?" Chrissie said. "Enraged would be more like it."

"Yeah, but if the jeweler yesterday was correct, Marielle here gave away at least 20,000 Euros worth of gemstones. I'd say his anger is understandable. There go the profits."

Marielle scrubbed at her eyes with the crumpled tissue and then drew herself up in her chair. Her face was white with bright red spots of color flushing her cheeks, but her dark eyes flashed dangerously. "Do you mean, *Señoras*, that I am working in crime? I am crook? I am not break the law on purpose. Will they arrest me?" Her anger rapidly gave way to terror.

Mom patted her arm. "Hush, dear. You won't be in any trouble. I know a very nice man who might want to ask you some questions though. Would you be able to do that?"

Marielle shook her head vehemently. "No. I am too scared. What if the bad *hombre* return to kill me?"

"We'll make sure that doesn't happen," Mom said soothingly. "*Por favor*, don't worry."

"Time to give Bobby a call," Mom murmured to Chrissie and me. She burrowed in her purse and fished out Bobby's cell phone.

"Before you call him," I said. "I have something else to tell you."

Three pairs of eyes were glued to mine. "The man in *Le Picnic*? The one who attacked Marielle?"

"Go on already," Chrissie said. "You don't always have to be such a drama queen."

"Humph. I am not a drama queen. If anything..."

"Kate," Mom said --- a warning in her voice. "Tell us."

"Fine. I saw a man in the doorway as we ran away from *Le Picnic*. The big boss from Paris? You'll be shocked to know he is the fourth man in the photos on the SD card."

"Are you sure?" Mom asked.

"Absolutely," I said. "It was weird hat guy. Same orange, purple and brown plaid hat. Same dark suit. Same furious expression."

Mom and Chrissie stared at me glassy-eyed and Marielle just looked perplexed, so I continued. "The big boss of *Le Picnic*, the one who knows about the smuggling, was with Inspector Claude Bouchard. In possession of a briefcase full of cash. Ties the inspector in almost conclusively, doesn't it? And now the big boss knows we had the picnic basket full of gems and the suitcase full of cash. I'd say he'd be more than a little anxious to find us and make sure we were dealt with."

It only took a moment for Mom and Chrissie to digest this new information. Then Chrissie squeezed Mom's hand. "Call Bobby," she said. "Now."

Bobby was furious. Oh, he was far too well-bred to scream or swear but his icy blue eyes and his clenched jaw spoke more clearly than words possibly could. He was waiting for us in the lobby of our hotel flanked on either side by a large associate. Each was about the size of a small Third World country and wore a stony expression that matched Bobby's. It would have taken a far more courageous woman than I not to be intimidated. Apparently my mother was that more courageous woman.

She sailed blithely up to Bobby and his compatriots and stood on tiptoe to plant a quick peck on his cheek. Bobby's shoulders lost some of their rigidity but he was not about to let her off the hook. "Good Morning, Laura. Where is my chocolate, then?" he said pleasantly but his smile was forced.

Ah, the man speaks my language--sarcasm. Somehow it made me sympathize with him.

His words stopped Mom. She flinched, momentarily nonplussed. "Um, what? Choco ...? Oh, I see. Well," she stammered as she looked up at him. "I.. um..we didn't actually..um..."

Bobby spat out his words between clenched teeth. "Let's not have this discussion here." He narrowed his eyes as he scrutinized the other hotel guests, turned on his heel and strode toward the elevator with everyone trailing behind. I chanced a glance at Chrissie and rolled my eyes. She shrugged and followed Bobby.

At the door to our room Bobby held a rapid consultation with his two mammoth compatriots and left them standing guard as we filed meekly inside and made ourselves comfortable on the beds. As Mom whispered to Marielle and guided her to the single upholstered chair, Bobby jerked a chair from under the desk, turned it backwards and sat down. He rested his elbows on the back of the chair and glared at us.

Finally when the tension in the room was almost unbearable Bobby snapped, his accent growing more pronounced with each word, "What in the name of all that's Holy were you thinking? Did you not understand that these are not tots playing pat-a-cake in the nursery? These are men willing to commit murder to protect themselves. If they tried to harm you what did you intend to do? Beat them senseless with your purse? Why could you not leave this business to me to sort out?"

"Robert. Bobby." Mom patted his arm placatingly. "How could we know what we would find at *Le Picnic* when we went there to make a *purely social* visit to return Marielle's blanket to her?"

Bobby wasn't quite finished. He knit his brows together and scowled, his eyes flashing bolts of lightening. "Laura. You lied to me. If you had told me your plans, I could have sent some men with you."

Mom squirmed under his gaze. "That's exactly why I didn't tell you. It was a *purely social* call. We didn't need bodyguards, did we girls?"

"Don't drag us into this," Chrissie said. "This was your idea."

Bobby heaved a huge sigh. He smiled, a bit grimly, at Mom. "Laura, did ye not think of my feelings?"

Mom was, for once, speechless. Her eyes went round as she stared at Bobby. He stared right back. Finally, she licked her lips and squeaked, "Feelings? Your feelings?"

"Yes," Bobby said, "I worry about you. Three attempts were made on your life yesterday. How do you think I would feel if something happened to you? Like it did to Emmaline."

"Oh." Mom looked chagrined. "I didn't think about it that way. I'm so sorry to have caused you concern. But we found some things and we wanted to pay a …"

"I know. A *purely social* call on Marielle." There was that sarcasm again. I liked him more and more.

Then his forehead crinkled as Mom's comment registered. "What things?" His tone was heavy with suspicion.

"In Christine's suitcase," Mom said. "Chrissie, show him."

Our suitcases were packed and stacked in one corner of the room. "I'm on it," Chrissie said and dug into her suitcase to retrieve the SD memory card and the folder of documents. At Mom's nod, she handed them to Bobby.

Bobby took his time looking over the documents and then turned the SD card over in his hand. "Would you mind telling me what's on this?'

"Better than that," I said. "I'll show you." I slipped the card into my camera and turned it on

Silently Bobby scrolled through the photos. Time dragged until he put the camera aside and grimaced. Shaking his head he said, "And you didn't think I should see these before you visited *Le Picnic*? What did you hope to gain?"

Mom hesitated. "Um, I guess I wanted to see for myself. Talk to Marielle. Find out if she knew anything about the inspector." She sighed. "I guess it wasn't such a good idea."

Bobby raised his eyebrows. "I would have to agree with that." He turned concerned eyes on Marielle who had almost been forgotten during the exchange with Mom. She was huddled in her chair watching us with big, frightened brown eyes. I wondered how much she really understood. She undoubtedly wondered what kind of crazy people she had fallen in with. She curled into a ball when Bobby addressed her. "Marielle? *Es ese su nombre*? Don't worry. I won't hurt you. I will see that you are safe. But first I need to ask you some questions? Would that be okay with you?"

His tone was kind and sympathetic and Marielle nodded warily. "*Si, señor*. I will try."

Gently Bobby questioned her and she explained that she hadn't worked at *Le Picnic* long. That she didn't know anything about Julio and Guillermo other than that they were temporary workers. That one basket was damaged and she wanted to do something special for us for our birthday and gave it to us. Here she teared up again as she realized that her generosity had caused all this furor. She told Bobby that Señor Obregon was the manager of the Barcelona office and that she had never met the man who had terrorized her today.

"I do not know this man," she said. "He comes today is *muy furioso* when I tell him the special basket is not there. I do not want to tell him I have made present of it, but he grabs me and rips my *blusa* and...." She broke down and started sobbing.

Chrissie handed her a tissue and as she cried softly, I decided it was time to tell Bobby about the man in the doorway. "Um," I began cautiously. "One more thing you should know."

Bobby sucked in a breath and blew it out. "You can't keep things from me, Kate, if you want me to help."

I nodded. "I know. As Mom told you we found the door to *Le Picnic* unlocked and let ourselves in when we heard Marielle screaming. When she ran out the door we followed her, but I looked back and ... he was there ... in the doorway. Crazy, insane, scary mad."

"Who exactly was in the doorway?"

I picked up my camera and found the photo I wanted. The one of Julio and Guillermo with the two other men. This was the clearest one I had of the man I had seen. "Him," I said.

Bobby took the camera and studied the photo and then he handed the camera to Marielle. "Is this the bad man from Paris who assaulted you? Take your time before you answer. I want you to be positive."

Solemnly Marielle focused her attention on the photo, turning the camera to examine it from different angles. Then she nodded slowly. "*Si, señor. Es lo mismo. El hombre de Paris.*"

Bobby plucked the camera from her fingers and scrolled through the photos until he found the one he wanted and returned the camera to Marielle. I was curious so I peeked over her shoulder at the fuzzy photo of the man we believed to be Inspector Bouchard snarling at the faceless photographer. "Have you seen this man before, Marielle?"

Marielle took plenty of time before she shook her head. "No, I'm sorry. I have never seen this one."

If I had expected a reaction from Bobby, I was disappointed. He stood up without saying a word, rotated his chair and shoved it back under the desk. "*Muchas gracias, señorita.* You have been very helpful. I will have you taken to safe place until we catch these criminals. Would you be willing to testify in a court of law about what you have seen?"

Marielle forced a weak smile and her hands shook as she handed the camera back to Bobby. But she mustered up enough courage to say, "*Si Señor*, I will." Then a horrified look crossed her face, erasing the smile. "What about my family? *Mi madre. Mi hermanita y hermano.* They are in danger also. No?"

"Don't worry," Bobby said. "I will have my men watch your house and the schools of your sister and brother. We will guard them until we find a safe place for all of you. We appreciate your help."

He stepped purposively toward the door but stopped with his hand on the handle when I called to him. "Wait. I have something you need to see."

I crossed the room and dropped the two nearly identical charm bracelets into his open palm. Wordlessly Bobby jiggled the bracelets, letting them trickle through his fingers from hand to the other. Finally he glanced up at me and waited for an explanation.

"This one (I tapped my bracelet) I found in my room in Nice. And Marielle was wearing this one today."

"Hmm," Bobby said. "Interesting."

"The charms are the same as the one I found in my ice cream in Nice," Mom interjected. "Remember? I gave it to you."

"Of course, I remember," Bobby said. "This is indeed an odd coincidence."

"If it is a coincidence," I told him. "Fifi had on an identical bracelet when we found her murdered in our train car."

"Is that so? I wonder...." Bobby began and then hesitated. "I'll definitely give these to the lab boys. Thank you for trusting me." And he opened the door and disappeared into the hallway.

A short time later Bobby, presumably having conferred with his associates via cell phone, ushered the two giant bodyguards into our room. We smothered Marielle with apologies for butting into her formerly peaceful life and waved farewell as the musclemen whisked her out the door. She shrugged off our laments with a brave smile. "*No es problema.* I must do what I must do. The bad men must be punish."

We sank into a gloomy silence as the door closed behind Marielle and her bodyguards. We stared into space --- each of us lost in her own thoughts --- until Bobby cleared his throat. "Ah hem," he said, his voice ominously low-pitched and emotionless. "Can I count on you to stay out of trouble while I look into some things? Or do I need to assign some lads to keep an eye on you?"

"Well," Mom said. "I'm sorry I worried you, but I would like to know what you think is going on. Can you tell us anything at all?"

"I'm sorry. I know you found yourselves in a mess, but I can't reveal anything at the moment. Perhaps later."

This wasn't the answer we wanted, but I think we realized that we wouldn't win a debate. And there had been those attempts on Mom's life. We couldn't ignore that. So we agreed to Bobby assigning some of his "lads" to follow us. We arranged to meet him that evening at the train station and cheerfully --- cheeks aching from fake smiling --- sent him off to conduct his investigation.

Chapter 33

Chrissie broke off a chunk of chocolate and popped it into her mouth. "I really don't need this after all the calories we've consumed the last few days," she said. She tugged on the waistband of her jeans.

"Don't worry," I told her. "It's a well-known fact that food which serves double-duty as an entrance ticket has no caloric value and, therefore, cannot cause weight gain." To prove my point I bit off a hunk of chocolate and chewed.

"I hope you're right," Chrissie said, "but I have my doubts. Although I've never eaten an entrance ticket before today." She gestured around the room with her chocolate bar.

I'd never been presented with an edible entrance ticket before either, but it seemed like an inspired idea. If anyone asked I would definitely encourage the practice at other spots.

After Bobby left us, Chrissie and I and our mother had decided to distract ourselves from our anxiety by visiting the *Museu de la Xocolata*, The Chocolate Museum. What the museum lacked in size --- it occupied a relatively small space --- it more than made up for in atmosphere. After we paid our fee we had been presented with chocolate bars and we munched them as we wandered through the exhibits with the tantalizing aroma of chocolate wafting in the air. Statues made entirely of chocolate were interspersed with the exhibits elaborating on the history of chocolate and the manufacture of the gourmet snack.

"Oh, look, it's Minnie Mouse," I said as we passed one glass-enclosed statue.

"There's Louis Armstrong over there." Chrissie pointed with her remaining nubbin of chocolate bar.

We lingered in front of a chocolate sculpture of *La Sagrada Familia*. "Looks harmless enough when it's made of chocolate," Mom commented dryly.

"But beware of falling M&M's," Chrissie added.

"How bad could it be if you got smacked in the head with a Hershey's Kiss?" I polished off the last of my chocolate. "Honestly, I could go for one right now."

Earlier we had left the hotel telling ourselves that everything was going to be just fine. Bobby was on the case. His "lads" were following us. The girls were in the capable hands of the MacTavish grandsons. All was coming up sunshine and Tootsie Pops. Now, though, with the chocolate Sagrada reminding me of yesterday's close call, my inner worrywart was surfacing to scream at me. I had her reeling from an overdose of chocolate and she was groggy, but she wasn't letting go. Were the girls safe? Were killers on our trail? Oh, God. Only one thing to do. Eat more chocolate.

So we stopped at the conclusion of our tour to sample some churros --- a kind of fried ladyfinger --- with thick hot chocolate to dip them in. We devoured the churros with cups of dark espresso to wash them down. When we were sated we sat back and regarded each other with the glazed eyes of the seriously overstuffed.

Chrissie wiped her mouth with her napkin. "The answer to any problem is always chocolate."

"Too bad Tessa and Casey missed this," Mom said. "They're going to be upset with us."

"I just hope," I said, "they're okay." I tried to sound calm, but I was beginning to get panicky. My inner worrywart was definitely recuperating from her chocolate coma.

We left the museum fretting about our daughters' whereabouts but trying to rein in our overzealous imaginations. A few doors down the street from the museum we passed a cheesy souvenir shop. Racks of t-shirts and coffee mugs blocked the sidewalk. Inside we saw more t-shirts in piles tumbling from uneven shelves and carousels of postcards crowded together.

"Oh, look," Mom said. Her eyes lit up. "Postcards. I haven't bought a single one the entire trip. I want to send some to the girls at the club."

I sighed. "You just want to make them jealous."

Mom chuckled. "Nothing wrong with that."

She hovered at the postcard rack debating her selection. I pulled out various cards as she twirled the rack around. Each offered an appealing view of some Spanish landmark. Cathedrals. Museums. Gorgeous sunsets over the city of Barcelona. Peaceful. Harmless. Until one card caught my eye. It showed a cemetery --- rows of headstones apparent in the distance --- fronted by a stone wall. And on the wall was carved a Skull and Crossbones. I plucked the card out of its slot and turned it over to read about the photo, but it was in Spanish.

"Hey, Chris." I tapped my sister's arm. "Look at this. What does it say?"

"I don't..." she began and then recognized what I was holding. "Oh, no. Let me try to read it."

While she puzzled over the Spanish words, I twirled the carousel to see if I could find another card showing a similar image. No luck.

"So?"

"Give me a second." She held the card gingerly between her thumb and forefinger. "Mom, you need to hear this too."

Mom stopped perusing the postcard selection and waited.

"Okay," Chrissie said. "It says that actual skull and crossbones have long been used to mark the entrance to Spanish cemeteries. This particular postcard was taken at...are you ready for this?"

Mom and I nodded impatiently. "Go on," I ordered.

"This photo was taken at the graveyard on Montjuic."

"We're surrounded by the dang things." I said. "Everywhere we go." I examined the postcard more closely. "I'm beginning to think someone is trying to tell us something."

"Yeah, like we're dealing with vampires and zombies and the undead?"

"Exactly. We thought the skull and crossbones charms were warnings. But what if they mean something else entirely?"

"Let's buy the card. Maybe we can learn more about skull and crossbones and Spanish cemeteries and God knows what else."

Mom stacked the postcard on top of the ones she selected for "the girls" and dug in her purse to find Euros to pay for them. "I have a brilliant idea. There's a business center back at the hotel. They have a computer we could use. Bobby and I saw it there yesterday," she said.

"Let the detecting begin," I said.

When we reached the *Placa Catalunyas*, Barcelona's large central plaza, we spotted a vacant bench in front of a water fountain --- an oasis in the midst of the snarl of pedestrian traffic and the cacophony of buses and cars. We sank onto the bench to catch our breath and to let Chrissie kick off her shoes. Immediately a band of audacious pigeons surrounded us hoping that we'd feed them. Mom shooed them away with her purse. "Scram," she said. "You're as rude as the girls at the club on free lunch Fridays."

Chrissie and I had to laugh at the indignant expression on Mom's face.

"I've been thinking," I said.

"About pigeons or the girls at the club?" Chrissie asked.

"Neither," I answered. "You said you gave Bobby the charm you found in your ice cream. Right, Mom?"

"Yes. The same day."

"Well, what did he say?"

Mom frowned. "Hmm. It's been a while now, but I don't think he said too much. The same things he said to you this morning. He'd show it to the lab guys." Mom tugged on a single curl --- a sure sign that she was thinking. "But I had the feeling that there was something he wasn't telling me."

"What makes you think that?" Chrissie asked.

"Little things. He has a quirky way of scrunching up his eyebrows and playing with his mustache when he isn't being entirely honest."

351

"Ah," Chrissie said. "You know him well. Anything else you'd like to confess to us about you and the sexy Scot?"

Mom fluffed her white curls and smiled a smug, self-satisfied smile. "Absolutely not." She tucked her purse under her arm and hopped off the bench. "We've rested long enough. Time to get back to the hotel and uncover some more clues." She plunged into the crowd and strode off with Chrissie and me jogging to keep up.

"Who is that woman?" I asked.

"I definitely believe we've created a monster," Chrissie answered.

Chapter 34

Chrissie scooted the wheeled chair away from the computer desk and flung her arms over her head in an enormous stretch. "Who knew there was so much information on the internet about the Skull and Crossbones symbol? It's fascinating."

I looked up from my own project. "So tell me."

The two of us had occupied the hotel business center for the last hour while Mom sat in the lobby around the corner writing postcards to her country club friends. Keeping busy, we agreed, was the best way to silence our inner demons.

"Well," Chrissie said, "there seems to be a difference of opinion about the skull and crossbones. It dates back to ancient times and originally it was thought to be protection. Then when the pirates adopted it and put the Jolly Roger on their flags it took on a more sinister meaning. The pirates thought of it as a warning of their evil intentions."

"Interesting, but what does all of that have to do with our bracelets?"

"Not sure." Chrissie rubbed her eyes. "The skull and crossbones is often used in Spanish cemeteries to mark the entrance to the graveyard. And, get this, it's also seen a lot in Scotland."

"Hmm. Scotland? That's unsettling, isn't it?"

"One article I read said that it sends the universal message that every human dies."

"Lovely. Warning or protection? Our choice," I mused. "I'll take protection."

"One other tiny thing I found out is that the skull and crossbones is also the insignia of the Skull and Bones Society at Yale. The society is a very big deal and its members include some really illustrious people. William Buckley, John Kerry and George W. Bush to name a few. They're called Bonesman."

"Yale? Didn't Bobby and Bouchard go to Yale?"

Chrissie nodded. "Hmm. You're right. I wonder if that means anything."

"Ask Mom." I laughed but I admit I wasn't feeling at all cheerful. We hadn't heard from Casey and Tessa all day and my inner worrywart was busy making dire predictions of doom and gloom. All this talk about skulls and bones wasn't helping my mood either.

As time crept by at the pace of fog my mom radar was on high alert. When I heard familiar voices and laughter I leaped up and charged into the adjoining lobby in time to see Casey and Tessa breezing through the door followed by the MacTavish grandsons. I swept Casey into a smothering hug. She allowed me to hold her for a bit, before, laughing, she pushed me away. "Get a grip, Mom. You act like you haven't seen me in a decade. I know you worry, but we're fine."

Tessa broke free of Chrissie's identical smothering hug. "We have so much to tell you. You'll die."

"Poor choice of words," Chrissie scolded. "What have you all been up to all day? We thought you'd at least call."

Tessa started to answer but just then we were interrupted by Bobby and his two king-sized compatriots. Bobby barked orders at them and his grandsons. "Robert, get those bags. Mac, call a cab. Ferdy, go up to Miss Laura's room and bring down the luggage."

Suddenly this officious creature morphed back into the more gracious and likable Bobby. Maybe the pressure of the situation was affecting him too. He scrubbed a hand over his face and heaved a sigh. "Ach. Sorry lads. It's been a long day. I'll tell you about it later, but right now we have a train to catch."

Mom showed up in time to catch his last words. "Bobby, I thought you and the boys were taking a plane from Barcelona. You said the overnight train took too much of your valuable time." There was the slightest edge to her voice.

Bobby grinned when he saw Mom. "Ach, Laura, my dear, I changed my mind. I cannot let you go on the train without someone to keep an eye on you."

"Hmm," Mom said. "I thought your lads would do it."

Bobby winked at her. "There are some things I need to take care of myself."

Chapter 35

I am sure that everyone at one time or another has devised a plan which seemed brilliant, but when it came time to set it in motion has that "what was I thinking?" moment. That's what happened to me. Ronda had seemed an inspired idea. The perfect end to our perfect trip. An elegant Parador in a quaint village. Gorgeous views. Cute shops and cafes. Even a renowned bullring.

But after all the adventures of the past weeks I was more than ready to trade an all night train ride for a luxurious and quick plane trip in Business Class. Not just that, but I was not sure about the entire venture to Ronda. A Parador? Just a rundown castle. Views? Seen a million. Shops? Well there's always Target. Cafés? My jeans were too snug already. And a bullring? Well, we know how my twin feels about bulls, so let's put her out of her misery.

No one else seemed to share my misgivings so I sucked it up and forged ahead, shoving my doubts to the back of my mind. Until, that is, Chrissie and I stumbled into our tiny compartment on the train. I was leading the way when I tripped on the raised track for the sliding door. I spun around to warn Chrissie and smacked her in the head with my shoulder bag. She, in turn, ducked as she tried to avoid my bag, fell over my wheeled carry-on and crashed into me. We ended up sprawled on the floor of the compartment.

"Smooth move," she said as she tried to stand up.

"Hey, you bumped into me."

When we finally managed to get untangled and hauled ourselves to our feet and looked around, we were shocked to find ourselves in a space about six by twelve feet. I've been in elevators that are larger. This sleeper was microscopic. Two bunks occupied the left hand side of the space with a bathroom about the size of a broom closet opposite. It would take some serious gyrations to get my five feet nine inch frame into it.

"Not too roomy," I observed.

"Well, at least we don't have to worry about fooling around."

"To whom are you referring?" I asked. "Tessa and Casey? Or Mom and Bobby?"

Both pairs --- as well as the MacTavish grandsons --- were bunking in the compartments adjoining ours. Bobby had used his influence to make the arrangements. No complaints there. So even though I was still longing for a sumptuous hotel room after a quick flight, I was determined to make the best of our accommodations and the entire train trip. Still it was unsettling to think of the girls and Mom sharing living space --- each with her own individual MacTavish.

I checked out the bunk beds. "Where there's a will..."

Chrissie giggled. "Stop. I can't think about it. Let's go find the dining car. It's got to be bigger than this and my claustrophobia is really kicking in."

Mom, Tessa and Casey were already seated at our reserved table in the dining car when we showed up. The table was covered with a white cloth tablecloth and set for five with heavy silver flatware and attractive red-bordered china. A porcelain vase held a bouquet of some sort of small red flowers that I couldn't immediately identify. Two bottles of wine occupied the place of honor in the center of the table. Things were definitely looking up. Maybe this train trip wasn't such a bad idea after all.

"Cool," I said as I slid into an empty chair and peered out the window. If I had expected to see masked bandits chasing us I was disappointed. There was nothing sinister to see. Just the usual pre-departure bustle of passengers scurrying toward the platform and workmen loading bags.

"Where are Bobby and the grandsons?" Chrissie asked as she looked around.

"They decided to check out the Club Car," Casey said. "Didn't want to disturb, as Bobby put it, 'Lassies' Night Out.'"

"Good," I said, "because we need to talk."

"Let's wait until we're underway." Casey jerked her head at our waiter who approached our table with order pad in hand.

A few minutes later the train crawled out of the station, picking up speed as we left Barcelona behind. A few lights shone in the silent countryside and a few dim stars sparkled above. We passed through a peaceful village --- the residents tucked into their quaint houses beside the tracks. A single drawn out *too-oot* alerted them that we were passing through. With nothing to see we concentrated on dinner.

We chatted idly while we sipped our wine and nibbled the crusty bread. After our salads were served and we commented on the crispness of the greens, the tanginess of the dressing, the overall deliciousness of it all, I put down my fork and leaned into the table. "I can't stand it another second. What big news do you have that we'll die when we hear?"

Casey snuck a quick conspiratorial look at Tessa and then shook her head. "Uh uh," she said to us. "You go first. Tell us about your day."

"Yes," Tessa agreed. "We need to build to the moment."

I sighed in resignation. Long experience told me they would never budge. "Okay. We'll go first." I waited until the waiter cleared the salad plates and served the soup course. Then I nudged Mom, "You tell them."

 Mom launched into a recap of our day's adventures. "It all began with Christine's suitcase..."

As the train sped through the hushed dark outside, the girls digested both dinner and the information that, taking turns, Mom, Chrissie and I served them. As her grandmother described Marielle's encounter with the scary dude at *Le Picnic*, I noted that Tessa was growing agitated. She shoved her plate away and fidgeted in her seat, eyes wide.

Eventually, Mom took a breath. "I guess that's about all. Oh, but I forgot to mention that we did spend some time at the Chocolate Museum."

"You what?" Casey exclaimed. "We missed that? Oh, man."

"Well," I said to her. "I promise we didn't enjoy it. We were too worried about you two."

I forked up a bite of chicken and started to chew, but my eyes drifted to Tessa's. What was wrong with her? She looked spooked. "Tess," I said, "you haven't said a word. What's going on in that pretty blonde head of yours?"

Tessa cut her eyes to Casey. Casey shrugged and blew a lock of hair out of her eyes. "Tell 'em, Tess."

"The whole story?"

"Your part of it for now."

Tessa tucked a strand of hair behind her ear and hauled herself upright. Flattening both palms on the table, she leaned forward and began speaking --- her voice hushed and tense. Both girls kept looking with trepidation at the other diners, who appeared to me to be totally oblivious to us. Tessa cleared her throat.

"Ladies and gentlemen of the jury," Casey whispered.

"Knock it off, Case," Tessa ordered. "I'm not a lawyer and never will be."

"Ri-ight," Casey drawled. "Tell the story already, before our ancient audience nods off."

Tessa scowled at her cousin. "Okay. So as I was saying..."

"Well, actually you weren't," Casey interrupted.

"Shut up," Tessa said, but she smiled. "I'm telling this. So, Casey and I planned to meet Mac and Robert for breakfast as soon as the dining room opened this morning. We figured it was the last day to hang out with them and we didn't want to waste a single minute."

Meet the grandsons at 6:30? Wow. These guys must be really special to get Casey out of bed, dressed --- and, I noted, very nicely --- and made up all by 6:30.

"... and when we got to the dining room, Mac and Robert hadn't showed up yet. But, at a table in the corner, deep in conversation, were two other people we knew," Tessa was saying. "Care to take a guess who they were?"

"Spare the suspense," Chrissie said, "and just tell us."

Tessa definitely knows how to work a crowd. She paused and drew in a deep breath and let it out slo-o-wly. "It was Inspector Bouchard and Casey's 'friend' Luc."

"Oh, I almost forgot he was supposed to show up in Barcelona today. I thought Bobby was meeting with him," Chrissie said.

We all turned to look at Mom. She turned her hands palms up and shrugged. "That was the original plan. I'm a little surprised that it was Luc having breakfast with him."

"You're surprised?" Casey interjected. "How do you think I felt?"

"I believe conflicted might be the term I'd pick," Tessa said. "So since Robert and Mac were late, Casey and I decided it would be rude not to go over and say hello. Right, Casey?"

Casey nodded and picked up the narrative. "Luc invited us to join them, but I said we were meeting the guys." She grinned. "I don't think he liked that much."

"So..." Tessa took over again. "We sat down and had coffee with them."

"What did you talk about?" I asked.

"The usual," Tessa replied. "The weather and our trip. I have to admit I thought it was odd that the inspector didn't ask us about the attempts on Nonny's life or anything about yesterday."

"Because he knew all about it already," I suggested. "Either he planned it or he heard it from us. Chrissie gave him a pretty thorough rundown."

"He did ask about you and your plans for today before we left to meet Robert and Mac," Casey said.

"What did you tell him?"

"Not much really. We said we didn't know your plans but that all of us were leaving on the 9:30 train to Madrid and then on to Ronda," Casey said.

"Oh, no," Chrissie exclaimed. "You told him that?"

"We didn't know it was a secret," Tessa said. "Are we in trouble?"

"No," Chrissie said. "Is that all?"

"Not quite. While we had breakfast with the guys we kept watching Luc and the inspector. They seemed awfully chummy. So we hatched a plan. We decided that when they left Mac and I would follow Inspector Bouchard. And Casey, who undoubtedly had her own motives, would tail Luc. Oh, and Robert could tag along."

Casey frowned. "No editorial opinions, Tess. Just tell them what happened next."

Tessa sat up straighter and fluffed her hair. "Well. Mac and I are pretty good at this detective stuff, if I do say so myself. We followed the inspector directly to *Le Picnic Francais.*"

Chrissie bit her lip. "Did he see you?" she said in a strained tone.

Tessa arched her eyebrows and flicked her mother an offended look. "Of course not. Do you think we're stupid? So, anyway, he met another guy at *Le Picnic.* They stood on the front step talking for about ten minutes and then they split up. The inspector left and the other guy went inside. Our job was to stay with the inspector, so that's what we did."

Tessa scooped her hair off her neck and fixed us with an earnest stare. "Which brings us to you and your story about the scary dude and Marielle. Do you think it could be the same guy? And he went inside and assaulted her."

"I think it's likely," I said. "What time were you there?"

"I'd guess about eight or a little before."

"We were there around eight-thirty. That would have given the scary dude plenty of time to go inside, wait until Marielle arrived and threaten her...all before we showed up."

"Too bad you didn't take a picture of him, Aunt Kate," Tessa said. "That would have been helpful."

I hoisted my purse onto my lap and sifted through the contents until I found what I wanted. I pulled out an envelope and held it up. "It wasn't really the best time to whip out my camera and ask for a photo op, but I do have these." I opened the envelope and spread out the contents --- prints from the SD card we found in Chrissie's bag.

Casey jabbed my arm. "You rock, Mom. Let's see."

Tessa reached for the photos. "Where did you get these?"

"Saved them to my camera and printed them in the business center while your mom was researching something else. But that's another story we have to tell you."

I sorted through the photos and pulled out several. "Here are some of the best ones." I tapped one with a fingernail. "As you can see, this one is of Julio and Guillermo. The kidnappers." I tapped again. "And this is obviously Inspector Bouchard." I picked up the last photo and handed it to Tessa. "Which leaves him. He's the one I saw in the doorway."

Tessa scrutinized the photo while the rest of us waited for the verdict. Finally, she handed it back to me. "That's the guy, Aunt Kate. The one we saw with the inspector outside *Le Picnic*. I'd recognize that awful hat anywhere."

"Bingo," I said.

"But the inspector could be simply investigating *Le Picnic*," Mom said, "not running an illegal smuggling ring."

"Maybe," Casey said, "but he doesn't have the authority to investigate anything here. We aren't in Paris. Or even in France."

"Good point," I said.

Our discussion was interrupted by our waiter clearing our dishes and offering us coffee and dessert. No one said much until after our waiter finished his duties and we contemplated the gooey chocolate volcano cake that was our diet-busting temptation. I took a tiny bite and sighed with pleasure. "Ooh. This is beyond awesome. How many calories do you think are in one piece?"

"It doesn't matter, Kate," Mom said. "It's a celebration. And celebratory calories do not count."

"Good to know," I said. And as we all dug into the dessert the tension dissolved along with the chocolate.

Casey ate about three bites of cake, dropped her fork back on her plate and pushed herself away from the table. "Seriously, you guys," she moaned. "Celebration or not, I think we have cornered the market on calorie consumption. I can't stuff in another mouthful."

Tessa looked up as she polished off the last bite of her cake. "If you're not going to finish your cake, Case, I'll take it."

Casey raised an eyebrow. "Really? You'll have to find a specially reinforced pole to dance on if you don't stop feeding your face."

"Spoilsport." Tessa glared at her and then both girls broke into giggles.

Casey wiped her mouth with her napkin and crumpled it into a ball. She toyed with her wine glass and then said, "So. Who do you guys think put the SD card and the documents into Aunt Chrissie's bag?"

"Our guess was that Fifi is the brains of the duo and she ordered Georges to do it."

"Why?"

"Blackmail?" I suggested.

"Again, I ask why?" Casey said. "Who were they going to blackmail?"

"The inspector comes to mind," I said. "But now that they're dead, he wouldn't have anything to worry about."

"That's it," Chrissie gasped. "Remember when we found Fifi and Georges in our train compartment?"

"Who could forget it?" I said. "You totally freaked about your jacket."

She shot me a dirty look. "Get real. I did not."

"Oh, okay. Relax. What about the train?"

"The inspector was there. Right there in the car. Funny how he got there so quickly, isn't it? Odd coincidence."

We stared at each other in stunned silence. Finally, I stammered, "Are you trying to say... Do you really think...? Could it actually be possible?"

"...that Inspector Bouchard killed them? Or had them killed?" Chrissie finished my thought for me. "Not a doubt in my mind."

Just then our waiter hurried over to the table and handed Casey a folded up piece of paper. "The *caballero* ask me to give to you, *señorita*."

Casey took the paper and smiled at him. "*Muchas gracias.*" She unfolded it, quickly devoured its message and pressed it into Tessa's hand.

Tessa read it and then nodded at Casey. What was going on with the pair of them?

"What's the note say? Is it from Robert? Or Luc?" I asked her.

"Be patient, Mamacita and all will be revealed in good time." She pushed her chair away from the table. "Like now. Follow me."

I shivered as a blast of air-conditioned air blew on the back of my neck. Maybe it was a premonition of something to come. Goose bumps prickled up and down my bare arms as I followed Casey out of the dining car and into the swaying passageway beyond.

I tottered after her as she bustled through car after car, not bothering to look over her shoulder to make sure I was still shadowing her. My heart pounded with apprehension and, yes, anticipation of what surprise she might have in store. Behind me I heard Chrissie huffing like a steam engine.

Casey finally reached the door to her quarters and stopped. She fished in her jeans pocket for her key, inserted it in the lock and released the door. She opened it and stepped back and motioned me to enter the cabin. Only a faint light shining under the bathroom door illuminated the space. Tentatively I squinted into the room and turned to look at Casey. She gave me a gentle shove. "Go on, Mom."

I stepped over the threshold and nearly had a heart attack when an oddly familiar voice floated out of the gloom. "*Bonjour, Madame.*"

"Who's there? Who is it?" My voice quavered.

"*C'est moi.*"

Who was this intruder in my daughter's room?

Suddenly Casey reached around me and hit the light switch. Light flooded the space. And I recognized that it was our suitcase-switching friend, Georges, reclining on the bottom bunk and Fifi swinging her red-stiletto clad feet from the top bunk.

"But they're dead," I protested.

"Obviously not," Casey said. "It seems that rumors of their death have been greatly exaggerated." She paused. "By Inspector Bouchard."

"Is this a joke?" I asked. "Because it's not amusing."

"It's not a joke. I promise." Casey swung her head from side to side as she scanned the passageway. "But let's get inside where we can't be seen or overheard."

Mom, Chrissie and Tessa huddled together in the corridor outside the door and Casey shooed us all into the sleeper. We squeezed into the small space while Georges and Fifi watched us silently. Casey took a position with her back against the door. "I can explain," she said.

"I'm waiting," I answered her. "This had better be good."

Casey slid down so that her back was against the door, her knees bent. She took a long, slow breath and blew it out. "Okay. Here goes. As you can see Fifi and Georges are alive and well. Not dead and buried like Inspector Bouchard told us."

"That much is obvious," Chrissie said, "but why would the inspector let us think they were dead?"

"I'm confused. Did they inspector really think they were dead? Or did he just tell us that?" I said. I wasn't convinced that Fifi and Georges were real and not figments of someone's imagination. Mine?

Casey inclined her head toward Fifi and gave her an encouraging smile. "Okay. I'll tell you what I know and then Fifi can tell you the rest. Okay, Fifi?"

Fifi's frizzy curls bounced as she nodded. She shoved one lock off her forehead with a shaking hand, never taking her eyes off Casey.

"So, here's the story," Casey continued. "Remember I told you that Robert and I were going to tail Luc?"

Lots of head bobbing in acknowledgment.

"And we followed him to the train station where he met Fifi and Georges arriving on a train from Nice. I almost didn't recognize them."

"I am master *illusioniste*," Georges interrupted with undisguised pride. "We are in disguise."

Casey gave him a frosty look and picked up her story. I studied her as she spoke. Her brown eyes sparkled and a tiny smile played around her lips. She was enjoying this. And, after all, why not? What twenty-something young woman wouldn't have a good time basking in the attention of two extremely good-looking potential suitors?

I pictured Robert and Casey hot on the trail of the mysterious Luc. Her words painted a vivid picture of the thrill of the chase and the heady feeling of discovering that the supposedly deceased were very much alive.

When Fifi and Georges appeared at the door of the train, Casey grabbed Robert's sleeve and pulled him behind a pole. "Robert," she whispered urgently. "That's Fifi and Georges."

"Do you know them?" Robert asked.

"Know them? I certainly do. But when I last saw them they were being hauled off in an ambulance after being shot in our train car. They're dead."

"They don't look dead to me."

"And Luc is meeting them? How weird is that?"

At the mention of Luc's name, Robert frowned. "So let's go. This is none of our business."

Casey tugged on his sleeve again. "Robert, we need to follow them. I want to find out what Luc's doing with them."

Robert started to object, but Casey cautiously poked her head out from behind the pole and seeing that Luc was concentrating on escorting Fifi and Georges away from the train, started after them. "I'll do it myself if you don't want to help me," she said.

Of course, chivalry is not dead and he wouldn't let her do it alone. Especially if it involved the handsome Frenchman. So Casey and Robert followed Luc and the French couple as they sped through the station. Finally, they turned into a long hallway with many doors along the length. Luc stopped in front of one door and knocked. Then the door was opened from the inside and the three disappeared into the space beyond.

"Let's go," Robert said. "They aren't going to come out."

Casey narrowed her eyes and pursed her lips. "I am not leaving. You are free to go, but I'm going to wait here if it takes all day."

Robert sighed. "I'll wait."

But as time passed, Casey's determination wavered. Standing guard in a deserted hallway dimmed some of the glamour of being ace detectives and she was about to give up when the door opened and Luc burst out of the door. His sudden appearance took Casey and Robert by surprise and they had no time to find a hiding place. Luc stopped when he saw them and then marched over to confront them.

"Why isn't this a pleasant surprise," he said. "Fancy meeting you here."

Casey blinked up at him, struggling to find something clever to explain why she and Robert were lurking in the isolated section of the station, but, failing that, said nothing.

"I don't suppose you'd care to explain what you think you're doing," Luc said.

Something about Luc's imperious tone annoyed Casey. Men. Seriously. So she blurted, "We followed you here. We saw you meet two supposedly dead people and escort them here. I wanted to find out why."

Luc ran a hand over his handsomely unshaven chin and sighed. "Casey, Casey, Casey, what should I do with you? You know I cannot tell you anything."

"I'm not leaving," Casey told him. She turned. "Right, Robert?"

Luc and Robert stared daggers at each other for a moment before Luc sighed again, his shoulders slumping. "Let me make a call. Wait here." And he disappeared behind the closed door.

When he reappeared he beckoned to Casey and Robert. "I made a few calls and it seems that we might be able to use your help after all. That is, if you are willing. Since you've already seen them...."

He opened the door wider and ushered Casey and Robert inside.

Seated in two straight-backed chairs facing a large black and silver office desk were none other than Casey's old acquaintance, Fifi, and the slippery Georges.

"*Bonjour*, Casey," Fifi greeted her. "I am glad to see you."

"Wow." Casey took a deep breath. "Not dead. Oh, wow. I'm so glad."

Casey was bursting with excitement as she finished her tale. Her eyes flashing. "So, that's it. Luc called Bobby and he arranged for these guys to take the train with us tonight. They figured it would be okay for Robert and me to hang out with them. Cool, huh?"

"Oh, very cool," I said, but something didn't make sense. "I don't get it. Why would Bobby allow two crucial witnesses to hang out with you? What about security? He won't let Mom use the restroom without an armed guard."

Casey chewed her lip and twisted her ring around and around. "Oh, did I forget to tell you? Robert signed up to work for Interpol."

"What? He what? Interpol?"

Casey rolled her eyes and gave me the "how can you be so dense" look. "He graduated with a degree in criminology. You knew that. And he always wanted to work with his grandfather. Ever since his grandmother died. He isn't actually an agent yet, but he will be. And Bobby trusts him."

I guess that explained why Bobby felt the girls were perfectly safe with Robert and Mac. They were soon-to-be cops.

"Mac, too?" I asked.

Tessa shook her head. "Jury's still out on that, Aunt Kate. He's considering it, but he hasn't finished school and he's a music major. Piano and guitar and bagpipes. He'd like his own band. So who knows?"

"I feel so much better now," Chrissie said. "If my daughter is in danger, Mac can beat up an assailant with his bagpipes."

"Mo-om," Tessa protested, but she smiled.

"What about Luc? How does he fit in to all of this?" I wanted to know.

Casey held up a hand. "Wait. Let Fifi explain this part. Then it will all begin to make sense."

Fifi drew herself upright and smoothed her skirt over her knees. One red stiletto slipped off her foot and dropped to the floor with a small thud. She stared at it for a few moments and then regarded us with wide, guileless eyes. "I must apologize to you. We get you involved and is not your fault. Georges he take a chance to switch the bags and then..." She lifted one shoulder in a shrug.

"No need to apologize, dear," Mom said. "Please go on."

Fifi gave us a wan smile. "*Oui*. We tell you how we meet two men who tell us they will pay us money to smuggle suitcase. Georges knows it will be huge problem to smuggle in bag," But we discuss and decide it is worth the try. We agree to meet the two men to pick up the bag. We are anxious and get to meeting place early. And, *voila*, find four men having rendevous. We have brilliant idea. We will take photos of the men. It will be information we can use to protect us."

Georges smiled smugly. "Is very good plan. Fifi says I should take photos with my camera."

"Ha," Fifi scoffed. "Is good plan until Georges is *tres stupide*. He gets too close and Inspector sees him. *Quelle problem.*"

"Still," she continued, "we are not sure is Inspector catching crooks or is crook himself. We think we wait. Pretend we have seen nothing. We meet two men who give us suitcase. Georges switch bag at airport. When the two men find out they are very angry."

"Then we make bad decision. We have the camera photo card and some documents Georges has taken and copied."

Georges broke in again. "I am *illusioniste*. Poof. Documents are mine."

"Shush, Georges," Fifi said. "I tell Georges to hide things in your bag and return bag to you."

Fifi's eyes swept the tiny cabin before she took a deep breath. "I know you are on certain train from paper in your bag." She looked questioningly at Chrissie. "What do you call it?"

"Itinerary," Chrissie answered. "I did have a copy of our itinerary in my suitcase. Go on, Fifi. Then what?"

"We go to train to wait for you and get photo card and documents from you. But before you arrive the inspector, he come. I think we can confide to him our story and he will protect us from the bad men. We think he will give Georges permission to travel."

She swung her foot and the other shoe plonked onto the floor. She gazed at it helplessly. "So. Inspector is friendly at first. Tells us to give him card and documents and he will make sure it goes to proper authority. But Georges does not have the information. It is in your bag." She looked apologetically at Chrissie. "We no can give papers to Inspector. He demands them. I now see he is not good man. He says we must tell him where we hide papers or we will regret it. Then time is up. Train whistle blows and Inspector gets very angry. He has a gun. Georges tries to get gun and bang Inspector shoots Georges. I try to run. And then he shoot me too." Fifi stopped talking, tears streaking down her face and her lips trembling. "Next thing I wake up in hospital with bullet in my arm."

"But not dead," I said. "Obviously. Why did the inspector tell us you both were dead?"

"Because we let him think we are dead," Fifi said with pride. "My sister is nurse at hospital. She tell everyone we are dead. Then she gets help and fix papers saying we died. She even has funeral. And cremates us."

"Wow, that was fast," Chrissie said. "And you fooled the inspector?"

"My sister she have much help. We are very grateful. A friend helps her take us to Nice. We stay with family there. Our injuries are not so bad and we get better. We owe him our lives."

"Luc? He's the one who helped them?" I asked.

"Apparently," Casey said, "Interpol assigned Luc to work undercover for Inspector Bouchard and he told Luc to go to the hospital and interview Fifi before she ..." She made quote marks with her fingers. "...died. When Luc heard her story, he called Bobby. Interpol made arrangements for Fifi and Georges to stay with Luc's sister in Nice until they could be transported to Interpol offices in Madrid for debriefing."

"Hmm," Mom said. "Then Bobby MacTavish knew the inspector's role all the time and used us to reel him in." She made a fist and thumped it against the wall. "I do not appreciate being lied to and used."

There was a tap on the door and Casey cracked it open and peeked out. Then she opened it the rest of the way to reveal Bobby and the grandsons standing outside.

"Did I hear my name?" Bobby asked.

"Whoa," Tessa said, "let's add eavesdropping to his list of transgressions."

"Bobby," Casey added, "you've got some 'splainin' to do."

Mom gave her granddaughters a pained look and then turned it on Bobby. "Yes, Bobby, you do have some explaining to do."

Bobby stepped into the sleeper. His grandsons followed. He took Mom's hand and bent to kiss it, but she yanked it away.

"Don't try your charm on me," she said.

Bobby flinched. "I'll explain later. I have many things to tell you."

Mom nodded, but sat with her arms folded across her chest and refused to look at him.

There was an awkward silence before Bobby turned to Fifi and Georges. "Let's get you two to your compartment. I'll have some lads stay with you until we reach Madrid. I don't want anything to happen to you. You might be in danger if Claude suspects that you are alive."

We watched in awe as Fifi and Georges donned their disguises. Before our eyes Fifi became a brunette with a smooth bob, her face shadowed by a large broad-brimmed hat complete with a veil. She slipped on huge dark glasses and a black trench-coat, but she slid her feet back into her trademark red stilettos. Georges transformed into a little old man with white hair and beard and a stooped posture. He buttoned his jacket to the chin, placed a fedora on his head, grabbed his cane from behind the bunk and peered at us through thick horn-rimmed glasses.

"That's awesome." Casey clapped her hands. "You are an *illusioniste*. Bravo."

Georges swept his hat from his head and bowed deeply. "*Merci, mademoiselle.*"

We bade them a final farewell and wished them luck, certain we would never see them again. As Bobby escorted them from the sleeper, Georges turned back and touched his hand to his forehead in a salute. "*Au revoir, mes amies. Bon Voyage.*"

And they disappeared into the passageway.

After Bobby and the French couple left we stared at each other in disbelief and sagged in exhaustion. What could possibly come next on this crazy adventure?

Mom announced that she was going to wait for Bobby in her compartment and Chrissie and I could see that Casey and Tessa wanted to spend some time alone with Robert and Mac. So we trailed apathetically out of the compartment, leaving the four young people behind.

In the narrow passageway we lingered for a few minutes replaying the entire episode.

I massaged the back of my neck with my hand. "Can you believe that Fifi and Georges are really alive? The inspector was very convincing when he told us they had died."

"Probably because," Chrissie said with a sigh, "he actually believed it."

"Bobby knew the truth," Mom said in an unforgiving tone. "There isn't any excuse for letting us believe they'd been murdered."

"Come on, Mom," I said. "He couldn't tell us. He had to protect them and the fewer people who knew they were alive the better."

"I suppose." Mom unlatched the door to her compartment and slipped inside. "But I'm going to tell him I'm disappointed in him."

"You go, Mom," I said.

When the door closed behind her, Chrissie turned to me. "I'm too keyed up to even think about sleep. Let's get a glass of wine and talk."

"Fine by me," I said. "Let's see if the bar is still open."

I followed her as she made her way through the rocking railway cars to the club car. It was dimly lit with a small bar at the far end and comfortable looking chairs surrounding round tables. The car was empty except for the bartender.

"Is it too late to get a glass of wine?" Chrissie asked him.

"*No problema, señora.*"

He poured red rioja wine into two glasses and we took them to one of the tables. We sank into the chairs, kicked off our shoes and sipped our wine in companionable silence. My twin plucked a peanut out of the bowl in the center of the table and popped it into her mouth. She chewed it thoughtfully with her eyes closed. Finally, she opened her eyes and made a face. "This is nuts."

"Crazy," I agreed. "Insane. All we wanted was a fun little birthday trip."

"No muss. No fuss. No daughters. No mom. No murder. No mayhem."

"Just the two of us, footloose and fancy free."

"Ha," Chrissie exclaimed. "Like that would ever happen. What were we thinking?"

"I have no idea, but we are in this up to our older-by-the-minute eyeballs so we have to deal with it," I said.

Chrissie drummed her fingers on the table and rolled her wine glass between her fingers. "Let's presume for a minute that the inspector is running a smuggling ring."

I nodded.

"I have a million questions about who, what, where, when, why and how," she went on.

I stared at my reflection in the window. "Let's take it one step at a time. The smuggling is a given. What? Gems. The how is to ship them in picnic baskets from *Le Picnic Francais*. Where? Overseas to the U.S. Who is a good question, but I'd say it's the inspector and the scary dude and Julio and Guillermo among a cast of hundreds. Why? Fairly obvious. Money. And if Luc is correct about the inspector's family maybe he does need money to pay hospital bills. They can be gargantuan."

Chrissie tossed another peanut into her mouth. "Mmm. Hmm. We think we know where they're shipping the baskets. Where do you suppose they're getting the gems? It can't be anything legal."

"Stolen, of course," I said. "But wouldn't Bobby and his lads at Interpol be aware of any unsolved jewelry heists? That would be the first place I'd think of to look for gems being smuggled and fenced."

"An unsolved crime means just that," Chrissie commented, her tone implying I was one cookie short of a sleeve. "One step ahead of the cops and all that."

I took a sip of wine and mulled over what she'd said. And then... I set my wine glass down with a thud and sat up in excitement. "Chrissie! What if the crimes aren't unsolved at all? What if it isn't whether a crime is solved or unsolved, but whether or not the stolen goods have been recovered by the police?"

She looked at me like I'd lost my mind. "Kathleen Kelly, what are you blithering about?"

"Okay," I said trying to rein in my enthusiasm. "Once I saw this movie about these rogue cops who stole stuff from the property room --- you know where cops keep stolen property. You've seen that on TV."

At her nod, I hurried on. "These cops basically stole the stolen property and then fenced it and no one was any wiser."

"Uh huh. So they committed the perfect crime?"

"Well, no-o-o. But it worked for awhile anyway."

"Do go on."

"What if the cop in question --- that would be Inspector Bouchard --- takes stolen gems from the property room. He smuggles them overseas and fences them there. Then he hires underlings to smuggle the cash back to France."

We stared at each other. Was it possible that we had stumbled onto the answer? I was surprised to find our wine glasses empty ... I didn't remember even drinking any. "I'll get us a refill."

I wandered over to the bar and the bartender poured more wine. On my way back to the table I noticed another customer had come in while we were immersed in our conversation. The man was slouched at the table farthest from us and hidden in shadow. He was half-turned away from us nursing a drink in a small glass and appeared totally caught up in the passing landscape. I dropped into my chair and jerked my head in his direction. "We have company."

"Uh oh. Maybe we should take this discussion back to our car. It isn't the kind of thing we want overhead by the wrong people," Chrissie said.

Something was bothering me. I studied the man at the table for a few seconds. He tugged on an earlobe. And I realized that he looked familiar. Too familiar. "Chrissie," I whispered urgently. "Don't be too obvious but look at that guy. I think I recognize him."

Casually, Chrissie draped one arm across the back of her chair and glanced sideways. Her eyes widened as she swung her chair so that she was facing away from him. She leaned across the table and hissed, "Inspector Bouchard. I'm sure it is."

"You saw it too?"

"The earlobe thing? Definitely."

I stood up. "Let's get out of here."

"I'm right behind you."

We race walked through the hushed cars fighting to keep our balance as the train swayed from side to side. I caught my heel and twisted my ankle as we stumbled through the pocket between cars --- the sound of rushing air echoing in our ears. I limped the length of the final car afraid to look back. After what seemed like a lifetime we burst into our quarters and latched the door behind us. I stood with my back against the door, breathing heavily and rubbing my throbbing ankle. Chrissie vaulted the short distance to the bunks and frantically peered under them and then into the tiny bathroom. Reassured that no thug with evil intentions lurked in our compartment, she sank onto the bottom bunk with her head in her hands. Her voice muffled she moaned, "Do you think he heard us?"

"I don't know. I didn't see him come in to the club car. I wonder how long he was there."

"Oh, God," Chrissie said. "What if we're right and what if he heard us?"

"Do you think he'd try to shut us up?"

Chrissie wrapped her arms around her chest and rocked back and forth. "What should we do? We're sitting ducks."

I hobbled over to the bunk and bumped her hip to make room for me to sit down. "We should tell Bobby we saw the inspector." But doubts crept in now that we were safely back in our sleeper. "Maybe it wasn't even Bouchard."

"Yeah," Chrissie agreed, sitting up. "It probably wasn't."

"Lots of people tug their earlobes. He isn't even on the train. He went back to Paris." I paused. "Oh, who are we kidding? It was Inspector Bouchard. We both know it. We have to talk to Bobby."

"Now?"

I looked at my watch. "It's really late. But I don't think we can wait until breakfast. As you said, we're sitting ducks. And I don't want to be a dead duck because we were too polite to interrupt Mom and Bobby doing whatever they might be doing."

" Eww. I don't even want to think about that. But one of us will have to go to their compartment and get him."

I grimaced at the thought. "Scissors, stone or paper? Loser goes."

She nodded. And for once her paper lost to my scissors. She pulled on her shoes and opened the door. "Be right back." And she vanished.

While I waited for Chrissie to return I stretched out on the bottom bunk and contemplated the underside of the mattress above my head. With my eyes half-closed I replayed our adventures. Suddenly my eyes popped open and I sat up, banging my head on the bunk above. "Ouch," I said aloud as I rubbed the sore spot. A hazy memory that had been floating on the edge of my consciousness abruptly came into focus.

I hopped off the bed and began to pace in the tiny space. Two steps one way; two steps back. I couldn't wait to tell Chrissie what I'd remembered. What was taking her so long anyway?

Just then I heard voices in the passageway, a muffled thud and then the door slid open. Chrissie slipped inside followed by Mom and Bobby. I quickly checked them out. Mom wore her soft pink robe with matching fluffy pink slippers, her glasses on a jeweled chain around her neck; her white curls were held back by a pink headband. Bobby was in jeans and a denim work shirt untucked with the top buttons undone. Both were slightly tousled, but presented more a picture of cozy domesticity than one of hot and steamy sex. Thank heavens. I couldn't possibly imagine my mother, for heaven's sake, having a romantic ... um ... interlude.

"Miss Chrissie says that you think you saw Inspector Bouchard in the club car," Bobby said.

I wrenched my thoughts back to the present with some effort. "Right. We did. At least we're pretty sure. But I just remembered something else and I think it might be important."

"Please tell us," Bobby said.

"Spill it," Chrissie said.

"So, Bobby, Chris and I were wondering about where the gems might have come from and how the inspector might have gotten his hands on them. I think I've figured it out."

"Go on."

"Do you remember when we first met Inspector Bouchard? At *Bouffe Tard*? Well, I thought he looked like Inspector Clousseau from Pink Panther."

They stared at me as if I had gone insane. Maybe I had a little.

"Do you remember what he did when he met us?'

"Said hello?" Chrissie answered.

"Don't be dumb. Besides that?"

"Can't say that I do," Chrissie said.

"Me either," Mom added.

"He did that courtly thing that European men do. He took our hands in his and he bent over and kissed them. All la ti da."

"So?"

"So what did he say when he kissed Mom's hand?"

"I don't know," Chrissie said. "What a lovely hand you have my dear?"

"Not quite. He said what a lovely ring you have, my dear."

Mom stared at me. "And then he told us he always admired nice jewelry, because his son is a jeweler and designs his own pieces. Oh my goodness."

"His son is a jeweler. Makes his own pieces. Oh my God," Chrissie exploded. "Do you all know what this could mean?"

"What if the inspector steals the gems from the property room and replaces them with fakes made by his son? I'm sure that no one would ever notice. It's not like they would get an appraisal once they had them in police custody." I grabbed Chrissie and we danced around the car while Bobby and Mom watched.

Bobby leaned back in his chair and rubbed a hand over his face. "I knew about his son. And it does all fit together. I guess I had hoped that Claude wasn't involved after all. But the evidence is starting to pile up."

No one spoke for a few minutes, then Bobby stood up. "And you're sure it was Claude you saw? When I spoke to him last in Barcelona, he was heading back to Paris. In fact, I saw him board the train before I joined you."

"We're sure," Chrissie said.

"It had to be," I agreed.

"Well, then," Bobby said, "I think I have to make a few calls." He started to open the door, but stopped when I called to him.

"Wait, Bobby. What about those skull and crossbones charms? Do you have any idea what they might mean? And where they might have come from?"

He smoothed his shirt and buttoned the top few buttons. "I have a few ideas. All I can tell you for the moment is that the gems used for the eyes are not genuine. They're fakes. Good ones, but still fakes."

I certainly didn't know what to make of this piece of information. Nothing made sense anymore.

"I'm going to take care of some things," Bobby said. "When I leave, lock the door and don't open it until I come back. I'll have some lads watch the door in case Claude did follow you back here."

And he was gone.

We stared at each other helplessly. What had we gotten ourselves into? Finally, Mom said, "I learned something else from Bobby that might be useful."

"Pillow talk?" Chrissie wrinkled her nose.

Mom gazed into space, a small half-smile played on her lips. Then she jerked herself away from her reverie. "Stop. I'll tell you what Bobby told me. And that's all I'll tell you two nosy boots."

Chrissie caught my eye and quirked an eyebrow. I did an exaggerated eye roll and forced myself to think calming thoughts. Ommm.

"Okay, Secret Agent," Chrissie said. "what did Bobby tell you about the whole smuggling thing?"

Mom straightened her pink robe and put her glasses on. "Well, you will both be astonished to learn that Bobby identified the fourth man in the photos. The scary dude you saw at *Le Picnic*, Kate."

Speaking softly and quickly, Mom poured out the story. Bobby hadn't recognized the fourth man so he turned the SD card over to his associates at Interpol headquarters. Bobby made prints and showed them around to some of the men in the field. One of the men recognized the scary dude.

"And do you know who it was who recognized him?" Mom asked.

We shook our heads.

"It was Luc. He met the inspector at grief counseling in Nice. Remember?" She didn't wait for us to answer. "And you remember that the inspector's wife died in the same terrible accident that left his daughter and two granddaughters so horribly injured?"

We bobbed our heads, eager for her to continue.

"When Luc saw the photo he immediately recognized the fourth man --- the inspector's son-in-law, the daughter's husband and the father of the two little girls. Luc told Bobby the son-in-law attended only one session and was very bitter. And Luc also remembered that he had been in the import/export business, but went bankrupt trying to pay the medical bills. He lost his business. Nearly lost his entire family. And his mother-in-law died. A terrible tragedy."

So the scary dude was Inspector Bouchard's son-in-law? You don't have to bash me over the head with a two-by-four. I got it. The family business became smuggling --- Inspector Bouchard had access to stolen jewels, his son designed jewelry and the final piece of the puzzle was the son-in-law in import/export.

"Whoa," I said brilliantly.

"Is Bobby going to arrest the inspector?" Chrissie asked.

"I can't say for sure," Mom said, "but he might bring him in for a chat."

"If he can find him." I shivered wondering exactly where the elusive inspector might be at this very moment. Camped outside our door posing as a security guard?

The three of us sat mute with only the sound of the train car rushing through the night to break the silence. Finally there was a light rapping on the compartment door. "Laura? Kate? Christine? It's Bobby. You can open the door."

Cautiously I unlatched the door and slid it along the track until I could see out. Then, reassured, I pushed it the rest of the way to let Bobby enter. He stooped to avoid hitting head on the ceiling and slouched against the doorframe. "It's all taken care of," he said. "I'll escort you, Laura, back to your compartment where you'll be safe. We can meet your daughters in the dining car for breakfast. I'll have one of my lads watch over them until then."

Bleary-eyed with fatigue, no one objected. Mom stood and allowed Bobby to take her arm. As he guided her out of our car, she looked back over her shoulder. "Good night, Nancy Drew. Good night, Stephanie Plum. Sleep tight."

We laughed. "Right back at you, Double 0 Seven."

The door swooshed shut and we climbed into our bunks to sleep a few hours of fitful sleep.

Chapter 36

When Bobby's lad chaperoned us to the dining car early the next morning we found Bobby and Mom sitting side by side with their heads together laughing. I stopped just inside the car to check them out. They certainly appeared cheerful and well rested. I couldn't help but wonder where they had spent the night. Together or not?

Bobby said something to her and my naive (or so I thought), prim and proper mother giggled. Seriously. Giggled. Mind you like a teen-ager. Chrissie stuck an elbow in my ribs and hissed in my ear, "I'm shocked. Look at them."

"I know," I whispered. "Have they no shame?"

Mom looked up and seeing us lurking there, waved and beckoned to us. We slid into seats opposite her and Bobby.

"Hey, you two crazy kids," I said.

"You're looking chipper this morning," Chrissie added.

Mom narrowed her eyes and frowned as we poured coffee from the carafe in the center of the table. "Behave yourselves."

Chrissie blinked innocently. "Us? I don't know what on earth you're talking about."

Mom studied us while we fixed our plates and made idle chatter with Bobby, her brows knit together in a fierce scowl. "I'm warning you. None of your twin thinking."

I grinned at her. "Oh, look. Casey and Tessa are here too." Sure enough, our daughters shared the table next to ours with Robert and Mac.

Casey wriggled her fingers at me and then turned back to the obviously much more engrossing company of the grandsons.

"So, Bobby," Chrissie said as she smeared strawberry jam on a piece of toast, "what did you learn about the inspector?"

"Is he on the train?" I asked.

Bobby took a long gulp of coffee and regarded us with serious blue eyes. "According to my sources he hasn't returned to Paris. It's likely, in view of what you told me, that he's been on this train. It doesn't appear that he's on the train at the moment, but we've made several stops so he could have gotten off anywhere along the line."

"That's wonderful," I said. "So you don't actually know where he is?"

Bobby shook his head.

"Very comforting," Chrissie said. "I feel so much better now."

Bobby's expression was grim --- his jaw clenched. "Don't worry. We'll track him down. He can't just disappear. In the meantime, my lads will keep tabs on all of you." He gestured at Casey and Tessa flirting with his grandsons at the next table.

He rose quickly from the table, bent to kiss Mom's cheek and studied us for a moment. "I have a lot to do before we reach Madrid. There are some details that need my attention. I'll see you all later." He patted Mom's shoulder and strode out of the dining car.

Mom watched Bobby leave with a bemused expression. Then she put her elbows on the table and leaned forward to get as close to us as possible. She raised both eyebrows and jerked her head to indicate that we should look over her shoulder. Her voice pitched so low that we had to strain to hear her, she said, "Don't be obvious, but there ... "She twitched her head again. "...are two of the things that need Bobby's attention."

I surreptitiously scrutinized the other passengers in the dining car. Nothing seemed amiss. Until ... I saw them. Two elderly couples at a table across the aisle. Grey haired and wrinkled, the women wore nylon track suits; the men baggy cargo pants and loose fitting shirts. All wore safari hats and one man wore a pair of thick horn-rimmed glasses. They were absorbed in reading their guidebooks. Typical tourists? Not exactly. Two of the elderly tourists were none other than Fifi and Georges. I never would have recognized them.

I leaned in to whisper to Mom. "It's them. Who are they with?"

"Bodyguards," she whispered back. "In disguise."

Chrissie's mouth hung open in astonishment. "Wow. That's bold."

I suddenly realized that the dining car was almost empty. I peeked at my watch. "Oh, dear. We'll be in Madrid in less than an hour. We need to finish packing. Let's talk more later."

Hastily we gathered our purses and sunglasses and prepared to leave. As we did, the two "elderly" couples passed our table on their way out. One of the two women, the dumpy one in the lavender suit, paused next to me. She shoved her sunglasses up so that I could see her eyes and winked. Fifi, of course. Then she gave me a thumbs up gesture and followed her companions as they exited the car.

"*Au revoir*, Fifi," I said. "*Bon Voyage.*"

Chapter 37

The little town of Ronda was everything we had hoped it would be. One of the oldest places in Spain, it clings to the side of the *Serrania de Ronda* Mountains. Its main tourist attraction is the gorge running through the center of town. And, our hotel, *The Parador de Ronda*, perched on the edge of that gorge and offered spectacular views of the river and tumbled rocks below. The town itself featured cobblestoned streets and Moorish architecture and a plethora of shops and ancient churches to explore. And we couldn't forget, either, the bullring, the oldest in Spain.

Our short trip on the train connecting Ronda and Madrid had been a bit gloomy. The girls were sad to say good-bye to the MacTavish brothers and Mom quietly read a paperback novel, keeping whatever she might be feeling about leaving Bobby to herself. So it was good to shake off our moodiness and emerge from the train station.

By the time our taxi dropped us off at the Parador our good spirits had been restored and we were in love with the surroundings and impatient to begin exploring. The Parador, itself, was elegant and upscale --- our last big splurge. Our rooms were amazing --- cushy queen-sized beds, hardwood floors, double sinks in the bathroom and, best of all, a balcony from which we could view the rushing river and stunning vista below. Leaning against the rail we breathed in the cool mountain air and looked at each other in awe. Then we exchanged a high-five.

"Wow," I said.

"Outstanding," Chrissie agreed.

"Yo, Mom." I looked up and saw Casey waving at me from the balcony outside her room.

"Good job, Aunt Kate." Tessa stood at Casey's elbow with her camera in her hand.

"Thank you, sweetie," I said. "Your mom and I are going to unpack later. We want to get out and do some shopping before siesta."

Siesta was perhaps our single biggest frustration during our stay in Spain. Other than attempts on Mom's life and scary dudes and all of that, of course. In Spain everything, and I do mean everything, shuts down between two and five in the afternoon. Shops, churches, museums all close their doors so everyone can nap. Or eat. Restaurants typically stay open so we'd done far more eating than shopping. Now it was nearly one and Chrissie and I wanted to get to the shops before they closed. Opportunity was knocking. So much shopping, so little time.

"Are the three of you coming with us?" Chrissie asked. "We don't have much time."

Tessa and Casey consulted briefly before Tessa called to us, "We'll skip it for now. We didn't shower on the train and we feel kind of grimy. We'll clean up while you shop and go to lunch with you when you get back. We'll scope out the best place to go."

"Sounds good," Chrissie said. "What about Nonny?"

"She's talking to Bobby on Casey's cell. You two go on. She might be awhile."

We didn't need convincing; Ronda was too tempting to resist. We ran a quick comb through our hair, tossed on our jackets and were out the door before you could say, "*Hasta la vista*." We paused to take pictures next to the water fountain in the sunny, cobblestoned courtyard outside the hotel and then dashed down the street, spurred on by the tantalizing sight of a street crowded with pedestrians and lined with shops.

The sky was bright blue overhead and the sun warm on our shoulders. We skipped in and out of shops, happily oblivious to everything but the beauty of the day and the array of goods within our grasp.

The hour flew by but we managed to spend a hefty pile of Euros on fashion bargains before the shopkeeper in the last store shooed us out the door and locked it behind us.

"Whew," I said as I sank onto a bench outside the shop. "That was fun."

"Exhausting, but fun. Aerobic shopping."

I swung my head from side to side and noticed that the pedestrian traffic had thinned considerably. Siesta had begun. My stomach growled. "Time to eat," I announced. "Let's go get Mom and the girls and see where they want to go for lunch."

Laden with shopping bags, purses and cameras, we strolled back to the Parador noting places we might want to explore later. We dumped our purchases in our room and drew back the heavy brocade curtains to let in the sunlight. I kicked off my shoes and fell backwards onto the bed nearest the balcony. "Hey, Chris. You can use the bathroom first. I'll call the girls and let them know we're back."

Chrissie toed off first one shoe and then the other and padded barefoot into the bathroom and closed the door with a thump. I rubbed my feet and stretched luxuriously before I rolled over on one elbow to reach for the phone. Before I picked up the receiver I noticed that the message light was flashing. "Hey, we have a message."

Chrissie poked her head out of the bathroom, toothbrush stuck in her mouth. "So listen to it, genius." She shut the door.

I found the instructions for retrieving messages in the desk drawer and punched in the code. And as the message began I nearly dropped the phone.

"Mom? Mommy? Oh, God where are you? We're okay. Don't worry. He hasn't hurt us, but he says…." Casey's voice on the answering machine quavered. Wasn't she shopping with Tessa? What was going on?

A male voice cut her off. Cold, flat and unemotional. *"I have taken your daughters. They are alive…for the moment. If you do exactly as I say, they will not be harmed. If not…"*

The frightening voice went on, but all I could hear was my heart pounding in my ears. My lungs collapsed. I couldn't breathe. No air in the room, in the country of Spain, in the entire universe.

A hand tugged at the receiver I had clenched in my freezing fingers. "Kate? Who is it? You look like death?"

Chrissie. I stared at her. I didn't want her to hear the sinister voice, but she had to. I jabbed at the telephone buttons. My fingers were shaking so badly that I missed the first time. I finally managed to get the message to play again. This time on the speaker.

As the terrifying voice filled the hotel room, Chrissie's eyes, glazed with horror, locked on mine.

"I have taken your daughters. They are alive, for the moment. If you do exactly as I say, they will not be harmed. If not ... I will kill them both.

"I have left instructions for you at the front desk. Do not call the police. You will not see your daughters alive again if you do. I am getting impatient. Do as I say. Do not try to fool me."

We stood paralyzed for a few seconds. Casey and Tessa were in danger. We had to do something.

"It's him," Chrissie breathed. "It's Bouchard, isn't it?"

My mouth was glued shut. I could only manage a nod.

"I'll go to the front desk," Chrissie said and, shoeless, flew out the door.

I paced the room unable to sit still, nauseated with fear. Cold rivulets of sweat dripped down my sides. By the time Chrissie burst back into the room, waving a sheet of paper, I was hyperventilating.

"What does it say?"

"Come to the bullring. Alone. Bring the documents and wait for instructions. Do not call the police. Do not call MacTavish. Your daughters are waiting for you."

"How do we know he has them?" I said.

Chrissie's face was the color of paste. "You heard Casey on the voicemail."

388

"We need to make sure they aren't safe in their room."

"I have a key. I'll go check," she said.

"I'm coming with you."

Chrissie edged into the girls' room ahead of me and gave a strangled cry. The two giants we had seen with Bobby in Barcelona were bound and gagged and lying in front of the door to the balcony. Chrissie crouched over one of them.

"Is he...he...dead?" I stammered.

"Don't know," she panted. "I'm going to do CPR." Using all her strength she rolled the giant over onto his back and pulled the gag from his mouth. He opened his eyes, moaned and then his eyes flickered shut. "Not dead."

I breathed a sigh of relief. "How about the other one?"

Chrissie put her fingers on the neck of the second giant. "I think I feel a pulse. We need to get a doctor."

"No-o," the first giant moaned as he opened his eyes again. "No police. No doctor. Call MacTavish."

"We can't," I told him. "Bouchard has our daughters. He said he would kill them if we called Bobby."

The giant moaned again. "You can't rescue them on your own. You need our help."

He had a point. Maybe we could use their help. "Let's cut them loose."

Chrissie disappeared into our room and returned brandishing a pair of manicure scissors. Frantically she snipped at the thick ropes but wasn't making much progress. The giant grimaced. "Those will never work. Unless you intend to trim my cuticles."

"You're right." Chrissie tossed the scissors aside and brushed a lock of damp hair off her forehead. "What do you suggest?"

"Call MacTavish."

"No. We can't. Don't you understand? He has our daughters." Her voice rose in hysteria. "He has Tessa and Casey."

"I'm really sorry." I said to Giant Number One. "We don't have time for a debate. You'll be fine until we get back."

Chrissie stuffed the gag back into his mouth. "I hate to do this, but we can't have you making noise and getting the police involved. I promise we'll call Bobby as soon as we have the girls."

The giant tried to twist away from her hand, but Chrissie was determined. "I apologize, but we need to get out of here." She patted his shoulder and stood up.

I tossed Chrissie's sneakers to her. "Put them on. There's no time to waste."

She stuffed her feet into her shoes and we exploded out the door and clattered down the steps. We raced through the cobblestoned streets dodging cars and pedestrians. Casey's face floated before my eyes. I imagined his hand holding a gun to her head as she begged for mercy.

"Hurry," I gasped.

"I am." Chrissie huffed out her words. "Will…we…make it?"

"We have to."

I shoved my hair out of my eyes. My vision was blurred with sweat. We finally reached the building and darted inside. We raced toward the door leading to the bullring, but a large guard in an unattractive uniform blocked our way. "*Señor*, I, we, uh, *como*?" Chrissie's command of Spanish, limited at best, had now apparently deserted her entirely.

The guard shook his head and pointed officiously at the ticket window. "*Señor, por favor*," she said, but he wouldn't relent. A few tourists were lined up to buy entry tickets. It appeared to be the only way we would get to the bullring so we lined up behind them.

"We don't have time for this." Chrissie shifted from one foot to the other. "Can't anyone make up their mind?"

A couple ahead of us debated which of many ticket options to select and the next in line had to have his credit card approved, apparently, by judicial mandate. We were nearly unhinged when we finally reached the window.

"Two adults," Chrissie said and shoved her credit card at the woman in the booth. She looked us over carefully before she pushed the entry tickets through the glass window and held up a hand. "*Un momento.*" Then she turned her back and pulled two headsets from under her desk and handed them to us.

Chrissie and I exchanged confused looks. What was this about? We hadn't asked for any headset. Did this woman work for the inspector? Were these headsets especially for us? A bead of perspiration snaked its way down Chrissie's cheek. Neither of us had nerves of steel. "*Para ustedes,*" the woman insisted and pointed the way toward the bullring.

"These must be the instructions from the inspector," I said as I adjusted the volume on mine.

Chrissie nodded and put hers on as we handed our tickets to the ticket taker. We hoisted our canvas tote bags onto our shoulders and, breathing deeply, stepped into the brick walled passageway leading to the bullring.

"Are you okay?" I whispered. "I mean with the bulls and everything."

Sweat dripped freely down her checks and made damp circles under the arms of her t-shirt. She squared her shoulders and looked me in the eye. "I'm fine. I have to be. Bulls are nothing to a frantic mom."

"I hear you. Let's go."

The voice coming through the headset droned on and on about the history of the bullring. It was built in the 1700s. Ronda's most famous matador was Pedro Romero. Blah, blah, blah. Facts which might have been fascinating under less challenging circumstances were only so much white noise. Where were Casey and Tessa? When would we get our instructions? The waiting was unbearable.

Chrissie shot me a questioning look. Anything? I gave her a shrug and two palms up. Nothing.

A sign on a double wooden door a few yards away indicated that it led to the bullring. Single doors to the right and left opened to the museum directly under the ring. The museum was filled with exhibits and displays and made a complete circle around the bullring. The sign above the right-hand door announced that this was the *Museo Taurino* and the voice in my ear directed me to enter. I looked at Chrissie and she pointed at the door. I nodded and we entered a dim, cavernous area. On the walls were huge paintings of matadors in full costume. Plaques in Spanish and English explained who they were and what they had accomplished.

The voice in my ear singled out one painting and was describing the artist's style and the period in which he painted. Quite frankly, I didn't care. If the artist, himself, had popped out of the ceiling above me, I wouldn't have batted an eye. I was totally focused on finding our daughters.

At my elbow a woman tourist pressed close to me. I stepped away from her, but she pushed even closer. Doesn't she know she's invading my personal space? How rude. I squirmed away but she stuck with me. By now I was really annoyed and I turned my head so that I confronted her and gasped. The woman at my side, wearing a voluminous black trench coat and a matching bucket hat pulled low over her face was --- could it be? --- Mom. What on earth was she doing here dressed as a bad imitation of an Agatha Christie character? I opened my mouth, but she put a finger to her lips to shush me. One hand on my arm, she drew me into the shadows next to the wall. She held her guidebook in front of her and tapped the page as if pointing something out to me. Our heads were almost touching as we peered at the book. "Don't let on that you know me," she hissed.

"What are you doing here?" I hissed back.

"Following the thugs that took the girls."

"Why didn't they take you too?"

"I wasn't in the room. I was outside talking to Bobby. Then I saw them marching the girls out and I followed them."

I didn't want to waste time asking about her disguise. Let's say Mom has her ways.

"Do you know where they're being held?" I asked.

"No. This place is a maze. I lost them."

I wanted to ask more, but at that moment the voice in my headset grabbed my attention. The flat droning voice of the tour guide was replaced with the suave, French-accented voice of Inspector Bouchard. Chrissie whipped around, her face reflecting fear. She heard it too. "Congratulations, Madames. You have done very well so far. I am quite happy with you. Please continue and I will give you further orders shortly. *Au revoir.*"

Chrissie began tugging me toward the next painting on the tour. I gave her sneaker a nudge with my toe, pulled her back beside me and Mom patted her hand. Chrissie jumped and jerked her hand away. She glowered at the woman in the trench coat and then flinched. She flicked a glance at me and rolled her eyes upward toward the ceiling. Of course. We were being watched. I didn't want to call any special attention to Mom so I turned on my heel to follow my twin. As I did I knocked the guidebook out of Mom's hand. I bent to retrieve it and Mom knelt down as well. For a few seconds we crouched together.

"Mom," I murmured. "Call Bobby. Call Interpol. We'll do whatever the inspector tells us."

Mom dusted off her book and returned it to her large shopping bag. Without another word or sign of recognition, she melted into the shadows.

I wanted to scream with impatience as we trudged through room after room with no further word from the inspector. We passed numerous exhibits of bull-related items --- capes, funky headgear and somber artwork featuring daring matadors. I stared at a display of sword thingies, decorated with colored cloth called *banderillas*, or little flags. Matadors use them to get the bulls' attention. Chrissie eyed the *banderilla* display as if she could imagine using one on a bull. She shuddered and I squeezed her icy fingers.

Only the monotonous voice in the headset kept us company as we dragged on. We exchanged a hushed word or two occasionally, but were mostly silent, each lost in our own desperate thoughts. My eyes anxiously flicked over each room searching for a clue, something, anything, that would lead me to my daughter. I could imagine her crying hysterically begging for us to rescue her. I had almost lost all hope when the inspector's cosmopolitan voice interrupted my chilling nightmares.

I jumped when I heard that voice. "*Bonjour, Madames.* Do you see the door to your right?" Involuntarily, I twisted my head to the right. "Yes, Madame. That is correct. The door just on your right." Oh, God, he *could* see us. Cold shivers tickled my spine. "If you will go through the door and wait, you will be given your next instruction."

The door was set in a recessed niche in the wall. On it were the words, "*Solamente empleados. Peligro.*" A picture of a bull was stenciled below. Chrissie hung back as I reached for the handle. "Here?" she squeaked, her voice shrill with terror. Danger. Bulls.

"Stay here," I said quietly. "It's okay. I can handle this."

She shook her head vigorously nearly dislodging the headset. "You aren't going alone. I've got your back."

Yeah, until a bull came along. But I didn't object. I needed her. We slipped through the door and looked around. We were at the very end of a long whitewashed hallway with red wooden doors spaced evenly along each side. The doors did not quite reach the ceiling and heavy rope was passed through an opening above the door and attached to the ceiling outside. We hardly dared to breathe. Chrissie clutched my hand. I tapped the headset with a shaking finger to see if it was still functioning. Nothing happened.

She pulled on my arm and I had to bend down so I could hear her tiny voice. "What do you think's behind those doors?"

"Dunno." And then I heard them. Snorts, snuffles, heavy breathing sounds. Bull sounds. There were bulls behind the doors. Mean, vicious, scary bulls. At that moment, I completely understood Chrissie's fear. Oh. My. God.

"Bulls," she wheezed.

"Stay calm." I squeezed her hand. "The bulls are in stalls behind big doors. They can't get us."

Chrissie's face was ashen, her eyes wide. "Says you."

Suddenly, Inspector Bouchard interrupted her burgeoning hysteria. "Welcome, dear friends. Perhaps you have guessed what is behind the red doors." His chuckle was sinister. "Don't worry. You are safe. Please proceed down the hallway to the door at the end of the hall. Go through that door."

My knees quaked as we slunk past the series of stall doors trying to ignore the assorted bull noises. The huge wooden door leading to the bullring was secured with a heavy iron latch. I struggled with it and then popped the release and slammed the door open with my palm using strength I didn't know I possessed.

Chrissie saw the girls first. Her scream echoed off the high ceiling. I peered ahead of me, my heart racing.

A large dirt floor. Empty bleachers circling it. In the very center, two tiny forms twisted toward us.

Our daughters. Casey and Tessa. Bound and gagged. Their eyes wide above the gags.

Just behind them a mammoth black bull pawed the ground and snorted as he tossed his head from side to side. Would he attack them with his giant horns? Or were they in more danger from the man dressed all in black who had a large gun pointed directly at their heads?

This could not be happening.

I started to run --- I had to get to Casey and Tessa --- but I hadn't managed more than a couple of steps before Inspector Bouchard stepped out from behind a red painted half wall at the back of the ring. "*Bienvenue*. I am glad you both could make it to my little *soirée*."

My throat closed up and I gasped for air. Chrissie's breathing was harsh and raspy. Both of us, paralyzed with fear. "What do ... what do you ... want from us?" I spluttered.

The inspector gestured at two facing benches similar to the one that Casey and Tessa were tied to. "*S'il vous plait*, let's sit down and we can discuss the situation."

My sister and I perched warily on the edge of one bench; the inspector straddled the other. He tugged his earlobe and put his elbows on his knees and leaned toward us. "We appear to have a small problem."

I smelled garlic on his breath and recoiled. I unsuccessfully tried to swallow the lump in my throat. Chrissie scooched closer to me, her fingers clenching and unclenching convulsively.

"You see," the inspector continued, "I seem to be in a bit of a quandary. My old friend Bobby MacTavish is convinced I have broken some laws. He wants to interview me and perhaps to arrest me. You know I can't let that happen, don't you?"

We looked like a pair of bobble head dolls, our heads jerking up and down.

"I believe that you have some documents that came into your possession with the aid of a certain Georges Laurent and his clever girlfriend, Fifi. *Est si vrai?*"

"We don't know what you're talking about. Please let Tessa and Casey go," Chrissie begged. "They're just innocent children."

The inspector sighed. "I wish I could, my dear, but, alas, I cannot do that. They are necessary, as you Yanks say, as hostages."

"If you let them go you could take us instead," I began. "We could..." I bit back further words as I saw the look of pure fury that darkened Bouchard's face.

"I know you have the documents I require. I will be most unhappy if you are unwilling to return them to me."

Chrissie flashed me a helpless look and slowly pulled her bag from her shoulder. Bouchard fixed her with a cold, calculating stare. "So, perhaps you do have something for me after all?"

Her voice rose several octaves. "Perhaps I have something to offer you."

"That's better. Please go on."

"We discovered a very large diamond hidden in the lining of my suitcase," Chrissie said.

We did? That was news to me? What other tricks did she have up her sleeve?

"If you let our daughters go free, we will give it to you," she went on. "Then you can sell it and get enough cash to travel out of Europe. You could go anywhere in the world. And Bobby couldn't find you."

Inspector Bouchard scratched his head, pretending to consider Chrissie's offer. I held my breath, hoping he'd fall for her lie. Or was it a lie?

Finally, he said. "That's a very intriguing offer, my dear, but I am afraid I must turn it down. I can't let the young ladies go or they will go directly to the authorities. Even if you had such a diamond on your person..." He leered at Chrissie's breasts. "...I wouldn't have the time to sell it and get out of Europe before my old classmate Bobby found me."

"We wouldn't tell him," I said. "We know all about your tragedy. We're so sorry about your wife and family."

At this, he appeared surprised. His eyebrows shot up and he tugged his earlobe. "What do you know about my family? And who told you?"

"I did," said a voice behind me. I nearly fell off the bench when I saw Luc Marin step out from behind another red barrier wall. "I told them, Inspector

Bouchard."

Luc? I was completely baffled. What was Luc doing here? Was he part of the inspector's smuggling ring, after all? That might make sense. My thoughts tossed around like clothes in the dryer.

"Ah, Luc, there you are," Bouchard said. "I was wondering what was keeping you. So you shared my secrets with the women, eh? Perhaps not such a wise idea."

"I wasn't aware that it was a secret, sir," Luc said. "I told them about my Annalise and your story just came out. I'm sorry if you wanted it kept private."

A dark, despairing expression crossed the inspector's face. "No, I suppose it is not a problem. It was a shock." He said up straighter on the bench and clasped his hands together. "Well, we must not waste more time. We must conclude this business."

I wondered how Casey was reacting to Luc's sudden appearance, but she was too far away for me to see her face clearly. I hoped she wouldn't be too devastated by Luc's apparent betrayal. But then it struck me with the force of a jack hammer blow, it wouldn't matter because we would all be dead. I tried desperately to telegraph my thoughts to Chrissie, but my twin telepathy was on the fritz and I couldn't reach her.

"So, Inspector," Chrissie was saying, "can we make a deal with you? Let us all go and we'll give you the diamond. As it happens, I do have it with me." She patted her bosom. "But you aren't getting it unless the girls are free? And the other documents? I have those too."

Wasn't she a little secret keeper? Who knew?

"We won't tell a single soul about any of this," Chrissie went on. "Right, Kate? Girls?"

I did the bobble head thing and Tessa and Casey made tiny head motions which could be interpreted as nods.

"Let me see the papers," the inspector demanded.

Chrissie shook her head. "Not unless we have a deal."

Inspector Bouchard considered it for a moment and then agreed. "Okay, you've got a deal."

Chrissie fished around in her bag and pulled out a bundle. What could be in it? Not the documents the inspector wanted. Bobby had those. What would Bouchard do when he discovered she had presented him with a bundle of garbage? I eyed Luc --- his face was impassive. Was he going to be any help? Chrissie made a big production of passing the envelope to the inspector, but as he was about to take it from her she jerked her hand and dropped the envelope onto the dirt floor. As the inspector bent to retrieve it, Chrissie bolted from the bench and darted across the ring. She sprinted past the two girls tied to the bench and disappeared behind the red barrier.

Too shocked to speak, no one moved for a few seconds. Then the inspector leapt to his feet and bellowed, "Luc, go get her and bring her back. Michel. Rene. Tie up this one." He gestured at me. "*Sacre bleu. Mon dieu.*"

Luc jogged toward the spot where Chrissie had last been seen. I didn't know whether to hope he found her or that she eluded him. The players in the game kept switching uniforms. It was hard to know who played on what team.

Chapter 38

One of the inspector's thugs grabbed me and as I struggled to get away I spotted a gun in a shoulder holster under his jacket. Crap, these guys meant business. I kicked and screamed but the thug was too strong. He lashed me to the bench with heavy ropes, stuffed a handkerchief in my mouth and dragged me and the bench to the center of the ring next to Tessa and Casey. My back was to them and I couldn't see their faces. I struggled to loosen the ropes that bound me but it was futile. The gag in my mouth was loose --- the thug had been a bit rushed --- and I could force out a few muffled words. "Are you two okay?" Behind me I felt movement that I assumed was nodding. I relaxed a little, telling myself that the girls weren't injured.

I watched Inspector Bouchard conduct a hurried consultation with two thugs and as they hurried off in opposite directions, I prayed that Chrissie wouldn't become their victim. I felt as if I was having an out of body experience --- observing everything from above. I saw the girls, and even myself, as if I were a bat on the ceiling. It was weird. I huddled there in a stupor --- my brain refusing to perform even the most basic functions. An escape plan was way beyond its feeble capabilities. There was no sign of Chrissie and the only coherent thought chasing through my addled brain was, "This is not good. This is sooo not good."

Time dragged with excruciating slowness before Luc reappeared and ambled across the ring toward the inspector. He flicked a quick glance our way, but never hesitated as he passed --- apparently oblivious to the plight of three women trussed up like Thanksgiving turkeys less than a yard away. I was dying, perhaps literally, to know if he'd been able to ferret out Chrissie. From his gestures as he reported to the inspector, I guessed his search was unsuccessful. Luc was doing a lot of head-shaking and shoulder shrugging. Bouchard waved his arms furiously, finally throwing his hands in the air and stalking away. Luc went after him and caught up a few paces away. They engaged in what appeared to be a heated discussion and then they shook hands. Luc strode out of the ring without a backward glance.

Whatever Luc had said to Inspector Bouchard had not been well received. The inspector stormed across the dirt ring and crouched so he was at my eye level and removed the gag from my mouth. A vein throbbed in his temple and his lips were pursed with suppressed fury. In a voice tinged with menace he said, "Madame Kate, I am very sorry that it has come to this. You shouldn't have tried to fool me with fake papers. I really did not want to involve you ladies in this unfortunate affair, but what can I do?" He did one of those "it's not my fault" shrugs. "It's out of my hands."

My mouth was so dry I couldn't make a sound. Bouchard pulled a water bottle from his pocket, uncapped it and held it to my lips so I could drink. I swallowed gratefully. "What are you going to do with us? We can't help you. If you let us go I promise we will never say a word to anyone about this."

His smile was sad. "Alas, my dear, I can't rely on that, can I? My men will find your sister soon. She can't hide forever. And then we will all wait together for my dear old friend Bobby to show up. It can't be long. I am sure someone has notified him of your predicament."

I was relieved to hear that until Bouchard continued, "You are my ticket out. My old *compagnon* will make the arrangements and you and your lovely sister will be my guests when I leave Europe for my exile."

"What if Bobby can't or won't make arrangements for you to escape?"

He shook his head. "Ah, but he must or ..." He dragged his fingers across his throat. "You understand?"

My stomach did a slow roll and I felt nauseated. I thought I might throw up on his shoes. Would have served him right. He couldn't mean he was going to --- gulp --- kill us. Or could he?

Inspector Bouchard stuffed the gag back in my mouth and rose to his feet.

He looked down at me and patted my shoulder. "I am so sorry but I must do what I must do." And he crossed the ring to confer with the two henchmen who had returned from an obviously fruitless search for Chrissie. There was more head shaking and shoulder shrugging by the two thugs before they hauled out their weapons and departed. Now I was completely freaking out and strained against the robes binding me. It was no use. I wasn't going anywhere.

Inspector Bouchard vanished for a moment and then reappeared holding something in his hand. He sauntered back to me as I waited helplessly. "It seems," he said, "that my associates cannot find your clever sister. I must give them some help. Perhaps she needs a little incentive to reveal herself. Do you think?"

What did he have in mind? I could only stare mutely as I imagined horrific scenarios.

He opened his jacket to reveal yards of red material which he swirled in front of my eyes. What on earth? Then it dawned on me. Red capes. The kind matadors use to incite bulls into a frenzy. But why?

Bouchard leaned closer to me and whispered, spewing garlicky breath in my face. "I don't want to leave you alone out here so I've found you some company." He grinned malevolently showing brown-stained teeth and stepped aside so that I could see ... bulls. Five of them being goaded into the ring by two thugs waving guns. Oh my. The inspector draped the red fabric over us with a flourish and then removed a container from his pocket. He unscrewed the cap and emptied the contents over our heads. It smelled vile --- a ghastly odor like decaying meat. Chilled drops slipped over my forehead and into my eyes. I blinked back tears but my vision was blurry and my eyes burned. My stomach clenched with fear.

His job done, the inspector gave us a mock salute and retreated to the side of the ring. As he ducked behind one of the barrier walls with the two henchmen on his heels, I figured it out. The barriers were protection from charging bulls.

We, however, were totally unprotected in the center of the ring. My entire body trembled uncontrollably.

The five bulls milled around at the end of the ring, perhaps confused by their unexpected freedom. One pawed the dirt and snorted. A take charge bull? They all seemed to be waiting to be told what to do. Unfortunately for us, one of the gunmen stepped out from behind the barrier and fired his gun several times into the air. The bulls raised their heads searching for the intrusion and spotting us in the center of the ring, charged. I ducked involuntarily as they headed our way, eyes flashing and hooves pounding. Oh, no, we were about to become a bull's snack.

Before we were gored by a raging bull, the herd skidded to a stop mere yards from us. They danced around and snorted and tossed their heads. Then they charged toward us a few more feet. And stopped. It seemed they weren't quite sure what to make of us. One of the bulls raced in a frantic circle while the others pawed the ground. They looked both angry and confused.

And that's when I saw Chrissie. She advanced on the bulls brandishing a *banderilla*, one of those little flag thingies we'd seen in the museum display. The bulls lifted their heads in, dare I say, shock. I'm sure they'd never seen a bullfighter quite like Chrissie in their careers as bulls. She waved her flag thingy at them --- at first timidly and then with more bravado. "Shoo, bulls. Shoo. Go way, bulls."

The lead bull stopped in his tracks and tossed his head, baffled. He snorted halfheartedly a few times as he eyed her. What kind of matador is this?

Chrissie edged toward him cooing, "Nice bull. Nice bully." Tears ran down her face and her hands shook, but she kept going. One of the bulls took a tentative step in her direction and she jumped back with a shriek. She dragged in a shaky breath and, hiccoughing, waved her flag thingy at the bull. "Go way. Shoo."

The bulls were flummoxed. What the heck was happening here? They lost their incentive to kill or maim and swarmed around our benches sniffing at the liquid Bouchard had dumped on us. Then they licked at it. Hmm. As bulls go, these were a pretty mellow bunch. More Ferdinand than ferocious.

I was so totally captivated by my twin's bullfighting prowess that I was startled when I heard the inspector applauding. He was perched on the top of the barrier wall, an amused expression on his face. "Bravo, Madame, bravo."

Distracted, Chrissie turned her attention away from the bulls, only to see two gunmen racing across the ring toward her --- their guns drawn.

"Well, done," the inspector called to her. "I'm so glad you could rejoin our little party."

"Don't shoot me." Chrissie dropped her "weapon." "I'll cooperate."

The bulls, alarmed by the sudden approach of the two gunmen, grew agitated --- tossing their heads and making scary snorting sounds. The take-charge bull stepped in front of Chrissie and the others circled her as the gunmen got closer. They seemed to have decided that she was more friend than foe. Chrissie patted one tentatively on his nose. "Good bull."

The thugs, momentarily rattled by Chrissie's protectors, managed to recover their equilibrium and scatter the bulls. One of the thugs took out a rope and tied Chrissie to my bench.

"Way to go, sis. You did good," I mumbled around the hanky in my mouth.

She managed a watery half-smile. "Thanks. I hope it worked."

"Of course, it did," I muttered. "The bulls didn't kill us."

One of the goons herded the bulls back to their stalls while the inspector strode across the ring to join us. "Nice performance, Madame. I quite enjoyed it."

I would have liked to slap the smug expression off his face, but my hands were tied. All I could do was wait to see what he had in store for us next.

I didn't have long to wait. A clattering sound came from the bleachers circling the ring. We looked up to see Bobby standing in the front row. And he wasn't alone. Armed men stood at attention with rifles trained on Inspector Bouchard. Bobby motioned for his men to stay in place and he swung his legs over the rail and dropped to the ground. He strolled across the open area, his hands stuffed in his pockets, his eyes on the inspector. When he reached us, he smiled a grim smile. "We meet again, Claude."

Inspector Bouchard offered a hand that Bobby ignored. "What took you so long, old friend? The ladies and I have been waiting."

"I had arrangements to make," Bobby said and made a sweeping motion with his hand to indicate the men with guns.

"I would have preferred that you came alone," Bouchard said. "But no matter. You will just have to make more arrangements. Ones to get me safely out of Europe."

"Now why would I do that?" Bobby asked in a conversational tone. "I believe we have you dead to rights on this one, Claude. All the evidence we need to convict you of smuggling gems out of Europe in picnic baskets. Quite a clever scheme, incidentally, but nonetheless, illegal."

"It was brilliant. The boys and I had a fine run there for a long time. Truthfully, I thought you'd figure it out more quickly than you did. I'm rather disappointed in you."

Bobby scrubbed a hand over his chin. "I was right then. You were playing a bit of cat and mouse with me."

Bouchard laughed. "It always was fun to try to outsmart you. Remember back in school?"

Bobby stuck his hands in his back pockets. "We were closing in on you but I knew it was you when the skull and crossbones bracelets started turning up everywhere."

Huh. What about the bracelets? I was mesmerized by the exchange.

Bouchard smiled. "So you got that did you? I wasn't sure you would."

"I know you never had much regard for my intelligence," Bobby said, "but those were extremely broad hints."

"Indeed. I needed to hurry you along a bit. Skull and Bones, eh? Those were the good old days."

Bobby shook his head. "But why, Claude? You didn't need to turn to a life of crime and I don't understand what you want of me. Was it all about the barony?"

The inspector sighed. "You would have saved us both a lot of trouble if you'd just accepted the offer and sold the place."

"What did you want with a barony in Scotland? And mine in particular? I don't get it."

"Well, old friend, you seem to have most of it figured out. The rest will come to you eventually." The inspector shook his head in resignation. Then he whipped a gun from his pocket and held it to my head. I gasped in shock.

"There is one little thing. I'll kill her if you don't make travel arrangements for me. Don't think I won't. I really don't have much left to lose."

I tried to jerk my head away but the inspector grabbed my hair and yanked it, holding me immovable against the weapon. "Tell your men to back off, Bobby. I'll shoot if I have to."

Hot tears dripped down my cheeks. He would kill me. I knew he would.

Bobby gestured for his men to stay put. "Where do you want to go, Claude? Don't you think you'll get caught sooner or later?"

"Perhaps," Bouchard conceded, "but not today. It's really not up for debate. Just get me a plane and a passport and a hundred thousand Euros and I'll be on my way. Oh, and Madame Kate, here, will be my honored guest as long as necessary." He paused. "Or until I am forced to end our relationship unpleasantly."

Oh, God. I tried to keep my eye on Bobby and Bouchard but the bullring swirled unpleasantly and a strange humming noise buzzed in my ears. Did

Bobby have a plan? He had to have a plan. Or had he walked into this without one? Trusting his old friend to do the right thing? I was going to die. And I wasn't ready. What about my underwear drawer? What were my friends and family going to say when I was gone and they had to sort it out? I wouldn't be there to explain about the thongs.

"You know, Claude, I would make a much better hostage than Kate," Bobby said. "Why don't you take me and let her go?"

Bouchard shook his head. "*Non, merci*, Bobby. Much as I'd enjoy a holiday with you like we used to have at university, I think Kate suits my purposes much better. Now why don't you get on it? My patience is running out."

"Fine," Bobby said. "I'll do it, but I'll need time."

"You've got one hour, old friend. Then someone dies."

By the time Bobby returned I had somehow achieved a zen-like calm, resigned to my fate --- whatever it might be. I had planned my funeral --- I hoped that Scott wouldn't have lilies in the church. I hate the smell of lilies. Oh, well, I wouldn't be bothered by them, now would I? I composed a touching eulogy that I thought would bring just the right note of sentiment and humor. Why didn't I write it before I left? I should have known I'd need it. My trips always turn out this way. I wondered how I was going to die. A bullet? Would it hurt? Of course, it would hurt. Would I take it like a man or a sniveling wreck? Oh, okay, a sniveling wreck. These thoughts weren't putting me in my happy place so I imagined Casey's wedding and her five adorable children. I had named them Brent, Barbie, Brad and Bruce and was struggling with little number five when Bobby strode across the ring. If he saved me from this catastrophe, I'd persuade Casey to name number five Bobby or Bobbie if it was a girl. The least I could do.

"All right, Claude," Bobby said, "I've got a car and driver to take you to a helicopter waiting outside of town. It will take you to Madrid where I have a charter jet ready. The pilot has orders to deliver you anyplace you wish." He handed Bouchard a briefcase. "In that case you will find a hundred thousand Euro and a new passport."

The inspector took the briefcase in one hand, the other held the gun against my head. "Open it, Bobby, and let me see." When Bobby did as asked, Bouchard nodded. "*C'est bonne.* You have done well. Now please untie Madame Kate and we will be on our way."

As Bobby bent to work on the knots on my wrists he whispered, "Don't worry, lassie."

Somehow I wasn't especially heartened by his reassurance. So far it hadn't amounted to much.

He finished unknotting the ropes and stood up. "One thing you should know, Claude." He looked the inspector straight in the eye. "If anything happens to the lassie. One hair of her head is touched. I promise you I will come after you and find you if it takes me the rest of my days. Count on it."

The inspector seemed unperturbed by that. "And if I'm followed, Robert, I promise you the consequences will not be pretty. Take warning."

He dragged me to my feet and twisted my arm painfully behind my back. His gun felt cold and hard against the back of my head and his breath hot on my neck. The scent of his cologne was overpowering. He forced me to march in front of him toward the exit across the ring. Bobby took a step or two with us and Bouchard stopped. "I don't think so, Bobby. I think you had best stay here. I don't trust you not to try something foolish." He considered for a moment. "Perhaps an unarmed escort would be helpful. Just to make sure I get safely to the car and am not mauled by a bull along the way."

"Whatever you want." Bobby signaled to one of his men. "Jack, leave your gun behind. I need you to see that my dear friend reaches the car outside."

When the inspector was certain that Bobby's lad didn't have a gun secreted on his person, the three of us set off. I shuffled my feet and tried to hang back but the inspector jammed his gun in my ribs and prodded me roughly to move. Bobby's guy, Jack, paced silently beside us, his eyes flickering everywhere. I chanced a look back at my family --- Bobby's guys were untying them --- and wondered if that was my final view. That made me furious. I would find a way out of this. No debonair French crook was going to keep me from Brent, Barbie, Brad, Bruce and Baby Bobbie. Not if I could help it.

We left the small bullring and made our way down a whitewashed hallway similar to the one on the other side. Again a series of red stall doors were spaced about four feet apart down the length of the passageway. I didn't hear bull sounds, though, which was oddly comforting. I was relieved the option of dying from a bull goring was apparently off the table. That still left a bullet. Crap. I was certain that the main bullring was directly above our heads. I imagined tourists snapping photos and enjoying the waning daylight. If only I could figure out a way to let one of them know what was happening to me right under their feet. Oh, sure. Nine-one-one wasn't operating here.

I looked to my right and left. I couldn't see anywhere to run or hide and the inspector's gun was pressed against the back of my neck anyway. Our escort, Jack, remained silent, but I prayed he was working on some escape plan. He was certainly better equipped than I. Inspector Bouchard, meanwhile, was intent on getting to the car without delay. He walked rapidly not giving us much time to divert him. I needed to slow him down, so I pretended to stumble and staggered to regain my balance. Bouchard was taken by surprise and nearly fell before he caught himself. He tightened his grip on my arm, pulling it upward. I was afraid he'd break it. "Don't try that again," he said in a raspy urgent voice. "I am out of patience."

My futile attempt had an unexpected consequence, however. We had come to a standstill at the far end of the narrow hallway and were facing toward the exit door. Suddenly from behind us came a screaming missile. It passed over my shoulder with a whistling sound and clonked the inspector on the back of the head. He went down like a sack of rocks and sprawled unconscious on the ground. Bobby's guy leapt on him and pried the gun from his stiff fingers. Then he reached into his own pocket, pulled out his cell phone and dialed. Was it really over? My captor lay unmoving on the floor and my bodyguard had him in a choke hold. He wasn't going to kill me after all?

"What on earth was that?" I asked Jack.

"Not sure, ma'am," he answered. "Rock? Bullet? There's no blood but he does have a decent sized knob on his head."

I stared at the inspector, out cold on the floor. Next to his head I saw the object that had knocked him out. I scooped it up and examined it in astonishment, because the small white missile I was holding was an object with which I am very familiar. It was...a golf ball! A golf ball? I whirled around to peer in the direction from which it had come. And saw my mother --- my former club champion mother --- jumping up and down at the end of the passageway holding an object in her hand that bore a striking resemblance to a golf club. She waggled the "club" at me.

"Fore," she called.

A SHOT IN THE DARK

Laura couldn't stop smiling. She knew that she looked like a doofus, but she couldn't help it. Winning the club championship (twice) had been wonderful, but this was so much better. She'd never dreamed that the golf ball she'd been carrying around until she could use it to clobber Bobby on the links, would be used to clobber the inspector and save the day. What fun it all turned out to be. This whole crazy vacation had been one adventure after another, but Laura hadn't enjoyed herself so much in ages. Wait 'til the girls at the club heard about this.

"I still can't believe you did that, Nonny." Casey plunked her wine glass down on the heavy wooden table and sprawled in her chair.

"You were awesome," Tessa agreed. "What made you think you could bring the inspector down with one shot?"

Laura beamed. She loved being the center of attention. She and her family were having dinner with Bobby and Luc at a restaurant carved into the mountainside that offered spectacular views of the gorge. But the panorama took a backseat to the postmortem discussion of what they had dubbed "the golf shot heard round the bullring."

"I've said for years that my short game is deadly." Laura laughed.

"You da mom," Kate said. "Nice nine iron to the head. I've never been prouder of your game."

Bobby swigged down some beer and skewered a piece of bread with his fork. He concentrated for a moment on carefully spreading butter and then regarded Laura with a somber expression. "I thought I told you to stay at the hotel and out of sight. What you did was reckless. You could have been killed."

Laura carefully placed her fork on her salad plate and looked Bobby in the eye. Time to put a stop to his nonsense. "But I wasn't now was I? And if you think for a single second that I would lounge around the hotel while my family is in danger, you certainly don't know me at all."

"Whoa." Bobby held up a hand in protest. "I didn't mean to imply ..."

Laura sagged. "I know you didn't. I had to do something, didn't I?"

Kate interrupted. "Where did you get a golf ball and a golf club of all things?"

Laura grinned. This was the good part. "I had the ball in my purse. It's one Bobby gave me from Troon."

"And the golf club?" Kate asked.

"That would be from me," Luc admitted. "But it wasn't a real club. I gave her a manure shovel to protect herself. It was the only thing I could find. She improvised."

"All those hours on the practice range turned out to be worth something." Laura smiled.

"And the bulls?" Kate asked.

"Wow, Mom," Tessa interjected, "you were amazing with those bulls. You were really, really brave." Tessa's eyes shone with pride.

Kate turned towards her sister. "You said something odd to me when we were tied to the bench. You said I hope it worked. What worked?"

"Oh, that. I was trying to create a distraction so that Bobby's men could get in place."

"With bulls? You're terrified of bulls. What would make you decide to dance with bulls, so to speak?"

"Wait a second," Luc broke in. He quirked an eyebrow at Chrissie. "You didn't tell me you're afraid of bulls. I could have thought of something else."

"There is no bull that would stop me from helping my family," Chrissie said.

"I'm lost," Casey said. "When did you and Luc have this conversation?"

"Oh, you don't know, do you?" Chrissie explained. "When I ran out of the ring, I had the element of surprise on my side, but I knew I didn't have much time to find a good hiding place before one of the thugs came after me. Lucky for me, Luc found me first."

Laura listened with shock and pride. Who knew her daughters were so brave? Her family astounded her.

Luc took over the narrative. "Bobby and the agents were on the way so I needed to create some kind of diversion. I figured turning the bulls loose would work. I hadn't counted on Madame Christine being so charming with them. She certainly captured Inspector Bouchard's attention." He grinned broadly. "And it was all the time we needed."

"Why bulls?" Casey demanded. "Bulls are scary and mean and dangerous. Aunt Chrissie could have been gored."

Luc chuckled. "Not by these bulls. I'm a farm boy. Spent a lot of time on my grandpere's farm."

"You what?" Casey's tone implied that he should have shared that information with her.

"Oh, indeed, yes. I was pretty sure that these bulls were ... er ... reject bulls. The ones who are more lovers than fighters --- preferring to woo the girl cows rather than swap horns with the other boys."

"Pretty sure?" Chrissie's voice was high and shrill. "You told me they were Ferdinand clones."

Luc looked puzzled. "Ferdinand?"

"Never mind," Kate broke in. "So, you told Chrissie to play matador after you convinced the inspector that it would be a great idea to sic the bulls on us?"

"Basically." Luc nodded. "Good plan, oui?"

"Good thing for you it all worked out, young man," Bobby said sternly. "You took a lot on yourself. Don't do it again."

"Right, boss," Luc said in an unconcerned tone.

Kate looked around the table. "Let's recap. So far we have Chrissie creating a diversion while Bobby's men get set. Bobby confronts the inspector and arranges his escape. I act as his hostage. What was supposed to happen next? Or was I going to be a human sacrifice."

"Now, Kate." Laura patted her daughter's hand. "I would never have let that happen." She took a long swallow of wine and recounted her part in the rescue.

Laura was returning to the room she shared with the girls after her long cell phone chat with Bobby. As she rounded the corner toward the room she saw Casey and Tessa being marched outside by two swarthy men. When she ducked her head into the room she found the two bodyguards hogtied and gagged on the floor. It hadn't taken an ace detective to figure out that something awful had happened.

Laura cut her eyes to Bobby. "Tell the lads I'm sorry I left them. I didn't have time to untie them at that moment. I hoped they would be okay. Are they okay? Oh, dear."

Bobby's lips twitched. "They're fine. Please go on."

Laura continued her story. She decided to follow the girls and the men to see where they were going. And frantically dialed Bobby's number. Again and again. When she couldn't reach him she trailed after her granddaughters until they reached the bullring. She hung back as the four entered the building by a side entrance and then crept up to the door and found it locked.

She started to head back to the parador to find Kate and Chrissie but just then she saw them in the ticket line. They disappeared into the museum before Laura could reach them so she bought her own ticket and followed.

"You should have seen Mata Hari here," Chrissie broke in to Laura's story. "Where on earth did you find that trench coat and hat?"

"I have my ways," Laura said. "So after I talked to you two in the museum I lingered in the shadows. I was surprised when Inspector Bouchard showed up. I wasn't sure what to do, but I thought he might be able to help somehow. But he went into the bullring and I saw Tessa and Casey tied up. And then Kate and Chrissie came and I could tell that he was up to no good."

"How did you see all this?" Casey asked her.

"I hid in one of the empty stalls. It had a window slit in the side that looked right into the little ring where you were tied up. When I saw Chrissie run out of the ring, I tried to reach her --- show her my hiding place. But Luc got there first. I wanted to hear what they were saying so I snuck up on them. I guess I'm not as sneaky as I thought and Luc saw me. He told me to stay hidden and he'd come for me later. So I did."

"Fine thing," Bobby said, "you listen to him and not to me."

"You don't answer your cell phone and what do you expect?" Laura frowned. "Anyway, after I watched Chrissie play bullfighter --- you were so brave, dear --- Luc came and told me to be ready to act when he needed me. As it turns out, he needed me to practice my short game as Kate and the inspector were leaving the ring." She folded her hands together and waggled them as if she was holding a golf club.

Luc raised an eyebrow. "I didn't exactly tell her to play a round of golf. I told her to cause a little disturbance so our agent could get a jump on the inspector. I had no idea that Madame Laura would be quite so successful."

"Imagine what I could have done if I'd had my five wood?"

Chapter 39

By the time we finished eating and polished off two more bottles of good Spanish red wine, it was late and our exuberance was waning and fatigue setting in. We decided to retire to our rooms at the parador before we fell asleep in our chairs. Bobby paid the bill and we lingered a few minutes to collect our things. I couldn't leave, though, without asking Bobby about a couple of things that still worried me. I pulled him aside.

"Bobby. What will happen to them? The Inspector and his son and son-in-law and to *Le Picnic Francais*? I suppose they'll go to jail. Your friend Claude tried to kill --- and nearly succeeded --- Georges and Fifi? Do you think he'll be charged with murder?"

Bobby came to stand beside me next to the window overlooking the gorge. He gazed out into the dark and then looked sideways at me. "I'm not sure, Kate. Interpol won't let him off lightly. His crimes are serious. Smuggling isn't looked upon favorably. As for attempted murder, I'm not sure. Georges admits it might have been an accident. You heard him say they fought over the gun, it went off and then Claude had to try to kill Fifi because she was a witness. I don't think he'll ever be a free man again."

He stared out again, his image in the window reflecting melancholy. "It's a shame really. Claude is fundamentally a good man. Oh, yes, in school in liked his women, good times, fast cars and a game of chance. But when he married Desiree he left all that behind. Became a good husband, father and grandfather. I don't believe he would have strayed outside the law if it hadn't been for that horrible car accident. He was an outstanding policeman for many years."

By now the others had gathered around to hear what Bobby had to say. Mom sidled up next to him and looped her arm through his. "What about the barony? He said he wanted you to sell him the barony?"

Bobby nodded and rubbed his chin. "Here's the sad thing. I probably would have sold it to him if he'd asked me instead of using an intermediary and then scare tactics. I am still not sure what he would have done with it though."

He sighed. "I'll find out, but it's too late for Claude. I'll see that his family is well cared for in spite of it all. They have had enough tragedy. I won't let them lose their homes."

Then he shook off his blue mood and turned to my mother. "Let's get the women's short course golf champion back to the parador. She had a tough match."

Mom smirked. "You're just jealous of my game, Bobby. When we play at Troon, we'll see who shoots par and who doesn't."

As we eased away from the window, I thought of one last question. "You and the inspector talked about the skull and crossbones charms. It seemed to mean something to both of you."

"Ach, yes, Kate," Bobby said. "At university we were mates. We were members of one of the more well-known societies at Yale. The Skull and Bones. When the evidence began to mount up against Claude and I accepted that he was the ringleader of the smuggling gang, I realized that the charm bracelets were his way of toying with me. He kept dangling them in front of me, daring me to figure out his scheme. He always did think he was more clever than he actually was." He rolled his eyes. "He never gave me a single bit of credit either. I guess that was his downfall after all is said and done."

Don't mess with Baron Bobby Hot Legs. Thank goodness.

Two days later we were at the Madrid airport checking in for our flight. Our brush with death and dismemberment by raging bulls and bad guys was slowly fading into a hazy memory and we were giddy with excitement to be on our way home. We received our boarding passes, relinquished our bags to be checked and headed for the crowd at security. As we zipped up our hand luggage and found our identification, I heard an odd noise.

I looked up, baffled. "What's that noise?"

"Weird," Chrissie said.

We scanned the check-in area and saw nothing out of the ordinary. "Must be coming over the public address system," I said.

As we strolled toward the security lines, the noise got louder. "What is it?" Casey asked. "It's kind of familiar."

"It's not music," Tessa said. "Is it?"

"Oh, yes it is," Mom said. "I know what it is."

At the same time we all recognized the sound --- bagpipes. We turned in the direction of the bagpipe music and our jaws dropped. There --- marching toward us --- were six bagpipers wearing kilts and piping with gusto. Leading the bagpipers was none other than Robert MacTavish, Baron of Troon. We burst out laughing. How perfect.

The bagpipers marched up to us and, at Bobby's signal, ceased playing. We hadn't seen Bobby since our last dinner in Ronda and hadn't expected to see him before we left. If Mom was sad about it, she never let on. But now her eyes lit up with delight and she hugged Bobby. "What a send-off you give a girl, Robert," she said with a brilliant smile.

One of the other bagpipers separated himself from the group and approached Tessa. "Don't forget me, Tessa," Mac MacTavish said as he bowed and kissed her hand.

Tessa threw her arms around him and laughed. "Oh, Mac. I won't. Don't forget to let me know when you'll be back in the states."

Mac took Casey's hand and kissed her cheek. "That's from Robert. He's sorry he couldn't be here himself, but Interpol interns don't get time off to bid fair lassies a fine farewell. He told me to tell you he'll be in touch. Very soon."

Casey smiled broadly and hugged him. "Thanks, Mac. Tell him I can't wait."

Suddenly we realized we were running out of time. The lines were long and we didn't want to miss our flight. This had been one very unique vacation, but it was time to return to the real world. We said our final goodbyes to the MacTavish men. The sound of bagpipes followed us as we made our way through security and toward our gate.

As we made ourselves comfortable for the long flight home, I turned sideways in my seat to face Chrissie. Champagne glass in hand --- you have to love Business Class --- I raised it to my twin. She lifted her glass and clinked it against mine.

"Happy Birthday, Chrissie."

"Happy Birthday, Kate."

CURTAIN CALL
A MONTH LATER

As I came in the back door, the phone was ringing. I dashed across the kitchen, dropped the pile of dry cleaning on a chair and grabbed it. "Hel-lo?" I said breathlessly and checked the caller ID. I carried the phone to the porch and plopped into the overstuffed chair, making myself comfortable for a long sisterly chat.

"Hey, what's goin' on?" Chrissie sounded upbeat --- little birdies singing in her tone.

"I just walked in the door with the last of Casey's dry cleaning. Honestly, you'd think she was moving into a four bedroom house rather than a tiny apartment with the amount of stuff she's taking."

"So how are things in Paris? Did she get the job she wanted?"

"Yup, she did. The photo agency loved her work. Casey's ecstatic to be back in Paris, her favorite place in the entire world according to her. Seriously, I'm not sure what she's happiest about, her job, her adorable apartment overlooking Notre Dame or the fact that a certain handsome Scot is living a short train ride away in London."

"Robert? He got his assignment? To London?"

"Uh huh. And he'll be spending some time in Paris as well."

"Do I smell romance brewing?"

"Maybe. Or maybe not. She's still seeing Luc and the girls, but only as 'friends,'" I said with a laugh. "Since Robert and he will both be in Paris occasionally, I'm not sure what's going to happen. Of course, Nice isn't that far away either."

"Hmm." Chrissie paused and I could hear her swallowing coffee. "So I guess that means Lester is totally out of the picture."

"Totally. I'm so relieved. This Paris thing is perfect for Casey. What about

Tessa? Last I heard she was debating going back to law school."

Chrissie didn't answer for a few seconds. "Hey, Chris, are you still there?"

"Mmm hmm. Here's the thing. Tessa says she might go back to school, but definitely not to law school. She says it's way too boring. Max is disappointed, but we agree that we have to let her lead her own life. Her own way."

"Wow. That's really mature of you," I told her. "Truthfully, I can't see Tess as a lawyer. Maybe a pole dancer, though."

"Funny you should mention that. Tessa's going into business for herself. She's opening a studio and is going to teach pole dancing. At least until she decides what she wants to do with the rest of her life."

I couldn't help it. I had to laugh. Pretty blonde Tessa was well-suited to that career. "Hey, Chris, I'm sure you're kind of upset, but ..."

"Actually, I'm not," she interrupted me. "If our birthday trip taught me one thing, it's that life is too short not to have fun."

"Where's this studio going to be? Close to home, I imagine."

"No. Not really. She's leaving today for New York to scout out locations."

"New York?" I said in surprise. "Why New York?"

Chrissie sighed one of those world-weary mom sighs. "Because that's where Julliard is and where a certain fun-loving Scot is finishing up his degree in music education."

I uncurled myself from my cushy chair and, phone in hand, went into the kitchen to warm the breakfast coffee in the microwave. This conversation was going to take more time and coffee to finish.

"Tessa and Mac?" Are they a couple? Has she seen him?"

"No and no," Chrissie answered. "According to Tessa they're just 'friends.'"

"Hmm. Are we going to have to visit our grandchildren --- if we ever have them --- in Scotland?"

"Who knows?" Chrissie said. "By the way, have you talked to Mom lately?"

"A couple of days ago. Why?"

"Because guess who's moving to Troon, Scotland, for the next nine months or so?"

My coffee mug slipped through my fingers and almost crashed onto the floor before I regained my grip. Regaining my grip on reality was more difficult. "She what? She never said a word to me. She isn't marrying Bobby is she?" My voice rose a few decibels.

"Calm down," Chrissie said. "According to Mom, this is purely business. You know she's always wanted her own interior design business so she told me she was going to 'take the bull by the horns' and just do it."

"Cute. But Troon? It's all about Bobby, of course."

"Sure it is. Mom says she and Bobby decided while we were in Europe that she shouldn't waste any more time. She's not getting any younger she says."

"So let her open her design shop in Florida or Michigan or Ohio. Why go clear to Troon?" But I knew. The rundown barony. Mom was enchanted with it and its possibilities.

"The barony," I said. "She loved that place."

"Bobby is the icing on the cake," Chrissie added. "Mom says they are just 'friends.'"

I cracked up. "Lots of our family have friends in Scottish places." I took a second to digest all this information. "When's she leaving?"

"Dunno. She said she was going to call you tonight so pretend you don't know anything about it. Okay? I'll be in trouble if she finds out I spoiled her big surprise."

"I'm not sure I'm that good an actress, but I'll give it a shot."

"What else is new?" Chrissie asked.

"Oh, wait. I do have news. Bobby called yesterday. It was business. It seems that Inspector Bouchard confessed to the whole smuggling scheme in return for immunity for his son and son-in-law. Bobby said that in view of the inspector's prominent position in the Paris Police Department, Interpol decided that an ugly trial wouldn't be in anyone's best interest. The boys won't serve any jail time. Just some sort of community service. And restoration of all the money they stole which will take years and years."

"What about the inspector? Will he go to jail?'

"Bobby said he would have to do at least ten years before he would be eligible for parole. And he told me something else that's interesting."

"I'm waiting."

"Okay. Guess why the inspector played the little game of hide and seek with Bobby and why he wanted the barony?'

"I have no idea."

"Bobby said he was going to use the barony as a secure place to hide the gems. It seems that the underground tunnel system met his needs and he thought Bobby would be a pushover."

"Makes sense."

"Here's the thing that's really unbelievable. Bobby said that the reason the inspector tried to maneuver Bobby into giving him money to leave the country was that he lost all the cash he had socked away in the offshore accounts."

"How'd that happen?"

"This is what you're going to love. Julio and Guillermo took it. Georges gave them the account numbers and they vanished with all the money."

Chrissie whooped in my ear. "Way to go, *caballeros*." She paused. "Not that I approve of crime or anything. Still, poetic justice and all that."

"I know," I said. "Guess we won't need to go back to testify after all since there won't be a trial. The statements we gave in Ronda will be enough for a judge to decide on a sentence. I have to say I'm kind of disappointed. Not that we won't be involved in a trial, but that we aren't going back to Europe."

Chrissie blew out a sigh. "I know what you mean. I think I was looking forward to another trip. Kind of dull here at home."

"Max is dull?"

"Not Max. Life. I miss crime solving."

"And the bulls?" I asked. "Do you miss them?"

"Kind of. How about you? And Scott?"

"Can't say I miss the bulls, but life in Ohio is a bit mundane. I'm back to tennis and Jazzercise and coffee and lunch. I'm thinking of writing another book. It's definitely ho hum, though."

"What we need to do," my sister suggested, "is start planning for our next birthday."

We sipped our coffee in silence for a while, thinking about possibilities.

"So," I said to her, "what should we do for our birthday next year?"

"Good question. Do you have anything in mind?"

"Let's do something less stressful and more relaxing than the last one."

"Sounds good."

"How about climbing Mt. Everest?" I asked.

"Or we could wrestle wild crocodiles in the Nile."

"Canoe down the Yangzee River?"

"Shoot wild boar in the African veld?"

"Anything," I said, "that doesn't involve traveling with our family would be more relaxing than those two weeks."

"Definitely," Chrissie agreed.

After we hung up, I made another pot of coffee, picked up the phone and dialed. When my friend Mary Linda answered, I said, "Hey girlfriend, Chrissie and I need you to help plan our next birthday adventure. We have some great ideas. Wait until you hear."

Made in the USA
Monee, IL
12 February 2022

91171774R30243